T0270449

The Picaresque of Imagine Purple

IMASODE IV:

Mayhem in Manhattan

Beth Fine

The Picaresque of Ímagine Purple

IMASODE IV:

Mayhem in Manhattan

TATE PUBLISHING
AND ENTERPRISES, LLC

The Picaresque of Imagine Purple
Copyright © 2014 by Beth Fine. All rights reserved.

No part of this publication may be reproduced, stored in a retrieval system or transmitted in any way by any means, electronic, mechanical, photocopy, recording or otherwise without the prior permission of the author except as provided by USA copyright law.

The opinions expressed by the author are not necessarily those of Tate Publishing, LLC.

This is a work of fiction. Names, descriptions, entities, and incidents included in the story are products of the author's imagination. Any resemblance to actual persons, events, and entities is entirely coincidental.

Published by Tate Publishing & Enterprises, LLC
127 E. Trade Center Terrace | Mustang, Oklahoma 73064 USA
1.888.361.9473 | www.tatepublishing.com

Tate Publishing is committed to excellence in the publishing industry. The company reflects the philosophy established by the founders, based on Psalm 68:11,
"The Lord gave the word and great was the company of those who published it."

Book design copyright © 2014 by Tate Publishing, LLC. All rights reserved.
Cover design by Rodrigo Adolfo
Interior design by Jomel Pepito

Published in the United States of America
ISBN: 978-1-63063-231-1
1. Fiction / Mystery & Detective / Women Sleuths
2. Fiction / Historical
14.02.06

Dedication

I dedicate this book series to my daughter Chelsea who is a quick study, clear thinker, and constant encourager. Those amazing qualities I have long admired and want to emulate more in my writing.

Acknowledgements

Putting this serial together would be impossible without assistance from computer experts, librarians, students, schoolteachers, parents, and proofreaders whose skills and suggestions make it better than I designed. Especially key to its development are two fine young readers, Avery and Collin, both home schooled. Their focus, reactions, ideas, and reports continually help this long project; and their encouragement makes me believe that an audience for an old-fashioned picaresque still exists.

Vicky Drake, assistant librarian in St. Lawrence, Newfoundland, helped with the Newfie dialect in Imasode-I. Riina Olvet, a library information specialist in Queens, New York, proved invaluable with the Estonian in Imasode-VII. Tahnya Sherwood, an elementary school media specialist in Atlanta, Georgia, came on board to help dovetail the series to curriculum. Kerry Chamberlain in Maine, gave me a home-school perspective. Until her recent death, Virginia Giles of Georgia helped in many unseen ways.

Tina Whittimore of Tri-Cities Web Solutions developed a new website for the print promotions. Justin Mulwee and Steve Chamberlain helped design earlier online versions. Shari Mauthner, a computer instructional designer at the University of Houston, has translated computer lingo. Chelsea Watkinson continues to plumb upcoming Imasodes to ensure they conform to the whole *Picaresque*. She also serves as behind-the-scenes coordinator, cheerleader, and brand developer.

Rick Ritts of Big Head Studios has brought the Imasode maps to life. Like a champ, he has fielded with good humor my many changes of mind. His added touches have come from his interest in the project.

However, the bulk of my gratitude goes to my incredibly patient editor, Rebecca Ensign of Gold Leaf Press in Detroit. Without her professional navigation over many years, this effort would have flown straight into the side of a mountain.

And now the many helpful and skilled editors of Tate Publishing have led me through the print process maze. I am grateful for their professional *rendering* of this burgeoning project.

Table of Contents

Information

Disclaimer

Although the story may mention real people and relate actual events of the historical era of 1969-1970, the characters operate in imaginary situations, only hint at factual accuracy, and speak of those times from their fictionalized perspectives. The suggested geography is relatively correct in the pictorial map and narrative descriptions. All real locations (e.g. Sloan-Kettering, Central Park, Sloppy Louie's, Friars Club, 46th Street Theatre etc.) are merely used as backdrops. No disrespect or offense is *implied* toward any of them. Therefore, none should be *inferred*.

Sensitive Material

Parental pre-reading and supervision may prove wise on all Imasodes after IMA II (especially III, V, and VII). On sensitive matters, the author *tempers* her viewpoint with genteel innocence and moral advocacy but without blinders and whitewashing, or base vulgarity and *prurience*. However in the 1960s, public education opened the gate to include once *sacrosanct* subjects into its curriculum. So, even though these are not always discussed directly, the Imasodes will not shy away from delicate issues:

Subjects bracketed below will appear in the current Imasode: alchemy, anarchy, [assault], [bad behavior], bigotry, [cheating], communism, dishonesty, disloyalty, drunkenness, [envy], espionage, ethnic cleansing, [*extortion*], fascism, fidelity, [gambling], greed, [guns], illegal drugs, integrity issues, [jealousy], job performance, [kidnapping], [lying], mind control, [moral lapses], murder/attempted, Nazism, pickpockets, poisons, politics, prejudice, protests, racial tension, religious faith, [responsibility], [revenge], rioting, shoplifting, smuggling, stealing, tyranny, union corruption, virginity, warfare, witchcraft, and work ethic.

Grade Level Appropriateness

Many paragraphs were sent through the Flesch-Kincaid Grade Scale via the MSWord Spelling & Grammar program and/or Blue Centauri, a free online consulting service. The range in early episodes, even with difficult *italicized* words and idiomatic sayings, scored from Grades 3.2 to 9.8. Of course, narratives scaled higher than dialogue, (even up to 11th grade+ range) when handling the more complex concepts, especially in later episodes

Most passages scored 70+ on the Flesch Readability Ease Scale and 5-10 on the Fog Scale. Strong readers should easily catch the gist of the stories. My test readers matured with the series and never mentioned any difficulty. Average readers, especially younger ones, may hit occasional snags. I have incorporated many context clues to help coax such readers to expand their vocabularies and comprehension.

Knowing readers may lose interest in the Biographies or may not initially appreciate the *amplified* details, I used the journalistic convention of putting less critical material at the end of each biography. Stylistically, in most cases, the reader may lop off latter paragraphs without losing critical points.

Instructions

Finding a Strategy for Tacking the Whole Series

To gain the needed background for each adventure and to discover if characters change when they pop up in future stories, read the Imasodes in sequence. To find clues to how a character's flaws or strengths affect his *temperament*, read the biographies during or before starting the story. To learn if a certain character has a biography, look at the List of Characters. Any name with an asterisk* beside it will have a biography in the Appendices. Sometimes when minor characters become major, they will have their biographies in later Imasodes. Some major characters have already had their biographies listed in Imasodes I & II, providing a good reason to hang on to previous books.

Choosing Your Mystery Solving Style

To have fun, skim the story without using the Appendices. Almost everything needed to solve the mystery, you can find within the story itself. When you come across something you don't understand, you can totally ignore it or say it aloud. Like a page-marker, the unknown item will echo in your head for future reference.

To get smarter, try using the Appendices. There, you'll find a wealth of information that explains items from the story: unfamiliar Clichés, Idioms, and Phrases as *two+ words* in italics; unknown Vocabulary will be noted as *one word* in italics. However, if you'll think back to when you first started reading, you often figured out strange words and phrases from context clues. The same holds true in the Imasodes.

When you hit abbreviations, historical *allusions*, famous people, events, scriptures, books, songs or shows of which you've never heard, turn to the Lookup Suggestions. These random items are organized there in categories and have one-liner explanations. Later on, if you choose to do further research, you will stretch your common knowledge bank and increase your understanding of past/recent history. If you don't find the curious item listed, it may have been listed in previous Imasodes.

Reading Dialect in Dialogue

Dialect dialogue is added for fun and flavor but can be a challenge. Therefore, always read aloud any crazily misspelled words that you suspect are in dialect. Sounding them out phonetically may help you understand what is being said. Some New England sounds continue from Imasode III: he-ah = here/hear; yu-ah = your; ahr = are; idear = idea;

New Yorkese words and phrases like: dawt'er = daughter; dem = them; dose = those; hoy'd = heard; lid'l = little; mattah = matter; mudder = mother; poison = person; stah-let = starlet; trav'l = travel; t'ree = three; turdy turd = thirty third; wh-ill = will. A sentence may read: "Wha cha spectin'…a parade? I hoyd yah…now, go on already! Riina has her own unknown dialect mishmash: darlink = darling; leetle = little

While walking her NY neighborhood, Ima imagines a speech by landlady Astrid. The author makes no pretense to use proper German vocabulary, syntax, or spelling but includes the below translation of Astrid's blurb for curiosity sake and hints at Imasode IX:

"Yes, you young Americans think I'm rich like Rothschild. But that's not right. During the awful war, we Germans learned to live like rats. So, I tell you something. A cold house will toughen you for life. Who knows the future? Now go have a nice cuddle time with Ímagine and leave me to my polka music."

Using the Illustrated Map of Manhattan

Each episode includes one pictorial map showing the geographical location and a few details in the story. You may want to look at the map before you begin reading. In this Imasode, you may find yourself referring to it often just to stay oriented and to grasp the distance between different parts of NYC. Ima moves from the Westside to Eastside, often walks across town, and rides subways or buses uptown and downtown.

Illustrated Map of Manhattan

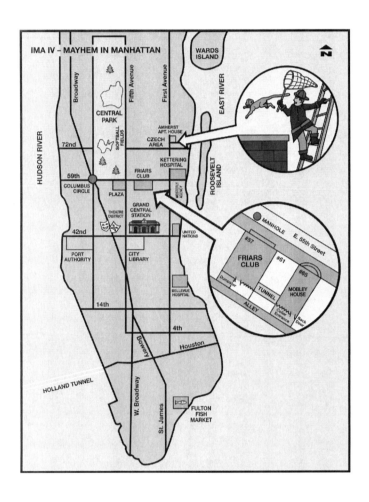

IMA IV – MAYHEM IN MANHATTAN

List of Characters

Arnie	Doorman at the Amherst
Feingold Family	Estonians escapees
Leo	Riina's father, a jeweler
Mariana	Riina's mother
Riina*	Ima's best school chum
Dollar	Cash's right hand man
Flannery	Superintendent at old apt.
Jarman	Butler at Mobley Mansion
Longwind Famly	English roots
Ímagine Purple**	Teacher/adventurer/new sleuth
Lionel Longwind*	Ima's father, famous baritone
Marsha Mushmouth	Owner of AAH
	Answering Svc.
Nelson	Nightman at the Friars
Nickel	Crewman for Cash
Officer Allrest	Precinct desk policemen
Officer Onfoot	Policeman on the local beat
Pennypinch	Smallest crewman for Cash
Primo	Play production manager

Pollibo Family	Italian immigrants
Maria*	Restorer of historical homes
Sal*	*Unscrupulous* hit-man
Val*	*Pugnacious* bookie
Quarter	Crewman for Cash
Sam Silencer	Sergeant at Arms at the Friars
Shelton Grape*	TV announcer/actor
Teresa Latimer*	*Stock* analyst, Lionel's fiancée
Underwood Family*	Sewer Constructors
Caleb/Cash*	Central Park vagrant
Vanna Belforte**	Young southern vamp
Wes Westerly*	Talent Agent/Ima's godfather

*Biography found in Appendices

**Biographies of main characters found in previous Imasodes.

A Prologue: Bad Memories

Having lived outside the United States during most of the 1960s, Imagine Purple and Savannah Belforte had no firsthand knowledge of the new hippy movement, only media descriptions. As reported, this new gentle generation of flower children had rejected the commercialism of America and sought more wholesome back-to-the-earth lifestyles. They moved to remote areas, built communes, and grew their own food. Their motto tried to *emulate* a popular song phrase, "Everybody get together; try and love one another right now," a motto very hard to follow.

So Ima and Vanna had anticpated peace, love, and gentleness in their first encounter with this newly *acclaimed* group but met with sore disappointment. While staying in a vacation cottage outside Canton, Maine, they got deeply deceived by some hippy neighbors who had fallen in with local gangsters up to no good. Thrown into a world of drug smuggling, car part fencing, and loan sharking, Ima and Vanna had some experiences that forever rocked their own naïve outlooks.

Recovery from such things would come slowly. Not only had Vanna gotten deep cuts on her face, cuts that would need time to heal; but also the young women's shaky friendship had ruptured again. Ima wondered if either of these would ever completely repair. They had *kept bad company* and felt the *ravages* of that old adage.

As excited as Ima and Vanna had been to meet some real hippies, their opinion had greatly changed. They discovered that in every *utopian pipedream*, a crackpot will emerge to stir the stew and set up a scheme that *panders to human frailities*. The old excuse that "the end justifies the means" had again trapped its victims with a lie.

• • •

The misadventures began when the two young women met Claude Gagnon, a handsome French Canadian guy who drove an unmarked white box van. They innocently accepted a ride with him from the Nova Scotia ferry to the American border in Maine. After that high point, everything went quickly downhill.

Ima and Vanna had believed the story that Claude raised houseplants on his organic farm in Canton, Maine. Unbeknownst to them, the truth was the word "farm" served as a *euphemism* for an illegal drug operation. Claude, along with the help of his pilot Swoopy and a self-appointed guru called Darwinia, actually grew and delivered marijuana.

After crossing the border, Ima and Vanna rented an old classic Hudson car and a vacation cottage at a gas station called Oren's Oasis. The next day, the two young women went out to explore the lay of the land around Canton but soon ran out of gas close to Claude's farm. After a strange initial visit, Ima lost all interest in returning to see his operation. But Vanna really liked Claude and let his accent charm her. So, one morning she drove alone over to tour the farm but soon became entwined in a series of precarious events.

Vanna met Rough Rod who originally loaned Claude the money to buy his farm. Unfortunately, Rod now held the *purse strings* and dictated the terms of repayment. Vanna, still believing the farm raised organic vegetables, encouraged Claude to let her father buy back the mortgage from Rod. That idea infuriated Darwinia. In fact she hated everything about Vanna.

Because Vanna was a pretty southern belle, stole Claude's attention, and wanted in on their business, Darwinia devised a *heinous* plan to get rid of her...permanently! While the men worked to free their tractor stuck in mud, Darwinia became irrational and struck down Vanna with a tire-iron. Then she dragged the pretty lady face down over gravel, thrust her limp body into a burlap bag, and left her unconscious inside the white van.

When Vanna had not returned to the cottage by evening, Ima called Sheriff Holland. Together they went out to search for the missing person but only found the missing car. Analyzing several clues left about the scene, they decided Ima's quasi-friend was undoubtedly in desperate *straits*. Supposing what might have happened to the victim, they traced her possible steps back to the farm. Their *suppositions* proved right. They found Vanna injured, *disoriented*, but alive in the van. Her rescuers took her to the cottage and set to repairing her serious facial wounds.

That night, Rough Rod found the old Hudson and drove it back to the farm with the plan to see how the operation fared. In a second moment of madness, Darwinia clubbed Rod, put him also a burlap bag, and stuffed him in the trunk of the Hudson. She thought that cinched the deal so Claude would not have to pay off the farm mortgage.

The next day, while Swoopy flew a delivery of marijuana to Quebec, Claude invited Vanna and Ima to take the old Hudson for a spin, all the while Rod kept knocking on the trunk. They crossed the Canadian border, *ostensibly* on an innocent daytrip. When they arrived at an airstrip, Claude got out of the car to join Swoopy who stood talking with their customer on the tarmac. Immediately, Ima spun around and headed for safety.

Back at the border when the patrolmen opened the Hudson's trunk, they found Rod Oregano and bags of marijuana stuffed inside with him. Ima and Vanna felt *ambivalent* about Rod's fate. Although he had participated in the farm's crime, they felt slightly glad he had not suffocated to death. The whole case came to a close when Maine's state police captured Swoopy and Claude who landed on the farm's airstrip.

With the two pot growers carted off to jail, the sheriff had one remaining issue: to arrest Darwinia for *assaulting* Vanna. Although the southern belle wanted to *avenge* the crazy northern guru for cutting her face, Darwinia went into a mad rage and set the barn on fire. When Ima pulled the blazing woman from the barn, the sheriff got his suspect. That ended both cases.

The sheriff had to confiscate the old rented Hudson as evidence in the drug bust because it too had participated in the crime. That meant the two ladies needed a replacement car. This time they went to normal rental agency.

• • •

Thinking their adventures at an end, the two young women returned to their summer cottage to rest. However, Vanna simply could not relax. Ashamed for letting Claude *beguile* her, she felt *distraught* and restless. How could she have been so reckless as to flirt with Claude? How could she even think of investing in his farm? And more than anything, how could she want to cut Darwinia or maybe even kill her, as revenge for the cuts on her own face? She felt *out of sync*.

As night descended, Ima struggled to soothe her on/off friend. Vanna began acting quite confused, almost beyond reason. With her nerves shot, she let every shadow and sound frighten her. *Cravenly*, she insisted on searching the cottage. In her mind, boogiemen lurked under the beds, in the cupboards, and behind every door. Before they retired for the night, Ima suggested they have a cup of tea by a wood fire. That temporarily calmed the atmosphere.

When they finally said goodnight, Vanna could not fall asleep. She imagined hearing a ghost speak. Terrified, she ran across the cottage, jumped in bed with Ima, and declared someone had sent an *apparition* to torment her. She reasoned that since she was a con artist that had *swindled* scores of people, her turn for punishment had now come. After all, Darwinia had also gotten her just desserts for many evil deeds.

Ima tried to explain the mysterious house sounds. First, she used a psychological basis, then logical, and finally spiritual. That last approach made the *irascible* Vanna flare up. She became *belligerent* and forbade Ima to mention the word God ever again. That command once again put the two *at odds with* each other.

Although Vanna had much to learn, so did Ima. Vanna craved peace of mind but despised her friend's advice on how to achieve it. Although Ima spoke words which in themselves held truth... and power to convince, she did not *temper* them with kindness. No salve came with their sting.

Instead Ima kept pushing hard to find answers to Vanna's fear. She seemed fixed on beating the details into clues as required by her sleuthing method. But that approach made Ima looked like a *prig*, a know-it-all...even a do-gooder who forgot that others had a right to choose or to reject. She would quote the Lord's words but then fail to *heed* His example of never forcing His way onto people.

Wisdom said to leave the southern belle alone to *stew in her own juices*. But Ima did not listen. Never yet experiencing so directly how heaven mysteriously worked things out, she used her new found faith like a weapon instead of a shield. Sadly, Ima would have to discover that her detective style could not solve everything, especially the mystery inside another person.

Early the following morning, Prudence Persnickety, the cottage's owner, showed up, uninvited. She began to *regale* them with historical ghost stories. That was the *last straw* for Ima and Vanna. They had grown completely fed up with the whole bad arrangement. Prudence had falsely advertised a quiet cottage and gentle countryside. It had in no way provided a restful, safe, or fun-filled retreat.

Disgusted, they requested a refund of the remaining three weeks deposit. Prudence, acting like a *drill sergeant*, insisted they return the cottage to a *spit and polish* condition. Then they could pick up their refund money at Oren's Oasis where they had originally rented the cottage and the Hudson. They did not welcome that thought of meeting Oren again after the drug bust.

It took a day and night for Ima and Vanna to clean everything to Prudence's standards. When examining their handiwork, they felt sure it should guarantee a return of their money. Early the next morning, the two young women packed the car, locked the door, and closed an unhappy chapter of their friendship…or so Ima thought.

Friendships, Impossible and Otherwise

In complete silence, Ima and Vanna drove down a narrow Maine road, heading to Oren's gas station in Auburn. Ima pulled in the driveway and heard the bell ring as the tires rolled over the cord. Strangely, no attendant came from the garage bays to fill up the gas tank.

Ima stepped to the main office door and tried the latch. It was locked. She knocked. No one answered. She squinted to look through the smudged window. The cash register had disappeared, and all the shelves lay empty of *stock*. Someone had made a hasty getaway!

Climbing back into the car, Ima informed Vanna of the situation. "It looks like this place closed up in a hurry. We did all our cleaning for naught. I guess we can kiss our deposit goodbye. Sorry. Will that leave you short of cash, Vanna?"

"You are such a baby...Little Lamby-Ivy Ima! Little-Miss-Pure-Mind! You don't get it yet? *Impecunious* will never describe me. I'll always have money. And if I ever run out, I have ways of taking what I need."

Feeling defeated, Ima swallowed hard. "I'm sorry to hear that. I thought this last adventure might change you forever, but I guess not."

"I may someday change and think like a...lamb; but for now, I choose to keep alive the wolf inside. Before softening up, I have some *scores to settle*."

Vanna the vamp had ridden back into town *on her high horse*. Her words penetrated like *pins in a voodoo doll*. Ima felt the familiar *impasse* return: the strain to conversation and the fading of a friendship. Why did Vanna work at being so mysterious... as if she enjoyed building walls around herself? What would it take to impact that wall or even better, to knock it down permanently? The process of caring about Vanna might end up with Ima denting her own head. A simple solution was to give up on Vanna, permanently.

"So," said Ima flatly, "I'm headed for Manhattan. Where can I drop you off? Portland is about an hour away."

"No, not there! The Boston Airport will do nicely." Vanna snapped back sharply, *dropping all pretense* of southern politeness toward her so-called friend.

"Good enough," replied Ima, determined to answer only the questions asked, just like at the border. But could she do that? She had begun to understand what it meant to be *one's own worst enemy*.

"I thought your dad is to be on tour for two more weeks," said Vanna.

"Well yes, but I'd rather be alone in New York than spend another night in Maine," admitted Ima.

Again they fell into a deep silence.

By late morning, they reached the Logan Airport in Boston where a curbside porter removed Vanna's large trunk from the rear of the car and put it on a cart. Ima watched as Vanna headed into the ticket lobby with the porter tailing behind her.

Suddenly, she realized that the vamp had carelessly left behind her shoulder bag and the kitty carrier. Hopping from the car and leaving the motor running, Ima grabbed the two items and chased after Vanna. "You won't get far without your purse. And you also forgot Boofy again."

Vanna looked back *petulantly* at Ima and sneered, "You're always in such a tizzy! I had planned to come back for all that."

"So you say now! But truthfully, Vanna, after your leaving both of them in my charge on the train and the ferry, I can't believe anything you say."

"So, you're calling me a liar? Is that what you really think of me?"

"I don't *harbor* bad feelings toward you; but frankly, I don't know what to think of you." Ima reached out to touch Vanna, "But, I do hope your life gets on an *even keel.*"

In a huff, Vanna roughly yanked her purse off Ima's shoulder. "Excuse me, the porter expects his tip." Then, without a word more, she turned abruptly and stormed off, exclaiming to the sky, "Delta, Delta, take me home to the delta where manners rule."

"No. Stop! Vanna, you forgot Boofy...come back." Hoping for assistance, Ima lifted the wire kennel for the crowd around to see. "You absolutely cannot leave your cat with me again. Is that clear? I love her, but she belongs to you. She's your responsibility."

Vanna turned *about face,* planted her feet in second position with arms akimbo, and waved casually. "Oh just keep her. She's good company. Besides, Tall Daddy's allergic."

"No way, I'm on vacation. I can't lug a cat everywhere I go. Please Vanna. Take your cat," Ima pleaded with a voice that faded in the noise of cars and travelers. She only got stares from passersby, but no sympathy.

Once again stunned at the *persistent,* willful behavior of this very tall, pretty, but rude young lady, Ima stood watching as Vanna disappeared into the airport lobby. Once again Ima had seen Vanna escape responsibility, leaving any inconveniences to whoever crossed her path?

Ima shrugged her shoulders and walked back to the car only to see it being *impounded* and hoisted onto a wrecker's hook. An airport policeman stood there writing out a ticket.

"Hey lady, this yu-ah car?"

"No, it's a rental. Really officer, I only left it...for a second."

"Look lady, it doesn't matter if want to leave yu-ah own car or a rental or even yu-ah papa's limousine at the curb. Ya can't! Understand? Ya gotta take 'em to the proper parking lots."

"Oh, of course. Normally, I would. Only my friend left her purse and her kitty in the car and I—"

"Yeah, yeah, I he-ah the sob story. Save it for my funeral. All I care 'bout is ya broke the law and ya gotta pay the fine."

"But, officer, don't you undersand. I was chasing down my friend before she disappeared," said Ima surprised, after their hassles, she still considered Vanna a friend.

"Yeah-yeah! Reasons a-hr reasons and rules a-hr rules. Ya got yu-ah idears...and I got my idears. Unless they match up, ya get a ticket," said the policeman, handing her the ticket and motioning the wrecker to continue towing the rent-a-car. "Now listen, young lady. Take this slip to the Avis counter and then get yu-ah life back on an *even keel*. Ya he-ah me?"

Ima nodded and thought how funny that he should use that same phrase she had just said to Vanna. Maybe she was so concerned about the *gaping holes* in Vanna's behavior that she had failed to see the flaws in her own. Then it hit Ima like a truck. Talk about gaping holes, in one hand she gripped the cat carrier but in the other, she did not hold her own *grip*. The valise that held everything for her trip had gone away with the car!

Ima ran a few car lengths down the curb, bumping into people and waving her arms to flag down the wrecker now speeding off. Unfortunately, he did not see her. She scooted into the airport lobby and down to the lower level to the car rental *kiosks*. Finding

Avis, she slapped her parking ticket on the counter and related what had happened.

"What are you driving?" the Avis clerk asked.

"A white Caprice," she answered, breathlessly.

"May I see your contract?" the clerk asked.

"It's in the glove compartment; but worse than that, my valise is still in the trunk. Can you stop the wrecker from *impounding* the car?"

"Oh, don't worry. The airport police love to cause a *hubbub* over parking infractions, but we have a *failsafe system*. The wrecker will actually pull the car over to our lot. I'll send one of our guys to collect what you left."

Ima sighed. "Lately, everything has backfired on me. Thanks for making this easier."

"You still have to pay the ticket," the clerk reminded. "We'll just add it on."

"Anything, just to get out of this mess," admitted Ima. She pulled her cash pouch from under blouse and paid the charges.

Then, with kennel and valise in hand, Ima hailed a taxi to take her to the Boston depot to catch a train down to New York. She sat back, poked a finger through the wire carrier and cooed to Boofy.

"Well, little puppy cat, you are quite the *resilient* traveler! You probably have no idea where you are or what's going on. So, let me give you a clue," Ima said, taking out the kitty to pet and comfort it.

"Now, I don't want you to think that Vanna has stopped loving you. You will always be good friends. But, the problem with Vanna is...she has too much on her mind...to give others even the slightest consideration."

Boofy curled up in Ima's arms, purred loudly, and seemed satisfied to lick the face of her temporary friend and maybe her new owner.

"So...I think we'll be spending a lot more time together. In a few more hours, you'll be in my old home; and tonight we shall both fall asleep on my old Jenny Lind bed."

. . .

Although the short trip from Boston to Manhattan had calmed Ima, the madhouse at Grand Central Station brought her unexpected joy and excitement. She smelled the grime in the air and heard the metal wheels rolling to a stop on the metal rails. Inside the covered terminal, rows of train cars ran *flush with* the boarding platforms. This made getting on and off much easier for passengers than Ima had found, climbing up and down the three steep steps of the Newfie Bullet.

With a style like nowhere else, the baggage handlers and porters bustled to and fro. Seeing the semi-organized chaos, Ima patted herself on the back for wisely not checking her valise or cat kennel. She entered the huge lobby designed during the heyday of trains. Its glass-dome and granite floor all looked and felt so familiar.

Grateful to have arrived home safely, Ima quickly forgot her woes from earlier in the day and scrambled down a couple of levels to the subway interchanges beneath the Grand Central lobby. She bought some tokens and went through the correct *turnstile* she recalled should lead to the same platform as long ago.

Various local and express subways screeched to a stop and then whizzed off again. For all the times she had traveled down Manhattan's West Side to Grand Central and taken the Lexington Line to her school on the Upper East Side, she believed she could do it in her sleep. Thinking so, she slipped into reverie and recalled her childhood days in the *Big Apple*.

Ima had loved growing up in New York City mostly because she had a great friend: Riina Feingold. Ima and Riina first met in nursery school. From then on, they were nearly inseparable and completely *insufferable*. They pretended to be twin sisters. Although they attended private school and naturally wore uniforms, they insisted on matching on the weekends too. They had a dress code for wherever they went: jeans to the zoo; fancy dresses to concerts; and baby doll pajamas to slumber parties.

Although looking nothing alike on the outside, they had similar thoughts on the inside and could finish each other's sentences. They even started their menstrual cycles within three days of each other. At first, they agreed to hate all boys until going to their first dance, which changed their minds. Then they decided to adore all boys, especially those their own age, and wished their school would go coed. At night, the girls had *marathon* telephone chats, which *exasperated* the Feingolds and the Longwinds. But on second thought, both parents realized that their children's relationship had more value than a few missed business calls.

At age twelve, Ima had the first tragedy in her almost perfect life, a tragedy that left a worse taste in her mouth than cutting twelve-year old molars. Ima's famous musical star father Lionel Longwind took a job in Michigan. To Ima that place sounded more like a foreign country than a state. She felt totally *discombobulated* having to leave her home in Manhattan and her beloved girls school. The cruelest cut of all came when she had to say goodbye to Riina, her best chum ever.! Yet Ima gradually admitted if her family had not moved to Michigan, she might never have met, fallen in love with, and married Sammy Purple.

A Chance Meeting at Grand Central

The bustling crowds moved from the subway trains and bumped Ima out of the way, stirring her from a childhood reverie. Since tokens now cost more than in the early 1950s she figured schedules and routes had also changed which meant she probably now stood on the wrong platform. Finding a staircase to the next sub-level, she started down but suddenly crashed into someone.

"Hey, watch it. Can't cha read? You're going down the up-side."

"Sorry, I got turned around," Ima said looking directly into the young woman's eyes. Suddenly, she pushed her valise to the other side and began to duck under the rail to get to the correct side but stopped short of her goal. "I can't believe it. It's Riina. Reenie Finklegel?" she uttered a forbidden name.

"It's Ímagine, Ímagine Hotwind Pickanose?" declared Riina, obviously returning some *arcane* insult.

"Is it really you?" yelled Ima to be heard over the *din*.

"You bet. It is I, in all my glory!" Riina spoke dramatically.

"I can't believe out of all the people in New York I'd see you right when I arrived. You haven't changed *one iota* since MaMadge's—" Ima interrupted herself and hugged Riina.

"And you still look twelve. Glad you're here. I need a partner in crime," quipped Riina.

They started to jabber and laugh loudly, which like a car accident stopped the flow of traffic going both ways. A host of objections soon blasted forth in typical Yankee lingo.

"Wha' ya think...ya own the staircase?"

"Get outa d'way. You're blockin' traffic."

"Hey, let a poison through."

"Watch out who ya go pushin' already, mista."

"Not you...I'm talking 'bout her...and the utter her."

"Hey, ya hoy'd da utter guy. Youse two...move it...I said."

"Who ya think both ya are...Lady Astor?"

"Yeh. This ain't the grand Waldorf-Astoria hotel...it's Grand Central Station."

Riina *glowered* at the complainers, gripped the collar of one, and quipped in her fake Brooklyn accent. "Hey, ya lid'l louse! I just hoy'd your mudder calling ya...so ya bettah already get a move on ya-self."

Then quickly Riina motioned Ima to follow her. Both ducked under the railing like kids. With Ima lugging her cargo and Riina going in front, the two long-lost friends went up the down staircase, giggling all the way.

After two flights in *counter-flow* to the crowds, Ima declared, "I've gotta stop a second and catch my breath."

"Okay, I've got a half-hour to kill. Let's go somewhere to talk," said Riina yelling over the noisy crowd and waving Ima toward the subway exit.

"But it'll cost another token to get back into the subway system," Ima called back.

"Be *audacious*. Live dangerously, or why bother to live at all."

"Right, audacious. Our parents went nuts when we learned that word," said Ima.

"So, let's duck under the *turnstile* and go upstairs to Nedicks for a hotdog."

"Neat-o Nedick's! How normal that sounds. Can you remember the last time we ate a Nedick's together?" asked Ima.

Still not seeming to notice how Ima struggled to *negotiate* the valise and cat kennel, Riina began to pull her old pal like a wagon through the crowds. Then suddenly, she let go Ima's arm and scurried ahead as if to pave a path for the bulk Ima carried.

Ima finally caught up. "I'd forgotten what it's like…how crazy… the crush of the crowd…the rush of routine…the urgencies… people with a million things to do on their lunch hours…folks looking for bargains with only a few bucks in their pockets to—"

"Yeah, pretty poetic stuff too!" Riina proclaimed to the air. "Eight million people means eight million stories, stories you'd never suspect! But, don't go asking anyone to volunteer details because…they've got a millions things—"

"On their minds," said Ima finishing the sentence. They were back on the same wavelength as when kids. "I know…New Yorkers only respond to a definite question."

"Yeah, even then you'll only get *Just the facts, ma'am* until you learn how to treat a real New Yorker. But there's even less chance of that happening because they're all out there running the rat race for everyone not living in New York City," Riina added, as if stating an *immutable* law of the land.

"Yeah, but shouldn't even rats have time for their fellow rats who've seen the other 49 states?" inquired Ima with a grin.

"You know, I think Michigan's made you mush. New York requires a tougher Ima."

"Oh, you want, tough. I'd like to see you make it in my recent adventures."

Finally they reached a *turnstile*. Riina went under, but Ima tried to reverse her way through. The cat carrier got *lodged* sideways. After wiggling it back and forth, Ima finally turned the carrier on end and managed to tug it to the other side, all whilst, Boofy mee…ooowed…loudly.

"What's that?" asked Riina.

"A kitty...and a very long story with its own urgencies," Ima said. "Say, since we're on the surface, we might as well find a place where we can sit and really talk."

"That cancels Nedicks," said Riina

"Right," said Ima, "I remember you either stand and eat, or grab and run."

"*No biggie*...let me think of somewhere else cheap and close," said Riina.

"Isn't there an Choc Full o' Nuts across the street?" asked Ima.

"Last I knew. Coffee sounds great," agreed Riina.

They pushed through the Lexington Avenue exit, jaywalked mid-block, and caused a couple of taxis to slam on their brakes to dodge them. Whereas Riina laughed at the tires screeching and drivers cursing, Ima almost froze solid in the street. She had forgotten how fast Manhattan cabbies drove. If policemen wore bulletproof vests here, pedestrians needed suits of armor.

A vagrant stood like an unofficial doorman in front of the coffee shop, begging for dimes and practically *accosting* customers. Ima and Riina figured he *obviously* had no concept of what a cup cost nowadays and probably planned to collect enough coins to buy a bottle of cheap wine for later. They did not assist him in his own destruction.

Getting past the beggar, the two old friends soon settled into empty places at a counter. While sipping hot cups of coffee, they watched all the typical characters coming in and out. Secretaries juggled bags of coffee to-go: marked for sugar, black, light, or light-light. Unemployed workers nursed a single cup while pouring over the classified ads. Semi-intellectuals sat doodling impossible *New York Times* crossword puzzles. Actor types excelled as master killers-of-time. They yawned often to exercise their faces and checked their watches as if waiting for an important appointment. Over in one corner sat an actress who kept admiring herself in her compact mirror.

"I feel a bit sorry for that girl over there. I suspect a sleazy director has wooed her here with the promise of an audition. Little does she know that no one in show business really holds meetings at Choc Full o' Nuts!" whispered Riina.

"New York constantly changes yet somehow stays the same. I've missed it all...and you...so much," admitted Ima. "I love this crazy place."

"Me too! Only an earthquake could shake me loose from living here."

"Well, that's not likely to happen! Remember the saying 'Old Amsterdam may be built on *poulder*?" said Ima.

"B-b-but New Amsterdam is built on a boulder" they said together and thumbed their noses at those annoyed by their antics.

"So, I've only got time for answers to a few questions. What are you doing here? Where's Sammy, and why do you have a cat?"

"Sshhhh! We'll get kicked out," whispered Ima kicking Riina's leg.

Joining the *ruse*, Riina whispered, "Okay. We'll pretend we're tourists just needing a cup of coffee until the next train. And let's say the carrier is my suitcase."

"Great idea," Ima lifted her coffee cup, clinked Riina's cup, and whispered a toast. "Here's hoping no one sees the furry object moving inside it."

"So...what's going on? I'm no cat, but you've revved my curiosity."

"Well, I'm here to visit PapaLi. I haven't seen him since MaMadge died. And this cat? Well, a lady dumped it on me at the Boston airport. I'll reveal that story in due time. As for Sammy, he got reassigned to Vietnam. So, I'm on an adventure," iterated Ima.

"Oh, Ima, that awful war! Aren't you terrified for him?" Riina asked.

"Sammy's a pilot, Reenie. Pilots go to war. Look, civilians don't understand how serious military matters can get. But, may we just...let go that topic for now?" Ima asked, waving her arm and letting go her coffee cup instead. It went splashing to the floor.

A huffy waitress walked around to the customers' side of the counter and began to dry up the spilled liquid with a floppy yarn mop. While leaning over to wring out the spilt coffee into a bucket, she peered more closely at the carrier.

"What's this? I've hoy—d of seeing-eye dogs but not seeing-eye cats? That's just ridiculous," chided the worker. "Besides neither of you looks handicapped."

Riina and Ima gulped and looked like two cats that had just swallowed a goldfish.

Ima tried to explain before being interrupted. "There's a logical answer for—"

"Save it for the city! Only handicapped...animals...are allowed in an eating establishment. You're violating a bunch of sanitation laws."

"But, Boofy's not handicapped," said Ima, the *perennial* English teacher catching an *obvious* misplaced modifier.

"What's that supposed to mean to me?" asked the waitress.

The two old friends glanced at each other and had the same thought. Riina grabbed the valise; and Ima lifted the cat carrier. Then both tore out of the coffee shop before anyone could ask more questions. They headed a little ways down Lexington Avenue toward 42nd Street but stopped at a newsstand. Unable to go an inch farther, they leaned over and laughed wildly until their *sides split*. Although many years had passed, these two had instantly returned to their prankish pre-teens.

"Oops, I forgot to leave a tip," Ima said *rummaging* around in her cash pouch and pulling out a quarter. "I'm going back."

"Throw it at her," ordered Riina. "That's what she deserves for nosiness!"

"You know me. I can't do that."

"Oh Ima, don't be *lily-livered*. Have fun. Get smarter. Live dangerously."

Ima ignored Riina's *protestations* and dashed back to the coffee shop. Looking to see if anyone noticed her, she put a tip on the counter, flashed out again and returned to where Riina waited.

"Well, did the waitress smile and gush with gratitude?" Riina inquired.

"Of course not! I'd never expect it. But, we'd better get lost in the crowd in case the manager comes after me for breaking the rules. You know how breaking rules hurts my stomach."

"Hey, you're back in the big city now. Minor rules get broken every day. That's how we survive. That's why the city keeps making more rules."

"That makes no sense. That only makes more rules to break," Ima iterated the logic.

"The more the merrier," Riina exclaimed.

"You mean. keep the citizens happy by letting them get away with something?"

"Yep. Now you're back *in tune*; and the *corollary* to that rule is...keep the police happy by letting them search for all of the worms in the Big Apple."

"I had forgotten what a terrible influence you are on me. Back in your presence for thirty minutes, I have purposely gone the wrong way on the stairs, ducked under a turnstile, jay-walked, spilt coffee, and broken city health codes."

"Stick with me, and I'll walk you right into a manhole," Riina added with a giggle and then looked at her watch. "Say, I better get going. I've got an audition in a few minutes."

"An audition? Well, great...uh...*break a leg*," Ima said, "Call my dad's home to let me know how it goes."

"Look, there's also a softball game tomorrow. Let's talk later. Love ya."

Riina handed the valise back to Ima, jaywalked boldly across the street, and disappeared into Grand Central.

• • •

Tired from the excitement, Ima decided to hail a cab instead of attempting the subway again. She gave the driver the address just off Riverside Drive and collapsed in the backseat. She soon realized that the cabby thought his customer a tourist who would not know the difference when he kept going south on Lexington. But he had sadly miscalculated. This cab ride was not Ima's *first rodeo*. She was *savvy* enough to know the driver's intention to *meander* around town to run up his meter. That plan she would *nip in the bud* by dropping a few hints.

"Whew! Can't wait to get home. Oh, by the way, you must be new to New York. Don't hassle going cross-town to Riverside. Just turn around, get on Madison, go uptown to 72nd and head through the Park to Broadway. Then go to 79th Street. I actually live just before Riverside."

She could see the driver's neck turn red. Upon getting her *subtle* message, he quickly corrected his route. His attempt to fool a native New Yorker had failed. "You're right, Miss. Sometimes I daydream and miss my turns."

Ima had travelled enough to know he hoped his mistake plus a cover-up lie would not affect his receiving a tip. But it would. Passengers groomed cabbies for the service they wanted, not vice versa. His *blatant* dishonesty matched by his naïveté would definitely cost him a tip.

"I love to daydream too; but on the job, it can be rather *precarious* to say the least," added Ima.

After following instructions and fighting traffic, the taxi pulled in front of a 1920s five-storied brick building with a curved stone front. Ima paid the driver the exact meter reading, nothing more. They both understood the system. Bad service meant no tip.

Lugging her valise and cat carrier, she slowly walked up to the entrance and waited for the uniform doorman to swing open the heavy gilded door. But no one came. Pushing with her baggage, she managed to pry open the door and enter the lobby. Not having seen the place since MaMadge lay dying, Ima gasped at the decor. Dried-up plants, faded curtains, and scuffed marks on the marble floors declared their past glory.

What a pity the landlord had neglected this old classic building. Her parents had owned their flat for decades and *subleased* it whenever they went away for extended periods. Lionel always claimed the old homestead worth keeping because someday every inch of Manhattan would be as priceless as a diamond from Tiffany's. Perhaps, he had not meant these precious inches that now resembled the Bowery more than Fifth Avenue.

Having no key to Lionel's apartment, Ima pushed the superintendent's office button and then spoke into the intercom. "Mr. Flannery?"

"Yes, who's there?"

"It's Ímagine Longwind!"

"Who?"

"Lionel Longwind's daughter! He's on tour for another week or so. I've arrived sooner than expected, so can you let me in? I don't have a key."

An old man in coveralls came down the dark hall, yawning and jangling his key ring. "Now, who did you say you were?"

"Ímagine Longwind...of 4C. Remember me? I played here in this lobby all the time when a child. Your son and I used to have marble *marathons* when you'd bring him to work on Saturdays."

"I think you're mistaken. My son is 30 years old. He never plays marbles."

"Probably not anymore," said Ima wondering if this old man had grown *senile*. "Let me see. Maybe you can remember my mom Madge Longwind? She taught at Farnsworth Boys School, around the corner?"

"No. My son went to PS 119. You must have this building mixed up with somewhere else. I've been here for 40 years."

"I know that Mr. Flannery. Many a time you unclogged our kitchen sink." Ima had few ideas left. "Maybe you remember that Christmas when the boys choir sang carols here in the lobby?"

"That sounds sort of familiar."

"Remember a few years ago when my mom was so ill, and Lionel had a role in *Camelot*? Remember how the whole cast serenaded MaMadge outside our window the night before she died? Remember the lobby overflowed with flowers for weeks? Surely, you remember some of this."

"Oh, that Lionel Longwind. Now I remember. Heartbroken he was...moved out not long after that."

"What?" said Ima, baffled and practically in tears. Her father had never said anything about moving. "Well...do you have any idea where he moved to?" *Dredging* up old times began to overtake her.

"Nope, but we can look him up. I'm sorry my lame brain upset you. Events get harder and harder to recall...and people...that's a whole other matter."

"By the way, where's the doorman?" Ima asked innocently.

"He's been gone a while, but we do have a night watchman. That's good enough for here, but he doesn't wear a fancy uniform."

Flannery walked over to the night watchman's desk. "Let's look for a phone book."

"Did he get lots of money for the flat?"

"Who?"

"Lionel Longwind. Did he get a good price for our flat?"

"Oh, no Miss Ima. This has always been an apartment house. People just simply stay here forever because...they pay cheap rents. It only seems like they own their flats, but they don't."

"I thought for sure we owned our flat!" said Ima, wondering if she were getting *senile* as well.

"You see, years ago a Rent Control Law forbade owners to raise rents in certain old buildings. Without much income on these huge properties, landlords can barely pay their taxes. They merely keep drains unclogged and light bulbs in the halls. That's why most of these old gems *deteriorate*. I'm hoping the Historical

Society will get interested. In the last few years, it's doing a lot to preserve the old look of New York."

"I wondered why everything looked so shabby," Ima admitted.

"Now about this predicament of finding your father," said Mr. Flannery, as he thumbed through the phonebook and squinted at the tiny print. "No Lionel Longwind listed. You know... most famous people have unlisted numbers."

"Oh, I've got his number. I just don't know now where he plugged in his phone. I mean, his new address," Ima sighed.

"And I don't know how to find where someone unlisted might live," added the old man.

"So, where do I go? I had planned to stay here tonight."

"Got any friends in the City?" asked Flannery, more clearer-headed.

"Of course. That's perfect. I just ran into Reenie. I could spend the night with her and find Lionel's apartment tomorrow. Let me see that directory."

Ima thumbed to the "Fs" and ran her finger up and down. "Good Grief, six pages of Feingolds and no Reenie!"

"Maybe she's married," Flannery suggested.

"She didn't say," Ima replied.

"What's her father's name?"

"Riina called him …. Uhh...something like la-la uh...lollipops. He was just plain Mr. Feingold to us kids, and that's been years ago." She stopped to think a moment. "It seems his name was maybe Lloyd or Leonard or Lenny or Larry...something like that." She ran her finger up and down the page, trying to jog her memory. "No, nothing sounds familiar. If I call all these, it'll take all night...so then I won't need a place to stay."

"Well, I can't let you camp out here in the lobby, but there's always the YWCA. That's where girls often stay when they first come to New York. We could call for a vacancy and rates," Flannery said.

"Might as well. The way I'm spending money, it won't last for my whole trip anyway. I'll be sleeping in doorways before long," Ima said sadly.

"Don't despair young Missy." Flannery found the Y's number and called, "Do you have a room available tonight?" He waited. "Uh-huh. How much with a cat? He waited. "She'll take it." He hung up and smiled. "They have room. It's $10, but no pets allowed."

Ima began to murmur under her breath. "A fine friend Vanna is. That stinker figured Boofy was an inconvenience to her, so she pawned the poor animal off on me."

"She doesn't sound like much of friend," surmised the old superintendent.

"Now, what am I suppose to do? Put her cat in a locker at the Port Authority overnight?"

"That's not a good idea," *interjected* Flannery. "Poor thing would suffocate."

Ima leaned down to open the carrier and found food, water, poop, and litter all jumbled. She pulled out the kitty and loved on it. "Poor Boofy. No one wants you."

Mr. Flannery saw Ima's *dismay* and offered to keep the kitty until she got settled in. After cleaning up the carrier mess, Ima opened a fresh can of food, brushed Boofy's fur, and tore a newspaper into bits to use for litter. That would have to work until morning. Fortunately, Boofy had almost hibernated during each phase of the trip.

Then grabbing her valise and thanking Flannery, Ima decided to hike over to Broadway and catch a bus down to the "Y." She held her head high and took long strides as her mother had taught her.

MaMadge repeatedly said, "Show the world you can defend yourself. Walk as if you have purpose and a definite destination. No one will want to tangle with you. That's a woman's first lesson of survival in Manhattan."

Stalked by a Manhattan Moose

Glad she had only her small valise to lug, Ima walked up the steps of the stately YWCA. Several big *moosey women* stood outside smoking. With short butch haircuts and humped shoulders to hide any sign of breasts, they looked more like men than women. Ima remembered similar type women hanging around the softball diamonds when she and Riina had played in the Central Park Junior Girls League. Their coach had warned the team whenever going alone to the restrooms, to steer clear of such strangers.

After checking in at the front desk, Ima went to a very clean but *Spartan* room. A bunk size bed stretched from a single window. A sink hung on the wall, with a mirror above. The desk clerk had informed her that bathtubs and toilets were located down the hall. Completely *depleted* from a long day of difficulties, Ima slipped on her PJs and flopped into bed, without going to the bathroom or brushing her teeth. No sooner had her eyes closed when a knock came at the door. She sat up abruptly.

"Yes?" said Ima *tentatively*.

"Do you want some company?" an anonymous voice said.

"What?"

"Do you want someone to talk to?"

Ima's heart pounded wildly. Did the Y have a sort of a *nighty-night* service, to tuck guests into bed? Had someone noticed her frazzled state and now offered counseling? Logically, the clerk would have surely listed such service with the other rules and *amenities*. Or Ima would have requested such help if it were needed, which it wasn't! This knock might only signal a mistaken room number. But Ima's inner detective sensed something not so innocent.

In the dark she automatically reached for a phone on the nightstand but found none. Then she recalled the Y only offered a common payphone in the hall. Calling the desk clerk to check on this *intruder* meant opening the door to go to the phone. She had no intention of making that mistake!

Ima decided to say nothing more. Then the person outside jiggled the door. If this someone meant her harm, he or she would have to bust the door down from its frame. Fortunately, Ima had double-locked it. After what seemed an hour of quivering, Ima finally heard footsteps fade away from her room. Finally, she fell fast asleep.

· · ·

Having a good night's rest gave Ima a clearer head to explore new options. She showered, repacked her valise, and made a few early phone calls to the names that now swirled back into her brain.

She had called Wes Westerly, but the answering service said his office would not open until 10. She'd be there by then and had no number to leave. As far as Ima could recall, Wes was the only agent her dad had ever had. Surely he would know Lionel's whereabouts. Besides, for years, Wes had been a close family friend, almost like a godfather to her.

That gave her the early morning hours to check other possibilities. She recalled a few of Lionel's old *cronies*. Shelton Grape came to mind, and he had a listed number. He sounded happy enough that she had called. Now doing TV announcer work more than theatre, Shelton admitted drifting apart from his actor friends. However, he thought that Lionel lived somewhere on the Upper Eastside.

"Thanks, Mr. Grape. At least that gets me to the right side of the island and narrows the search to a few less million residents," Ima said with a giggle in her voice.

"Look, I'll keep inquiring. Meet me for lunch at the Friars Club. Let's make it one o'clock. I may have more answers for you," Shelton remarked.

"That is very gracious of you. Thank you again. See you soon," she said.

When checking out of her room, Ima learned that the YWCA had strict security and forbade loiterers in the hallways. Not surprisingly, the desk clerk confirmed that the Y did not provide roaming counselors. Ima patted herself on the back. Her instincts had been right.

Scooting down the old brick steps, she sighed with relief that no one, male or female, leaned against the building or waited to *harass* her. She struck out to catch a cross-town bus to First Avenue and very soon broke into her Manhattan stride. The exercise felt so refreshing to her travel weary body that she decided to walk all the way to the Westerly office. Besides, being on the sidewalks gave her an eye level view of sights rarely seen by tourists. She bought a pretzel to munch, looked at trinkets in the street peddler stalls, and visited a tiny gallery with pictures on the walls in a narrow alley between buildings.

• • •

"Imagine, darling," said Wes, welcoming her *effusively*.

"Mr. Westerly, thank you so much for seeing me *on the spur*."

"What is this Mr. Westerly jazz? When did I stop being your Uncle Wes?" he said, the *consummate* host and constant entertainer.

"Never, I hope," she said.

"I guess not. I was the one who met your folks at the station when they got back from Lionel's tour in Ohio. Remember? I held you my arms while the porter got the trunks." He laughed at himself. "Of course, you don't."

"Right. I have a pretty good memory but not that good," Ima said with a giggle.

"My-my, you've come a long way since I saw you last."

"Uncle Wes, I haven't changed that much since—"

"I know, but just indulge me. I want to take a good look at you. Remember how you used to model for me when you were little. You know, you'd spin around and bow."

Ima strolled down between the couch and desk, pretending to be in a fashion show and holding out her simple *pinwale* skirt as if it were airy *gossamer*. She whirled round and fell back onto the couch laughing.

"My dear Ímagine," said Wes, wistfully. He began to sing in a French accent like Maurice Chevalier. "'Thank heaven for leettle gerls, for leettle gerls get beeger everyday' and you have!"

"You're such a tease, Uncle Wes. I've missed that about you."

Then he seemed to eye her with a talent agent's glint. "Now, that you're *all growed up*, as they say down South, you've turned out too short to be a top model; but your face is still cute as a button, perfect for Disney films."

"Uncle Wes, I teach school now and am very happy doing so, I might add," she said.

"Schoolteacher...mulepreacher! You still look like a teenager to me," he said with *obvious* flattery. "Say, when did we last meet?"

"At MaMadge's funeral a few years back."

"Oh, yes. A tragic loss...but what I meant was when did you leave here?"

"When I was twelve, PapaLi moved us to Michigan. Don't you remember? The Interlochen School hired him to teach musical comedy? Then during the summers, he acted in Shakespeare plays—"

"At Stratford-on-the-Avon in Ontario. Of course. I tried to talk him out of that, but you know Lionel. He wanted to kick his career in that direction. I think when he returned to New York, the experiment or experience helped in the long run."

"Not for me. I felt lost in Michigan. Except for meeting my husband and going to college there, I have always considered New York my true home."

"I know, sweetheart. New York draws like a magnet."

"Or if you're a gangster, concrete boots will at least keep you in the New York Harbor, right?" Ima added with a teasing glance. "You know, like in the movies?"

"That's right! Best not get on the wrong side of the *mob bosses* here, or you're doomed…also like in the movies," Wes said, pointing his finger like a gun. "So what can I do for a young lady who could have a Hollywood career but chooses to teach?"

"Help me find my dad. Where is he?"

"On tour with *Guys and Dolls,*" Wes said matter-of-factly.

"So, you are still his agent!"

Wes nodded and then cocked his head. "Unless you know something I don't."

"No, I'm so glad you are. I was hoping so," she said.

"Well, I don't understand why you're here. Didn't you know he'd be out of town?"

"Oh yes, but I needed to come on earlier than expected. I got here last night and went to our old flat off Riverside. Much to my *chagrin*, the super said Lionel moved out right after MaMadge died. You know Lionel. He never writes any letters; and on the phone, he never mentioned it. He only talks about work," said Ima, *exasperated*. "So, tell me, where does my father live nowadays?"

Wes stood up and remarked, "I'll take you there right now. Give me a few moments to call the answering service. My assistant just quit; and unlike Lionel, I like those close to me to know my whereabouts."

Wes and Ima caught a cab to pick up Boofy from Mr. Flannery and then crossed back to East 74th Street at First Avenue. They pulled up before The Amherst, a contemporary apartment house that stood oddly among old tenements most likely waiting for the *wrecking ball*.

"Lionel's choosing to live in a high-rise surprises me. My folks always loved the historical architecture of the West Side," Ima lamented.

"I know, but I think all that reminded him of Madge. He just wanted a clean start. So, do you want me to go in?" asked Wes.

"No, I can manage. Thank you, Uncle Wes. You've helped me so much already."

"Oh, bosh," he said, obviously dismissing any effort on his part. "Okay, I'll go back to the office and take care of business. But we could meet for lunch at Sardi's, if you like."

"Thank you, but Shelton Grape has already invited me to the Friars Club."

"Grape? Hmmm," said Westerly scrunching his face. "Well, then I'll join you there to keep that wolf at bay."

They both laughed. Noting his curious comment about her lunch date, she pecked his cheek and got out of the cab. The cabby set her baggage on the sidewalk and then drove off. Ima stood there a moment, wondering if this place had a doorman or just a night watchman too.

Suddenly, Arnie, a football-player sized fellow in a maroon uniform, bounded out of the door. With an instant smile and greeting, he swooped up her valise and carrier, not noticing the cat inside.

"Let me help you, Miss," said Arnie. "Visiting someone?"

"No, my father lives here; and I've come home," Ima announced with a sigh.

"Which apartment?"

"I don't know. He's moved here since I was last in Manhattan. Please, just take these up to Lionel Longwind's apartment."

Arnie checked the binder on the reception desk. "Sorry, Mr. Longwind is out of town and left no instructions about a visitor."

"You're kidding. I'm Ímagine Longwind, his only child, here to visit. I know I'm early, but it shouldn't matter. His home is my home!"

"I wish I could help, but we have rules to safeguard our regular tenants. I can't simply let some *random* person into Mr. Longwind's apartment."

"I'm not some random person. I am his totally exhausted, longing-for-a-hot-bath-and-about-to-cry, daughter," Ima said, struggling to hold back her tears.

"Now, now. Let me talk with the manager, Miss Gibralter," Arnie said, disappearing.

Moments later, a tall, *intimidating* woman marched out, carrying a clipboard. She planted her feet in stone and glared at Ima. "Imogene Longwind. Never heard of you. Do you have some identification?"

"My name is Imagine, but I'm not famous like my PapaLi." Ima pulled out her passport.

"Well, this says Imagine Purple; but I don't see Longwind on here."

"Because I'm married! My passport application has my maiden name Longwind, but the state department chose not to use it on this document," said Ima, amazed at the manager's manners, or lack thereof.

"This is all very *unorthodox*. I'll have to call Mr. Levi," she said and went back to her office, mumbling all the while. "Imagine Purple? I can't even imagine seeing red if I got mad for being given a crazy name like that...indeed a cruel mark for life."

Meanwhile Arnie tried to calm the situation. "Don't worry," he said, pointing to the *officious* manager. "Everything will turn out okay. If you can't get past the manager, I'll call the owner myself. Mr. Levi is a real pussy-cat."

Ima gulped in gratitude to this kind doorman, "And does the owner allow pussy-cats in his apartments?" she said discreetly pointing down to the cat carrier.

"He does. Miss Gilbraltar doesn't. Say a prayer. Leave the rest to me." Arnie winked and moved his mountainous body to block the manager's view. "Just watch. God not only moves mountains but the Rock of Gibraltar as well."

Soon the manager returned. "Strange...but Mr. Levi approved your request. You must have *some kind of pull*."

"It's nice to have a famous father." Arnie winked at Ima, and Ima winked back.

"Well, in any case, I hope you enjoy your stay in New York. It is my duty to inform you that this is a quiet place: no subleases, no move-ins, no loud parties, no casual sleepovers, and no pets," she said, turning to head off.

Ima could not believe she stood in front of another Prudence Persnickety...with another list of rules.

Arnie whisked up the baggage and motioned Ima to follow him to the elevator. He hit the 8th floor button but not quickly enough. Miss Manager stuck her clipboard between the doors before they closed.

"Do I smell cat urine?"

"Oh yes, the best perfumes are made with it. I wear Joy. What do you use?" said Ima.

"I have my own unique scent formulated by an *exclusive* perfumery on Fifth Avenue."

"Do you mind telling me your perfume's name?" Ima asked without real interest.

Miss Manager glared at Ima "Surely you jest. A lady never shares her secrets with a stranger." Puffed up with her own power, she pulled out her clipboard, allowing the elevator to ascend.

The phone was already ringing loudly when Arnie opened the door to number 801. He quickly placed Ima's things inside the doorway and scurried back to the lobby, probably to *face the music* from the manager. Meanwhile, in totally unfamiliar territory, Ima followed the ringing to a phone on the kitchen wall. She grabbed it and hoped the party would not hang up before she could answer.

"Hello!"

"Ima, glad I caught you. It's Riina."

"Reenie, I'm so glad it's you. How did your audition go?"

"I'll fill you in later. First, a favor. Can you play ball this afternoon?"

"What? Are you kidding?"

"No, for real! Some of us actresses formed a team for the city league. Anyway today, we're short...a shortstop. We really need to win this game for a chance at the playoffs. You used to be a great shortstop. Could you help us out?"

"I haven't played softball *since Hector was a pup*," admitted Ima.

"It's like typing or riding a bike. You never forget how. So, meet me before seven at the East Diamonds in Central Park. Wear jeans. I'll bring you a team shirt. See ya," Riina said and hung up before Ima could *refuse*.

Fancy Lunch and Softball Bunch

Ima looked around her father's one bedroom apartment wondering where she would sleep. This cookie-cutter space was a *far cry* from the grandeur her family had once occupied off Riverside Drive. Although spacious enough, the living room made her parents' furniture looked *dowdy* against the sleek white plaster walls. The smell of cigarette smoke hung in the living room. How she wished Lionel would quit...if not to help his health...at least, to save his voice.

Scattered unpacked boxes and ill-set furniture told a story about her father. Lionel had never moved in properly. He had given no thought to having company or grouping seats for conversation. Ima surmised that without the female touches of MaMadge, Lionel did not consider this space his home, just a *flophouse* between tours.

Stacks of unopened envelopes represented months of mail. Ima judged from the short, neat stacks that Arnie must have emptied the Longwind mailbox once a week when PapaLi went out of town. Upon seeing many restaurant bills, Ima *presumed* her father ate out most meals. In this personal mystery, she felt her detective sense served a good purpose.

Audition notices were strewn around on the dining table which probably now doubled for his desk. Lionel had circled an open call to replace the role of Jud in a revival of *Oklahoma*. He had made a note to check on possible cast openings in the newly premiered show 1776. She promised herself to see that musical during this visit. It pleased Ima to think her father still tried out for good roles but took lesser ones in between. She knew how actors survived in the *dog-eat-dog* business of theatre. She made a mental note to ask Uncle Wes about Lionel's next in-town job.

Framed awards and certificates lined the floor instead of walls. She thumbed through and noticed one commemorating a *Friars Club Roast* given him last year. She gasped, "Oh, good grief, the Friars Club! I forgot all about my lunch with Shelton Grape," she looked at a clock and dashed downstairs. Arnie hailed her a cab, and she flew away.

• • •

In 1929, Martin Erdmann built an *august* English Renaissance structure as his residence. It sat on East 55th Street between Park and Madison Avenues. The Friars later purchased his home for their Club House in 1957. The outside of the building bore a stone *façade*; the inside had an equally masculine appearance with heavy paneling, *balustrades*, and crown moldings fit for Mad King Ludwig's Castle. Although the first floor dining room allowed guests, it only hinted of the promise of splendor held up the grand staircase. But the upper floors remained open *exclusively* to members.

The aging but ever dashing Shelton Grape stood just inside the lobby. Ima thought he looked dwarfed by his surroundings, like the *sexton of a great cathedral*. Grape seemed nervous as he waved to Ima as if she might have forgotten him. Instead, she instantly recognized him because in many ways, he resembled

Lionel. Both *svelte* and sauvé, they often competed for roles. But whereas, Lionel, a singer by reputation, had turned more to acting; Shelton, an actor by training, had moved more to announcing.

Shelton approached and kissed her hand but lingered longer than she preferred. "We'll take lunch in the lounge instead of the dining room."

The steward led them off to a cozier area with dark tables and deeply *tufted* chairs.

"It will be quieter here and much easier to talk," Shelton explained to Ima.

Shelton ordered baked sole to be de-boned at the table, asparagus tips, *wilted endive salad,* and a bottle of champagne. Ima could think of nothing to *warrant* such an elaborate celebration except her finding Lionel's apartment!

"By the way, I hope you weren't put out too much trying to find my father's address. Wes Westerly saved the day, and I'm all settled in now."

"Oh, yes, he does consider himself a savior. In fact, he called to say he would meet us for dessert after his office duties. I think he phrased it...as to save you from my charms," Shelton said, laughing but showing signs of being *miffed.*

"Oh good, it will be fun to visit with Uncle Wes a bit more," Ima exclaimed but noticed her comment seemed to irritate Shelton. She found him a rather strange duck, especially upon seeing him *bristle* at her words of fondness for Westerly.

"Oh yes, I'll grant you he is fun, quite the comedian...but finds it hard to buckle down to the drudge of work. Now he has no choice but to run the business himself. It seems his assistant has up and quit."

Ima wondered about Shelton's bitter tone. "So I take it you are no longer represented by his agency?"

"Quite the contrary. I remained with him as a favor. In fact, I've brought other prestigious actors into his stable. Every single *ten percent commission* he takes off our labors, keeps him in the lifestyle to which he feels entitled."

"But he keeps you busy, right? Your career has gone well?" asked Ima.

"Splendidly. Thank you for asking. I've done the Crossword Puzzle Show on TV for years now. Sadly, the *scuttlebutt* is that it may move to Hollywood. I'm not really a California type, but if duty calls! If not, Westerly will have to *drum up* a new gig for me."

Shelton's arrogance made Ima uncomfortable. His *cynical* words rolled from his lips like melting wax. She wondered if they might hit the air and fly back onto his face to form a mask.

"So, what can you tell me about Lionel's career," she inquired.

"Well, I had hoped you could tell me," Shelton replied, with teeth gritted.

"I would; but truly, I know nothing. My father could win the world's worst pen pal award. I guess no news is good news, right?" said Ima, struggling to be upbeat.

"One could say the good news about your father is he remains as *perennial* as an apple tree, blossoming year in and year out! With his good looks, good voice, and good diction, he gets any role he wants...and will probably die on stage."

"Oh, PapaLi would like that. It'd be so dramatic to die on stage like Richard crying for 'A horse. A horse. My kingdom for a horse.'"

"How literary of you! Do you act as well," Shelton inquired but rolled his eyes into his head, as if ready to ignore her answer.

"No, PapaLi is the actor in my family; but I was an English major and still recall Richard III's speech before dying on stage." Ima tried to speak kindly to this difficult man. "Still I think that would prove a better way to fade away on stage than in bed like Camille does." Ima laid her hand across her chest to mimic the famous gesture of Greta Garbo.

"The worse way of *dying on stage*...is when a play flops." Shelton said *ruefully*.

"Yes when critics pan a play, it's so sad...for the cast, the crew, the audiences that never got to see the play or make up their own minds." Watching Shelton's face, Ima instincts said that Shelton must have recently lost a role or had his play close. She had no desire to embarrass the man if she had guessed right. So, she steered the conversation in a new direction, hoping that Wes would arrive soon and bring some sunshine.

"Yes, that's why I'm glad for my regular gig on Crossword. Otherwise, it's difficult to pay one's bills as an actor."

"It must be. But let's say...a play does have a long run...and you are cast in the role of a villain. Why that's the best of all worlds...almost like the old saying a *coward dies a thousand times*. The actor gets to die on stage...every night...for years. As good an actor as I bet you are, you could *milk* the death scene for all it's worth." Ima almost blushed because she had switched from honest to *obsequious* discourse which made her feel as slimy as Shelton's words began to sound.

"But dying too soon...can severely limit an actor's lines." Although Shelton tried to make a joke, his remark sounded *petulant*.

"Well...uh... uh...but villains don't always die or even stay villains. For instance, let's take Nathan Detroit in *Guys and Dolls*," Ima added.

"You can have him!" Shelton declared *condescendingly* and snooting his nose in the air . "I cannot figure why a refined gentlemen like Lionel chooses to play that ruffian."

"I think, in the theatre, that's called acting!" exclaimed Ima.

"Oh, yes...I did not mean to *imply* that Lionel—"

"I'm sure you didn't. But if PapaLi only played Englishmen with stiff-upper lips, directors would think him a *hack*...instead of the great actor he is. Though he might dislike playing *stereotype* roles, he dislikes unemployment even more. So he usually accepts anything that's not sleazy. That policy has given him a long career of playing the *stock* characters of Shakespeare and Moliere as well as creating great roles on Broadway."

Ima felt awkward defending Lionel who needed defense as much as an alligator needed armor. Even so, she found Shelton's comments oddly *pejorative*. He seem to alternate between criticism and compliments. She could not figure if he despised Lionel or just tolerated him. Had Shelton had a *falling out* with PapaLi and maybe with Wes as well?

Shelton *bristle*d a moment and then *segued* into another subject. "Well, I can say one thing about Lionel's role as your father. He certainly *sired* a lovely daughter."

"Well, thank you, Mr. Grape. How kind of you to say so," replied Ima, accepting the compliment, if indeed it was that instead of flattery as she suspected.

"So, what's happened in your life since you left New York?" Shelton asked.

"There's nothing much to tell. I'm a schoolteacher married to an Air Force pilot. When Sammy got assigned to Viet Nam, I had a choice. I could sit around and *pine* for him or put our goods in storage and assign myself to a year's adventure."

"Well, aren't you the cutest and bravest young thing ever. I mean, to put your life on hold and suffer the inconvenience of this horrible war. That is hardly the usual American Dream for a young couple."

"Oh, I'm used to military life. Some of us are designed for it."

"Well, I think with your pixie face, you were designed for the movies."

"How flattering! Wes said the same thing today. But, really, I'm not the type."

A long lull came. *Obviously* these two had little more to talk about beyond *superficial* matters. What a strange, gushy, and nosy man, Ima thought. She almost felt pity. His unreal demeanor disturbed her. Her teacher mind grew exhausted with adjectives that fit him: *pretentious*, too *solicitous* and *inauthentic*. What was he pretending to be? She wanted to ask for the real Shelton to stand.

With a long lull in the conversation, they both seemed relieved and tended more to their food. After a few bites, Ima looked squarely at Shelton and smiled as innocently as she could *muster*. Feeling probed and prodded as if in a medical exam, she had almost lost her appetite and wondered if others felt the same negative effect as he had on her. Her detective antennae began to poke through her carrot colored hair. She would do some probing of her own before this meal ended. Shelton's attitude indicated either a cover-up for something bad or a *ploy* to win her favor to get back into Lionel's good graces?

"Oh, please Ímagine tell me more about yourself, your interests, passions."

"Well, I enjoy traveling and—"

Just then, as if on cue, the *maître d* ushered Wes Westerly to their table. Although not unexpected, this new arrival clearly *irked* Shelton and pulled Ima's focus away from him.

All smiles, Wes shook Shelton's hand and gave Ima a quick peck on her cheek. "How's my girl? Settling in?"

"Fine, Uncle Wes. Thanks to you and Shelton, I'm getting my Manhattan *sea legs*," Ima said, letting her eyes show gratitude for saving her from her current host.

"Good to see you in person, Shelton. Phone calls never replace face to face," Wes remarked, sitting down and pulling his chair close to Ima.

"Well, I haven't received many phone calls from you either lately. How's business? Any Broadway offers...I mean anything in the *offing* for me?" teased Shelton, obviously surrendering control to Wes who had lightened the mood.

"Why yes, Shel, contracts keep piling up on my desk. I just can't decide which role best suits you," Wes ended the joke and patted Shelton's back. "I'm waiting for someone to write a movie about a TV game show." They all laughed politely.

"Uncle Wes, I noticed Lionel had circled an announcement for *1776* and one for a *revival* of *Oklahoma*. Are they still in casting?" asked Ima.

"Nothing concrete yet. Just some recasting going on! I'm still pushing on that," said Westerly.

"Lionel always said you were the best agent in New York," Ima smiled and squeezed his hand.

"Wes, I'm also interested in that *1776* show. Throw my hat into the ring, will you?" said Shelton. "By the way, there's a card game here tonight. Can we count you in?"

"Sure, as long as Val Pollibo is not invited," remarked Wes.

After finishing dessert and coffee, the group broke up. Ima thanked Shelton for the lovely lunch, hugged Wes, and walked off toward the cheap shoe district. She needed sneakers for the softball game but figured to borrow a glove. Usually the equipment bag had extras. She actually felt excited about the game and hoped to pull her weight or at least not to embarrass Riina.

• • •

That evening, Ima walked on 72nd Street over to the park and got there in time to see the 6:00 o'clock teams take the field. She introduced herself around as Riina's friend, the substitute shortstop. They all welcomed her gratefully. While several young women played catch, others jogged around. The pitcher and catcher carried on a heavy-duty warm-up. Soon Riina came running across the meadow wagging an extra Guilders team shirt like a flag.

"Why do you call yourselves the Guilders?" asked Ima.

"We all belong to SAG, you know, the Screen Actors Guild," Riina replied.

"Oh sure, like PapaLi belongs to," Ima said.

"Now go change in there, but beware of any big moosey women." Riina laughed and pointed Ima toward the restroom. "Remember they're bad news and worse ballplayers."

"And the subject of childhood nightmares," Ima replied quietly and ran off.

• • •

Pretty actresses *comprised* Riina's team. Although at auditions, they competed as professional rivals, tonight they joined together to beat the other team, not to model uniforms. Cleats replaced cute sandals. Golden and brunette curls got tucked under ball caps. Sweat and dirt smudged their faces. Muscles flexed ready for action!

A *hodgepodge* of spectators formed the fans of the Central Park League. Businessmen, heading home late, often crossed through the Park just to watch the antics of the ladies' softball teams. Early evening athletes would stop *ostensibly* for a breather. But their real intention was to admire how such lovelies could whiz strikes like Juan Marishal and hit homers like Mickey Mantle.

Because so many teams had joined the league, the games could only last about an hour. That gave enough time for three innings of play and required everyone to give maximum effort. The umpire flipped a coin. The Guilders lost the toss. The Sliders chose the premium position...that is, getting to hit the field first, instead of the ball. As a strategy, teams usually liked to have *last bats*, which gave them another chance to score with no *recourse* for their opponents.

The ump dusted the home plate and said, "Play ball."

The Guilders huddled, prayed for players' safety, and broke with a cheer. Up first, Riina entered the batter's box. The next Guilder batter *stood on deck*. If taught correctly, a player kept her eye on the ball and swung her bat to match the timing of the pitcher's throws. The Slider pitcher had a *windmill delivery*. It proved too hard and too fast to hit so the first three Guilder batters went three up...and three down. No one even touched the ball, much less got on base.

Still, with a burst of enthusiasm, the Guilders picked up their gloves and ran onto the field. The infield began to chatter to boost the pitcher.

"OK, Pinky! Time to turn their luck."

"Ditto their inning."

"I vote three up and three down."

"Yeah, you can do it."

"You're the one."

The crowd whistled and chanted in *wild abandon*. A row of vagrants formed the game's most curious group of fans. They yelled *unabashedly* for their favorite team of good-lookers.

"Don't give an inch."

"Pretty is if pretty plays tough."

"Sock 'em with a Killer pitch."

"Serve that girl a syrup sandwich."

When the first pitch popped up to the infield, Ima caught it with ease. That play instantly *stood her in good stead* with the rest of the team. The chatter sounded nostalgic to her.

"Atta girl."

"Ima nailed it."

"Way to go."

"Ima's an ace."

"Ima-Ima-Ima-Ima," shouted the team and crowd alike.

Then Ima started chanting, "Pinky-Pinky-Pinky pitch the ball."

The second batter got on first base with a bunt and started faking a leadoff. The pitcher looked back at second base and nodded. The catcher, pitcher, and first base stood ready for a stolen base and a double play. Either could happen, and then Guilders would be back at bats.

Pinky threw a fastball. The batter chopped it down, and Ima picked it up on the first bounce. She whipped the ball underhanded to the second baseman who whirled around and threw to first base. The ump yelled, "You're outta there. Both of ya!"

First inning down with a score of 0-0. The crowd rooted and whistled loudly. The second inning made a *carbon copy* of the first. At the top of the third inning, a wild ball hit the first Guilder, sending her to first base. The next batter walked; this signaled the pitcher's arm was growing tired.

Ima felt the weight of the world on her head when she entered the batter's box. Having properly timed the pitches, she thought her swing could connect with the ball if the coach didn't call for a change-of-pace. The pitcher wound up and let go a very fast ball. Ima swung at the first two. The Guilder on second stole to third. Then the pitcher got really wild, so Ima let three balls pass. Now it was a *full count*.

Riina called from the bench. "Swing like you're lightning! She's fast, but you're faster. The fastest bat in the West...I mean the East."

Ima stepped out of the batter box and raised her hand for a time-out. She walked over and exchanged her bat for a Louisville Slugger with a fat grip. She marched back to the box with confidence.

The pitcher wound up, let go the ball, obviously heard a bat crack, and instinctively ducked as the ball sailed out to center field. The two Guilder base runners passed home, and the crowd went berserk. Even though Ima got called out when hitting third base, it had been worth it. The next two batters struck out.

The Sliders came in for their *last bats*. Quickly, they had two strikeouts but then got a base-on hit. Hoping for a rally and a chance to live up to their name, they got excited when their next batter hit what looked like a homer. However, the Guilder's leftfielder backed up to catch the high fly and spoiled the Sliders' hope of sliding into home.

The game ended with a 2-0 score. All the teammates grabbed soft drinks from the ice chest, shook them, and had fizz fights just like a bunch of boys. Ima ended up rolling on the grass with Riina spewing foam into her face.

After their celebration, Ima ran over to the restroom to wash off the sticky soda. As she approached, a big woman stuck out a hand and foot to block the doorway.

"What's the password?" asked the *Amazon*-sized woman, half-teasing.

"*Open sesame?*" said Ima, playing along at first.

"It's not that easy, you *dolt*! Use your imagination," demanded the Amazon.

"I don't want to. Just let me by, or I'll report you to the coach."

"Go ahead. He's a friend of mine," bragged the moose.

"You're just saying that," Ima said.

"Go on...ask him. I dare you," the Amazon declared.

Realizing she had shown weakness by arguing, Ima got quiet to pray quickly and think clearly. Then she stared at the bully's face with its beady eyes, red blotchy cheeks, and greasy hair swooped back into ducktails like a *hoodlum*. Ima had a flash vision of this Amazon wrapped in a pink baby blanket.

The moose took a step forward, "Why don't you just settle down and be friendly. Wouldn't you just like a little company?"

"Not yours! Not ever! I'm *known by the company I keep*, so I don't want yours."

"Don't you want a friend?" said the strange moosey woman.

"No thanks. I've got plenty of friends."

"But not here in Manhattan, right?"

"You don't know that," Ima declared.

"All you Midwest girls come here but don't have a clue about big city life. Helping little lost lambs like you is sort of a mission of mine. I provide an older shoulder to cry on, so," said the woman drawing still closer, "so, I ask you again, real nice-like. Wouldn't you like a little company?"

With that phrase ringing in her ears and her heart pounding in her chest, Ima backed away, "Now, I know who you are and where you hang out. I'm gonna find a policeman and tell him how you came to my door last night and that you're *harassing* me again today."

"You fool," said the woman, pushing Ima to the ground. "No policeman takes girls like you seriously." The Amazon started dragging Ima by the feet into the restroom. Then, assuming a *stance of dominance* over Ima, she put one foot on her victim's chest, "Shut up about going to the cops, or else I'll make you and your face very sorry."

"No, you won't." Ima used every ounce of energy she could *muster* to roll the opposite way, out from under the foot of the *assailant.* Scrambling to her feet and not looking back, Ima whirled from the restroom and dashed back to the diamond.

Sadly, all the Guilders and Sliders had left. The spectators had thinned a bit, and two new teams *spanned* the field. Ima saw no one familiar except one shabby man who had watched their game. *Distraught,* she approached him.

"Sir, I need help."

"From me?" the bum said, taken aback.

"Yes, please. It's getting dark. Would you walk me to the edge of the park?"

"You want me to walk with you?" the man answered, looking *incredulous.*

"Yes, you seem like a decent person who might help a *damsel in distress.*"

"Of course, I'd be glad to do it...honored in fact." He noticed Ima sweating from more than the exertion of the game. He picked up the signs of fear she *exuded* from the restroom ordeal. "By distress, do you mean that some man bothered you?"

"Not a man...a big woman...dragged me into the restroom!"

"Oh, that type! They always hang around girls' softball games," he said.

"I know. My coach warned me when I first played ball at only eleven years old."

"You can't be too careful," the old man advised.

"Well, normally this wouldn't have upset me. I can take care of myself, but I think this woman is stalking me."

"Stalking you?" he inquired.

"I'm almost positive she's the same person who knocked on my door last night at the YWCA. As if that were not unnerving enough, now today she attacks—"

"Well, Missy, Old Cash will see you safely through the park. I know my way around here and can smell a mugger three blocks away."

As unlikely a man as most would trust, Old Cash rallied to the request. His chest swelled. Ima smiled as he extended his arm to her. Together, they struck out through the trees toward Fifth Avenue. In a short while, the Park suddenly darkened. The ball diamond lights no longer shone behind them.

"Better stay close, Missy."

Ima's heart rate sped up again. Here she was walking somewhere in the woods of Central Park, surrounded in the pitch dark and walking with a stranger. What if he planned to mug or rob her? Had she asked help from the wrong person?

Cash sensed her discomfort, pulled out a flashlight, and kept heading in the same direction. "Don't worry. You stick to Old Cash."

Arriving to the park's edge, they stood at East 72nd Street and Fifth Avenue and saw that all of upper Manhattan had gone dark.

"Oh great, another New York Blackout," Cash exclaimed. "Now, don't fret. I'll get you where you need to go."

Even though the street lamps and traffic lights did not work, the taxi headlights provided enough light for them to see. Cash moved out into the busy street and started waving his arms wildly to stop cars so Ima could cross. Upon seeing two random people out in the middle of the road, several taxis screeched to a halt. That allowed Cash to escort Ima to the far side. When he offered to show her the rest of the way home, she smiled but declined.

"No need to bother you further; but thanks for guiding me this far."

"Well, if you want to go alone, at least take my flashlight. Now don't take any chances, and avoid all strangers," he said, waving goodbye.

Turn It Back On

By the time Ima made it back home to E. 74th Street, the last colors of dusk had faded. Although the Amherst stood as dark as the other buildings around, she could discern the form of Arnie coming toward her and shining another flashlight to direct her feet.

"Now, isn't this a romantic way to end the day?" he teased.

"Is it really a blackout?" Ima inquired.

"Looks like it, at least for our end of the island," Arnie replied.

"I know. It's so eerie," said Ima. "How long do you think this will last?"

"I don't know. We had a really huge blackout in 1965. It lasted days. Traffic clogged the streets. People got trapped in the subway and train tunnels. Workers got stranded overnight in elevators stalled between floors."

And all in the dark...how *disconcerting*," she remarked.

"And with no electricity, the air conditioning went off in the big skyscrapers including ours. At least older buildings had fire escapes and windows that opened. People *clamored* outside and joined thousands roaming around."

"I bet they felt relief," said Ima.

"You bet, because once in the streets, they had some light. Car headlights helped a while until batteries *waned*. Believe me, it was frightening stuff at first. We didn't know if America had been attacked or what. Finally, some folks with transistor radios heard that the whole eastern corridor had lost its power. Soon, that news traveled by word of mouth from Manhattan to Staten Island...to all the *boroughs*."

"Did people relax, knowing the reason?" Ima asked.

"Well, I'm not sure how relaxed they felt; but they got really creative. Musicians performed in the streets. Stores shoved sale bins onto the sidewalk. Candles sold out fast. Restaurant owners moved their tables and chairs outside. The whole city took on a festive air like an *impromptu* New Year's party."

"I bet it was dark enough for you to see the stars?" asked Ima.

"Yes, and that's a rarity in this city," replied Arnie.

"As Charles Dickens said *it was the best of times; it was the worst of times.*"

"Yes, exactly! People stopped to talk to their neighbors, as rare a thing as you see now. So, Ima, besides a weird ending, did you have a good day otherwise?" Arnie asked.

"Yes...and no. Yes...because I had a good lunch and a great ball game."

"Who won?"

"We did. My team played great," added Ima.

"So what's the 'no' part of today?" inquired Arnie.

"I was stalked and almost mugged," she said, tears in her eyes.

"New York's a tough place for a woman to be out alone."

"Arnie, my would-be mugger was a woman," Ima said *ruefully*.

"That's a new one. Manhattan has so many kooks. You almost need a different type armor each day of the week," advised Arnie.

"I better drag mine from the closet and polish it before going out again. What saddens me the most is how easily I got scared. I grew up here! I know better than to look like a helpless china doll! But her beady eyes—"

"Don't relive it," said Arnie trying to comfort her. "You'll soon be back walking your Manhattan stride. All you need is to rebuild your confidence and resistance. Two weeks of sleep and you'll be good as new."

"That's perfect advice considering the last two weeks I've endured. Thanks Arnie."

"Well, Miss Ima, I need to get home to check on my own family. It looks pretty dark up Harlem's way. "

"Absolutely, they'll be worried sick about you. Can't you call them? Phones don't usually go out with the electricity," Ima commented.

"I've tried...can't get through. All the circuits are jammed," Arnie replied.

"Well, be safe. I'll see you tomorrow," Ima scooted into the lobby which proved much darker than outdoors. She defined the outlines of several people whose lit cigarettes moved around in the air like fireflies. She thought it funny that even in the dark, people gestured with their hands when they talked.

Absentmindedly, Ima edged her way to the elevator door, pushed the up button with her flashlight, and stood, waiting for the door to open. After a few moments, it hit her. If the lights were out, everything else electric was too. So, she padded the walls with her palms, fumbling to find the stairwell. Slowly, she climbed the eight lonely, pitch-black flights of steps. She stopped occasionally, groaned slightly, and rubbed her aching calves. They had had more exercise in the last few hours than in a month.

Once into Lionel's apartment, Ima shined her flashlight on several boxes to see if any of them contained candles. She found a few but had no idea where Lionel kept matches or cigarette lighters. Instantly, she had a flashback to the Maine cottage and began fumbling to find the broom. Breaking off a straw, she lit it from the pilot light of the gas kitchen stove. *Voilà!* Ima had *improvised* a match just like Vanna had done.

With candles lit, the room had a nice glow. She opened the windows and looked out into the night. Large groups of people, all with flashlights, clustered at the corner. Laughter rose up to her ears. The evening had turned into a party, just like Arnie's description of the first blackout. Tonight though, a halo glowed over lower Manhattan where the blackout had not reached..

With no electricity, Ima could not watch TV or play the stereo. Since it was too early for bedtime, she drifted over to the grand piano and began to noodle a few old show tunes her father once sang. In no time, she heard a knock at the door. At first, she froze. Oh no! Had that moosey woman followed her home?

Ima did not know whether to answer or not. She could buzz the doorman, but Arnie had already left for the day. Since she hadn't had a chance to meet the night man, did she dare take a chance? Looking through the peephole, she saw an older couple standing outside the apartment. "Yes, who is it?"

"Your next door neighbors."

"Yes, what do you want?"

"To be neighborly," they said in *unison*.

Hmmm. Ima thought that quite curious. New Yorkers weren't exactly famous for their neighborliness. "Look, it's been a hard day—"

"But the night is young, and we heard music," the woman said.

"Oh, is my playing bothering you?" asked Ima.

"Not at all. We thought a party had started," the woman said.

"A party?" Ima asked.

"Exactly! Since there's not much else to do in the dark, we thought we'd bring a bottle of wine to celebrate the blackout."

"Or at least…wait it out together," said the man.

• • •

The next day, Ima woke up refreshed and feeling more *resilient*. She looked out the window and saw traffic flowed as usual. The electricity crisis seemed over, but she flipped a light switch just to make sure. She reheated a frostbitten bagel from Lionel's freezer and had a cup of coffee to gag it down. After breakfast, she bounded out to take some clothes to the cleaners and to check the lay of the land.

Everywhere she looked, she saw signs written in a foreign language. Until now she had not noticed the neighborhood's Czechoslovakian influence. Narrow 4-storied brownstone houses lined East 74th. Most had pillows and *duvets* sticking out of their windows. The sight of linens airing this way reminded her of when she and Sammy lived in Germany, a sight that sent her into an instant reverie:

> The landlady Fraulein Astrid Stenglestall was a fresh-air fiend. A model of German efficiency, she clicked through her daily household chores, breathing deeply throughout. She opened all the windows and thrust her quilts and covers slightly outside. Then she mopped her kitchen floor, remade the beds, and did her morning exercises. About midday, she hooked a basket on her arm and walked off to the market to buy food for dinner.
>
> Since both Ima and Sammy worked during the day, the cold house never bothered them until returning home at night to their 50° flat. Ima had told Sammy, "Fräu Stenglestall thinks we're a couple of wine bottles that need to stay cellar-cool." But Sammy had great patience in the face of *Saxon blockheadedness*. Almost every evening, he went down to practice his German in conversation with the landlady. He dropped hints about raising the house temperature by suggesting he go to the basement and stoke the boiler so it could send up more heat to their radiators.
>
> *Frugal to a fault*, Fraulein Stenglehall only laughed, unconvinced. "Ya...du junge Amerikans tink I'm reich like Rothschild. Doch, das ist not rechts! During dat awfuhl war, we Chermans learnt to live like rats. Zo, I tell you sumpting. Unt kold house veel toughen you up for life. Who knows das future? Now go haben unt nice knuddeln mit Ímpajene and leaf me to my oompapa musik."

Sammy would describe how Astrid would always smile broadly, pat his hand, and shoo him back to their apartment, with words that sounded like *the world is your oyster*. Understanding about half of what she said, he acknowledged Fraulein Stenglehall was his only military defeat.

As Ima daydreamed, she accidentally stepped off the curb. A car swerved to miss her. A loud horn honking pulled her back to the reality of contemporary East 74th Street life. The cabby shook his fist and yelled something like, "Hey lady, chur mudder oughta teach cha not to play in da street."

In the same block sat the old Jan Hus Presbyterian Moravian Church. A bi-fold placard sat out front and welcomed the homeless to dine in the church's soup kitchen. Ima took note. The next time she saw Old Cash, she would tell him about this place. She might even come one day to help fix food. Maybe she could walk around the Park wearing a *sandwich man* placard to advertise the free food.

A few steps down into the church's *daylight basement* led to double doors of the American Savoyards. Faded notices announcing productions of Gilbert & Sullivan operettas flapped loose. Cater-cornered across the street sat the Phoenix Repertory Theatre. Ima figured Lionel selected an apartment in this location because it had so many nearby outlets for his talent. Maybe his future looked brighter than she had first thought.

After surveying the surroundings, Ima got into the full swing of urban life. She went to the butcher for meat, the green grocer for fruits and vegetables, and the supermarket for staples. With the pantry *stocked*, Ima started in on the apartment which looked mostly like a bachelor's war zone.

She scrubbed the bathroom and kitchen, vacuumed carpets, mopped floors, dusted tables, and arranged furniture. Deciding the grand piano fit the dining area better than the living room, she called Arnie to help roll it there. She reset the dining table and chairs at the entry that had mirrored walls to make it look wider. Now with daylight, she found more old candles and plopped them into candlesticks at each end of the table. Ima stepped back to admire her handiwork.

The next morning she asked Arnie to remove the hall closet doors and take them to the basement. The exposed area formed a perfect nook for the desk which currently sat crammed in a corner of Lionel's bedroom and stacked high with boxes of books. Playing librarian, she lined the *tomes* of poetry and plays onto the closet shelves above the desk. She tacked his certificates and awards on the back wall and pronounced the redecorated space a man's proper study!

The apartment had taken shape after only two hard days of cleaning and rearranging. Now, Lionel would return to a real home! Unfortunately, poor Boofy's furry world had turned into upside down *chaos*. Terrified by all the vacuuming and scrubbing, the kitty disappeared for days. The only signs of life were food eaten and poop deposited. When Ima started to pull clothes from Lionel's closet, she found the quivering kitty that had secreted itself safely into a shoebox.

In order to wash clothes, Ima had to go the laundry room in the basement, a place that gave her the creeps. She felt skittish being down there alone. That new feeling dented her usual bravery. In spite of all her preaching to Vanna about not having fear, Ima had now experienced it from a new, unexpected enemy. How strange to think of fortifying herself against a woman! Ima could still feel the park bully's hands pushing her to the ground and dragging her. She had to admit the strangest fact of all: this woman had threatened her face, the same threat Darwinia had used on Vanna in Maine. Indeed a strange coincidence!

Ima pondered how to build a back-up system for emergencies. Until Lionel returned, she would form a habit of telling Arnie her whereabouts, whether she went downstairs to wash clothes or down the block to shop for food or out to visit friends.

• • •

By the end of her first week in Manhattan, Ima felt accomplished...
but lonesome. She wished she had gotten Riina's phone number
at the game. Just then the phone rang. She answered it quickly,
"Hello."

"*Stop the presses.* It's Reenie. Get dressed," declared Riina.

"I can't believe it's you! Not a second ago, I thought about
calling," Ima said.

"What's da matt-ah? Did ya break off your fingers playing
ball or did da mob cut 'em off so ya couldn't dial a poison?"
quipped Riina.

"No! I wanted to call but didn't know your unlisted number."

"It's not unlisted. I still live over with LeoPops."

"Leo. Of course. I just couldn't remember your dad's first
name. I kept thinking, it was Lollipops. As for Feingolds, do you
have any idea how many live in New York?"

"Well, lucky for you, we're back on the same wavelength,"
declared Riina.

"So, do you want to come over and talk about old times?"
Ima asked.

"Forget that! I have a fabulous *agenda* for the Dallying Duo!"
replied Riina.

"You goose. What are you talking about?" asked Ima.

"Saturday at the Met! I've got matinee tickets this afternoon
and standing room for *1776* tonight," announced Riina. "What
cha say, we grab dinner at Nedicks."

"I'm not sure I have anything fit to wear to the opera,"
Ima replied.

"Don't fret. It's gonna rain. So, dress code of the day will be...
drum roll please."

Trying to match Riina's zany mood, Ima tapped rat-a-tat-tat
on the phone receiver.

"*Trench coats!* They fit all occasions," proclaimed Riina.

"So, we dress *incognito* like foreign diplomats?" Ima inquired.

"Yes, darlink. Incognito never-r-r-r goes out of style. But, lettuce make eet morrrre like Spyware," Riina rolled her tongue and spoke an unknown European accent.

"Right. We'll be Bond girls or better yet...Bond twins."

"Yes, darlink. James's saucy leetle sidekicks."

"You haven't changed a bit since your were twelve," declared Ima with a giggle.

"I hope not because...'A, I'm adorable; B, I'm so beautiful (sic).'"

"And 'C, you're still crazy as a loon,'" Ima chimed in on the old tune. "I guess keeping company with the likes of you will make me crazy too."

"So be it. If you're crazy enough to wear the required outfit, be waiting downstairs in 45 minutes," Riina said. "I'm swinging by in my limo."

"Limos and hotdogs?"

"Yes. Also, always in style!" Riina exclaimed.

"Still using that old method of splurging on one, scrimping on the other?" asked Ima.

"You bet. That's how the rich stay rich," replied Riina.

"Okay, if I can't persuade you otherwise, you get your way today. As long as I can wear my purple shoes, I'll dress however you say, go wherever you want, and eat whatever you choose. But tomorrow, I'm in charge!" Ima said and hung up.

Reviewing Recent Events and Past History

La Bohème was Ima and Riina's favorite Puccini opera. Although three hours of opera tantalized their ears, it numbed their backsides also. When the two young women exited the Metropolitan Opera House, rain *pommeled* them.

"Let us seek *refuge* and *repast*...in yon subway station!" Riina spoke as if quoting Shakespeare. "A royal feast awaits us at Sir Nedicks?"

"Is that still the only *bill of fare* available underground?" replied Ima.

"No. We could dine on pretzels with or without salt?" suggested Riina.

"How can you constantly eat such horrible foods," remarked Ima.

"Well, 'Mares eat oats and does eat oats, and hungry actors eat hotdogs.'"

"I surrender," said Ima throwing up her hands. "Hotdogs it shall be."

"Believe me, most starving children would love a quick Nedicks."

Finding a stand, they were soon downing their chilidogs and onions. "Um-um good," smacked Riina.

"I just don't get your fascination. Those wieners are far from *kosher*," Ima noted.

"I'm Jewish but not Kosher. My food is a total *hodgepodge*," declared Riina.

"Maybe you should consider eating more kosher style because what goes into these wieners is one step above dog food."

"Penelope Arf-Arf at your service," she spoke in a mock-British accent and held her hands up like dog paws.

"Never mind. Tell me about your audition the other day," said Ima. "Did you get it?"

"The director laughed at my reading. Wes said the man loved me, and I'll know for sure by Monday."

"So, you're with The Westerly Agency too?"

"Always stick with the best!" replied Riina.

"Lionel's been with him for years. I've always loved Wes. He's been more like a godfather. He also represents Shelton Grape."

"Hmmm, Grape...Grape?"

Ima imagined Riina running names and faces through her wiry-haired head file. "You know, the host of 'Crossword Puzzle,' the man I lunched with the day of the game?"

"Oh, that Grape," replied Riina wrinkling her face like a raisin.

"Do you disapprove?" asked Ima.

"Well, you know the rule about the company you keep," Riina warned.

"It was lunch, not a date. But, never mind him. What was the audition for?"

"Procter & Gamble. But hey! Soap commercial today...soap opera tomorrow!"

"I'd hate being stuck on a soap, playing the same character for years," Ima remarked.

"Darlink, a soap opera role answers a girl's prayer and fills her bank account. Imagine how hard it is to look this gorgeous for auditions everyday, rain or shine. I stand there in line, looking all *svelte* in my spike heels but get rejected as too gorgeous or too plain; too short or too tall; too skinny or even too fat. Can you believe that!"

"I can't imagine anyone daring to think you're the slightest bit plump."

"Right, you know I'd rather *ride the rails* than look like one."

"So, you wouldn't gain weight, dye your hair, or sell your soul to get cast in something regular?" asked Ima.

"No, but I would trade artistic value for a food upgrade: from hotdogs to steak!"

"But isn't that a *compromise* of your true beliefs?" Ima persisted, *egging on* Riina.

"Yeah, yeah...compromise...dum-pa-mise," Riina teased.

"Riina, you wouldn't really give up your *scruples* for a job, would you?"

"Not normally! Most times my acting talent wins out so I don't have to stoop to any *unscrupulous* practices."

"Acting is a tough business! I've seen PapaLi wrestle in it his whole career."

"Yeah, but I bet no producer ever *insinuated* that Lionel was an *easy girl*," said Riina.

"An easy girl? I haven't heard that cliché in years," Ima remarked.

"Believe me, it still fits. Some producers continue to *dangle a carrot* of success in front of would-be starlets, but not to me! I don't buy their line. I'd rather lose a role than my reputation on the old *casting couch*," Riina explained.

"I bet once those girls lose their looks, they spend their success money on a *shrink's couch* trying to lose their guilt," Ima predicted.

"And believe me it's harder to get rid of guilt than acne. If my talent can't win the role, it's the wrong one."

"But you won't feel guilt for taking a soap role you don't really want?" Ima asked.

"No, mostly I'd take a soap role because I want my own apartment and fewer auditions."

"So, 'As the World Turns,' you will be 'Young and Restless' and fight 'The Secret Storm' to 'Search for Tomorrow' until you find 'The Edge of Night,' or land up in 'General Hospital'?" iterated Ima, reciting the afternoon schedule of soaps.

"Hey, that's pretty good. Who writes your material?" asked Riina.

"I come from a long line of imaginations," replied Ima, taking a bow.

"So enough about me!. What have you done since the game?"

"Cleaning house mostly! But you'll never guess what happened at the park after the Guilders left." Ima related the story of being stalked by an Amazon in the restroom."

"No kidding!" Riina laughed. "Like the moose we joked about as kids?"

"Except it's not funny anymore," reported Ima, suddenly visibly shaken by the recent memory. "Fortunately, I found a nice vagrant to walk me through the Park."

"So, your answer to the moose problem was to jump *from the frying pan into the fire*...from a stalker to the arms of a mugger? Don't you read the newspapers? A *derelict* in Central Park would gladly roll you for your wallet... any time day or night."

"Old Cash may be a bum but not a *derelict*. He remained a perfect gentleman."

"OK, the bum's a great guy. He even won the *Man of the Year* award. But Ima, promise me you won't take any more chances like that. You're not yet in the swing of things. The city has changed a lot since we ran the streets like carefree *banshees*."

"Rinna, Cash is the least of my worries. That woman who cornered me is the real issue. She's the same one who knocked on my door at the YWCA."

"Oh, okay. So, if the moose cornered you, we should track her down and corner her. Let's see how she likes that delicious development," said Riina, rubbing hands together with delight.

"Delicious for you, maybe, but just talking about it makes me lose my appetite for this hotdog."

"Stuff it in your purse for later," Riina said. "That's a starving actress trick."

The two grabbed a train down to the station closest to the 46th Street Theatre. As they climbed the subway staircase, a big moosey woman started down the other side. When right alongside Ima, the moose threw out her elbow into Ima's ribs, knocking her into Riina. Ima groaned and whispered in disbelief, "Riina, Riina...that's the one! She's following me. It's as if she knows where I'm going before I do."

"Ima, you're imagining things. You look like Mata Hari. Who could possibly recognize you? I hardly do, and you're my best friend."

"No, really, I've got to get smart about this and think logically. The downtown Y is just blocks away. Such random meetings aren't coincidental. I need you to help me find some clues. Would you return here with me tomorrow to see if we can trace her path?"

"Is that what you meant about my owing you tomorrow?"

"Actually, I was just trying to keep up with your chatter."

"Okay, I'll do it for a small bribe, say with pie-a-la-mode at the automat?" Riina said.

"Okay, my treat, after the show," agreed Ima.

"What we need though is a new disguise, one she's never seen...that is, if she truly did recognize you. Probably, she saw your carrot-colored hair."

"How about I wear a Sherlock Holmes earflap hat to cover up my hair? A fun shop around Times Square must have something like that." Ima asked.

"Too obvious! I *nix* that idea," declared Riina.

. . .

The new musical *1776* still packed the 46th Theatre with enthusiastic audiences. For veteran theatre attendees like Riina and Ima, standing room served as the perfect solution. Although their feet might get tired, they liked being behind the *orchestra section*. It offered the best of both worlds: a great view at a low price and enough space to jump and jive with the music, without disturbing others in the audience. But jump and jive did not describe this historical musical at all. Instead it left Ima and Riina feeling patriotic and wanting to wave a flag or eat apple pie.

They headed to the Horn and Hordart Automat at Times Square, a *perennial favorite* of their childhoods. Before going in, they stopped outside to watch a giant Camel Cigarettes' belch billboard giant smoke rings. When tourists began to cluster around them, the twosome ducked inside the restaurant.

The automat looked and operated the same as it had twenty years before. Still Riina began to review the process for Ima. "Okay, here's the routine. I go to a cashier for coins. I put the coins in slots beside tiny windows displaying foods, and then I pull—"

"The lever like a slot machine?" teased Ima. "And you keep putting money in until you win a piece of pie?"

"Sort of...but you only put in more change...if you change your mind and want to choose another, more expensive piece of pie," Riina continued to iterate instructions.

"I'm sure it's like riding a bike or playing ball and will come swirling back to me."

"Right! So, you go first while I stay on guard for the moose," Riina announced.

"I don't really want apple pie. But to keep with tonight's patriotic theme, I'll eat blueberry to make my tongue and lips blue," pronounced Ima.

"And I shall eat cherry pie in memory of the old Washington myth about his cutting down a cherry tree. Besdies, cherries should turn my teeth blood red which ought to scare any moose away," Riina added to keep the charade growing.

"Unless red attracts moose like it does bulls?" Ima asked.

"Naw. That's only a bullfight myth," declared Riina.

"So, we have blue and red. Now, we need white to complete our color scheme."

"How about vanilla ice cream on top? You promised pie a la mode," Riina reminded.

Both satisfied with their dessert choice, they selected a table near the front door so as to keep an eye on who entered. Gradually the teasing ceased, and they grew more reflective.

"You know, Riina, I can't stop thinking about that musical. I never realized how much our forefathers argued over every little point. They held to their principles and *refused* to *compromise*," Ima remarked and kicked Riina under the table.

"Is that dig meant for me because I want an easier job on the soaps?" Riina grinned.

"No, I meant it seriously. We take our freedom from England for granted," said Ima.

"I know. History books made winning our independence seem so inevitable...automatic or even *irrelevant*. I used to read the assignment but could never figure what the big deal was. To me freedom looked pretty easy to get," said Riina, unusually *pensive*.

"Me to...except I did get excited when Mr. Watermeyer had our class signed a *mockup* of the Declaration of Independence. Remember?" Ima recalled.

"Yeah, I liked that part; but even putting my name on a dotted line did not impact me on what those signers risked. I never imagined the deep discussions and disagreements they had like in the play tonight." Riina cocked her head in thought.

"No heartaches...no dying soldiers...no confusion over what our country should look like or stand for or mostly...what breaking from England really meant to regular folks," Ima iterated.

"I remember the chapter that described bitter cold weeks at Valley Forge. To me those words lay flat on the page as if describing a day of falling down at the Central Park skating rink," said Riina. "I'm not proud to admit this but my Walt Disney brain saw those muddy roads as ribbons of chocolate pudding instead of *impassable* trails that stalled wagons and clogged horses' hooves. How did exhausted soldiers ever *traverse* such slippery paths on foot. As an actress, I'm usually able to imagine things... to put myself in other people's shoes. But on this one, I get stuck in the mud of my mind."

"Riina, that's very poetic. I think actors in plays and movies do a splendid job of recreating such scenes. Yet, we, the audience, leave the theatre and soon drop the passion felt for the reality just *depicted*."

"Well, not tonight! I must admit I felt a sense of what guts it took for those men to add pens...and guns...to their complaints," said Riina.

"I wonder how they knew their decisions were right for us in the future?" asked Ima.

"Or even...for their own families, right then. Think about it. Most of their parents or grandparents left England long before the War of Independence. For our folks it was different. It's only been a few decades since my parents came to Ellis Island from Estonia in the 1940s."

"Right. Same with Lionel. He came from London in the mid 1930s, and by then, America had been established for 150 years!"

"That's why I can't imagine in the 1500s how people came in blind faith to set up colonies... to become Americans, trusting that a better life in a better land would make it worth their hardships." Riina looked far off. "Think about it."

"I am...if I understand what you mean. For me it's hard to comprehend that the colonists were not even Americans yet. They were Englishmen who believed their English king was wrong. Families broke up over their loyalties. Some chose to stay under the king's rule and not to fight against him," iterated Ima.

"Bunch of *turncoats!*" Riina quipped, as if a bit tired of being serious.

"Riina, I think you mean Loyalists. They were colonists too. They just chose a different set of hardships. Many of them were Black men who decided to move north to Nova Scotia," Ima iterated facts from memory. "It was a hard choice, not a simple one."

"You mean not something simple like choosing flavors of pie," said Riina, blushing.

"Right. That makes us sound sort of frivolous, doesn't it," added Ima, happy to have a friend who could make her think, as well as laugh.

"I'm so glad we saw *1776* tonight. It is a solid play with solid ideas and is about something real. Nothing frivolous about it! I predict it will have a long run," Riina said pensively but then grinned broadly, acting more like her old self. "It's a shame it has no strong girl parts to try out for."

"So, do you think *1776* will win any Tony Awards?" asked Ima.

"*Indubitably!* Ron Holgate as Richard Henry Lee is a *shoo-in,*" Riina said with confidence. "The play could sweep the Tony roster. It's got all of the right elements: good story, good music, good acting."

"You mean, terrific acting? I bet Lionel could play any one of those roles," added Ima.

"I hear through the grapevine, Howard di Silva has fallen quite ill. An *understudy* had to sing his part on the show's LP recording."

"Which part was he tonight?" asked Ima.

"Ben Franklin! You know, if I were a man, I'd *pursue* that role."

"Me too," agreed Ima. "Franklin is like a devil's advocate... *ornery...ambiguous... cantankerous.*" She struggled again for the exact adjective. "He seemed to push the other men into thinking harder...more clearly!"

"In acting school, we learned that the audience reacts best to arguments...and villainy," Riina said, wiggling her fingers evilly.

"That's almost what I said to Shelton the other day. In real life, I don't like villains; but in a drama, they add the flavor and mystery," Ima admitted.

"I think Lionel should go for the Franklin role. He's got the commanding presence."

"But not the body type or hairline," said Ima.

"A leetle padding here...a leetle nose putty dare...unt good wig on top...so nutting's impossible!".

"Okay, Miss-Theatre. That takes care of the pudge and *pate*. How about height? In paintings, Franklin looks of medium height, but PapaLi is rather tall."

"A good director would keep him seated or have him standing alone," Riina remarked.

"But several scenes showed him standing in a group," Ima reminded.

"Then, I'd advise him to slump a lot," said Riina.

"That pose sounds so attractive! You better stick to acting not directing."

"Well, acting is my *forte*. In fact, my specialty is *improvisation*. Remember as kids how we'd set a scene and play it out?"

"I remember how great you could do that," remarked Ima.

"You weren't half-bad. After all, you're half Lionel, the actor and half Madge, the teacher."

"Yes...but I followed more the steps of MaMadge than PapaLi."

"Well, even so, let's try to make history come alive right now."

"You mean reenact one of the scenes from the play?" asked Ima

"No. I want you to pretend to be an imaginary teacher, and I'll be a student."

"Right here. Right now! People will think we're nuts" exclaimed Ima.

"Why not. It's Saturday night. All the crazies are either out there or in here."

Although not thrilled at the prospect, Ima knew to resist one of Riina's ideas would prove useless. "Okay, you win." Ima cleared her throat and began, "Boys and girls, please open your history books to the chapter about the Loyalists."

Riina groaned. "Do we hafta? History is so boring, *dry as toast* without jazz and jam."

"Well then, I'll personalize it. Are there any Loyalists in your family?"

"Sure. My folks are loyal to the soda pop and toothpaste they buy."

"Not that kind of loyalty. Ever heard of the book, *Fight for the King*?"

"Did they make a movie of it?" asked Riina, perking up in the chair.

"Maybe. But the author *injected* fictional flavor to stale textbook facts."

"Oh, yeah, like *Three Muskateers* spiced up French history?"

"Exactly. That's why historical fiction helps you understand the past."

"Because it stirs real and fictional people into a pot and reboils history?"

"Good. So, if we also add mystery to this recipe, we have a *Gourmet goulash*."

"Hey Teach, we're making a food…metaphor here, right?"

"Right." Stopped in her tracks by that crack, Ima burst into laughter.

"Hey, you broke character," chided Riina. "An actor never *breaks character*."

"Couldn't help it! You nailed it. That' exactly how kids put things together."

Bagging a Moose

Last night, before saying goodbye, the old friends had agreed to meet at the Feingold's apartment at 1:00 on Sunday and be ready to track down the Amazon. So, the next morning, all set to go sleuthing with Riina, Ima had just enough time to attend church first. She walked over to Jan Hus Presbyterian and sat down quietly in a back pew. When the service began, to her surprise it was all in Czech. Not understanding a word but trying to go along like a good sport, Ima hummed the hymns and smiled at folks in the congregation. They looked back at her as if she had come from outer space. So, Ima hummed more quietly. At the end, many shook her hand and, in broken English, invited her to come again.

• • •

It was a beautiful July day, so Ima strolled over to Madison Avenue and down to 65th Street. She had not been to visit the Feingolds in over fifteen years. Their apartment now looked like a magazine feature.

Leo, a very *frugal* jeweler, had in the 1940s worked long hours and saved his money to open his own business. Ima remembered how at the *drop of a hat*, he used to give lectures on hard work and thrift. Following his own advice, he had made a very comfortable living for his family. But when Leo learned how to invest his money in other businesses, he became not only successful but also quite wealthy.

The Feingolds now lived in an upscale cooperative apartment house. When Ima arrived, the maid ushered her onto a narrow terrace where the family sat, waiting. Soon a huge seafood salad was place before each one, and the group dispensed with the *superficial* niceties. Off like a horse race, everyone ate and jabbered at the same time. Leo and Marianna Feingold *doted* on Ima but also threw out a *barrage* of questions about her life. Then just as abruptly, they stopped to listen intently to her answers.

"Ah, our leetle carrot-haired gal is now big enough for the stew," said Leo with his immigrant accent still lingering. "How wisely you must have invested to be able to trav'l the world now. Oh, Ima, Ima...may you always be prudent and save-save your money for a rainy day. I promise if you do, you wh-ill ne'va starf...like people did in the war," he added, almost spitting out his words.

"Leopops, please don't start in on Ima. You'll drive both me and her *Bonkers in Yonkers*," complained Riina.

"And you shouldn't listen to him about saving money?" teased Mrs. Feingold.

"Yeah, Ma, I hear him," replied Riina. "But, I've heard it all a hundred times."

"Well, I must tell you how proud we are of you, darlink Ima... already a schoolteacher, married to a successful man, and coming to New York to check on your poor father...now that your poor mother has passed. Such a good dawt'er...and so independent," said Mrs. Feingold, glaring at Riina who still lived at home.

"Stop with the *incessant comparisons!*" exclaimed Riina in her flippant way. "All this *fawning* over Ima won't make her sign adoption papers. So, you're stuck with just me." Riina motioned to Ima that they should leave. "Let's went, Cisco."

"Okay, Pancho," said Ima reciting the Cisco Kid's usual response to his sidekick.

"Ma, the meal was delissshhhh, but we gotta go, *capish?*"

"Thank you for a lovely lunch, but we really must do our sleuthing," Ima confirmed.

· · ·

Ima and Riina walked down to the Plaza Hotel on 59th at Fifth Avenue and then over to Columbus Circle. There they turn south on Broadway with a plan to survey the whole route to the *theatre district*. But in only a few blocks, they passed the old YWCA. Ima grabbed Riina's arms, dug in her fingers, and gulped unconsciously. She felt *vulnerable* again but hated to admit it.

"You act like the Y was a torture chamber instead of a ladies hotel," quipped Riina.

"If you had seen that woman's beady eyes, you'd understand! That moose must have thought me a teenager or else she'd never have risked assaulting me."

"We'll assign you a bathroom buddy for the next game," teased Riina.

Fortunately, they saw no suspicious characters loitering about the Y steps. Perhaps, even evil respected Sunday. They passed over a subway grate that sent hot air blowing up their legs. Both began to act like Marilyn Monroe in the famous movie scene where her skirt blew up uncontrollably. And for a moment, they laughed uncontrollably which broke the tension inside Ima. But, a bit farther down, Ima felt her discomfort returned when she spied a bunch of big moosey women *skulking* outside a *bawdy dive*.

As planned, the two old friends split up. Riina walked ahead and ducked behind a street vendor's stand to watch. Ima, with her carrot-colored hair flopping loosely, strutted directly toward and then on pass the target. Instantly, the same mannish woman from the park separated from her group and began to tail Ima.

Riina pulled a camera from her tote bag, stepped into the open, and quickly clicked a picture framing Ima in the foreground and the moose behind. Then Riina ran over to Ima, grabbed her arm, "Oh, there you are, darlink. Unavoidably delayed, I *presume*?" She said, steering Ima away and chattering idly. "I saw you coming down the street and I got the cutest, candid shot of you, ever... absolutely ever. You'll love it. Oh...and...I love your hair style and that cute outfit...get it at Macy's?"

"No, Gimbels," said Ima, as they walked briskly around the closest corner.

They hid in a *recessed* doorway to see if anyone followed. Although their hearts raced, they had succeeded in getting a picture of the stalker. So far, their little *ruse* had worked. Now, they would find the nearest *police precinct* and turn over the evidence.

• • •

A uniformed officer stood at the precinct intake counter and looked annoyed as Riina waved a roll of film in his face. "And what am I supposed to do with that?" he asked.

"Develop the picture inside to get the evidence, of course," said Ima.

"Ladies, we don't develop people's pictures. That's Kodak's job," he said, refusing to take the roll of film.

Ima looked at his nametag. "Let me understand you, Officer Allrest. You wouldn't even do it if that meant preventing another crime?"

"We're in the business of *prosecuting crime* not preventing it," he said.

"But we've already done a stakeout, collected clues, and pegged the crook," replied Ima. "All you need to do is swoop down and arrest her."

"What she means is we just *bagged* ourselves a moose," said Riina.

"Then I should arrest you two for hunting out of season," the officer said.

"We're wasting our breath, Ima. We'll have to do this *flatfoot*'s work for him."

"It's really too bad he won't get a promotion for saving the city from a ruthless gang of Amazons, bent on attacking young innocent girls," declared Ima.

"Or worse!" Riina began to over-dramatize. "The headline will give him nightmares."

"Headline...what headline?" asked Officer Allrest, completely *discombobulated*.

Realizing Riina had dropped into another improvisation, Ima decided to play along. She took a hairbrush from her purse and held it up like a microphone. "Yes, I too would like to know to what headline you refer."

"The one that will read, 'Young Girls Dragged Off Against Their Will.' And the article to follow will give chilling descriptions of mere children being forced into a *den of iniquity* and having their *innocence stolen*."

"Oh, no," said Officer in despair.

"Indeed, 'innocence stolen' sounds too poetic for a news item. The English teacher in me thinks a more accurate, persuasive word would be *defiled*. Do you agree, Miss—"

"Miss Feingold. That's F-e-i—"

"But don't you remember 'i' before 'e' except after 'c' or in words like 'neighbor' and 'weigh' is one of the main spelling rules," remarked Ima.

"Well I never follow rules," declared Riina.

"So who does this news article blame for such injustice," the officer shyly inquired.

"Well, the police of course!" Riina said, winking at Ima and giving a toothy smile.

"And I promise you such *dereliction* of duty will be mentioned," remarked Ima.

Then unexpectedly, Riina put her act in high gear, hopped on the counter, and leaned across to tickle the officer's chin. "You see, Officer Allrest, you have an opportunity to prevent having the department's reputation *besmirched!*"

"And saving girls from a most unsavory experience...at the same time," Ima added. "Believe me, I know."

"I don't envy you, if your supervisor discovers that you *refused* to help us," said Riina.

Embarrassed by Riina's crazy *antics*, Officer Allrest threw up his hands in surrender. "Okay, okay! I *get the picture*...umm...no pun intended. So, give me the film. I'll ask the lab to handle it."

"Excellent. *Right off the bat*, I saw you as a leader of men," Ima replied.

After writing a description of the *alleged* culprit and filling out a report on the incidences at the YWCA and the park restroom, Riina and Ima felt proud to have done their civic duty, even if in a rather *unorthodox* manner.

By Monday evening, the police had picked up suspects to put in a line-up. Ima came down to the precinct to identify the culprit. In the safety of a darkened room, Ima viewed five lookalikes through a *one-way glass*. All had on ball caps which the sergeant made them take-off to reveal their faces. That made the choice more obvious.

The beady eyes and blotchy cheeks of one suspect served as a *dead giveaway*. The police arrested the moose for attempted *assault* and whisked her off to jail. That ended the case and Ima's fear that the woman would ever cross her path again.

• • •

Early the next morning, Ima had her first real sense of freedom and relief since arriving in Manhattan. She could now begin her New York life. First on her list was to return to the Jan Hus Church to help in the soup kitchen for the homeless. Some Czech folks who struggled to welcome her on Sunday, now smiled to see her back so soon.

The room had a cafeteria-style setup, with steam tables and rows of banquet tables. Assigned to serve bread and drinks at the end of the line, Ima got to see everyone coming by. Suddenly, she saw a familiar face. Old Cash passed through, holding his plate out for ample servings of stew.

"Cash. Cash," Ima called out and waved.

"No, miss. We don't charge for this food," said one of the church ladies.

"Oh, I know, but that's my friend's name," she said, smiling in reply.

Cash stuck out a hand to greet the lady, "I'm Cash Underwood, and this cute little lady is my new friend, Ima Purple."

"Of course, you're Cash. I've seen you before. I'm sorry," she said, obviously too embarrassed to look him in the eyes.

"So, you already know about this place?" inquired Ima.

"Been coming for years," he admitted. "They serve good food here."

Once the line thinned out, Ima went to sit with Cash at one of the long tables. She told him about the line-up and pointing out the culprit.

"An *attempted assault* is a serious offense. If the judge follows the law, that woman won't bother anyone for a while," he spoke as one who knew.

"Listen. I can't tell you how much you helped last week, rescuing me in the dark. If you ever need anything, you call me at this number," Ima handed him a slip of paper. He read the note, then chewed it up, and swallowed it, much to her surprise. "What are you doing?"

"I follow the spies' code so your number won't fall in the wrong hands," he laughed heartily. "Now, give me no thought. I've got someone watching over me," he said, pointing upward.

"Me too," agreed Ima, winking.

"Well, I'm off to the kitchen to wash dishes. Gotta earn my keep," he added.

Next day, Ima woke up early and returned to the soup kitchen to help prepare food for lunch. After a few hours, she walked down to the Westerly Agency.

Wes opened the door and greeted her warmly. "Ima, what a surprise."

"Oh, Uncle Wes, do you have time to talk?" she asked.

"Always to you, sweetheart."

"Well, it concerns PapaLi. I went to see *1776* last weekend. It inspired me and made me wonder about future cast openings that might fit PapaLi? I heard—"

"I'm already on top of that rumor. I've got him lined up for an audition as soon as he returns later this week."

"This week? Oh, I can't wait to see him," exclaimed Ima.

"Few people know this; but earlier this spring, the producers wanted Lionel to try out for several parts. But his *prior* commitment to the tour made it impossible for him to consider it. Those are the breaks in show biz," said Wes.

The phone rang, and Ima instinctively reached for it. Wes got to it first and excused himself to the back room.

• • •

"The Westerly Agency," said Wes speaking quite spoke low in case a new visitor came to the office next door. With the talent business so competitive and actors often very jealous, he found it easier not to reveal when others had auditions and bookings.

"It's Riina Feingold on the front lines…reporting back to the general's headquarters."

"Riina, how did the soap commercial go?" inquired Wes.

"Full of bubbles. The director loved it and wants me to demo a variation on the same theme. I felt like a music composition."

"This could be the break we've been waiting for," Wes remarked calmly. "Let's celebrate. Meet me at Sardi's. I have someone who needs a local friend."

Learning to Play People's Game

Most of her life, Ima knew of Sardi's as a hangout for celebrities, journalists, and actors. Anyone who wanted to see and be seen by others of the same *ilk* showed up there at night. Directors might search for a fresh face to cast in a TV sitcom. Broadway producers might find the latest *It-Girl* to star on the Great White Way. But primarily, Sardi's remained the oasis for *playwrights* with opening night jitters. There they would wait for early newspaper editions to hit the newsstands. A critic's review could make or break their play's success.

Whereas the night crowd had connections to entertainment, Sardi's day customers revolved around the axis of commercial advertising. Account executives, talent agents, voiceover announcers and on-camera spokesmen gathered there for lunch. In their trade, the star on the TV screen was the woman *attesting* to the best vegetable oil or the man touting the latest new cars.

For the few minutes it took to read a script at a studio, an actor got paid a modest session fee. The real money came later in *residual paychecks*. That meant, for every minute his picture showed up on TV or his voice echoed on radio, he got paid more money…without having to do more work. This had happened because actor unions fought to secure such *coveted* plums for its members.

Talent agents met at Sardi's to discuss their stable of clients with ad producers. An old legend still circled that moviemakers had discovered a cowboy named Gene Autry sitting on a soda fountain stool at a drugstore. No one knew if that myth held any truth; but with that hope in mind, many actors came regularly to Sardi's to promote themselves. Some unemployed performers paraded around looking for temporary *gigs*. Others hoped to land a job as an *exclusive* speaker for a single product: the best *boon* to anyone's career in commercials.

• • •

Riina stood in front of Sardi's and howled when Ima climb out of a taxi with Wes. He smiled when the two young women hugged before he ushered them inside.

"So, you know each other?" Wes wondered.

"Since diaper daycare days," quipped Riina. "Wes, don't you remember I first met you at Mrs. Longwind's—"

"Of course, I had forgotten all—"

The *maître d* interrupted and welcomed them *effusively*. "Ah, Mr. Westerly, your table waits," he said leading Wes and his two attractive female companions to the *coveted* captain's table.

"I haven't been here since MaMadge's…" Ima said, tearing up.

"Oh how I loved your mother and still miss her sorely," said Wes.

"I know, Uncle Wes. Me too," said Ima biting her lip. "And at the wake, when we ran out of food?"

"No complaint here. I had plenty to eat. It was all delicious," added Riina.

"Remember when you ordered me to go to Sardi's for more food on the pretense that the staff here was too busy to bring it to us?"

"Yes, I'm sorry if I seemed unreasonable. I thought getting away might help you think clearly. Madge's death shook you up so," he explained.

"You were right. That's when I learned you had Sardi's *cater the wake*."

"Well, someone had to be host. Your father was a wreck," noted Wes.

"People came from all over. Except for the sad reason, I'd have called that week-long wake the best party of my life," Ima said wistfully.

"Well, if you want to hear a really-really sad story to bring you to tears, I-I-I haven't been to Sardi's since my-my-my 14th birthday! That's half my life," Riina admitted, trying to shift the conversation away from death.

"How is that sad?" inquired Ima.

"Because over the years for all other special occasions, we only go to the Estonia House. My mom loves to practice her folk dances. I tell her *oom-pa-pa* music fit fine in the old country but is completely *passé* here. I tell her to go to Studio 54, a really cool place where really cool people do really cool dances like the Jerk and the Swim." Then Riina did sit-down versions with choreographed hand-movements.

"I think the jerk fell out of fashion," remarked Ima.

"Maybe so, but the chiropracters did a booming business with all the *whiplashes* the jerk caused," said Wes, grinning and rubbing his own neck.

"Not the way I do it," said Riina, giving a few more sit-down jerk motions.

"Riina, how'd a New York gal like you survive a Jewish father and an Estonian mother?" said Wes.

"Or *vice-versa*. Riina is a psychiatrist's dream case, right?" Ima stated.

"No, I think such warring natures inside grow character and give a person an advantage," said Wes. "I bet *destiny* has plans for her...for fame and fortune or—"

"Or the funny farm," added Ima.

"Or a homeless shelter! And, I'm telling you both the truth. If I don't make it big pretty soon, my folks threaten to kick me out," said Riina.

"Keep hanging on, Riina. If you must stay, ask them to let you sublet your bedroom. But, assure them, one day, directors will *clamor* to hire the comedic face and unique dance steps of another Fanny Bryce." Wes put his fingers beneath her chin.

"Really Riina, no one ever makes me laugh more than you do," Ima added.

Riina stood, *pirouetted*, and bowed. A slight applause rippled across the dining room. Just then Shelton Grape suddenly appeared behind her. He took her hand, twirled her, and reseated her beside Wes.

"A party...to which I was not invited?" intoned Shelton.

"Oh, Shel, please join me and share the *genial* company of my lovely young guests... so fresh and full of life. Beside them we look like stale bread?"

"Speak for yourself!" Shelton muttered and remained standing, *impervious* to how his *imperious* manner stopped all conversation. He seemed unaware that he often acted like royalty, expecting common folk to speak only when spoken to first. "Stale..indeed."

"Uncle Wes stale? Never. He's still the life of any party," Ima declared.

"Well, I won't interrupt...this party! I just wanted to ask if you had any news on *1776* re-casts. The Richard Henry Lee's role interests me a lot."

"Yes, yes, Shel. I'm on it. You'll know as soon as I hear anything."

"Oh, by the way, Wes, the regular game is at the Friars again tonight."

"I'll be there if Val Pollibo isn't invited," Wes said.

Shelton sniffed with a high nose but did not leave.

After a lull in the conversation, Riina decided to *inject some levity*. "Oh, by the way, Ima, the regular game is at the East Diamonds tonight."

"I'll be there if that Amazon isn't invited," Ima played along.

A little confused by the double conversations, Shelton lost his *train of thought* a moment before continuing. "Pollibo will come, invited or not."

"So, correct that. Withdraw his name from your guest list," Wes remarked.

"He'll still come whether he's on or off the list. You know how guys like him operate," Shelton admitted.

"Look, Shel. Here's the truth. Pollibo spoils the fun. Once he started *horning in* on our friendly games, they stopped being friendly. I'm losing interest. Do what's right, or I'll find a table better fitted to my pocketbook," Wes said.

"Harrumph!" Shelton sneered and quickly turned to leave, *inadvertently* bumping a waiter holding a tray. Surprised, the waiter fell forward and tried to *stabilize* his load. Hot chowder spilt from a bowl, bulged over the tray edge, and slurped down onto Shelton's sports jacket.

"Now see what you've done, you careless *oaf*! You've ruined my jacket."

"Sorry sir. Sardi's will have it dry-cleaned. Please accept my apology, and please know your guests' meals are on us," the waiter said graciously, hoping to please as well as sooth this *irate* customer.

"Who said these were my guests?" Shelton demanded to know.

Making a mountain out of a molehill had caused Shelton to lose his usual public *persona*. Instead of a cool, calm character, he began to sweat, noticeably. His eyes bulged. Polite *civilities* on the surface could not mask *seething hostilities* underneath.

Ima could not believe how instantly Shelton had grown *contentious*, so ready to pick a fight. His quickness to blame and not to forgive puzzled her. She wondered what really went on inside this strange man?

Wes noticed how uneasy Ima and Riina seemed by the *altercation* between Shelton and the waiter. So, he took center stage and with a gentle *reprimand* to his client, restored order. "Look, Shel, I must get back to my guests. So please, either join us or stop making a public scene!"

Now more subdued and probably needing to lick the wounds inflicted on his ego, Shelton slithered into the booth next to Ima. He looked embarrassed but not defeated.

So that *cooler heads would prevail*, Wes ordered iced tea all around instead of cocktails. He knew the *catalyst* of alcohol usually inflamed such situations.

Shelton *mustered* his courage and pretended to make amends for his bad behavior. Turning to Riina, he asked a simple question that set off another unexpected scene, one that neither he nor Wes quite understood, "So who are you...an actress?"

Acting very *demure*, Riina said. "I'd like to think I'm an actress, but no one takes me seriously."

"Accept it. You're a natural born comedienne," Ima *goaded* her pal into another instant play.

"Am not!" exclaimed Riina, accepting the challenge.

"Are too," replied Ima, keeping the rally going.

Faking an argument, Riina knew how to *up the ante*. "No, I'm a serious ac-tor," she said, exaggerating the "tor" syllable.

"In your dreams, maybe," said Ima.

"*Turncoat!* I would expect my best friend to be on my side."

"Not on this point," retorted Ima. "Face the facts: you're just plain funny! I'm sorry to say it, but good friends tell each other the truth."

"Then, you're fired as my best friend," Riina announced.

Playing along, Ima spoke in her teacher tone. "The truth is undeniable. You've been funny your whole life."

"You're just saying that to make me give up my goal."

"I'll prove it. Remember when we were ten and that camera shop man on 42nd Street photographed us and then sang that old song 'You ought to be in pictures.' He meant you."

"I wish that were true, but he was looking straight at you," Riina insisted.

"Not me. I've never wanted to be an actress on the stage or screen," Ima iterated.

"Maybe not, but to him you were a great discovery. He thought you ought to be in pictures or cartoons or the circus because of your orange hair, just like the clown Betty Hutton played."

"You're mixing the story all up. Jimmy Stewart was a clown and Betty Hutton was a trapeze artist," said Ima.

Riina began to sing, "The daring young girl in the strapless costume."

"Now you're mixing up the song too. It's 'The daring young man on the flying trapeze," Ima corrected.

"Man or Ma'am. Can of Spam! Facts don't change. The shopkeeper said you looked like Betty Hutton with her carrot-colored hair and big mouth," Riina added.

"That's all wrong. He called you Wiry Locks, a steel wool version of Shirley Temple."

"And he called you a *hybrid* of Flopsy, Mopsy, and Cottontail who ate so many carrots you turned orange," declared Riina.

"Your memory is as fuzzy as Cottontail's...uh-uh cotton tail. So I'll tell you again, you're the one who wanted to be an actress... funny or not," remarked Ima.

"Well, maybe you're right. Maybe one day, I'll be a great actress...the next Greta Garbo." Riina put her hand across her chest. Then grinning openly, she slapped the table. "And Ringo Starr agrees that 'They're gonna put me in the movies.'"

Whereas nearby customers had stopped eating to watch what appeared to be an *impromptu* audition. Shelton rolled his eyes and appeared to judge the display as *insipid* and amateurish. As the scene extended for quite a while, Wes finally stood up and waved a white napkin between the young ladies.

"*Peace Pact. Peace Pact.* The point is you're both right. From now on, I will market Riina as a comedienne who can act."

"Wes, that crimps my style! How can I get *top billing* with a tag like that."

Ima chimed in. "How about: Riina is an actress who just happens to be funny."

"Hey, Ima, I like that fine! I like it a lot," admitted Riina.

"You've got good instincts! Want a job as my assistant?" Wes offered.

• • •

That evening at the Friars Club, the regular players had their usual, friendly game of poker. When Val Pollibo joined, he wanted to *up the ante* above the game's usual limit. Wes took his winnings and walked toward the door. Val called him a sorehead and a *welcher* for leaving. Such name-calling only confirmed Wes's opinion of this most unwelcome player.

• • •

A mile or so away in Central Park, another game went on. The Guilders were playing softball, and Ima once again filled in as shortstop. Old Cash and his vagrant chums lined the diamond to cheer on the pretty girls. When the team won, Riina and Ima invited Cash for a victory hot dog from a nearby street vendor's wagon. On a park bench, they ate the simple *bill of fare* and chatted quietly.

"Listen, you guys. I need your advice. The coach offered me the shortstop position for the rest of the season because the regular player has gone off to Hollywood to make the *pilot of a new TV show*."

"Great. You're the fastest infielder we Guilders have had in awhile."

"And the cutest in my book," said Old Cash.

"Such prejudice you two have," said Ima, squeezing both their hands.

"So, what's the problem? You want Coach to get on his knees and beg?"

"Of course not, but for one thing, I'm not sure how long I'll be here. Another is I have to be working in show business to qualify as a Guilder."

"Well, Wes did offer you a temporary job today. I say, take it and *let the chips fall where they may*," declared Riina. "The Westerly Agency belongs to all the acting unions so that should cover Wes's employees as well."

"Sounds as if an answer dropped into your lap," agreed Old Cash.

"But, I'm a schoolteacher. What do I know about showbiz?"

"Ima, it's *no biggie*. You grew up in it. Take the job. Wes will teach you *the ropes*."

Learning the Ropes of Showbiz

Thursday morning, Ima walked down the twenty blocks to the Westerly office. She carried her valise like a briefcase to reflect a sense of importance to her job. When she arrived, Wes had just started on his second cup of coffee.

With big smiles, he welcomed her. "So, you're gonna accept my offer. The glitter of show biz hooked you, didn't it?"

"I guess so. Can you make me into an assistant talent agent in a day?"

"It may take a bit longer, but you're a natural. The most important thing to remember is to give performers a lot of attention. They thrive on it. That's why I keep my *stable of clients* small and *exclusive*. You'll know them all in no time." Wes handed her a list.

Recognizing a few actors' names from her childhood, Ima grew excited. "I know some of these people. So, what exactly will I do with them?"

"Hold their hands mostly. Other than that, you will answer calls from casting directors and suggest which of our people might fit a role. They'll think you're a *greenhorn* with no *moxie* about this business, but you just barrel through with the blurbs I'll give you to practice. You will keep the audition schedule and contact clients about appointments. Sometimes you will book studio time to make demo tapes. On the money side, you'll compare their checks to the *union book*, and mail out their money, minus my 10% fee."

"Lionel taught me a little about that," said Ima.

"You may get periodic calls from clients who fuss over my part of their money. But deep down, they know that without me, their little talented toes would never get in many doors. I'm sure Lionel also taught you that always *pull is better than push*. In this business it's not who has the most ability but who has the most contacts."

"Uncle Wes, please be patient. I usually teach adolescents and preteens so working with adults will be a challenge."

"Not really. Performers often act like preteens, even preschoolers at times."

Ima laughed, "Well, at least I'll love the accounting part of this job. Arithmetic has always come easy to me."

"It will all be easy unless we run out of coffee or I must run out of the office. Then it works like this: While I entertain producers to get jobs for my clients, you must be me."

"Like a *stand-in* in the movies until the star arrives? Or like an *understudy* in a play, I get to play your role?"

"You play my role...except this role is real, not one on stage."

"So, you entertain the producers and have all the fun while I do all the hard work?" Ima asked with a tease in her voice.

"The hardest thing is you must tippy-toe around the *delicate ego* of actors," he admitted.

"You mean learning who to leave alone and who to give a swift kick? That's the same as with students in a class."

"See, what good instincts you have," he said with a belly laugh. "I must warn you that a few may act paranoid and accuse you of not putting their names in for auditions."

"I got that feeling from you-know-who at our lunch yesterday."

"If you mean Riina, she's a delight. But, Mr. Grape will zap your strength. He thinks I'm his personal manager not his agent but is unwilling to pay 25% for the difference in those services. Don't fret. I'll help you deal with him," Wes advised, patting her hand.

"Lots of love, attention, and distance, right?"

"You've got it. At least an arm's length," said Wes with a chuckle.

"So, tell me about your other clients...I mean...our clients. What kind of jobs do you...I mean we...get for them?" Ima asked, realizing she had just become part of something Wes had built from scratch.

"I do manage a couple of musicians who *score movies* and *write jingles* for commercials. Most of my actresses work in soap operas. I have DJs, puppeteers, cartoon *novelty* voices, and a few models. But fashion has grown too iffy, too competitive for my taste."

He flipped through a book of bios and *photo composites* of his clients. "I also represent a few directors who do documentaries. Many have converted from film to videotape. Now Ima, if you want to make your mark in this business, I *recommend* learning about videotape. It's a wide-open field: the wave of the future."

Then Wes motioned her into the hall. Since his office was at home, he stored his filing cabinets in the tub of his extra bathroom. Ima laugh out loud and wisely decided to make notes to define all the do's and don'ts of the workplace. She wrote in large letters, "Never turn on the shower."

This crazy job looked like fun but had serious parts too. Wes showed her his filing system for voice-over and on-camera demos tapes, which had been jumbled completely out of alphabetical order. That she could remedy easily. After all, she did know her ABCs. In fact, she saw several places where her talents would be handy.

"Okay, I think I understand so far. What else?" she inquired.

After I take a producer or casting director to lunch and sell him on an idea of using one of our clients, you follow up the meeting," Wes instructed her.

"How? What do I do?" Being a student differed from being the teacher.

"You will send an appropriate demo on audiotape or videotape.

"You mean those in the file drawer?"

"Yes...and when we run low, order more from the studio listed on the back of each. Also, if a producer asks to see a demo on film, you will need to order a *kinescope*. Okay, now for the bulk of my business!" declared Wes.

"Whew, you mean there's more?" asked Ima.

"Oh, lots more. I only have a few flashy moneymakers. My *bread and-butter* clients are my old radio *cronies*." He showed her a composite photo of twenty voice-over announcers. "They have *mellifluous* voices, but their aging faces no longer fit TV work. Believe it or not, you hear these fellows behind most every commercial on today."

Ima studied the faces and acknowledged a few of them. "Don't tell PapaLi, but my all time favorite radio actor played *Luigi*. I loved that he portrayed an immigrant going to night school to learn English? We all cried the night Luigi became a citizen."

"Oh yes. J. Carrol Naish did a terrific job with that role."

"Do you represent him?" Ima asked eagerly.

"No. Although I wished so, he belongs to another agency," said Wes.

Ima continued to point to various actors. "What an honor to help you with these actors. As a child, I met most of them. PapaLi often called them sub-stars and old *troopers*."

"Old *troupers*, exactly! And do you know why?"

"Because they were altogether in the army?" she asked.

"Good guess but no cigar. He meant a unit of actors, not soldiers," replied Wes.

"So that type of *trouper* is spelled differently," surmised Ima.

"You Longwinds drive me crazy with your proper word usage."

"A talent which you don't like to represent?" she asked.

"But...I guess it's my *cross to bear*," replied Wes.

"So, why do you represent mostly old troupers?"

"Because advertising executives love them! They never arrive late or quibble about money. They simply walk to a microphone, sight-read a script in one take with no errors, and save thousands of dollars in studio costs, the opposite of overnight sensations."

"PapaLi called those guys, hot-shots and *flashes in the pan*," Ima added with a giggle.

"And for good reason! Some careers stretch over decades and others last only a few years or months."

"I know. Some cute actor or actress appears in a movie but then is never seen again."

"Until learning the secret of endurance! The old performers have practiced their craft until their whole *persona* says 'professional.' The hotshots also call themselves professionals but end as expensive amateurs in studio. There're one-hit wonders with minimal talent, strutting about, making demands, and taking all day to record a simple 60-second spot." Wes concluded his tirade in one breath.

"Whereas the new guys will get better as they learn *the ropes*, the older actors like Lionel and Shelton already are—"

"Real pros! At least you're dad still is *viable* and *virile*."

"And Shelton?" Ima inquired.

"As much as I hate to say it, Shelton has become a stinker lately. He's cranky, jealous, and hard to manage. At times I want to *sic* a bulldog on him; but I guess in the main, he's a decent chap. I just wish he knew how lucky he is to have the announcer's job on a popular TV game show. Honestly, he'd be hard to place anywhere else," Wes explained.

"I know. He seemed so agitated yesterday," said Ima.

"Hmmm, yes. I think he's over his head in...oh, let's not waste time on him. There's too much more for you to learn."

"I never knew you did all this. I simply thought of you as Uncle Wes."

He smiled warmly to her and continued. "First off, so you won't exhaust yourself trying to get jobs for our clients, you need to understand that normally, only 10% of all actors in America work at any one time. But, we usually beat the odds."

"How can do you do that?"

"If my guys, or rather our guys," Wes stopped to include her, "stay *Johnny-on-the-spot* and never miss an appointment, they usually work almost everyday. Now that's money in their pocket and mine as well. That's the reason why I constantly keep their names in front of producers."

$$\bullet \quad \bullet \quad \bullet$$

On the way home, Ima's head swirled with names and union rates and audition dates. She felt too tired to cook, so she bought a few slices of pizza from an open storefront nearby the Amherst. When she got home, she flipped on the TV and flopped on the sofa to eat her simple supper. Soon thereafter, *recumbent* with throw pillows tucked all about her neck, she fell asleep watching "The Beverly Hillbillies."

About midnight, she awoke with a start upon hearing a key in the front door. Her heart leapt to her throat as she ran to the kitchen, grabbed a skillet, and hid in the broom closet.

"Whew. Home at last," said Lionel flipping on the entrance light. "Hey, what's going on? Where's the piano and—?"

Ima jumped out of the closet and ran to the doorway "PapaLi, welcome home. I wasn't expecting you until tomorrow, but I love you, love you, love you for coming a day early," she hugged him and couldn't let go.

"Eemagene, Eemagene!" Lionel said, hugging her tightly as well and starting to pick her up but stopping himself with a groan. "Oh, I'd better not. The trip home about wrecked my back."

"Are you okay? You must be exhausted," she inquired.

"Never mind me. Let me have a good look at you." He pushed her away and shook his head in disbelief. "You look marvelous."

"You always say that. Any sane person would say I look a fright standing here in my PJs."

"Oh, if I must prove my sanity, I'll say your crazy carrot-colored hair sticks out like twigs in a bird nest."

"I know. At night it gets that bedtime, slept-in look."

"But really, nothing matters except my little girl has made it safely to Manhattan."

Ima hugged him again and then spread her arms out to present his re-arranged apartment, "Ta-dum! What do you think?" she said, hoping he liked the more *aesthetic* look of his home.

"It looks like your mom dropped by to make the apartment a home for you."

"Not for me, PapaLi. For you!"

· · ·

After the usual office *cordialities* of coffee and personal news, Wes gave Ima her first assignment of confirming his lunch date with the producer of *1776*. After that, he continued the training session for her new job. He informed her that J. William Tyler Advertising Company had an upcoming campaign on a new sports car designed by some ex-Ford engineers. Everyone wanted a piece of that cake. Everyone hoped that this prototype might succeed as quickly as the Mustang had in '63.

Wes gave Ima a standard *blurb* to memorize for when she talked to casting directors. She practiced the speech until she felt comfortable with the advertising *lingo*. Then when ready, she called Janet, the casting director at JWT. "Hi, I'm Ima Purple—"

"You're a purple what?" Janet replied *brusquely*.

"What I mean is my name is Ímagine...Purple. I'm Wes Westerly's new girl," Ima said, trying to sound upbeat.

"Oh, Wes's new girl? You sound too young. What's Wes doing...robbing the cradle?"

"No, I meant I'm his Gal...Friday," said Ima, politely.

"Sure honey, you call it anything you like if that makes you happy," said Janet. "So, Miss Ima Purple, I'ma gonna turn you over to my secretary. She'll set up an appointment for you to come in and fill out an employment form as a favor to Wes for his new girl."

"No, you misunderstand. I'm not applying for a job. I already work for The Westerly Agency. I'm his new...assistant, and I've called you to find out what type talent you need for your upcoming sports car commercial." Ima stayed remarkably composed even though she realized Janet had shown mastery of the *intimidation* game.

"Oh, I get you now. Okay, take this down. We need a solid voice but with gravel in it. No disc jockey types but good-looking enough for on-camera, if we decide to go that way. Did you get all that?"

"Yes, I did." Ima said boldly if only half-confidently. Although Janet had been very *patronizing*, Ima decided not to strike back but to learn from this experience.

"Okay. Now, it's your turn to shoot. You've got five minutes to empty your gun but don't try to send any duds in my direction," said Janet.

This woman's abrupt manner rattled Ima. But, taking a breath, she slowly gave the rehearsed speech. Then feeling like a real talent agent, she began to *pitch* several actors and announcers from Wes's roster of clients, hoping she had chosen appropriate ones. Unbelievably, she got auditions for two of them. With a silly grin on her face, Ima hung up. Her first attempt at selling talent had proved a success.

• • •

Lionel arose late the next morning, had some coffee, and read aloud the note Ima had left. "I'm working temporarily for Uncle Wes. He may have good news for you, so call him whenever you wake up today. Otherwise, I'll be home after six. Then we'll celebrate. Love from Your No-Longer-Imaginary Daughter, Ima."

Before dialing the Westerly Agency, Lionel pondered the note and felt proud that Ima had the *moxie* to work in his strange career field. However, he wondered if Madge were still alive, would she show delight...or chagrin over Ima's choice.

Lionel showered, shaved, and called Wes who said to meet him at Sardi's. They would be lunching with the producing staff of *1776*. Dressing quickly, he dashed out onto the sidewalks, happy to be home in Manhattan. Most *savvy* actors rode to auditions in taxicabs. That gave them privacy to exercise their faces and pinch their cheeks to look ruddy and vital. Instead, Lionel walked halfway to get color in his face and then caught a cab the remaining way. Before entering Sardi's, he repaired his windblown hair and tie.

While having a light meal, the men discussed Lionel's taking an unusual job as a general *understudy* for several historical character roles. That way the director could ease him into the play's cast. Since Lionel could act, sing, dance, and do dialects, he could serve like a utility ballplayer. They planned for him to sit on the sidelines until a main role opened. Even so, as *proficient* an actor as Lionel was, the production manager Primo suggested he meet a few times with their acting coach. Lionel's British accent needed toning down to fit America's colonial times.

Two Nights on the Town

Ima dragged home Friday evening, totally exhausted after only two days of work at The Westerly Agency. Instead of showbiz *stars in her eyes*, she saw *stars before her eyes*, like Wiley Coyote falling off a cliff and landing on his head in a *Roadrunner* cartoon. Though teaching required flexibility and sleuthing called for focus, showbiz had turned her brain into mincemeat. All day she had to catch and categorize a flurry of details from casting directors, producers, studios, and Wes's clients. Fielding so many details did not resemble playing shortstop with a few pop-ups. It felt more like trying to catch pellets from a shotgun.

Ima had no idea how to apply her intuition to this new job as she had done when solving mysteries. As dizzying as her day had been, it did not compare with what awaited the moment she opened the door. Unprepared for Mr. High Energy, she had forgotten all about her father's eternal *exuberance*. There stood Lionel in the living room, dressed in a tuxedo and ready to go out and celebrate Ima's visit.

"We have much to be happy about tonight. We're both back in Manhattan. You have a new job, and I start *1776* rehearsals on Monday," said Lionel beaming.

"Wes told me. Oh, PapaLi, I'm so happy for you," replied Ima.

"Hurry up and get dressed. I made reservations at La Toque Blanche, and we'll go dancing at the Algonquin afterwards. Sound good?"

"Incredibly so! Believe me my heart wants to do that tonight, but my body feels *bushwhacked*. Could we do it tomorrow instead? I will borrow one of Riina's spectacular dresses and promise to make you proud," she said, begging off.

"Of course, darling Eema. We'll do that. But tonight, I'm in the mood to go out. So, if you don't mind, I'll call a friend."

• • •

Teresa Latimer pushed the buzzing *intercom* to let Lionel into the lobby of her high-rise apartment. She quickly glimpsed herself in the hall mirror. The black crepe dress with its *plunging V-neckline* and her ankle strapped patent heels made a perfect outfit for dancing. Opening her apartment door, she stepped into the hallway just in time to see the elevator door roll back and Lionel exit. She gave him a coy peck on the cheek and twirled to model her dress. "What do you think?"

"You look like a million dollars, but then you always do" he said, pulling her in to kiss her warmly. "I've missed you so much, Terri."

"How would I know?" she said awkwardly, pulling away. "It's been months since you've written or called so I—"

"You know how I am: all business on the road and all yours when at home," he said, trying to gentle her into his eager arms.

She looked him squarely in the eye, "Okay, you're forgiven. But, if we don't get going soon, my feet may skip dinner and head for the dance floor."

Lionel laughed and pulled her in close again. "You do know that it's your sense of humor and not your beauty that attracts me, don't you?"

"That is a *backhanded compliment* if ever I heard one," she said hooking his arm and tugging him toward the elevator.

· · ·

The intimate atmosphere of La Toque Blanche immediately relaxed both Lionel and Teresa. The efficient waiter respectfully left them alone for their reunion.

"I've got terrific news. My daughter Ímagine has arrived."

Teresa blinked. "Oh, darling, how will she react to seeing you with me and not her mother?"

"Eema misses Madge but wants me to live happily ever after."

"I hope you're right, and I hope she likes me," Teresa said.

"I can promise she won't like you," he said, looking for effect.

Teresa cocked her head and scrunched her face. "Why?"

"It's a fact. She just won't like you…she'll love you!"

"What an awful tease, you are," Teresa said letting her lips brush across his freshly shaved face. "So, what are you going to do now that the tour is over?"

"Well, let me brag a bit. Today I got hired as the general *understudy* for all male leads in *1776*."

"That's a great show. I can almost see you doing it as a one-man show. So, how on earth can you step down to being an understudy after so many starring roles? You're an actor's actor."

"No, I'm just an actor who would rather work than sit home, waiting for a bigger role to come along. Wes has taught me that *longevity* in a theatre means more than stardom. Besides, with so many men in the cast, someone's bound to get tired or sick and quit."

After eating scallops drenched in butter, French onion soup, and baked snapper, Lionel and Teresa declined the tempting dessert cart. They decided to dance off some calories first, maybe even do a little *jump and jive*.

The Algonquin had timeless décor and broad age in *patronage*. Many guests came weekly. Some greeted Lionel, asking about his recent whereabouts. Shelton Grape, also among those out for the evening, came over to Lionel's table. He had a date with Letitia Parkwood, a highly-touted scholar from Columbia University.

The pasty lady seemed stiff and uncomfortable, perhaps even *pedantic*, preferring books to people.

"Lionel, my old friend, how did the tour go?" Shelton asked but allowed no time to hear an answer. "By the way, I auditioned for projected openings in *1776*. You more than anyone knows how fickle and easily bored the leads of a big hit like that can get."

Lionel attempted to comment, "Yes, I know—"

"Oh, and have you heard the producer has hit some snags over keeping the show at the 46th Street location."

"No, how sad. That theatre is such a good *venue*," Lionel replied.

"I'm resuming voice lessons to beef up my range for the predictable loss of one of the leads. John Adams and Franklin have lots of lines. I particularly like the Jefferson part, but I think the director liked my reading of Richard Henry Lee the most."

"Oh yes, Lee is a good role but a bit young for us old hoofers to—"

"Of course, Lee is very young at the time of the play, but I think with my range and proper make-up, I could create the illusion nicely. The director said I might need to understudy until there is a shake-up in the cast. Anyway, I'm waiting for a callback. You know how tough it is *vying* for roles these days."

"Well, Shelton that's good news. I hope you get a part," Lionel said without revealing his own good fortune. Lionel smiled, thinking how Wes had promoted both of them for the same roles. Good ole Wes looked out for good ole Wes. As long as he got his 10% from one of them, it didn't matter.

Shelton put his arm out to Terri but looked at Lionel. "You don't mind if I steal a dance with your lovely date."

"Well, yes I do; but she's free to make her own decisions," Lionel said.

Teresa looked back and forth between Lionel and Shelton. Lionel saw her unexpected pain and eased the silent awkwardness. He stood, took her hand, and placed it in Shelton's open palm. "Handle with care," he said. Then graciously, he offered his hand to Letitia, who understood nothing of the *undercurrents* between these three. Both couples glided stylishly onto the floor and did a smooth Fox Trot, a step all learned in their youths.

· · ·

That night Teresa had a terrible time going to sleep. She puzzled over her reaction toward Lionel once Shelton had shown up. Although she admitted both had charm, she could not help comparing other things about these two men. They had a similar appearance but a very different manner! Whereas Shelton had a courtly air, Lionel was more *cavalier*, almost like a buccaneer. Whether on the stage or dance floor, he stole hearts on land rather than treasure at sea. She recalled that once Lionel had gone on tour, Shelton had quickly started calling her for dates. She enjoyed his company but never encouraged him. To consider him anything but a friend would be a mistake. She loved Lionel; but she wondered if the still-grieving widower would ever choose her to replace his first love. During the evening whenever his eyes had met hers, she had seen a gulf between them. She wanted Lionel to respond to her silent plea not to compete for her with Shelton as they *obviously* already did in their work. But Lionel seemed *oblivious* to the issue.

· · ·

Saturday morning, Ima arose early to fix breakfast. While she prepared an omelet with garlic, peppers and cheese, Lionel made a pot of coffee and brought a pile of bills to the dining table. While eating, they chatted about old times. Ima brought him up to date on Sammy and told him about her adventures since leaving Newfoundland.

Finally, leaving Lionel to face the bills alone, Ima headed for the Feingold's apartment to find an outfit for the upcoming evening. Riina and she had always been the same size. At first, their mothers tried to keep their clothes separate, quickly returning whatever got borrowed or exchanged at a *prior* sleepover. Gradually it grew more and more *futile*. They simply trusted that every outfit visiting one closet for a spell would eventually find its way back to the home rack.

When Ima got there, Riina had already spread several gowns onto her bed. Ima glanced through them and held a few up to get a general idea.

"This one is divine," said Riina pulling up a blue *A-line* with a boat-neck.

Ima tried it on and said "Too Jackie Kennedy for me!"

Riina held up a red collarless shantung evening gown with *empire waist* and long sleeves, "This is a *man-killer!*"

Ima *nixed* it immediately, "Too *femme fatal* for me. Now if you were dressing my new friend Vanna, you would find her vampish enough to do that dress justice, but not me. Remember, I'm an old married lady now. I have no interest in slaying men or men slaying dragons over me."

"Picky, picky!" declared Riina, pulling out another dress. "Okay, how about black silk? This is the perfect dress for all weathers, for all occasions, and for all emergencies."

"No, black is not my color. Got anything in purple? It helps people to remember my married name!"

"You are too boring for words. Must you act so predictable?" asked Riina pushing through the hangers and pulling out a long purple satin sheath with a high Victorian neck and deep-cut bare shoulders A row of covered buttons down the entire back completed the elegant outfit.

"Oh please! That one, that one," voted Ima. "It's gorgeous!"

"Only if you promise not to sweat," joked Riina. "Also, you must wear my matching pumps, not those horrible purple walking shoes."

"Look, when you travel light, you have to choose comfortable shoes that can take hard wear and go with everything. Besides, they are, after all, purple."

"Yeah, maybe so, but they would destroy the whole effect of this dress," said Riina.

"That's why I came to see you, Miss Diva of Dresses. After three years in Newfoundland, I have lost all fashion sense. Up there warmth served as my only style."

The purple dress fit Ima like a glove, not in a tight clinging way but *chicly* falling around her small curves. Riina pulled out the latest in a strapless bra with pushup padding. "Here, slap this over your chest so you won't look like a little girl wearing your mommy's clothes."

Ima obeyed. It did fill out the *bodice* correctly. With her pink pearls from Sammy, she would be all set for a glamorous evening with her father.

"Now that looks divine," Riina said.

"Thanks Reenie. I'll think of you when I whirl around the dance floor."

"Say, what plans do you have for tomorrow afternoon?" asked Riina, always ready with a scheme.

"I hadn't thought that far ahead. It's Lionel's first weekend home. After two nights out, he may want to stay in."

"Not him, silly. You," said Riina.

"What are you, my social secretary? Have you mapped out every minute of my visit?"

"Oh, Ima, I've got a confession. If you only knew how great it is to have my best friend back for a while...to have someone to do things with."

"Me too!" she hugged Riina. "So, what did you have in mind?"

"Okay. I belong to this group that takes free tours around the city, you know like Yankee Stadium and backstage of the Met. Well, tomorrow we're touring the sewers of New York!" Riina said holding her nose.

"Talk about divine sounding," Ima joined in holding her nose.

"No, really, it'll be fun. We won't be inside pipes, just inside the workman's passages. Think about it. Haven't you always wanted to go down a manhole?"

"Absolutely, top of my list to Santa," Ima declared.

"Okay, meet me at one o'clock sharp, tomorrow at the Central Park South manhole across from the Plaza. And do not wear my purple dress. Jeans will do nicely."

• • •

Because La Toque Blanche was his favorite, Lionel wanted to take Ima there as well. The *maître d* Pierre gasped at the lovely young woman on Lionel's arm and seemed surprised to see the illustrious *patron* returning again tonight...and with a different woman.

Seeing Pierre's alarm, Lionel quickly introduced Ima, "This dazzling young lady is my girl."

"Your girl?" asked Pierre who, being French, of course, never blushed at any romance. However, he did look slightly puzzled.

"I mean my little girl, my daughter!" Lionel said.

"Ah, oui! I see zee resemblance," he said leading them to a quiet table.

Lionel quickly ordered shrimp cocktails, spinach salad, crabbed stuffed snapper, and a bottle of champagne. Afterwards, they lingered contentedly as long as the waiter kept pouring the French-roasted coffee. At almost ten o'clock, they took a cab to the Algonquin, with plans to dance off the delicious meal.

To be festive tonight, the Hotel Algonquin had hung a mirror ball over the dance floor. After a few slow dance tunes, the band broke into jazz for a few swing numbers. Now wide-awake, the crowd jumped to its feet and started doing the Lindy.

When Lionel proudly escorted Ima onto the floor, several men without dates *tagged his shoulder* to cut in. Seeing her delight, Lionel reluctantly *relinquished* his built-in partner. But still playing his role as father to the belle of the ball, he pointed out her ring finger to whoever invited her to dance. He figured that ought to *preclude* any misguided flirtations.

One eager fellow invited Ima to jitterbug. His style resembled more *calisthenics* than dancing. He lifted her above his head, slid her down through his legs on the floor and then *retrieved* her back to an upright position. Over and over, he spun her in and out like a yo-yo. During one such spin, he accidentally let go of her hand and sent her sailing into a *ringside table* which just happened to be Shelton Grace's perch.

"Ima, so nice of you to drop over...for dessert," he said trying to make a joke since she had landed in the middle of a melting *Baked Alaska*.

As he helped her off the tabletop, she said, "Oh, Mr. Grape. I've spoiled your lovely dessert."

"And it has spoiled your lovely dress," Shelton said.

"I'm so embarrassed," said Ima.

"Oh, don't be silly. This is definitely the right party to join." Then, motioning to the pretty lady at his side, he said, "I suppose you know Teresa Latimer?"

Just as Ima reached to shake hands with Teresa, Lionel appeared to rescue his daughter. He had been so busy *cutting up the rug* with other friends, he failed to notice his most favorite one had come with...his least favorite. Bewildered, Lionel looked at Teresa and then at Shelton.

"Oh, here again tonight, Lionel?" asked Shelton, extending his hand.

"Yes," he said, trying to cover his *obvious* hurt. To smooth the strained situation, he nervously shook Teresa's hand instead. "I hope you both have a nice evening." Then offering his arm to Ima, Lionel said as if in a Shakespearean play, "Come Eema darling, let us away to the dance floor!"

"Oh, please PapaLi, let's go home? This evening is a total *debacle*. I've ruined Riina's dress, and she's liable to disown me if these stains won't come out."

As they turned to leave, Shelton called out, "By the way, Li, while you were away, we switched the weekly games to the Friars Club. See you there, Monday or Wednesday or both."

"Oh, sure, thanks for reminding me," said Lionel.

Meanwhile, Ima's jitterbug partner stood by totally *mortified*. He had humiliated her by causing a soft landing in meringue. Now, shrinking to chipmunk-size, he scurried over to the bar to *drown his sorrows*.

• • •

The next morning, Lionel bounded out of bed, dressed quickly, and came to the couch to shake Ima awake. "I forgot it's Sunday. Hurry up, we'll be late for church. I have to run ahead to find out what the choir plans to sing today. See you there!"

"Where?" asked Ima.

"Jan Hus!" said Lionel.

"You speak Czech?"

"No, but I sing Czech!"

Ima quickly showered to shake off the food fiasco of an inglorious Saturday night. She slipped on a mint green linen dress also borrowed from Riina. It looked fairly good with her old standby purple walking shoes, which would carry her through the storm sewers later in the afternoon.

When Ima walked into the service, some of the soup kitchen people waved for her to sit with them. Much to her surprise, Lionel sang the offertory solo. Although for her, the sermon was in *gibberish*, the same spirit of God dwelt in this place. She felt comforted by the common faith among the people in the pews. At the end of the service, she felt proud that so many in the congregation waited in the *narthex* to congratulate Lionel on his return. She watched them talking with their hands, trying to be understood. They all seemed to love and appreciate him. Suddenly, Old Cash came up.

"Hi, Missy, back again?"

"Why yes. I plan to make this my church while visiting."

"I've been coming...or going here the last little while. I like the people even when I can't understand a word they say."

"I know. Isn't it crazy how that works? So, are you a member here?"

"Oh, nothing like that. Are you?"

"No, but you see that man over there?" Ima pointed to Lionel.

"You mean the singer fellow?" Cash asked.

"He's my father. He belongs here," Ima declared.

Cash looked at her for a moment wondering what she meant. "I heard he is famous, so do you think I don't belong here?" he asked, *furrowing* his brow.

"What?" Ima asked in shock.

"Well, if someone famous goes here, do I belong somewhere else?"

"Of course not, Cash. You belong here more than anyone. You are like Jesus to me. You helped me in my troubles, and you're so kind to people...and you clean up after the lunches and—"

"Well, we're mighty lucky to have a famous man in our midst," Cash said.

"He may be famous to some, but he's just plain ole PapaLi to me," she *reiterated*.

"Well, I want to buy you and your papa a chilidog, that is if you don't mind eating with the likes of me," said the Central Park vagrant.

"There you go again, putting yourself down. We've broken bread twice before. You're my friend, and I choose my friends very carefully," Ima declared.

"Me too," he said, patting her shoulder. "So, you'll come?"

"The truth is today Reenie and I plan to take a tour of the storm sewers. I have to meet her in less than an hour. May I have a *rain-check*? Or maybe you'd like to come along."

"Thanks for the invitation, but I've spent enough time underground. I'd rather be outdoors where no one tells you what to do," Cash confessed.

"So, do you go down there to keep warm in the winter," Ima said, trying to imagine the lifestyle Cash must lead.

"Something like that," Cash muttered, evading direct eye contact.

Monkey See...Monkey Do

Ima ran back to the apartment to change into jeans and reconsider her shoe choice. Her new sneakers would certainly work better for climbing in the sewers; but, on the other hand, they would get filthy. So, with her old faithfuls on, Ima struck out for the *highbrow* Plaza Hotel to take the lowbrow sewer tour. Crossing Fifth Avenue, she saw Riina with an assembled group standing midway the block and awaiting orders to 'go below.'

Crawling down a manhole sounded as easy as a monkey scampering up and down a coconut tree. But easy, it was not! The manhole had a narrow opening with a steep ladder inside. The guide went down first to catch the next one descending. Each person who followed assumed the role of body catcher, in case anyone's foot slipped.

Most areas felt dampish and cool; but whenever the tour group passed a subway vent, hot air blew into the tunnel just as it had on the sidewalks. Since a recent rain had drained off and no water main had broken lately, only a little water ran down the center of the giant concrete passage. Still to keep dry feet, everyone stayed on the flat ledge of one side. Of course, a few show-off rebels chose to *straddle* the stream.

The first stop on the tour was under Carnegie Hall. The guide motioned them into a semicircle. "Close your eyes and pretend you're a chamber choir making your debut performing the ancient melody, 'Greensleeves.' Peasants used it for the Morris Dance, and Christians made it into a Christmas carol." The guide began humming the tune, but most everyone sang "What child is this?" A few stragglers attempted to dance in the cramped space. Strangely, the *unison* voices and clunking feet echoed against the hollow concrete *ducts* giving the song deep and powerful overtones.

Then they backtracked and walked beneath Saks Fifth Avenue. "Don't tell anyone you were at Saks on Sunday. You might be arrested for breaking New York's Blue Laws."

"It's not like we can buy anything from under the store," said a tourist.

"Yes, yes, of course. Just a little underground humor," said the guide. "Okay, let's head to Rockefeller Center."

"What's next? Do we pretend to be Christmas trees in the plaza?" quipped Riina.

"No, you're going to dance at Radio City Music Hall or at least under the big stage."

Riina took that cue to organize a chorus line. "Okay Rockette cadettes, we've no time to rehearse so just follow my lead and sing along. We're gonna steal the Sunday show." She urged the female tourists into a chorus line, had them hook arms, and told them to kick the *can-can.*

"Monkey see. Monkey do," said Ima, amazed how at home Riina looked staging a dance routine even in the worst of places: the sewers.

The ladies gave a *valiant* effort to follow Riina's vigorous, high kick routine, but most fell on their duffs laughing, glad they had worn jeans, especially the one who splashed into the drain water.

"So, Ima, tomorrow, I want you to add this to my bio. Say something like I briefly toured with the Rockettes or—"

"Sure, Reenie," Ima said, playing along. "I'll say you danced underneath the same lights as the Rockettes of Radio City Music Hall fame…way, way under."

. . .

When the tour finished, Ima invited Riina over to PapaLi's apartment. She found a note from Lionel, saying he had gone to Teresa's apartment and would be home late. With the place all to themselves, the young women decided to relax and take it easy. Ima fixed a light *repast* of apple walnut pancakes with sausage, her favorite Sunday night meal.

After dinner, she showed Riina the disaster that had happened to the purple dress. Riina touched the encrusted white stain and licked her fingers, "Do I taste meringue?"

"And ice cream and other gooey stuff. Oh Reenie, I'm so sorry. It was an accident. My body went sailing across the room and landed in a Baked Alaska. I'll have it cleaned tomorrow. I hear Royal Cleaners claims to have removed the *damn spot* from Lady Macbeth's hand."

"Ridiculous. Cleaning would cost a fortune, probably more than the dress did. Don't fuss," she slipped into her mixture of New York dialects. "It's had good mileage…gone to turdy t'ree openings and hoyd lots of compliments. So, I should worry about it? Neither you nor I should worry for nuttin' about it. Maybe I'll win an Oscar for the biggest costume mishap of 1969? Only thing I regret is missing your performance."

"You mean my disaster. I was *mortified* and still am when I see what happen to this gorgeous gown," lamented Ima.

"Forget about it, already! I bought it at a lid'l resale shoppe in Greenwich Village! It's probably hot, stolen off the back of a stah-let or fell off some gangsta's twuck."

"Oh Reenie, you're the fastest forgiver I've ever known."

"With a face like mine I need mercy so I gotta forgive fast," Riina joked and made a grand Garbo gesture, "So, I *bequeath* this purple gown to Ima Purple to clean or burn or wear or start a new marbleized fabric fashion."

"Well, I want to return your mint green dress before anything happens to it. I did wear it to church and got lots of compliments," said Ima, hanging it on the front door so Riina would not forget to take it.

"The question is, did it *repent* and get *redeemed*?" inquired Riina.

"I'm not sure your dress understood the sermon. Does it speak Czech?"

• • •

As the evening drew on, the young women still had the sewer smell in their nostrils. Although it was mid-July, Ima turned off the air-conditioner and opened the windows for fresh air. They dragged dining chairs to the window and put their feet on the sills. Ima sat, brushing and loving on Boofy. The poor animal, shoved from *pillar to post* for weeks, acted skittish around a new stranger. After sweet talking it and stroking its ears, Riina finally coaxed the kitty into her lap. Both seemed content.

Lionel's apartment looked out on a 1920s nondescript, six-storied apartment house that was one grade above public housing and probably never had a *heyday*. Unlike those Westside rent control buildings which Flannery said the Historical Society might want to preserve, this one possessed no *redeeming* or aesthetic features. During the Depression this brick blob had probably become a *tenement* for poor folks and never recovered from that needed assignment. Riina and Ima discussed its likely future and the scheme to replace it with another 1960s nondescript 20-storied apartment house like the Amherst. Perhaps even tonight in a fancy restaurant, developers chewed on steak, *chomping at the bit* to demolish this eyesore.

No matter how ugly the structure was, it could support a reasonable life for its current tenants who called it home. They had adapted to its antiquated plumbing, *frayed* electrical wiring, and the inconveniences of no elevator or air-conditioning. They had found answers to their own complaints, like tonight, a night almost too hot to breathe.

The two young friends watched while folks climbed out windows of their flats and sat on fire escapes to catch whatever breeze blest the concrete canyons of East 74th Street.

Kids held lemonade glasses in hand, and the adults sported beer cans. Almost instantly, bags of chips tied with long strings got passed up and down to whoever could grasp the cord. The evening had turned into a block party!

Suddenly, the tenants began yelping and stretching their necks to look up at the top edge of their building. Kids pulled on parents' hands and pointed at some unknown commotion on the roof. Some received orders to sit down. Others dropped water bombs down to the sidewalk. One unruly girl dropped her lemonade glass down four stories to see what would happen. When it crashed into a hundred *shards*, she was *banished* back to her family's hot flat and would have to miss the rest of the fun.

Captivated by the free, *impromptu* entertainment, s*cores* of Amherst residents, including Ima and Riina, leaned out of their windows.

"Everyone over here is looking at everyone over there. It's crazy," said Ima.

"Everyone looks like baby birds leaning out of their nests and waiting to be fed."

"No, there really is something on the roof over there. Everyone's pointing to it, but I can't see it," remarked Ima.

Riina began putting on an act, pulling back in and turning her nose up in the air. "Such riff-raff. It's all sooooo undignified, tish-tish!"

"You *bourgeoisie* snob. I thought you loved mingling with the masses," said Ima as she also pulled her head back in. "I'm going to get Lionel's binoculars for a closer view."

After peering out and still not seeing anything, Ima passed the glasses to Riina. She dropped the snob act and took a quick glance.

"Being a New York BOI, I know when to be quiet and when to yell. This is definitely a loudmouth moment!" Riina said to Ima and then called outside. "Hey, what's going on?"

"There's a monkey on the roof," said an unidentified voice.

"A monkey?" Riina inquired.

"Probably loose from the hospital," another voice informed her.

"Which hospital?" Ima asked, not knowing the neighborhood yet.

"You know... the one doing research on monkeys!" said someone.

"Oh, good grief," said Ima, letting out the teacher tucked inside. "Well then, don't touch it. Leave it alone. It might have an infection or a rare disease."

Soon after, several firemen arrived in a truck. While a few went inside, the others stayed outside. One climbed up the ladder from the truck to get a better *vantage point* for catching the beast. The news of the event spread quickly. Soon several hundred people lined the intersection of 74th Street and First Avenue.

More fire engines arrived. Taxis, bogged down in the traffic jam, soon drove up onto the sidewalks to get around the growing crowds. One taxi knocked over a fire hydrant, making all the children squeal on such a hot evening. Kids scurried over to take a shower bath in the free flowing water.

Then the games began. Two firemen on ladders tried to calm the terrified animal. Meanwhile, the other half of the firemen came panting out onto the roof after climbing six flights of stairs. When a roof fireman came to the edge, the monkey jumped onto the next tenement over. Unbelievably, the crowd cheered. Then the truck moved down to that building and dangled a fireman over the terrified animal. Feeling trapped, it jumped back to the original building. Again the crowd went wild and routed for the monkey. It had made a monkey out of the fireman.

"Pretty smart little guy," said Ima.

"Smart, maybe but...still...it's a far stretch for me to believe I came from that!" declared Riina.

"Right, that'd insult the monkey! So what do you think they'll do after they catch him...put him on trial?" asked Ima with a giggle.

"And-and-and he'll...need...a good lawyer," Riina sputtered with bursts of laughter.

"Right!" said Ima, joining in the fun as she caught on to Riina's *drift*. "He'll need the best attorney possible."

"Let's g-g-get him Clarence D-D-Darrow—"she interrupted herself with the hilarity of that idea and gasped between guffaws.

"Exactly. Clarence Darrow...for another Monkey Trial," shouted Ima, laughing so hard she almost fell from her chair.

The *volleying* match with the monkey on the roof lasted over an hour. Finally the fireman claimed victory. Crowds dispersed quickly. Kids went inside to bathe, and fire escapes soon stood empty. This sight *surpassed* the best night ever on TV.

With the excitement over, Ima and Riina both admitted that New York had given them great childhoods and prepared them to have satisfying lives as adults, a fact the kids across the way would someday appreciate.

"Although we grew up before blackouts and stalkers and muggers, I now agree that a woman should not walk home here. Manhattan isn't safe anymore. I'll get you a cab."

After Ima called for a cab, the two friends headed down eight flights of stairs instead of taking the elevator.

"Ahhh-just can't get enough of that tunnel love," declared Riina taking a deep breath and coughing. "Pew! I still have that sewer smell in my clothes."

"I know. I didn't want you stinking up my fancy elevator," quipped Ima, giggling.

Soon out under the canopy to wait for the taxi, Ima and Riina grew philosophical.

"You know even though New York may be less safe, nowhere but here would you have ever seen any monkey business like tonight's" remarked Riina.

"Agree, and no one here, rich or poor, has any excuse for getting bored," Ima said.

"Oh, Ima, you absolutely must move back," declared Riina. "Don't you miss it?"

"Yes! But Reenie, my year of adventures has just begun. I want to see the world."

"I mean after that. Maybe Sammy could ask to be assigned to Brooklyn's Navy Yard."

"Oh, Brooklyn now has its own navy?" she asked teasing because of her friend's wrong arrangement of words. "Don't you mean the U.S. Navy's Yard located in Brooklyn which we just happen to call the Brooklyn Navy Yard?"

"You English teachers drive me nuts," remarked Riina.

"Evenso, Sammy belongs to the Air Force, not the Navy."

Just then a cab drove up, and Lionel popped out. Although he looked a bit shaken, he smiled at the young women. "Riina, how nice to see you. What are you doing here?"

"Just waiting for my cab, Mr. Longwind," Riina replied.

"Here, take mine. It's all the same," he said.

"No, we called for one; so, I'll wait. It's only fair," replied Riina.

"But cabbies never miss a return fare," said Lionel. Puzzled, he waved off his taxi. At the corner two people hailed it, proving both systems worked.

"So, Ima, were you waiting up for your old man?"

"Of course not, PapaLi. But you do look terrible. Are you okay?" said Ima.

"No, Teresa gave me very unhappy news. But I can't let it discourage me. I must be strong...very strong if I am to play

George Washington or Thomas Jefferson or Benjamin Franklin or whoever else might drop out," he said, hugging Ima.

"Are you sure you're okay? You'd tell me if you weren't, right?"

"Yes, but I'm fine. Money and women come and go, but family is forever," Lionel confessed.

"Does that mean you broke up with your lady friend?" Ima asked.

"Oh, nothing like that. I'll tell you about it later," Lionel said.

"Say, Mr. Longwind, welcome back from your tour and congratulations on your new role or should I say roles?" said Riina. "The news should hit *Variety* this week, but Ima already told me early."

"Yes, but I'm afraid our fellow actor Shelton Grape may be an unhappy chap about that and...the fact that Teresa and I are now engaged. What a double whammy!" Lionel announced his news like an *actor's aside*.

"So you got engaged instead of breaking up?" Ima gasped and hugged Lionel's neck. "Oh, that's wonderful."

Riina joined in the gasping and hugging as well. "I can keep that a secret."

* * *

Returning to the apartment, Lionel heard the phone and grabbed it, "Hello?"

"It's Teresa. I just wanted to wish you a good night's rest and an excellent morning's rehearsal. I know you'll bowl them over!" declared Teresa.

"Thanks for your vote," he said.

"And darling, don't worry about your investments. *Stocks* go up and down like fever. I'll keep my ears and eyes open. Just don't panic. This is an unwise time to sell."

Lionel hung up and felt grateful that Ima had not heard that side of the conversation. He didn't want his daughter worrying about his finances.

Friends Only at the Friars

The rehearsal went well on Monday. Both the producer and the director of *1776* knew they had hired a pro. Lionel needed no *coddling*, no prodding, and no cheering section to do a job he fit perfectly. Even so, it was not uncommon for agents to show up to give their clients moral support. So as a courtesy, Wes dropped by the 46th Stage Theatre before going to Sardi's for lunch.

When Wes returned to the office that afternoon, Ima broke from her other duties and handed him a stack of messages. "I deposited all the checks; and as we speak, all clients active on today's schedule have gone to their studio sessions or auditions," reported Ima.

"See how your efficiency makes me only a fixture around here?" he said.

"Oh, that's pushing it. I'm not ready to take over. I can manage the *superficial* tasks but talking directly to casting directors unnerves me. Some of them treat me like a child and insist on talking only to you."

"Ima, that's just a power game they like to play," Wes said, chuckling. "They'll settle down once they realize you're really the one in charge around here."

"By the way, how did Lionel's rehearsal go," Ima asked.

"You know your father. For him, every day he wakes up is his very best day. He's a pure pro, and every word or motion coming from that man is pure gold."

"Acting and singing have remained his passions since his twenties," Ima iterated.

"Before becoming an agent, I also worked as an actor, for no less than 25 years. Yet, I could never master myself or focus the way Lionel can. I don't know how he does it," confessed Wes, thumbing the pink messages. "Hmmm, Shelton's called three times."

"Yes, I know. He wants to know the outcome to the audition," she iterated.

"I must say, I don't relish telling him he lost the job...and lost it to Lionel."

"He's a pro too. He'll understand?" Ima said innocently

"No, he won't," Wes said, shaking his head uncomfortably. "I better meet him this afternoon for drinks. Would you set it up?" asked Wes.

"Where do you want to go to...P.J. Clarke's...at the usual time?" asked Ima.

"No, it's too crowded that time of day for what I need to do," decided Wes. "Besides, that's where Shelton meets his bookie and other creeps like Val Pollibo. If my news makes him angry, Val will side with him and want to fight. It would not be a pretty picture."

"I'd think being in public would help control the situation?" asked Ima naïvely.

"No, Ima. That's a cue for the famous movie line, *Let's take this outside.*"

"Well, so far Shelton has been quite sweet to me," said Ima.

"That's his mode when he wants something. But you don't know him yet. When he doesn't get his way, he's unleashes a nasty *temper*...also not a pretty picture," said Wes.

"I can't imagine what Shelton could want from me," she said quietly.

"Probably to grill you on why Lionel got this job, and he didn't."

"How could anyone think I would have any influence over any director's choice much less over anything, especially over what PapaLi might do...at anytime?" inquired Ima.

"Facts don't matter when Shelton has his eye on something." Wes shook his head.

"So, Uncle Wes. We're back to square one. Where do I make a reservation?"

"Let's make it here at The Westerly Den," he said, pointing to his living room downstairs. "Shelton can *grouse* and grumble all he likes. No one will hear."

"Simple enough. I'll leave a message with his answering service and let you know when he confirms," replied Ima, showing her efficiency.

Nodding, Wes started toward his desk but then turned back. "Ima dear, since you're working with me, I need to let you know honestly how this business works. If it sounds as if I'm *badmouthing* a client, I'm not. I'm telling you the truth so you'll be prepared."

"Uncle Wes, I know you're not a gossip," she said.

"It's more than that. I want to groom you to have fair judgment about people's talent. It takes a distinctive taste to cast actors in the proper roles. I'm sorry Shelton missed this chance, but I'm pleased for Lionel. He'll do the agency proud. You see, no real contest ever really existed. The producer only gave Shelton an audition as a courtesy to me."

"But why?" she asked.

"Whereas Lionel has a vocal quality found only in the best actors...that is with equal parts of gravel and *timbre*, Shelton always sounds like an announcer."

. . .

Shelton never confirmed the appointment with Wes. He needed to save face after reading in *Variety Magazine* that *1776* now had hired Lionel as a general understudy for all roles. The battle lines had changed. Shelton needed a new *strategy*. He intended to get a *pound of flesh* one way or another, perhaps beginning tonight at the poker game.

• • •

Wes and Lionel met for dinner at the Friars Club and planned to join the friendly poker game later. When they crossed the lobby and entered the dark paneled card room, the game had already begun. Players had cards in hand and colored poker chips sat in *denomination* stacks before them. *Ostensibly* for this friendly game of cards, the dealer had called the stakes a bit above *penny ante poker*. Everyone, except Shelton, smiled and appeared relaxed for their weekly game.

"Well, if it isn't my personal agent with his favorite client," Shelton said *snidely*. "So, after your little private dinner meeting in which I'm sure you made glorious plans for Lionel's future, you decided to grace our humble table with your presence?"

"Shelton, I have no favorites, just people who honor appointments better," said Wes.

"Well, I told Ima I'd see you here! What? Did little Miss Favorite Client's Daughter forget to tell you?" Shelton scoffed.

Tired from the long day, Lionel already disliked the *tenor of the conversation*. "Shel, do you plan to throw daggers or deal cards? If we're not going to play, I have lines to learn and things to do at home."

"Yes, yes Lionel, you are such a busy actor," Shelton said, starting on a monologue and increasing his volume. "I'm sure you're overloaded with learning dialogue for so many roles. It's like *Russian Roulette* to know which cast member will drop in his tracks first. Let me see. Will it be John Adams or Hancock or Ben Franklin or Tom Jefferson or...oh my, no, help us all...please not Richard Henry Lee?" declared Shelton, more vicious with each name. He then turned to Wes and blurted, "So, how long have you known Lionel got the job I wanted."

"Since Friday," said Wes.

"And just when did you plan to tell me that I lost the audition? Tonight, so I'd be embarrassed?" Shelton oozed *acrimony.*

"No, Shelton, today...at the appointment with me that you ignored! I did not extend a casual invitation to have cocktails but requested you meet me privately to talk business...about your future with my agency," Wes said.

At that very moment, Val Pollibo darkened the arched entry. He looked like a *sinister* portrait, *encased* in the massive English *fascia* and carved moldings. The ornate frame clashed with his typical *hoodlum attire.* "So, boys, are you getting up a game?"

"Yes, a friendly game for members and their guests only," said Wes.

"Well, I'm a guest," Pollibo said, stretching his massive arm to form a gate across the doorway.

Wes glared at Shelton, "I thought you took care of this. Now I will," he said, leaving the table and going to the door. Pollibo blocked the exit by moving side-to-side so that Wes had to duck under to get out.

In perfect timing and with clipboard in hand, Sam the on-duty *Sergeant of Arms* appeared behind Val, "Sir, please step out of the way." Val refused.

"What is your name?" Val kept silent like a crook *waiting for his lawyer.*

"Glad you came, Sam. I was just heading off to find Security. This man's name is Val Pollibo and is not one of us," declared Wes.

The Sergeant looked at his clipboard and saw no such name on the guest roster. "Sir, this is a private club. I must ask you to leave right now."

"But Mr. Pollibo is on my guest list," Shelton said, jumping to Val's defense. "I thought Friars was a civilized club. Is this how we treat visitors?"

The Sergeant looked again at his clipboard, "No, Mr. Grape, you are mistaken. Perhaps the office removed him, so you must re-submit his name for approval. I'm sorry, but this man must leave for now."

Shelton approached Pollibo and led him out to the sidewalk. "I'm sorry about the mix-up. Give me a moment to straighten out this matter."

• • •

In a half hour, Sam returned to say he had made an error and apologized *profusely* for the disturbance. "After reviewing the records, I discovered Mr. Pollibo is indeed on the list of another member, but not Mr. Grape."

"You mean another *fink* is among us tonight?" Lionel said, looking at Paul and Tim, two other Friars at the table who often joined the weekly games. Still with a fan of cards still spread in their hands for the game in progress, they looked bewildered more than embarrassed.

"What other member would choose a companion like Val Pollibo?" asked Lionel whispering discreetly to Wes.

"Who knows, but obviously Sam has had his mind changed," remarked Wes.

"A little friendly *goon* persuasion," said Lionel, mimed some *arm-twisting*.

When the dismissed guest and his patron Shelton returned to the game room, everyone prepared to play cards. Shelton doubled his *façade of propriety*.

"We should make amends for the humiliation inflicted on Mr. Pollibo.

"How about he show us a little humility for letting him stay," said Wes.

"That request doesn't fit Val. He's a proud man. I say we show him great hospitality and *set the stakes of the game* high enough to interest him to stay," said Shelton.

Lionel looked at Wes, "Let's not! I vote for the lowest stakes possible...so low that this goon will *take his marbles and go home.*"

"Low sounds just about my style. Besides, I like to play poker so much, I'd even play for matchsticks or jelly beans," Wes teased.

All three new players gathered chips to join the game. Lionel and Wes sat strategically so the only chair open for Val was between them. In that position they would keep their eyes on Val's sleeves in case he tried to cheat. Shelton dealt a new deck.

"Hey, Shel, we haven't finished our other game. There's twenty bucks riding in the pot," said Paul.

"Twenty bucks...oh, what big risk-takers you have here at the Friars Club," said Val, laughing *derisively.*

"Let's call that a practice game...which doesn't count. The pot stays. Now let's get down to serious cards," Shelton declared with an edge to his voice.

"Says who? I want to see what you and Paul had in your last hand," replied Tim, revealing that he had a Flush. "Now, show me your cards."

Paul showed a Straight, and Shelton opened his old hand to a Full House, "So, I won, anyhow." He started raking in the pot but stopped. "No, I'll leave it. You suckers can win it back." His small victory puffed him up.

Lionel looked at his new hand and opened with a quarter. Both Paul and Tim had nothing in their hands so each asked for a card. Shelton passed. Val looked at Shelton, and Shelton looked back. Then Val said, "I'll take that and raise you a buck."

"So Shel, are these the *high stakes* you threatened us with to ease the pain of this big tough guy?" *goaded* Paul. He got no reply.

Wes looked at his cards and raised Val fifty cents. However, suspecting Val was a rat with poison on its teeth, he asked, "You do understand we play family style here?"

Again, Val looked at Shelton, and Shelton looked back, "No, I play only *bookie style*," Val spoke in a raspy voice, trying to *intimidate* the others.

· · ·

Winning their third game, the Guilders were *on a roll*. The team members decided to go out to celebrate. They didn't care if the public saw them in grungy uniforms with ball caps pulled down on their faces. Nothing could tarnish the image of these *up and comers*. No one yet knew who they were. Besides, not even their own mothers would recognize them under the dirt and grime.

Since the Central Park ballgames hailed from the *exclusive* part of town, the team decided to balance the evening by going slumming in the Bowery. Down there for sure, no one cared what you wore. Ima asked Old Cash if he wanted to join in the fun, but he answered almost as curiously as when she asked him to go on the sewer tour.

"I love that you young girls invite me to go places with you; but honestly, I've spent too much time down there with drunk friends dying in my arms. But keep asking. It makes me feels... like a regular fellow."

Riina and Ima hugged Cash warmly and dashed off to catch up with the other players.

The team rode the subway to St. Mark's and then walked over to Sloppy Louie's on South Street close to Fulton Fish Market. If not for its great popularity with locals and tourists, Louie's would have been shut down by the City Health Department long ago. It violated every food sanitation code on the books.

The crowd was noisy; and the fish, always fresh and deep-fried. Louie's made its claim to fame for dust and grease ringlets that hung from the ceiling like Spanish moss from live oak trees in Louisiana.

Riina turned to Ima, "And the coffee shop worried about our breaking sanitation codes with one small kitty?"

"I know. Talk about a *double standard*. Look at the filth everywhere," said Ima. "But it's fun for folks to come here...at least once."

"Take my word for it. I know New York politics. Some inspector receives regular payoffs to overlook code *infractions*. That keeps the tourist money rolling in."

"You're so *cynical*, Riina," declared Ima.

"Yeah, just call me a silly ole realist."

"I'd rather be a silly ole optimist," said Ima.

"Okay, Pollyanna, there's room for us both in the boat," quipped Riina.

Having won their game, the Guilders now worked to win the loud-and-rowdy award at Louie's. From the moment they arrived, they continued jumping up, topping each other's volume, and cheering themselves onto an all-city victory.

Soon their *raucous* behavior started an unfortunate avalanche. Uninvited, gooey *curlicues* like black spaghetti began dropping down from the ceiling. Though this *phenomenon* rarely happened, the dinner guests welcomed the surprise with delight. Waiters quickly replaced diners' plates with fresh ones. The manager made a short announcement to inform the crowd that reporters and cameramen would arrive soon to cover the story.

A few *novice* Guilders grew concerned over what such *publicity* shots might do for their careers. Although on the ball field they loved letting down their guard, vanity and beauty still remained their meal tickets to the world of show biz.

Now working for an agent, Ima stood and tried to reassure them, "Look girls. Most publicity is good publicity, especially when it comes for free. Newspapers will forever link your names to something funny...not disgusting or illegal. Just think about it. Chicken Licken claimed the sky was falling, and you saw that happen right before your very eyes."

Riina stood and pushed Ima back into her chair. "Excuse my friend Ima. She lives most of the year in happy la-la Newfoundland

and teaches young minds to think. That the law allows her to roam loose in Manhattan is a scary enough thought to keep you from ordering dessert for the sake of your waistlines," remarked Riina who waited for a ripple of laughter before sitting down

Even with Ima's explanation and Riina's encouragement, two very new actresses wanted to protect their reputations at all costs. So, they *split the scene* to avoid being plastered across the newspapers, looking less than their best. Even so, the majority of the diehards relaxed and considered the event pure *serendipity*, a chance to land their names and photos on the *New York Times* front page. Next month they might be on Broadway or in Vogue which would change the public's opinion of them.

Moments later, reporters did actually appear and concentrated on the Guilders' table. The interview covered not only the greasy ringlets falling from the ceiling but also the ones from under their softball caps. Those who stayed gladly gave their names as long as the team's recent winning streak got publicity in the papers as well.

After short interviews, the players finished their meals and left. Riina grinned and rubbed her hands together. "Okay, let's stir up some mischief."

"You're *incorrigible*," Ima said.

"Well...why not? We're out for the evening anyhow," Riina announced.

Ima thought otherwise but agreed. "Okay, let me tell you what I want to do. By the time PapaLi gets home tonight, I'll be asleep. I have to know how his first day of rehearsal went. So let's go by the Friars."

"Sounds good. Then we can walk to my folks from there," suggested Riina.

They caught an uptown bus, transferred to get to East 55th and soon bounded into the Friars Club, like two lost little kids. Sam, now manning the front desk, checked out every stray that entered. He looked *askance* at the two oddly dressed young women.

"Are you here for try outs as ball-players in *Damn Yankees* or as urchins in *Oliver*?"

Delighted that Sam had played along at first, Ima and Riina answered together, in their best Brooklyn accent, "For both of dose, already."

"Well, sorry, the Friars Club is no longer New York's Central Casting Office for old *musical revivals*."

"So you know showbiz?" asked Riina hoping he would stretched out his story.

"Everyone here is attached to showbiz in some way, but what's your excuse? This is a private club, members only," he said, less warmly.

"We know. I had lunch here last week," said Ima. "Don't you recognize me?"

"No. Are you tourists who lost your parents? If so, I must inform you, the Friars is also no longer New York's Lost and Found Department."

"Nope, I've not lost my father. He's here playing cards. But he may have lost some money in the poker game that's going on," she said with a lilt.

"What's his name," asked Sam.

"PapaLi, but you know him as Lionel Longwind?" said Ima.

Acting ready to end this discussion, Sam went quickly to the card room and disappeared. Moments later Lionel emerged and headed toward Sam's podium up front.

"What are you two ragamuffins doing here?" asked Lionel.

"I couldn't wait until tomorrow. We came by to find out how your play rehearsal went...and to brag on ourselves for winning the game today."

"Great news. And as far as the rehearsal and dialect session, all went well, in fact much better than this poker game," he said with a rather curious look on his face.

"Well, don't lose my inheritance. I may want to move back to New York; and it's so very, very expensive here," Ima said, hugging him.

"You girls be careful of muggers," he said with a strained smile.

"Believe me. We will. By the way PapaLi, it's already late. I'll probably stay over at Reenie's and just wear something of hers to work tomorrow."

"That's a good plan," said Lionel. "So, let's have lunch tomorrow?"

"It's a date, and will you feed Boofy when you get home tonight and in the morning too?" Ima asked.

He nodded and gave her another strange look. "Sure, leave Boofy to me."

"PapaLi, are you okay? You're not ill or something, are you?"

"No, never better. See you tomorrow."

Riina and Ima exited the front door and slowly step away from the club.

• • •

Sam, the Sergeant of Arms, stood at his lectern and watched Lionel head back to the game. Just then a man in dark attire hurried from the card room, pushed Lionel aside, but offered Lionel no apology for the abrupt action. As the *brusque* man came closer, Sam recognized him as Val Pollibo with whom he had dealt earlier. Val's behavior disrespected Club rules. Friars represented the elder statesmen of the acting profession. They normally practiced *impeccable* manners toward members and expected all guests to *adhere* to that standard. Sam now deeply regretted forging this rude man's name onto a guest list. In so doing, Sam had *compromised* his job and the club's reputation; but even more so, he had disappointed himself.

• • •

Ima felt uncomfortable when a man sprinted from the Friars' front door, stopped abruptly, and looked from side to side. She could not imagine any reason why a complete stranger might be after her or Riina for that matter. But, ever since the YWCA and Central Park encounters, she took no chances. If only for curiosity sake, she motioned for Riina to follow her toward the corner of 55th before looking back to see if he had followed them or had only come outside for some fresh air. She watched intently.

The stranger lit a cigarette, checked his pockets for something, and then began to pace back and forth. Soon afterwards, another man seemed to appear out of nowhere. Man Two approached Man One standing outside. They dressed similarly and talked using similar hand gestures. Then just as abruptly as he had arrived, Man Two took away Man One's cigarette, snuffed it with his foot on the Friars' steps, and entered the Club.

"My instincts tell me, those two men are the cause of Lionel's poker game not going so well," surmised Ima.

"And my gut agrees with your instincts," replied Riina.

How To Out-Weasel Weasels

Ima grew concerned when Wes never appeared in the office the entire next morning. She went about all the duties she had so far mastered. Mid-morning, the casting director from the advertising agency doing the soap commercials called to say that Riina's new demo would be recorded at studio late Wednesday afternoon. Ima relished the privilege of calling Riina to announce the good news.

"You have to be at studio by 4:00," Ima said matter-of-factly.

"Oh no, so sad! That means I'll miss our game," Riina said, *feigning* regret.

"Poor you! But we know you'll be with us in spirit, right?" inquired Ima teasing.

"Which position will my spirit play?" asked Riina stretching the idea.

"Probably in right field where the fewest balls go," replied Ima.

"I hate right field. I like the action around second base."

"Well then, *kill two birds with one stone*. You could be at the game in time if you're efficient at studio. Just knock 'em dead by doing the script in one-take," Ima advised

"One-take. Are you nuts?"

"Wes told me producers like actors who only need one-take. That's how the old-timers from radio do it and keep getting hired.

"My dear, I'm not from the radio days. I'm from the today's theatre-world," Riina drew out the word dramatically.

"Look, if you're smart and do it in one-take the producers will be impressed and want you back for a hundred more commercials," said Ima.

"But, I am artiste! You cannot rush a masterpiece," giggled Riina.

"Okay Miss Picasso. But I thought you were also a professional! Shall I call the agency back and say you've declined the job?"

"No, you've twisted my arm. The show must go on," admitted Riina.

"By the way the green dress you forgot on Sunday will now be lunching with Lionel and me at that cute little bistro close to the 46th Street Theatre."

"I'm *green with envy*. But don't worry about me. While you *hobnob with the hoity-toity*, I'll burp down a Nedick's dog with the *hoi polloi*," Riina proclaimed.

• • •

Having arrived to the bistro first, Ima selected a back table for privacy. When Lionel walked in, he looked gray and tired.

"You look like *death warmed over*," she declared.

"I feel the age to match it," he said.

"What's the matter?"

"I never went home last night, and Wes is probably still at the game."

"I wondered why he hadn't left me a note at the office. So, that also means poor Boofy had no food?" she asked in a mock-scolding tone.

He sighed. "Oh, I'm sorry, Eema. The game went on and on... just like in the movies when the saloon never closed."

"But the Friars does!"

"Yes, but the staff ignored us because...because...oh, never mind. Then when morning finally came, I *begged off* to go...to uh-uh...my rehearsal," stammered Lionel.

"Oh, PapaLi. Your health is more important than some silly game."

"My health is the least of my problems. You have no idea how behind I am on my bills...and now... this," he said, yawning widely and letting his voice trailed off.

"Didn't the tour pay you well?" she inquired.

"Oh, I always make big bucks when I work," he said.

"More than *union scale?*" she asked naively, trying to use the showbiz lingo.

"Oh, darling Eema, I always make much more than that. The problem is I also spend it. You see, MaMadge used to bank most of my money to build us a *nest egg*. Knowing how all that finance jazz confused me, she kept me *on a tight leash*."

"MaMadge spoiled us both royally," Ima said patting her father's hand.

"She was your mother; but darling, she was my lover, my whole life. I miss her more than I would my eyesight...except for today, when I look at you."

"But you have Teresa now," Ima coaxed him into unfamiliar territory.

"Oh yes, and she's wonderful. You'll love her once you know her well."

"So, what are you saying...Teresa is not yet your *chief cook and bottle washer* like MaMadge?" asked Ima, trying to understand.

"In fact that's the main problem! Madge and I rarely went out except on special occasions. She complained about the noisy crowds. Don't get me wrong. I loved her cooking; but she herself took the prize for making noise whenever she did fix a meal."

"I remember," Ima said, giggling. "She'd bang around in the kitchen like a one-woman street band."

He smiled and blinked away a tear. "Anyway, once she died, I started dining out mostly. You can imagine the charges I have made all over town. You know how pricey New York restaurants are."

"I'm surprised they don't *comp your dinner.* Doesn't the mere *prestige* of your coming to their restaurants attract other customers?" Ima inquired.

"That would be great. But, they figure the opposite way. I'm famous, so I must be *rolling in dough like Rockefeller,*" Lionel replied.

"I still don't know what you're trying to say," Ima reiterated.

"I'm saying I'm deep in debt...drowning in fact...way over my head. So last night, thinking I could catch up, I *got suckered in* by a gangster, an *intruder* who hustled us all into a *high stakes* game."

"A gangster?" Ima remembered the discussion at Sardi's when Wes told Shelton not to invite a certain man. "Does his name sound like Pucinni...you know the composer? Or maybe something like Pulucci?"

"It's Pollibo, and he's one of Shelton's *cronies!*" remarked Lionel.

"Yes, Val Pollibo, Shelton's bookie who hangs out at P.J.'s," Ima recalled.

"You know about him?" asked Lionel looking stunned and rubbing his tired eyes.

"Only what Wes has told me. I guess weasels run in packs like wolves."

"Our regulars have known each other for years, and all play a good hand of poker. So when this goon dropped in but played a very average game, my antennae went up."

"Oh that happens to me all the time," she said.

"Well to me it signaled that something was wrong. After a few hands, the guy hiked up the *winning pot* which made no sense based on how he played. The first time he did that, I suspected he had a super hand."

"Or was bluffing," added Ima.

"Of course, bluffing goes with poker territory; but this bluff had a twist. Val started acting antsy...as if he needed to empty his bladder or get some air. He got nervous and began to sweat. Then without apology, he stopped the game and left. Ten minutes later, he returned...all refreshed, as if he had just taken a shower."

"Do you think he's on drugs and went out to *get a quick fix* or something?"

"No, but he did have a lot to drink...more than two of us guys," Lionel remarked.

"Well, did he win?" asked Ima.

"No, that's the strange part. Shelton won almost every hand. Somehow this Pollibo guy swayed each game over to Shel," Lionel said, *quizzically.*

"Hmmm. So, Shelton did most of the winning. To me that sounds like a clue in a mystery," remarked Ima.

"No, there's no mystery. Those guys play *cutthroat poker.* I've heard of it but never seen it done, much less been in a game of it. Anyway, now I'm in a tough spot. I have to go tonight to win back my losses. At least I've figured out their system."

"Please don't, PapaLi. Let's figure another way to pay bills besides gambling," *implored* Ima. "I've got my first paycheck coming soon, and we can save money by eating at home. I'll cook supper every night if you'll stay home. Teresa won't mind not going out on the town. She'll see what you're really like if you just relax and watch TV. Besides, that's free."

"You're sweet, Eema; but I have to do this my way," said Lionel, looking at his watch and then wiping his mouth with a napkin. "Sorry darling. I have to get back to the rehearsal. At least I have a job."

"How can you work all day and play cards two nights straight? Do you want to drop in your tracks?" asked Ima.

"Don't worry. I'm strong as a horse!" he said and dashed away.

When Ima returned to the office, she called Riina to ask for some detective help. She related Lionel's suspicions about the not-so-friendly card game. "I need help to set traps for two weasels: one named Shelton Grape; the other, Val Pollibo."

"Good. Let's dress up as gun molls in *low class outfits* and go back to the Club again tonight to see what we can learn."

· · ·

Wearing fishnet hose, spike heels, side-split skirts, tight blouses, and berets, Ima and Riina *traipsed* the ten blocks from the Feingold's apartment to the Friars Club. Of course, looking rather *risqué*, they attracted lots of whistles and catcalls on the way.

As soon as they hit the Friars lobby, Sam stopped them. "You two back again?"

"We're on a mission," said Ima.

"We don't need any missionaries here. Like I told you last night, this is not Central Casting. Besides, the Club doesn't allow in bawdy girls who look like rejects from auditions of *Guys and Dolls*. For your information, the tour just ended so you're out of luck all way round."

"Sam, don't you think I know the tour ended? After all, Lionel played Nathan Detroit. But just because he played the role of a fictional gangster, why is he now playing cards with a real gangster here at the Friars."

"Never. Ours is an *exclusive* membership. No gangsters get past me."

"Please, Sam, let us *kibitz* the game for a moment," Riina begged.

"No. Double no! Leave them alone. They're having a poker *marathon*."

"A poker marathon? Why...to see who could *lose his shirt* the fastest?" Ima asked.

"No, it's a first time event for the Club. I hope we continue each year," Sam replied.

"Until the whole Friars'roster is so broke it can't pay dues?" inquired Riina.

"No...because half the winnings will go to the actors' pension fund, which your father and I may need for our old age."

"Now, Sam does that marathon cover actresses when they grow old as well as actors?' asked Riina. "I could support such an annual event if it helped me in the long run,"

"No, you'll have to fend for yourselves...get your own act together for when you grow old instead of *horning in* on our plan," Sam declared rather rudely.

"Sam, somehow you've grown meaner and older and less fun just while we've stood here tonight," said Ima.

"Right. You've lost your charm and sense of humor! But I'll help you find them in the Lost and Found if you'll let us watch the game for a few minutes." Riina circled to his side, looked in his ear, and pinched his nose.

He waved her away like a fly. "No. You cannot go into the game. That's final."

"Well, can we at least use your ladies room," asked Riina.

"No. Gun molls are not ladies," answered Sam.

"Well, can we at least have a drink of water?" asked Ima.

"No, we're not an oasis for camels. There's water in the gutter for the likes of you. Now scoot," he said, motioning them outdoors.

Outside, Ima and Riina *loitered* a moment at the Friars entrance. Unfortunately, dressed in such flashy clothes, they again attracted the wrong type of attention. Several passersby whistled at them, so they ducked around the corner onto Madison to revamp their plan of attack.

"I'm wondering how we could get inside the Club and into that game," asked Riina.

"I think Sam is onto us, but I still feel that those guys on the porch last night hold a clue to what's happening inside tonight?

"Me too. That scene has intrigued me all day," Riina admitted

Just then Ima noticed a manhole nearby. "Hey, there's a manhole just before the corner. Think about our underground tour:

"Manhole...gutter...sewer...tunnel...water!" Riina's face lit up.

"Didn't we come at least this far underground on Sunday?" asked Ima

"I'm way ahead of you. I saw a manhole close to the Friars Club entry," replied Riina

Looking both ways to assure no car would hit them, the two gun molls stepped onto the street. With no traffic in view, Ima tried to pry open the manhole by herself. Then Riina joined her. They could not make it budge.

"It's too heavy. We'll never lift it alone. Hmmm! Maybe we could pretend to drop something valuable down the gutter grate," proposed Ima.

"Pretend, nothing," Riina removed her gaudy bracelet and dropped it so it would roll into the gutter. She yelled, "Oh woe is me. Dear grandmama's bracelet."

Both young women got on their knees and started reaching through the grate with no real intention of grasping the bracelet-in-despair. Then they boldly went back to the manhole and *ostensibly* tried to raise the cover. Two pedestrians going by ignored them.

"Oh, I broke a nail," Riina wailed and waved down a man. "Hey there, Big Boy. I bet you're as strong and helpful as you are handsome."

Taken aback by her compliment, the man said, "Well, I do *calisthenics.*"

"I knew it. Then you must be very strong," said Riina feeding his ego by feeling his biceps.

"Do you ladies need help?" he asked.

"Yes, my grandmamma rolled into the gutter...I mean her antique bracelet...rolled down there," Riina stammered. "We must get into the sewer to *retrieve* it; but alas, we can't lift this manhole cover."

"And we're absolutely frantic," added Ima, joining in the ruse.

In seconds the man had the manhole cover off. While Riina fluttered her eyelashes and thanked him *profusely,* Ima started climbing down the hole to the sewer tunnel. "I feel like Alice in Wonderland going down the rabbit hole. But I bet she wore sensible shoes, not spikes," said Ima.

"Alice wore Mary Janes like all little girls in the Northern Hemisphere," said Riina.

Except for Ima getting her heel stuck in one rung and Riina snagging her fishnet hose, they handled the steep ladder like champs. Once underground, they heard the man replace the lit. That sound committed them to a new folly. Light came only from weak ceiling bulbs spaced periodically. They got a bit turned around trying to figure which way led to the correct corner above, on the surface. Finally agreeing, they went to a connecting bend and curved a hundred feet or so back to the Friars Club.

Once there, they chose to shinny up the ladder one at a time. Riina took the *first watch*. Ima feared for Riina who teetered near the top of the ladder. Then she watched Riina use all her might from her hands and head to raise the heavy cover.

"Ima, I don't have enough strength to prop open the lid to get a clear view of the Club's front door."

Just then a car whizzed by in the next lane over. That *close shave* obviously scared Riina because she skidded down the ladder, missing half the rungs. "Good grief. I think my skull just got shoved onto my neck. I'm done. It's your turn."

They exchanged places. Ima crept up the narrow ladder and used her upper back instead of her head to lift the lid slightly. Although that part of her body proved stronger, she had to crook her neck sideways to see over the lip of the manhole. For just a second, she glimpsed a man standing out in front of the Club and smoking a cigarette. The scene resembled the same as last night. She wondered if this could be the infamous Val Pollibo stepping away from the card game for a smoke as PapaLi had described at lunch?

Her whole upper body soon throbbed. When she wanted to quit, something told her to hang on a little longer. Just then she saw another man walk up. He had on a *fedora*, which shadowed his face. However, when he took it off, she realized that the two men resembled each other. No...they were actually identical! What a nasty looking pair they made with greasy hair and pock marks on their faces. So excited by this insight, she forgot her pain and quickly descended the ladder to report to Riina.

"Reenie, remember last night?" Ima's voice echoed against the walls.

"What? I can't understand you with the echo. Talk more softly," Riina replied.

"Remember a second man suddenly appeared, put out the first man's cigarette, and then went into the Friars?" asked Ima.

"Nasty looking fellows and dressed almost alike," Riina said, nodding.

"Yes. Dressed alike because...they're identical twins!" declared Ima.

"How cute! Mommy still chooses outfits for her middle-aged darlings?"

"Probably," Ima laughed briefly. "See, I knew something was going on here. At lunch PapaLi said the Friars had let in a goon named Val Pollibo who—"

"The guy Wes and Shelton talked about at Sardi's?" asked Riina.

"The very same, and Lionel said Val Pollibo continued to *up the stakes* until the pot got large. Then Val began acting strange and suddenly left the game. Lionel figured the man had an urgent bladder, but now we know the truth. He came outside to smoke, and to meet with his twin brother who—"

"Who exchanged cards or brought a fixed deck," Riina surmised.

"Or loaded his sleeves with aces and kings." asked Ima.

"Or somehow else...they cheated the other players" declared Riina.

"So let's get logical about the 'somehow else.' Exchanging cards seems too *obvious* to me," remarked Ima.

"How about exchanging information?" asked Riina.

"That's good, Reenie. Man One tells Man Two how the game is going and what he thinks is in each player's hand. They *strategize*, and then the better player goes back in the game...for the kill?" surmised Ima and proposing a few options.

"They're *card sharks*. They don't want to kill. They want to win?"

"No, somehow these guys fix it so Shelton wins most of the hands. Lionel called it *cutthroat poker*," Ima explained.

"You're good at this clue-stuff, Ima. Really good," admitted Riina. "Well, what about this *scenario*. Since the game has high stakes, maybe Man Two brings Man One more money to bust the game...or to gang up on a weaker player who then must withdraw because the game has gotten too rich for his pocketbook."

"If so, Man Two would have only dropped off cash and left," Ima said.

"It must take a bundle to stay in such a high-stakes game. I know Lionel is well-off, but gambling can use up cash pretty fast," declared Riina.

"To tell you the truth, Riina, PapaLi is broke. He only has his fame to use for credit," Ima revealed.

"Personally, I'm surprised the Friars allowed such a game to occur," Riina said.

"You heard what Sam said. Half the winnings will go to pensioners."

"Ima, that sounds fishy! Do those guys look like *philanthropists*?"

Ima ascended the ladder and raised the manhole lid enough to poke out her nose once again. She called down to Riina, "Nope, to me they still look like *run-of-the-mill* thugs." Though her back ached, she *persevered* to watch a bit longer. The men stopped talking. Man One left. Man Two went inside. Or was it *vice-versa*. Having missed half the scene, she could not tell for sure, which was which.

Having witnessed enough to form a theory of the crime, Ima and Riina decided to leave. They did not want to embarrass themselves by surfacing in front of the Friars Club, so they scooted through the sewer and around the corner to the original manhole. Then crammed together on the ladder, they used all their strength to shove the manhole completely open. As they did, a policeman's feet greeted them.

"Good grief, I've heard of girls lowering their morals...but sinking down into the sewers? How low can you go? Is this a *limbo contest?*" said Officer Max Onfoot. As soon as he assisted them from the manhole, he handcuffed them both.

. . .

At the police precinct, Officer Onfoot and his two *apprehended* gun molls stood at the intake counter and called out to the man on-duty. However, the officer with his feet atop his desk seemed keener on resting...than arresting. To the young women's surprise, the snoozing man was none other than Officer Allrest.

"Oh no, look who it is. We'll never hear the end of this," said Ima.

"Never fear. Riina's here. I'll *cajole* him into releasing us," Riina replied. "Remember he was *putty in my hands* on our last visit."

"What-what-what's going on?" said Officer Allrest coming out of a deep sleep.

"Just need you to do some paperwork," said Officer Onfoot.

"Sorry folks. My body's still on day shift, but I just got put on night duty and can't stay awake," said Allrest scrambling to the counter and pulling out arrest forms. "Now, who are these lovely...lovelies!" he said sarcastically after looking the two young women up and down.

"Two *degenerates* I found crawling from a manhole," said Officer Onfoot.

Allrest put on his glasses for a closer look at the two ladies and recognized them immediately.

"So, what's this disguise supposed to be?" asked Officer Allrest.

"Gun molls! Fooled you, didn't we?" declared Riina proudly. She shinnied up on the counter to twirl a loose curl on Allrest's forehead.

"Going undercover with the mob, are you?" the officer asked, smoothing back his hair that Riina had mussed.

"Yes, and we're close to breaking up a gambling ring," declared Ima.

"And so what's the police supposed to do this time...twiddle its thumbs and let you take all the credit for single-handedly shutting down organized crime in the City of New York?" he said, weakening from all of Riina's attention.

"No, but didn't we bring you good evidence that led to the arrest of that dreadful female *predator*?" asked Ima.

"How could I ever forget," Allrest said throwing up his hands. "Officer Onfoot, there's no use arguing with or arresting these two. What would we charge them with... good citizenship for reporting crimes?"

"But they were in the sewers without authorization. They trespassed on city property. At least we could book them as public nuisances," declared Onfoot, wanting to make his monthly *quota* of writing tickets.

"I agree they are nuisances," admitted Allrest. "But nuisances also have the exact type personality to find clues on our nuisance cases. As much as they irritate us, they also help. So, it's useless to arrest them."

With mercy much too lenient for Officer Onfoot's taste, Officer Allrest released Ima and Riina, warning them, "May we never meet again under any circumstances!"

"But Officer Allrest. You're our only police connection," said Ima.

• • •

When Ima got home, she quickly peeled off the gun moll outfit, put on her PJs, and flopped on the couch. Exhausted yet *pensive*, she reviewed the day's trials and successes.

Boofy, looking rather forlorn, hopped onto her lap but got no response. Soon, the kitty jumped down and nipped Ima's instep. Still no response. Then the kitty started a loud, *incessant* meowing until Ima got the message.

"Oh, poor Boofy-Boofy. I forgot you. Lionel forgot you. No food and no company for two whole days! You must be starving," Ima picked up the kitty and cooed to it sweetly. "Let's find your favorite," Ima said, opening a can of tuna and spooning out half of it.

As she watched the cat eat, Ima remembered she too had not eaten since lunch. Looking in the kitchen, she found the *cupboard was bare*. She boiled some eggs and chopped up veggies to make a quick salad.

While eating her supper, Ima pondered how her visit to Manhattan had brought nothing but *mayhem*. In Boston, she had hoped to get her life on an even keel. So far, everything grew more and more *out of kilter*.

Starting tomorrow she would reorganize. For one thing, if she started cooking regular meals to help Lionel economize, she would need to shop for groceries more often. Resolved, she flipped on the TV but fell asleep almost instantly.

Upon rising the next morning, she could tell PapaLi had not come home to sleep. She hurried off to work and found Wes had not slept in his bed either. How had these two men, so important to her, been hypnotized by such a foolish timewaster and money waster as a card game? She could not imagine any real reasons to excuse their behavior. They had good lives and weren't known to be foolish or greedy. So, why had card playing become an overnight vice? What lay behind this choice that could eat up all their money so quickly?

Before beginning her regular duties at work the next day, Ima called the 46th Street Theatre, only to hear that Lionel had not shown up yet. She left a message and then called the Friars. She asked for Sam but learned that he did not come in until three.

"By chance is Mr. Longwind there playing cards?" inquired Ima, hoping.

"The cardroom is empty right now, Miss," said the on-duty man.

"Well, do you know what time last night's game broke up?" Ima asked.

"Not really. The night man could tell you, but he's gone home."

"Well, let me ask this. Would you mind calling the Westerly Agency if Lionel or Mr. Westerly come into the Club later today?"

"I guess I could," said the on-duty man.

"Please do. I would appreciate it so much," said Ima leaving the agency number. Still at *square one*, she decided to call Teresa about coming for dinner.

"Hi, Ms. Latimer, it's Ima, Lionel's daughter. We met Saturday night?"

"Of course, Ima. Please call me Teresa. What do you need?"

"To save some money," Ima stated plainly.

"That's always a good idea," Teresa agreed.

"Well, I have a new plan to economize. I'm going to fix more home-cooked meals for PapaLi. So, would you like to come to dinner tonight?"

"I'd love to, but I'm afraid that *infernal* poker game is on again tonight."

"I don't get it. Lionel has so many new and good things in his life like his job at *1776* and my visit. Can you tell me why he hasn't come home yet?"

"If you're hinting that he spent the night over here, I assure you we plan to be married before moving in with each other."

"Oh, I'm sorry. I didn't mean it that way. You're one of the new good things too. What I meant was, PapaLi has been alone for a while and not used to checking in with anyone. Still, I'm concerned. He's been gone for two days, and Wes has left me alone in the office for two days. I don't know enough about his business to actually run it. I'm so *buffaloed* by all this. Have you seen either of them?"

"Not since yesterday. We all had a quick bite after Lionel's rehearsal, but then they went back to the Friars. I think Shelton and Lionel are in a feud or some sort of contest, and I'm afraid it's over me," Teresa said sadly.

"Shelton puzzles me," admitted Ima.

"Me too. This morning he phoned to ask if I would go out of town this weekend. I had to say no and to *add fuel to the fire*, I had to tell him I was now engaged and no longer free to date him. His voice turned icy cold, and he started saying strange things. He said although he had lost me and lost the *1776* audition, he would not lose the poker game."

"They seem to hate each other. What do we do? We can't very well send them to the principal's office like bad little boys," said Ima.

"Stay busy and calm. Things like this usually work themselves out."

Disturbed by Teresa's word "usually," Ima declared, "Yes, if such things have a divine purpose. But this situation has no such appearance."

"In any event, I congratulate you on your economy campaign. I know all about Lionel's finances because I am his *stockbroker* at E.F. Hutton. That's actually how we met. He needed my help to manage his money."

"Oh, does he ever! Thanks for helping him."

"No thanks needed. It's my business. He's a client but also the love of my life."

"Then, I guess it's okay to share some family history. You see, MaMadge came from thrifty roots and watched over PapaLi's *expenditures* like a hawk. If she hadn't, by now he'd be a charity case, considering the way he spends money."

"Or the way he's lost money at poker this week," Teresa added.

"If he doesn't stop, he'll be joining the bums over at Central Park. Then the closest he'll get to any actors will be to watch the showgirls play softball," Ima said, half-laughing. "That reminds me. We have another game tonight."

"Well, Ima, I will share something with you that Lionel might not. Right now, the *stock* market is shaky. His investments have lost value, and he's worried. Men his age have heart attacks when they worry too much."

"Poor PapaLi. He's getting it from all sides."

"He'll be okay. The other night I advised him to ride out this setback, to curb his expenses, and not to sell any *stock*. So, you see we are thinking alike. Your new economy plan will also help him a lot," said Teresa.

After the conversation with her future stepmother, Ima admired the great concern she had heard in Teresa's voice. That settled Ima's mind. Although she would always miss MaMadge, she approved of Teresa. Lionel had again chosen someone who loved him in spite of his flaws.

Halfheartedly, Ima busied herself around the Westerly office. She surprised herself how much more quickly and confidently she handled the clients' money this week. After matching the agency checks to the actor's pay rates in the big *union book*, she made out deposit slips and ran a few blocks to the bank. Getting air into her lungs invigorated her. She realized it was lunchtime and even disgusted herself by grabbing a Nedick's *on the fly*. It actually tasted good.

• • •

The stage manager picked up the phone and answered gruffly, "Yeah, 46th Street Theatre, backstage."

"I've a message for the producer," said Sal Pollibo. The line went on hold.

"Hello. Primo, here. The producer's out to lunch. Who's this?"

"It doesn't matter. Just listen. Tell the producer over there that I have under my thumb, the most recent addition to your *1776* cast," said Sal.

"Which means?" inquired Primo.

"Which means...my thumb just cocked the gun that my hand holds against Lionel Longwind's head. My trigger finger may get itchy and lose its grip if my ears don't hear exactly what they want to," said Sal ending his long list of *body metaphors*.

"Which is what?" Primo asked.

"You have two choices," Sal said.

"Which are what?" Primo asked.

"Either you send me by messenger, $30,000 in cash to cover a few of his business related expenses, or—"

"Or what?"

"Or you can send me a blank *full-run contract* offer for Shelton Grape to replace Lionel Longwind in your little patriotic play," said Sal. "You can get Shelton for a little less, which should appeal to your pocketbook."

"We don't pay ransoms, and we don't hire untested actors," said Primo.

"Well, let me *up the ante*. Perhaps my idea for you to hire Mr. Grape might appeal more to your sense of personal safety," Sal advised.

"Look, thug, we don't respond to threats, and we don't *negotiate* with mobsters. Besides, actors like Shelton Grape are a *dime a dozen*. He's certainly not in the same league as a star like Lionel Longwind. However, whether Lionel stays or goes is our decision and on our terms not yours."

"Perhaps you need time to consider your options. How about we meet after tonight's play. Does that suit your busy schedule?"

"Or what?"

"Or you'll find blood is harder to wash off dirty hands than to remove it from white sheets," Sal threatened coolly, without losing his *temper*.

• • •

After returning from lunch, Ima decided to call the 46th Street Theatre again to see if Lionel had shown up yet. She learned he had not, a fact that made Primo sound *miffed*. Ima thought maybe the man had had a bad day.

"Well, Mr. Primo, would you mind asking Lionel to call his agent's office whenever he does arrive?" she said and quickly hung up to answer the second line that now jangled.

"Westerly Agency," she said.

"Ima, I've got—"

"Uncle Wes? I'm so relieved to hear your voice. I've been worried about you and PapaLi. Where are you?"

"Sweetheart," said Wes sounding *stilted* as if he were reading from a script. "I don't know what to say except that Lionel had a heart attack last night and they rushed him off. I'm with him now, so will you take care of business? I'll get back to you as soon as they let me...I mean...as soon as I know something."

"But Uncle Wes, where is my father? I should be with him if—"

The phone went dead. Her head went dead. She sat in complete shock, unable to think straight. Her heart clogged her throat. She could barely breathe.

After several minutes, she pulled out the yellow pages and found a long list of hospitals. Except for the one from where the monkey escaped, she couldn't recall the location of any others. Then she began to remember the famous ones like Mount Sinai and Columbia Presbyterian but did not know which had a reputation for handling heart patients. She vowed to herself that Lionel would have the best specialists in town, no matter what it would cost. She could use her adventure money if necessary.

Exasperated at how much had suddenly landed on her shoulders, she had no attention left to give to the business. She called Actors At Home, the agency's answering service and asked the operator to monitor her office calls while she tried to find Lionel.

Marsha Mushmouth, the name Wes gave the owner of AAH, took the phone from her assistant, "Let Marsha handle it. Now Ima, what's the problem?"

"I need the answering service to watch the other phone while I call all the hospitals to find where my father is. Wes said Lionel had a heart attack and was rushed off during the night. Marsha, where would that be to? Where would an ambulance take someone in the middle of the night?"

"Well, if Lionel were a pauper or a crazy loon, it'd be to Bellevue. But he's saner than I am. Now sweetie, listen to me. You've got things upside down. The best way to organize this is to depend on us to find Lionel. It's what Wes pays us for anyway. Let me call all the hospitals. I know this town better than the mayor. I'll get back to you shortly."

"Oh, thank you Marsha. I was—"

"You were hoping for a little motherly advice, yes? So, boil some water, fix a cup of tea, and take 10 deep breaths between each sip. I know actors. They like to hide, but I'm used to finding them. So, leave it to Marsha to dig up the facts!"

Ima fixed the tea and, as best as she could, did a bit of work. She called several casting directors to inquire about upcoming auditions. As hard as it was to be fair-minded, Ima even *pitched* Shelton for an airline advertising campaign. She silently wished he'd be asked to audition, win it, and fly off into the wild blue yonder, never to interfere with her family again.

Then Ima thought Riina might know to which hospital an ambulance would take Lionel. She called the Feingold home and told Riina the story.

"Definitely not to that monkey hospital!' she said. "Say, my folks' friends have heart attacks weekly. It's the new status symbol, sort of an excuse for time off. Mom will know their friends' favorite home away from home. I'll call you back."

Ima wanted to call Teresa but almost felt relief when the secretary answered. Ima thought it unwise to relay such bad news through a third party, so she left a message for Teresa to call back.

Suddenly, Ima stopped in her tracks. Two mysteries had just dropped into her hands, uninvited and unrecognized until full blown. She had no problem finding and arranging clues but held a pitiful record at applying them. She repeated her basic mistake of not seeking advice about what the clues could mean. Once again, thinking she could handle matters herself, she had ignored her greatest secret weapon: How many times would she follow this pattern until it became automatic for her to stop to *ponder and pray* first and then to organize all the details?

She felt right down stupid. After quickly *repenting* of her pigheadedness, Ima had a breakthrough. Something echoed in her ears. "Rushed off. Rushed off," she thought aloud. "What does that mean? I had assumed Wes meant to a hospital, but could it be somewhere else? Maybe he meant somewhere close-by? Hmmm."

Within an hour, Marsha called back to say her operators had called the entire list of hospitals. "We've checked Manhattan, Bronx, Queens, Brooklyn, and Staten Island and the shores of Long Island. So far, your father is not registered anywhere," the efficient Marsha reported.

"Oh I had hoped—"

"Now don't you worry, Honey. That'll give you a heart attack too. Marsha will keep checking. Some emergency rooms are slow to record admissions. After all, their business is saving lives, not recording life histories. Also since Lionel is famous, he may be listed under an assumed name. I'll check every angle."

"Thank you, Marsha. And I'll let you know if I learn anything too," replied Ima.

Just as she hung up, the other line rang again. This time it was Riina.

"For heart attacks, go straight to Columbia Presbyterian, pass 'Go' but do not collect $200," Riina recited the familiar Monopoly phrase.

"Thanks Reenie, but the answering service has already called all of the hospitals in all *five boroughs*. Marsha did not find Lionel at any of them."

"Oh, Ima, what's happening?" Riina said without her usual quip.

"I'm not sure. Wes said Lionel had been rushed off. What else could he mean?"

"I don't know…off to a hospital seems logical? I can't think of anything else," Riina said quietly.

"At the end of the call, Wes said he'd 'get back to me when they let him,' but he stopped in the middle of the sentence," Ima recalled.

"Good ole Wes always calls back. So who is the 'they' in that sentence?"

"Good clue, Riina. My sleuth's instincts wonder if the 'they' means those *sterling characters* we saw from the manhole last night," answered Ima.

"If so, maybe rushed off means off the island of Manhattan," said Riina.

"But why take Lionel to another borough?" asked Ima.

"Look, big crime bosses have big estates on Long Island and in New Jersey where they're out from *under scrutiny* and can cover-up a deal that's gone bad or hide—"

"Yes. Or hide hostages where no one would ever think to look?" said Ima, as if assembling puzzle parts. "Riina, I think if those guys would go to so much trouble, PapaLi has something they want more than money."

"Even so, once they get whatever it is, they might still *dispose* of him like in the gangster films. You know, bury him in a Jersey junkyard or put his feet in cement and dump him the East River?" Riina iterated the possibilities.

"Reenie, that's too horrible to *contemplate*," said Ima, getting quiet and letting wheels turn in her head. "But you've given me another gangster idea. When we lived in Michigan, folks told us about *bootleggers* who got so rich that during Prohibition they bought giant mansions in the fashionable district of Grosse Point east of Detroit."

"So, we're back to concrete feet! That's always the favorite way thugs get rid of people," stated Riina.

"I guess you have more close mafia friends than I do," said Ima, needing to clear her mind with a bit of humor.

"You bet. My life's one big crime scene," Riina announced officially. "So what about Detroit?"

"Right, we *essayed* way off topic. Let's get back to Detroit and stick to my point. Well, it seems that tunnels ran between these mansions. Mobsters brought whiskey over from Canada and stored it in cellars. Others brewed bathtub gin in their houses and trucked it out from another.

"Tunnels...smunnels. What's that to do with finding Lionel?" asked Riina.

"Stay with me a moment. The midtown Manhattan mansions around 55th Street were built about that same time just before the Depression. What we need to know is, who owns the houses in the Friars Club block and if any tunnels run between them."

"How do you propose we find that out...break into City Hall?" asked Riina.

"We don't have time to go to jail. Even so, I think the New York Library has that kind of information," said Ima, planning her strategy as she talked.

"This is getting complicated," Riina declared. "Indeed, a true *imbroglio*."

"Exactly! But wait. We need to split up tasks. Look, I know you've got a session at studio this afternoon, but first would you do me a favor?"

"It depends, Ima. I love Lionel, but this demo is very important to me."

"I know, Reenie. But think about it. Right now, I'm closer to the Library and your apartment is closer to Central Park. We need re-enforcements. If you'll find Old Cash and ask him to bring some buddies here by 4:00, I'll run over to the Library and read up on those homes."

"Aw, Ima, I don't wanna run around the Park looking for Cash. I'll get all sweaty for my big performance."

"It's your liquid voice they want, not your gorgeous face," Ima coaxed.

"But I only have an hour to spare before I must start my vocal exercises and primping routine," Riina iterated.

Without even seeing Riina, Ima could hear her friend's resistance and imagined her standing in a dramatic pose.

"Then let's reverse roles. While I find Cash, you get all ready and go do the research. That won't require sweat. The Library is air-conditioned and only blocks from Soundman Studio. After the session, you could meet us here."

"Deal! If time allows, I'll even drop the information by beforehand."

"And I'll call Jan Hus to see if Cash is helping with lunch today. If not, maybe someone there will help me find him. You know, Reenie, I'm catching on to what Wes said. If the director casts the best actor for each scene, he'll have a hit. Now, I think we're in the correct roles. Anyway, pray we all connect," Ima hung up and quickly called the soup kitchen.

Fortunately, Old Cash had stayed to help wash dishes again. Ima's voice sounded raspy and breathy from talking so much.

"Ima, calm down. What do you need?" Cash asked.

"I'm having to ask people for favors today, and I need your help too."

"Do you want me to fill in as shortstop at today's game?" he joked.

"Oops, I keep forgetting about the game. Life has become too *topsy-turvy*."

"If my favorite girl isn't playing, what may I do for her otherwise?"

Ima filled him in on the pertinent details of the card game, the suspicious twin brothers outside the Friars Club, Lionel's heart attack, and Wes's strange call.

"Can you collect some friends and meet me here at the office around 4:30? We need to plan an underground attack," iterated Ima.

"Leave it to me. Old Cash knows the underground better than the devil."

• • •

A little after three, Riina bounced in, waving her research notes. "I found the whole subsurface scheme for that area. I almost stole the architectural plans from the Library."

"Please Reenie, you have a demo; and I don't have time to *bail* you out of jail. We must dedicate every minute left to finding Lionel and Wes. I am beginning to believe we can solve this mystery before tragedy strikes them," Ima said anxiously.

"Okay, here goes. These old houses are masterpieces, built to last 300 years. They have solid foundations, copper pipes, and the best electric wiring available in the 1920s. These homes aren't flimsy like the stuff built now. You know: apartments today; *tenements tomorrow!*"

"Riina, can you spare me your historical home tour until next Sunday? Right now, I need to know one thing. Are there any tunnels?"

"Not exactly tunnels. Most houses on that block of 55th have cave-like compartments once used as coal bins. Now with today's furnaces, owners probably use the space for storage."

"Are any of these houses near the Friars?"

"On that side of the street, two houses have never used any coal but still had the deep open places built. The Martin Erdmann House, bought by the Friars in 1955, is one. The other is two doors east."

"Who owns that one?" asked Ima.

"I don't know. The deed information was missing."

"Hold on, let me call Marsha at Actors At Home. She's a genius with numbers and addresses," Ima said, quickly calling the answering service.

"Hi, it's Ima again from The Westerly Agency. May I speak to Marsha?"

"Hi Ima. It's Marsha, here," she said. "Have you found Lionel yet?"

"No, but I have another idea...another project. Can you help?"

"Shoot!" said the *seasoned* operator.

"Is there some way to cross reference addresses to people's names?"

"Sure, Honey. We do it in emergencies to help the police and firemen."

"Well, this is not exactly an official emergency like that; but it is urgent that we find Lionel," Ima said.

"Do you have a name, address or phone number?" Marsha asked.

"Nothing complete. I need an address on the odd number side of the street, two doors east of the Friars Club at 57 East 55th Street.

"Be back soon!" Marsha said. After a moment, she returned to the line. "The residence belongs to Maria P. Mobley; street address number is 65."

"Maria P. Mobley. Thank you again. You do save lives just like the emergency room." Ima hung up. She sat there with a serious look. "Who do we know that knows all the wealthy people in town?"

"My mother knows some, but the Times knows them all," said Riina.

Ima quickly dialed the New York Times and got the information desk, "May I speak to a society columnist, please?"

"One moment while I connect you," said the operator.

"Society Page, *debutante* in training," kidded a secretary who answered.

"Do you have a file on someone named Maria P. Mobley on East 55th?"

"Hold on while I check with the research department," she intoned snobbishly.

"Absolutely," Ima's eyes widened toward Riina. "She's calling the research desk."

The secretary came back on the line, "Are you referring to Maria Pollibo who married David Mobley in 1945?"

"Yes, I think that's the one," gulped Ima, barely able to contain her shock.

"Mrs. Mobley's name appears often in our paper. Was there a particular reference you needed?"

"Not at this time. What can you tell me about her generally?" asked Ima.

"Her bio says she is a great *patron* of the arts and heads up several charities. Would you like a list?" said the secretary, incredibly full of free information.

"Thank you, but our association mostly wants to know about her *ardent* passions and most noteworthy accomplishments?" replied Ima.

"Well, it says since her husband's untimely death, she devotes herself to the Historical Society preserving her own neighborhood and other landmarks."

"How admirable! How about her children?" Ima continued the *feint*.

"Children? Hmmm. Children? According to my notes, she has no children and never remarried. She does have close family ties in town. We have photos of her twin brothers escorting her to numerous gallery shows and play openings."

"Well, thank you for your generous help. I think Mrs. Mobley will be an excellent guest speaker for our group," Ima hung up, delighted with all the *gratuitous* information. "Hmmm," Ima said, turning to Riina. "Guess what? Maria P. Mobley is Maria Pollibo Mobley."

"Mother of the darling twins?" asked Riina resisting a giggle.

"No, their *doting* sister," replied Ima. "Hmmm. Somehow that clue seems too obvious."

"It did come rather easily," noted Riina

"Maybe so we'd jump to an obvious but wrong conclusion," said Ima.

"Well, that could be a big mistake," Riina surmised.

"In fact that's my typical mistake. Instead, I need a giant *ponder and pray* to get real insights and to *ascertain* how Maria fits into all this."

"Well, maybe easy isn't always wrong. Didn't you conclude quickly that those two men were twins once you saw them together the second night?" asked Riina.

"Yes, but Lionel had already told me that Val Pollibo got antsy and left the card game the night before. He had already planted that seed or weed in my mind," replied Ima.

"So, after we discussed the possibility of their being twins, wasn't it easy to *extrapolate* that the two had probably switched places?" inquired Riina.

"Yes, but we still don't know that for sure. All we do know is Val Pollibo has played poker with Lionel two nights in a row and that Maria Pollibo Mobley lives two doors down from the Friars and just happens to have twin brothers," replied Ima. "Hmmm. We are getting close."

"So, how easily did Man Two drop from the sky onto the Club's front steps the first night?" asked Riina, following Ima's logic.

"Very easily! He probably lurked in the shadows until we turned to head for the corner. And then suddenly he was there?" Ima recalled.

"So, the plan has worked so far!" Riina concluded.

"Right. It was easy for you to *get the scoop* on the house and for me to find Cash and to get the society report. So together we've pegged a connection between the Mobley House and the Friars Club. All in a day's work!"

"But mine's not over. Gotta scoot. I still have that demo…and the studio's down dare at Turdy-turd stweet."

"I hoyd ya. So, go already! Whatcha want, a parade marchin' ya down dare?" Ima said, playfully in her best New Yorkese.

Strategy for Conquering the Block

When Riina left, Ima scanned the library notes. She felt restless having stayed inside rather than going out to look for Lionel herself. But she *conceded* that only in the last few minutes had she gotten the foggiest notion where she might look. Besides, she had needed to stay put in case Wes called again.

Inside her mind, Ima let her instincts tackle the *classic crime formula* of weapon, opportunity, and motive. Raising money for charity by gambling seemed a matter of poor taste, but hardly a crime. If the marathon card game proved to be what it pretended, the weapon was surely a *stacked deck*. And if the Pollibos lived only two doors away from the Club, they certainly had opportunity and easy access to infiltrate and cause a *ruckus*. But naming a motive stumped her.

The only possible motive Ima could currently imagine was Maria's passion for restoring historical landmarks. Perhaps she resented the Friars for turning the Martin Erdmann mansion into a semi-commercial operation. Maybe Maria had urged her brothers to undermine the Club's reputation.

The phone interrupted Ima's crime analysis. She grabbed the receiver, hoping to hear news about Lionel and not Cash *reneging* on helping her. "Hello."

"Ima, this is W-W-Wes-s-s," he said, with a tired, hoarse voice. The phone line had static and a bothersome echo.

"Wes, where is PapaLi? Marsha called every hospital in town."

"He's not...in a hos-hospital. "He's-He-s-He's..." the echo resounded, compounding an already a bad connection.

"He's not dead, is he?" asked Ima, desperate to hear good news. "He's not dead...oh, please, God, no."

"No-no-no, d-d-darling, but he's in deep-eep-eep...in deep-eep-eep...trou-trou-ble."

"Then he needs a doctor and needs to be in a hospital," Ima insisted.

Wes whispered to reduce the echo. "It's not that kind of trouble. Now listen to me. How much money do we have in the bank?"

"What a thing to ask right now when my father is seriously ill."

Wes must have put his hand over the phone because some muffled talking filtered through from the background. She heard Wes say something like, "Give me some-m-m time-m-m-m. Give me m-m-more time-m-m-m. I can get it-get-get-get it."

"Wes, what's going on? I can't understand your words with that echo."

"We're in deep-eep-eep."

"Yes, I know. Deep trouble! So I must come to PapaLi. Where is he?"

"No, we're in deep-eep-eep," repeated Wes, sounding more strained with each word.

"Uncle Wes, please tell me where Lionel is!"

"If you want-t-t-t-to know, don't talk, Ima. Just listen," Wes dropped his voice to a barely *audible* volume. "Just tell me the b-b-bank b-b-balances."

She fumbled through the file and pulled both ledgers. "With today's deposits minus checks made to the clients, the business account has $3,062.

"You're j-j-joking," he whispered, and then his voice rose. "There was over $12-12-12,000 on F-f-friday. I-I-I withdrew o-o-only…" Then again his voice dropped to a whisper, "F-f-forget it! How m-m-much is in the other?"

"Let's see, with all your bills paid, the personal account shows $1,700."

"Forget that. I need real money. Where can I get that? They want big money."

"They…meaning the Pollibo twins?" Ima dared to ask.

Wes said nothing for a moment. "Yes…I'm in that deep… deep…and need $10,000. Lionel is in deep-deep. B-b-but he's their *cash cow*…no…their *golden calf*."

"Cash cow? What?" asked Ima, not comprehending what Wes meant.

"F-f-forget it, Ima. Tell me, d-d-did you m-m-mail client checks yet?" he whispered.

"No, but I promise to drop them in the mailbox after work. Don't worry, Uncle Wes. I'm taking as good care of your business as I can."

"No, please don't!"

"No, don't take care of your business. I don't understand," said Ima puzzled.

Wes choked out his words in a bare whisper. "No…t-t-t-transfer to my p-p-personal ac-c-c-count what you h-h-had on the books before writing ch-ch-checks to the cl-cl-clients. Then, h-h-hold their envelopes until new money comes in. I'll c-c-cover them later this week."

"But Uncle Wes, that's the clients' money. We can't write checks on that!"

"You don't know the h-h-half of it. Just d-d-do what I said, or you may n-n-never see Lionel again. Now g-g-go to the bank and g-g-get me all the c-c-cash you c-c-can."

"But the banks are already closed for the day."

Now completely desperate sounding, Wes whispered, "Ima, l-l-listen to me. Pollibo has called in his *markers*. You've g-g-got to get me c-c-cash. We're deep-deep-deep in."

"Uncle Wes, I've got $8,000 in travelers checks back at the apartment, but I don't know where I can get anymore."

"No. L-l-lionel will need all that. He owes even m-m-more to these g-g-goons."

Unwilling to betray Lionel's confidence about his own unpaid bills, Ima now understood how much stress had mounted on top of her father. "No wonder he had a heart attack. No sleep, *cutthroat poker*, and now losing gobs of money," Ima iterated.

"Ima, the heart attack was a lie. They m-m-made me say that. I'm sorry if—"

Suddenly, a loud whap came through the phone as if someone were using the receiver to hit Wes in the face. He groaned lowly, "Ima, just d-d-do it …tr-tr-transfer all the m-m-money." The phone went dead.

Sitting at her desk, completely stunned, Ima did not hear the doorbell ringing at first. When the sound finally registered, she looked at the clock. It read almost 5:00 o'clock. She opened the door to four scruffy men and Cash.

"Ima, we got here as soon as we could. Tramps don't normally travel during traffic times," he said, making a bit of a joke. "Let me introduce you to my friends. This is Dollar, my right hand man and these are Quarter, Nickel, and Pennypinch."

"Welcome gentlemen and thank you for coming. I feel better now that you're here," Ima spoke almost formally to show them respect. "A couple of you look familiar from the softball games."

Though shabbily dressed and smelling of body odor and liquor, they nodded and looked ready for action. Each held a crowbar.

Ima did not know whether they planned to pry open manholes or hit people over the head. Motioning them to sit, she *reiterated* the latest information about Lionel and Wes' big poker losses.

"I thought the heart attack story rang true. Lionel hasn't slept since Sunday. I figured his blood pressure had soared and that his nerves must have *frayed* so as—"

"At least Lionel is not sick, and your boss Wes sounds worried but alive," said Cash.

"But Cash, we need a plan to combat these...gangsters," Ima said.

"Believe me, gangsters like you described are usually interested in only one thing–to getting any money owed them!" Cash exclaimed.

"And believe me, both PapaLi and Uncle Wes owe a bunch. For Wes alone, I've got to come up with over $10,000 in cash."

"Whew, that means they've been playing pretty high stakes!" Cash said.

"Just the length of the game is enough. Think about it. It's gone on for 2 days. That's plenty of time to *lose your shirt* and—"

"And your pants...so they couldn't break loose and run away." said Cash seeming to blink in disbelief that he had joked again at such a time.

"Right now, I've lost my sense of humor," said Ima trying to smile.

"Sorry I didn't mean to jest or sound *calloused*. It's my way to stay calm," he gulped his words and looked embarrassed. "So, how much does your father owe?"

"Wes didn't say exactly...only something about Lionel being their *cash cow* and a *golden calf.* It didn't make sense. All the words jumbled together with an echo. I could barely understand him," admitted Ima.

"Hmmm. A golden calf is like an idol!" Cash deduced.

"Yes...and the ladies used to call Lionel a *matinee idol,*" she remarked.

Cash pondered the ideas. "A *cash cow* makes quick-and-easy money, but an idol is something to which others make sacrifices. Those are scary words with definite meanings if I've interpreted them right!"

"All I know is Wes kept repeating that they were both in deep-deep-deep, and I should get money if I wanted to know where Lionel was. Oh, Cash, I think he meant PapaLi is in deep trouble...in deep debt," Ima said almost on the *verge* on tears.

"Could he be deep in something else, more than a poker debt?" asked Cash.

"Something else? Or somewhere else...deep...with villains holding them in deep, dark shadows," Ima exclaimed.

"That could mean a kidnapping," remarked Cash.

"I know, but kidnapping grown men for a ransom sounds so melodramatic. Why would these thugs *go to such lengths* and...for what reason would—"

"And that's the something else," Cash stated calmly.

"That's what Riina and I thought at first...that maybe Lionel has something else they want. But after talking to Uncle Wes, I'm sure it's only about money."

"Missy, this is serious. You need to go to the police," Cash advised.

"And I will as soon as I know where Lionel and Uncle Wes are."

"So, how do you plan to find him? Knock on every front door in town?" asked Cash.

"Well, at least knock on every front door in the same block of 55th Street as the Friars Club is located." Ima paused and had a slight taste of Fig Newton in her mouth.

"Off Madison?" inquired Cash.

"Yes. You see, Cash, I can't say why; but I sense PapaLi and Wes are *stashed away* close by, but deep...out of sight...maybe in a secret place." She had a flash reverie of the sewers and another slight taste of Fig Newton.

"Ima, a secret place is just that...a secret...that we don't know," said Cash.

Ima stopped to listen to a word buzzing in her head. "Deep, deep...somewhere deep, deep," she repeated in a whisper but remained puzzled. That clue needed turning inside out and upside down. She began to drift off but fought to stay alert.

"Okay, if these guys only want their money, they may rough up Lionel and Wes to scare them...and you," Cash said.

Ima's attention returned to the discussion, "Rough them up," Ima exclaimed. "But, to what purpose?"

Cash spoke calmly but with eyes widened. "Think about it. Friendly persuasion...to get their money. But if the reason is the something else we have yet to figure out, then there is no telling what these thugs might do."

"Let me put this together. On the phone, I heard someone hit Wes," she said, fighting off fears that lay just beneath the surface. "What if they did that to PapaLi...to ruin his handsome face?"

"Now I'll ask you, to what purpose?" asked Cash motioning her to continue her *train of thought.*

"Again, I'm thinking that the something else is something they want...something Lionel already has," replied Ima. Suddenly, her mind darted off, *essaying* other concerns. She blinked repeatedly, yet no longer hearing or seeing Cash and the Central Park fellows.

Ruining faces seemed to be the latest trend in *assault.* Darwinia had scarred Vanna's face and then the moose lady had threatened to hurt Ima in the same way.

So, if it wasn't money that these thugs wanted, what was the something else? Who else gained something by putting Lionel *out of commission*? PapaLi had already missed rehearsals today which might *jeopardize* his job. Hmmm! Shelton had wanted a part in 1776 too. Of course! Shelton! Could this hostage scheme and demand for money have something to do with that? Or did the competition Teresa described between Shelton and Lionel figure into this scene? Did jealousy now *verge* on violence?

If so, did Shelton *harbor* enough hatred to have his gangster cronies cause Lionel real harm? Could he have *instigated* this whole ordeal? Ima licked her lips, craved a Fig Newton, and said under her breath, "I bet that's it."

"Missy, you are a thousands of miles away...as if traveling with those astronauts headed for the moon right now," Cash observed.

"I'm sorry, Cash. My mind goes on safaris...into dark jungles," admitted Ima.

"*Don't borrow trouble* that may not even exist," he said wisely. "There's enough evil to fight today."

"I know you're right. Well, anyway...moving on. Let me tell you about my tunnel theory. Do you remember the Detroit gangsters during Prohibition?" asked Ima, leaping to a totally new subject.

"What on earth are you talking about?" Cash shook his head at this *non sequitur.*

"Never mind, I'll tell you later. I must be logical...I need to stay with one idea at a time." As straightforward as her statement was, Ima seemed rattled as she picked through Riina's notes. "Stick with me. This mystery grows more complicated by the hour. What I need right now is to *decipher* these sketches Riina drew from architectural plans of houses built around the Friars' Club."

"I worked in that area years ago. Let me study the sketches a moment." Cash scratched his head, following the drawings and notes as best he could.

Strongly resisting, Ima still almost drifted off again into her world of swirling thoughts. Wes's word "deep" continued to echo in her mind...just like his words had echoed on the phone...and just like the tour guide's words had echoed against the concrete walls of the sewer...deep, deep, deep. Was that the message? Was that how she had first gotten her idea about the tunnels? How curious it all seemed. Were Wes and PapaLi hidden deep somewhere like the sewers? She must know soon, before hidden deep...meant buried deep.

She tried to be polite and remained quiet. Finally, Ima could wait no longer to ask her questions. "What I need to know is, could any underground tunnels exist on that block? If so, where are the entrances? I mean could someone be hidden in a concrete tunnel? Could someone somehow go from a house basement into the city sewers without coming outside? Don't water pipes in the basement end up in the street sewers?"

"Goodness, no! Those are sealed systems, totally separate," he said laughing and motioning to his friends who had spent many a cold night below streets.

"You mean the sewers aren't like subways changing directions at different levels?" Ima continued her illogical crusade and logic.

"Not exactly! Street sewers only handle the gutter overflow from rains. House drainpipes intersect with a much deeper system. Otherwise it would have been too stinky to take your crazy sewer tour last Sunday" Cash teased. "Where on earth did you get this idea?"

"Remember I told you how Reenie and I poked up from a manhole and watched two suspicious men last night? Well, their last name is Pollibo. We think they are the poker cheats everyone owes. Then today, we learned that their sister Maria Pollibo Mobley lives two houses down from the Friars."

"Coincidence or convenience?" Cash mumbled.

"Or both. That made me think the Pollibos had hidden Lionel and Wes below the Mobley house. And now that I keep hearing Wes' voice echoing the words 'deep-deep,' I'm more convinced than ever that he's down deep somewhere...in a manhole...a secret passage or some type of tunnel close-by the Friars...or the Mobley cellar. That's why, for me, the sewer sounded like the perfect route to get in there unnoticed."

Nodding to his pals, Cash said, "She's in love with the sewers!"

"Well, how else can we get deep down in, then?" asked Ima.

Cash sat down behind Wes' desk. "Let me think," he said, biting his lip in thought. "Most fine old New York homes have steps up to the front door which opens to what they call the first floor. That height allows a *daylight basement* underneath, where once upon a time servants lived and cooked for the families. Often below that was a root cellar or a sub-basement for storing coal or wood for fuel."

"That's exactly what Reenie discovered in her research. Wes's brownstone has one here. Bedrooms are up here with the office; living room and kitchen are downstairs! And beneath the down staircase is a door with a ladder to the cellar where Wes keeps junk. But then, isn't that at the same level as the sewer Riina and I were in last night?"

"Ima, forget the sewers! Maybe you'll understand this. Out in front of most *street-level buildings* are sidewalks with basement doors so drivers can drop goods at the curb. Some basements even have elevators to go below."

"I've seen porters lowering boxes and racks of clothes at some storefronts."

"Well, in an old *exclusive* area like East 55th, folks didn't want boxes or coal delivered to the front sidewalk. Believe me, Old Cash has experience with this."

"I believe you, Cash. You sound very experienced about such things," said Ima.

"You bet. Well, homeowners wanted delivery men to go round back where a kitchen door or a cellar door or both would be," he said.

"Good grief. Are you now suggesting we knock on all the back doors in town?" asked Ima.

"No, but just as you said about front doors, we should at least knock on those in the block we're discussing," *conceded* Cash.

"So, do you agree with me? Do you think Lionel and Wes could be close to the Friars but deep underneath somewhere?" she asked sincerely.

"In fact, they may actually still be hidden at the Club itself," surmised Cash.

"I don't see how. The staff would have noticed if two men were being kept against their will or rushed out in the wee hours of the morning."

"Okay. So, we need to narrow our search somehow," Cash advised. "Then we could eliminate the Friars completely?"

"I'm not sure. I called this morning...yikes," said Ima. "I completely forgot to call at three when Sam came on duty. It's almost six now."

• • •

Ima quickly dialed the Club and hoped Sam would give her some fill-in information to assemble this puzzle into a clearer picture.

"Friars Club. Sam Silencer, Sergeant of Arms. How may I help you?"

"Sam, this is Ima Purple. Please don't hang up. It's very important."

"Before you ask, no, Lionel is not here playing poker."

"I know that. He's being held by the Pollibos until his *marker* is paid," said Ima.

"The name is Pollibo, not Pollibos," Sam corrected her.

"No! Pollibos means there are two men named Pollibo," said Ima in her schoolteacher tone. "They're twin brothers. You saw both but never realized it. Anyway, they cheated all the players with their twin scam and have now taken Lionel and Wes hostages."

"I don't know about all that; but you better steer clear of Val Pollibo, whichever one he is. I've felt the power of his *strong-arming* until he gets his way."

"Sam, it would be easier if we could talk in person. Will you help me?"

"No, helping you always causes trouble. We don't want any trouble here," Sam said, ashamed, wanting to *wiggle out* of his part in this fiasco.

"Well, you've got it whether you want it or not," she declared.

"I don't want you stirring the pot. I can handle this amount of trouble fine," he said.

"You can? Did you get my earlier message about yesterday's game?"

"What about it?" asked Sam.

"If you don't get messages, how can you expect to stop a scam?" Ima asked.

"There's no scam here, just a marathon poker game to help build the pension fund."

"Do you really believe that?" she asked. "Does Val Pollibo look like someone who gives money to charity?"

Weakening from Ima's *barrage* of questions, he began to *divulge* what he knew about the poker game. "Look, no one now on duty was even around after eleven last night. We'll have to wait till the night shift arrives to *get the scoop*. I will tell you the scuttlebutt around here is Shelton and Lionel had a big blow-up."

"I need to know about that, right now. Is there any chance I could call your night replacement at home?"

"He's probably asleep. He isn't due here until 11:00," replied Sam.

"That may be too late to prevent a tragedy," said Ima with true concern.

"Don't be so dramatic!" Sam chided.

"Then would you call him at whatever time you think he starts getting ready for work? In the meantime, we're coming," she said and hung up.

• • •

Ima hung up the phone and turned back to Cash who now stood with the other men, waiting for assignments or dismissal.

"Well, fellows, you heard my side of the conversation. We can't eliminate the Friars yet. I think Sam will help us, maybe reluctantly but at least postitively."

"Good. And I've got a beginning solution for the other house. We need a fact-finding mission. Since panhandlers often go down alleyways and knock on back doors for handouts, we won't look unusual. Maybe a few angry dogs will object, but swanky neighborhoods are usually generous. So, what if you distract the residents at the front door while we *reconnoiter the rear?*"

"*Reconnoiter?* Wow Cash, I'm impressed. I don't ever remember using that word in a sentence, and I'm an English teacher."

"Well, isn't that exactly what we'll be doing?"

"Yes sir! So, while you go to the Mobley backdoor in the alley, I'll go to the front door and ask a few innocent questions. Perhaps a few details will leak out," Ima said, walking over to the bay window and looking out onto the street. Suddenly, she saw Riina, all smiles, popping out of a taxi and rushed to welcome her at the front door. "Your face tells me the demo went well."

"They loved it and signed me for a year's contract on the spot. Ima, I'm on my way. My first spokeswoman account for a soap product to boot!"

"Without Wes *perusing* the contract first? Oh, Reenie! That's not wise," Ima warned.

"Aw, he'll love it after a leetle perusing and *schmoozing* the producer,," said Riina.

"No. Wes will have a fit but never mind. He's in no position to complain. We'll deal with it later. Here's the plan. We're all going to the Friars neighborhood to do more investigation. First, I've got to go home to get lots of money and to eat a Fig Newton before I faint. Could I come by your apartment to get into a disguise?"

"Sure. What do you want...the Mata Hari look again?"

"No. How about the look of Lois Lane, girl reporter?"

"Perfect, and I'll bring my camera and be your sidekick photographer." Riina ran back down the front steps, waving to the taxi she had just dismissed.

Looking out the bay window, Ima watched the antics of Riina jumping in. "I bet the backseat is still warm."

"Or sweaty on a hot July day like this," said Cash, looking up from the sketches.

Ima looked back at the men in the room, who looked back at her orders. How on earth would she use them effectively? She had never assembled an army before. Had she requested them to come along too soon? She shook her head. No. Lionel and Wes had been missing all day. The time to act had come. This mystery kept twisting, and she struggled to retain all the facts. Having others onboard was bound to help.

"Cash, would you and your men meet me at Madison and 55th in about an hour?"

"Sure, you can count on us," he said. "About seven then?"

"And eat beforehand. It could be a long stakeout," said Ima, handing out money."

• • •

Ima took a taxi home, got her traveler's checks, and quickly ate a cookie, an apple, and a slice of cheese. Grabbing her *trench coat*, she dashed over to the Riina's home to complete her disguise. The young women wore *bowler hats*, with reporter cards slipped in the side. They looked as if they had just stepped out of the newspaper movie, *Front Page*.

They walked down ten blocks to 55th and saw Cash and his buddies waiting at the proper corner, just west of their destination. The group finalized their plans and split. The young women took the front sidewalk route past the Friars to the Mobley mansion. Cash's platoon of vagrants marched down the rear alley to the Mobley's back door.

• • •

Cash had remembered correctly. Every house on the alley had a slanting ground-level door to a cellar and a normal backdoor to a *daylight basement*. When he saw a dumpster behind one backdoor, he *presumed* that had to be the Friars Club. Surely, no private home had enough *refuse* to need major pickups. Cash told his men to take cover behind the dumpster while he continued two more doors east to the Mobley house.

He knocked on the back door. A maid answered and looked at his clothes.

"What do you want?" she said with an uppity air. She acted as though she held the same station in high society as her employer.

"Could you spare a few scraps for me and my friends?"

"I'll see if Cook has sumpin' for ya," she scoffed and left the doorway.

With the maid gone, Cash signaled Dollar to come quickly and check on the Mobley cellar door.

Together the two men flipped back the metal door flaps. In the last light of evening pouring into the cellar, Cash watched as Dollar descended the rickety stairs.

"Cash, there are two men down here. This seems too easy."

"Tell 'em the plan."

"Fellows, don't be afraid," Dollar advised. "We're Ima's friends. Just stay put while I tell the others you're safe," he said, starting back up the cellar stairs to the outside.

At the very moment Dollar's head poked above the cellar door, the maid returned to the backdoor.

"Hello, hello. Mister, your food," called the maid.

Motioning Dollar to duck back down the cellar steps, Cash moved swiftly back to the backdoor to block the maid's vision.

"Thank you. God bless you," Cash said sincerely, taking the bag of warm food.

"Now be gone wid cha," she said *condescendingly* and slammed the door.

Cash, stunned by the maid's rudeness, stood at the Mobley kitchen door for a moment.

Dollar closed the cellar door. "Those men are prisoners... gagged, blindfolded and tied down to chairs. But I think we can get them out of there with no problem."

"What's the area like?" asked Cash.

" The room is narrow and has a door at the top of a ladder... probably to the kitchen," replied Dollar.

"Good. Go fetch the others. Send Quarter to the corner to tell Ima what clues we've found so far. The rest of you guys come back here. I'll keep watch."

• • •

Currently unable to see or speak, Lionel had no idea where he and Wes were or how long they had been there. He felt sure that each of them had recent events running through his own mind. He figured if they could compare details to form a collective memory, their *perceptions* of what had happened would prove identical:

Lionel knew that the poker game had stopped in the wee hours of Wednesday morning when Shelton had announced that all the players had to pay up. Val Pollibo had allowed everyone except Lionel and Wes to go on home. They had lost sizeable amounts of money, more than they had in their bank accounts, much less in their pockets. He recalled Val standing over them with a gun while someone else blindfolded and gagged them. Then they were rushed away in a car. After what seemed hours of driving, the car had stopped abruptly.

Lionel had felt someone stick a gun in his ribs and force him out of the car. He assumed Wes received the same treatment. Both unable to see, they had no idea where they had ended up nor recognized the sound of metal flaps opening until someone forced them down rickety steps into a cold, damp room that smelled of mildew. That unknown person had tied them to a chair and then disappeared in what seemed a different direction.

Things had gone along uneventfully except for twice when a wooden door opened from somewhere above, and footsteps came down creaking rather than rickety stairs. Then a man spoke gruffly to Wes and *goaded* him off somewhere. Lionel recognized Val Pollibo's voice but could only imagine the meaning of the other sounds: ropes being untied next to him, scuffles going up, a wooden door opening higher above, and a muffled voice whispering from a perch but still close by. He figured Wes was sitting on some landing and talking to the Pollibos.

During hours of despair, Lionel had sat quietly, deep in thought. Suddenly, again there was the metal clanging sound and steps coming down rickety steps. A moment of hope replaced his feeling of terror. A friendly voice pierced the air, claiming to know Ima and promising to return soon. Then after sounds of rickety steps and metal clanging, silence reigned again. Lionel assumed a potential rescuer had entered and departed by the same way his captors had brought Wes and him.

Shortly after the hopeful voice had spoken, footsteps from their earlier tormenter again descended into the cellar on the ladder from the Mobley's kitchen. He untied the captives from their chairs, retied only their hands, and told them to get moving. The voice sounded like Val. Then Lionel heard a makeshift door sliding and felt the goon's gun barrel goad him in the ribs. He figured the other scuffling feet ahead had to belong to Wes.

• • •

Without free hands to help balance themselves, the hostages stumbled along, scraping their faces and shoulders. Some places in the tunnel grew so narrow the men had to sidestep single file. Close to the end, the ceiling dropped very low. Several times the men crashed their heads. Although Val failed to caution them to duck and crawl on their knees, he never forgot to warn them of the gun pointed at their backs. In great difficulty, Lionel and Wes *negotiated* their way through this long hole in the ground to an unknown destiny. Suddenly, voices came from overhead or up ahead. Now quite *disoriented*, the captives could no longer determine directions.

Val knew those sounds came from the Friars' Club end of the tunnel. He had made that exit hole smaller than the entrance and paid the wine steward to put a long table in front to mask it with a tablecloth.

He whispered to his captives to stay still...as if they could run away under these circumstances! Val needed to lay low until the *coast was clear* before moving the hostages into the Friars' cellar. Then he planned to lead them up to the alley where Sal promised to have the Caddy waiting.

• • •

Lionel strained to recognize the voices. He heard muffled talk about Chablis and Cabernet. Wines? Then he also sensed voices behind him in the tunnel. Was someone bringing up the rear? Had the *captor* changed plans? Did he intend to toy with their minds, trying to drive them crazy? Would he kill them at the end of this tunnel? Were they merely prisoners escaping from their cellblock into death row?

Lionel mulled over the whole situation and reviewed his good fortune. Yes. Lionel's winning the girl and the job had doubled Shelton's loss and turned the longtime *cohorts* into rivals. He had seen Shelton's jealousy transformed into revenge toward him and rage toward Wes. He imagined that Shelton wanted now to change their fortunes radically, thus *getting two birds with one stone*. For that to occur, Shelton had used a *rigged* card game as a unique weapon: He had invited the Pollibo goon to sit in, a goon who now seemed determined to *wreak havoc* on Lionel's life and loved ones. If Val killed him, what would happen to Ima or Teresa?

• • •

When Dollar returned to reopen the cellar door flaps, he could not believe his eyes. The two hostages had disappeared. "They're gone!" he exclaimed.

"Not possible," gasped Cash coughing and trying to catch his breath. The excitement had made him feel a bit weak, but he shook it off. "I've stood here the whole time. No one's gone in or out of the Mobley cellar."

"Then explain how two men can turn to dust?" puzzled Dollar.

"I think someone must have shifted them to another location in the house. A place this big must have gobs of rooms," surmised Cash.

"Well, I'm not in the mood to be hauled off by the police for breaking and entering a fancy house," declared Dollar.

"No, but it couldn't hurt if you took another look for clues in the cellar," Cash suggested. "I'll stand guard."

· · ·

Accustomed to Cash's leadership, Dollar did not balk but simply led his crew of vagrants down in the ever-darkening cellar. He left open the metal doors to get the day's last remaining light. They patted the rough cellar walls, unsure of what they should find.

"This reminds me of my cell up at Sing Sing," said Pennypinch said.

"Yeah, me too! Some guy would always brag about digging a passage from his cell to the outside prison walls," added Nickel.

"Of course, he only had a spoon from the mess hall to dig with," added Pennypinch, sniggering.

"Hey, maybe there's a button on the walls that responds to the code phrase, *open sesame*. You know, like in the old horror movies when mummies came out of secret passages or knights in armor fell down the stairs," Nickel teased.

"Keep it down, fellows. We need to feel the walls to see if an opening even exists. Those two men cannot have disappeared into thin air," declared Dollar.

Just then Nickel found a break in the wall, clumsily covered with a sheet of plywood. "Hey, like this!" he exclaimed, sliding back the makeshift door.

"Good work, Nickel. Now, you go up top to stand guard while Pennypinch and I go in the tunnel," said Dollar, turning to Pennypinch. "The short guy goes first. I'll follow."

For a couple of minutes the two men moved easily through the hole until it dropped to shoulder height. Dollar bent over and went a little farther, but they both stopped upon hearing voices up ahead.

"Pennypinch, I'm going back," whispered Dollar. "You go on as far as you can, but don't take any chances. Ima wants clues, not dead heroes."

Dollar backed out of the tunnel and exited the Mobley cellar. "You're not gonna believe this. The two men have indeed disappeared."

"Then we must report that back to Ima before going on with the plan," said Cash, just as Quarter ran up, excited and breathing heavily.

"I didn't see *hide nor hair* of those two girls."

"Well, go back and check again," ordered Cash. "If Ima comes, tell her the two men Dollar found in Mobley's cellar have gone somewhere else."

"What? I never got to tell her we found them in the first place," lamented Quarter.

"Go on now. Just tell her both: we found them, and we lost them," admitted Cash.

Quarter ran back to the head of the alley, looked to the corner and returned, "I still don't see Ima or Riina up that way. Their side of the plan must have stalled out too."

"Okay, we'll follow our part as far as we can," said Cash. "Let's go back to the Friars' dumpster and stay behind it for now."

Coaxing the Reluctant

Concurrent to Cash's back alley scene, Ima with her notebook and Riina with her camera, stood waiting at the Mobley mansion front door. The butler swung open the heavy oak door and looked them over with a sneer.

"Hi, my name is Ima Purple, and this is Riina Feingold. We are freelance reporters interested in historical architecture. We're interviewing people on this block. Might we speak with Mrs. Mobley this evening, or could we make an appointment to come back in the morning?

"Mrs. Mobley doesn't speak to strangers, or you must be *recommended* for an appointment," he said, as the lady of the house suddenly appeared, peering over his shoulder.

"What's this, Jarman, two poster children for my pet project?" said Maria.

"Oh, hello Mrs. Mobley, my friend and I are a freelance team reporting on historical homes that have been preserved from the *wrecking ball*. Like you, we too have an interest in saving old homes, especially on the upper eastside where many Czechoslovakians originally settled?"

"Oh, yes," Maria Mobley said in a very snobbish voice. "But those brownstones are mostly *ramshackle*."

"I'm shocked you feel that way, given your love of period architecture," said Ima.

"The Heritage Committee never considered the period for those buildings anything but totally unremarkable," Mrs. Mobley declared.

"Oh, how sad!" said Ima, cocking her head in disbelief. "Surely you agree that home is home to the people who love it. In fact, the tenants across the street from my own apartment building want to save their old structure because they've never lived anywhere else. We figured with your influence, you would help them."

"You figured wrong, and you *presumed* on my good nature," said the lady.

"I've got some snapshots of these folks' sacred bricks and mortar," chimed in Riina. "Maybe if I showed them to you as soon as they're developed—"

"And maybe if you could help us to get private grants and city permits or learn how to *salvage* old architectural *facades*—"

"You'd realize how worthy a project that would be," added Riina.

"Yes. Didn't you have those same struggles while restoring this magnificent house?" inquired Ima, pointing to the facade and fanning her hand in the air.

"Well, my dears, you just said the very words that define what is and is not worthy of being *salvaged*," she said, haughtily. "You *can't make a silk purse out of a sow's ear*."

"But won't you please, please, at least help us try? We'd *covet* any worthy advice you'd deemed...worthy to give us," urged Riina, trying to sound sincere while sliding her foot in to block the doorway.

"Young lady, thou shalt not covet!" said Maria, self-righteously.

"Oops! One of the Ten Commandments, right? I once heard about them long ago!" said Riina obviously pretending to repent. "What I meant was a *picture paints a thousand words*."

"Oh, yes, I agree it does," said Maria.

"And as a photographer, I would love to see any old pictures of this house before you completed the *renovations*."

"So would I," said Ima, moving her body against the door and changing her *tactic* to keep this interview alive. "I'm wondering if most homes on this block have basements? Do you? If so, is it divided into livable spaces? Are servants' quartered there? Do you have a subbasement or a cellar? Do you keep coal down there? Is it terribly dirty?"

"You ask more questions than anyone could ever answer comfortably. I think you need to learn more about being a reporter and leave the historical restorations to me," Maria declared.

"Well then, might we just take a peak at your handiwork? I've heard fabulous things about your house," Ima asked, switching to flattery to get inside the Mobley mansion.

"And I hope to sell a series of home photos to *House Beautiful*," bragged Riina.

"Oh, yes. Just so you'll know. I'm planning a feature article on rough spaces like basements and cellars that have been made more livable and more *aesthetic* by little touches of an artist's hand, such as yours," added Ima. "Do you have a cellar?"

"My *colleague* and I would just love to see it. We promise to be very grateful...and very quick," Riina said in an edgy tone just shy of begging. "The society pages would absolutely eat up this story, especially if we combined it with how charitable you were to add your vast knowledge to help the Czechs revive their neighborhood over on the Upper Eastside."

"Well, since you put it that way, Jarman, show these young ladies upstairs, this floor, and the basement," her voice grew nervous and halting. "But not the cellar!" she whispered. "The boys have a project ongoing down there."

After a quick tour of the first and second floors, Ima and Riina swooned at the *opulence*. They saw antiques tastefully arranged about the spacious rooms. The crown moldings at the ceiling and carved window cornices resembled more a palace than a normal *domicile.*

Jarman then showed them to the basement which contrasted greatly to the first floor. Few improvements had come below. Dingy walls, chipped plaster, and ancient kitchen equipment only echoed of glory days gone by.

Then the team went into their special modes. With her crazy brand of chatter, Riina distracted the butler as she had Officer Allrest at the precinct and Sam at the Friars Club. That ploy freed Ima to open the cellar door located in the same spot as in Wes's brownstone. With great *agility,* she climbed down the ladder. Her manhole experience had groomed her for this steep entry. Below she found a tunnel-like room made of damp concrete and with a smell that reminded her of the sewer tour. She mused that even if her sewer idea had proved foolish, it had gotten things rolling in the right direction.

Ima looked about the dim room. On the far side and close to the ceiling of the outside wall, she saw a slanted, double cellar door slightly ajar. The crack allowed a little light to pierce through and fall onto two empty chairs. How curious! She could not imagine anything but cases of wine enjoying this deep hole... certainly not humans sitting around talking?

So, why would the Pollibos choose to sit down here and talk about a project? Perhaps their dastar*dly* deeds required complete darkness? Suddenly, she heard muffled voices coming from a sidewall. She edged her way over. But unfortunately, Jarman interrupted her search for more clues.

"Say, Miss, what are you doing down there?" Jarman said *curtly.* "Did you not hear Mrs. Mobley call the cellar *off-limits?* Your tour is officially over!"

The two young ladies thanked the butler for his time and asked if they might exit through the backdoor, just to get a lay of the land. However, Jarman insisted they satisfy the old superstition: leaving from the same door they entered.

Ima and Riina dashed down the mansion's front steps, giggling over how they had *hoodwinked* most of the Mobley household. They ran to the west corner where all had agreed to re-gather. But, looking both ways, they saw no sign of Cash or his crew.

"We should wait for them. They probably hit a snag in the plan," Riina said.

"Or real trouble. My instincts say something has gone wrong. Not knowing what Cash may have discovered, we can't proceed with our plan" remarked Ima.

"So what do we do, oh great Ima of the North?" asked Riina.

"Let's pray," Ima said, grabbing Riina's hand.

"You mean right here and right now, just like before our softball games?"

"Exactly! But this time, we'll do it for the safety of Cash's crew and all the honest players in this dirty game! Let's ask for the next step. That way I know we'll remember something that could lead us to Lionel and Wes," remarked Ima.

"You know I'm game for almost anything, but what is all this praying jazz lately? Are you becoming a nun? Or are you dying?" asked Riina half-serious and half-jesting.

"Of course not! I'm healthy as a horse. It's only that since we were kids, something has changed in me, something wonderfully easy to accept but very hard…no, almost impossible to explain at the same time."

"You seem just the same to me," Riina remarked.

"Maybe on the outside but not on the inside! I don't know about you and your folks, but mine never talked much about following God. Now I'm trying to let Him lead me through everything, but I keep running ahead."

"Even a half-breed Estonian Jew knows how that will make you *run amuck*," said Riina.

"Right. But there's another thing you don't know about me. It fits into this idea. See, when I moved away to Michigan, I missed you terribly. My only friends were books. I got hooked on mysteries. Then I decided to study to be a sleuth. I made up my own logic, which made it easier to see details and *decipher* leads," boasted Ima.

"Well, Sherlock, just call me your own Dr. Watson," Riina teased.

"Not by half. Sherlock would have quit his occupation if he had had as many failures as I have. I can quickly see the details others miss, but then I struggle to put them in order or turn them into clues that prove my case. This may sound silly, but I decided to pray about clues. Strangely, answers started coming. Then if I found more details, I needed still more answers. In fact, I needed a type of minute-by-minute...in touchness," admitted Ima.

"In touchness?" teased Riina. "This phrase from the lips of an English teacher?"

"You know what I mean. Tell me, who else but God knows what's about to happen?"

"Right! Who else would have known your mother would die so young. Frankly, I don't understand it because she was a good person! Both your parents always tried to do right—"

"And brought me up to think that same way too," remarked Ima.

"So, what's wrong with that?" quipped Riina.

"Nothing, except I never knew how they felt inside...about the God thing."

"The God thing?" asked Riina. "What's that?"

"That's what my friend Vanna called it," said Ima realizing she had said 'friend.'

"Sometimes, I even wonder about all that," admitted Riina.

"Look, I'm thrilled to know Lionel joined Jan Hus Church and I hope that—"

"If wild Moravians can't penetrate his thick skull, he needs brain surgery," said Riina, grinning and looking at her watch. "But we *digress* from the task at hand. So, I hoyd ya. So, stop the *dawdling* and start to praying already!"

Lord, help us to find PapaLi and Uncle Wes." Ima paused and then turned to Riina, "Without knowing Cash's back door results, I feel nudged to return to the Friars' front door, our original target. Maybe Sam has the full story on last night's card game.

The young women walked in to find the Sergeant of Arms behind his desk as if behind a gunner's station. He seemed *steeled* against them, ready to reject whatever they offered.

"So, it's you two again. What are you supposed to be disguised as this time?"

"Reporters!" Riina pointed to her hat placard.

"Two Lois Lanes! Where's Clark Kent?" he said sarcastically.

"He's protecting Metropolis from a meteor," Riina quipped.

"Now Sam, I told you I was coming, and you said you'd help," Ima reminded.

"I can't help. Auditions for Superman closed years ago. It seems you two have struck out like most New York actresses," he said in an unfriendly manner.

"Not completely," Ima said with determination. "This disguise won us a tour of a neighbor's home. By the way, did you know the Pollibos live two doors down?"

"For the umpteenth time, it's Pollibo not Pollibos!" Sam exclaimed.

"Be nice Sammy. That's not helpful. You did tell Ima you'd help. I'm a witness," said Riina, circling his desk to tickle his bald head. "Now, do you want folks to remember you as the most cooperative Sergeant of Arms the Friars ever or the one who *reneges* on his promises?"

"Please Sam, we need your help more than ever," Ima *entreated*.

"What do you propose I do?" said Sam.

"For one thing, did you call the night man about Lionel?" she asked.

"He said he'd only talk to you and only in person. Someone muzzled Nelson," Sam admitted, looking to and fro in case that "someone" might overhear.

"Muzzled? You mean someone got to him and paid him off?" asked Ima.

"Of course! That's how those guys operate," said Sam. "Do what they say or else they threaten you."

"And did they?" asked Riina rubbing his head. "I'll show 'em another 'or else' of my own."

"Or else they *grease your palm* with an *incentive* to keep your mouth shut," Ima surmised.

"Yes, I admit it, *much to my chagrin*," said Sam, nodding.

"You knucklehead!" declared Riina thumping his *cranium* like testing a coconut.

Sam blushed and rubbed his scalp. "But so what if I did? What does it have to do with Lionel anyhow?"

"I'll tell what you obviously don't know. Lionel has not been home from the card game for two days, nor has Wes been in his office. But today, he called to say my father had a heart attack and was rushed out."

"Maybe it's true. I heard the same *scuttlebutt* circling here today," Sam spoke more kindly than before. "Like I said on the phone, I don't know the details."

"Wait, there's more. Wes later called back to say it was all a lie. Then he began saying that they were in deep-deep-deep, deep in."

"Oh sure. That's an old gambling term," offered Sam, shamefacedly. "It means you're deep in debt...deep into the bookies for lots of money."

"Talk about lots of money, that's what Lionel lost here last night. But I think there's more to it. When Wes kept repeating the word 'deep,' it seemed like a signal, as if he wanted to tell me something else...like where he was? He said they rushed Lionel out.

"So, who are the 'they' in this story," Sam asked.

"The Pollibos. Aren't you following any of this?" quipped Riina.

"It's Pollibo not Pollibos!" said Sam

"Forget that, Sam. What I need is your help with the 'where' in this story. Wes said they rushed him out, but to where?"

"To the hospital, I guess?" asked Sam, innocently.

"No need to. They lied about Lionel having a heart attack!" said Ima "So where else would they rush him and Wes? Somewhere out of sight...to hide them?"

"Somewhere down deep...like into a cellar?" Riina peered into his eyes and answered for him.

"What if right now, Wes and Lionel are deep in the Friars' cellar or in the walk-in cooler or worse yet, the freezer. Isn't that worth investigating?" asked Ima.

"There's no way. We only allow staff down there," declared Sam.

"Well, maybe the staff got strong-armed or muzzled like Nelson," Ima said.

"Or got paid off to keep this a secret...like someone else we know," added Riina, twisting her finger from his balding head to his ear. "Please Sam, we need more facts."

"Please let me search below just to ease my mind?" asked Ima. "It could save a life or prevent a death because I can't come up with all the money Wes and Lionel owe the Pollibos."

"Bo not bos!" said Sam as if he could not resist correcting Ima one more time. Then, almost as quickly, he *acquiesced* to her request. "Okay."

• • •

Leaving Riina at the reception desk, Sam steered Ima through the Friars lobby and took the elevator down to the basement. The kitchen staff bustled about, too busy preparing meals for the dining room to notice the *intruders*. As Sam crossed to open the cellar door, the wine steward came bursting forth, mumbling to himself as he dusted off several bottles.

"Chablis and Cabernet...I must remember to order more Chablis and Cabernet," the wine steward said and then looked *askance*, shaking his head. "I would not take a lady down there. It's miserably cold!"

"Thanks for your concern, but my trusty *trench coat* will keep me toasty," Ima said boldly. Nothing could dampen her will to see what lay below.

While descending the steps, Ima heard scuffling feet and metal doors scraping. By the time she hit the cellar floor, she saw a last foot leaving the stairs to the street level. Then a gunshot rang out. Glass broke. Wheels squealed.

Ima called up to the kitchen. "I heard a gunshot. Sam, quick. Get the police!"

Whirling around, she stumbled over Pennypinch who was in the process of crawling from under the table set to conceal the tunnel opening.

"What are you doing here? Did you fire a shot?" asked Ima.

"No, Miss, someone else. But, we found your tunnel! I followed it to here and hid, there under that table," said the squatty fellow, pointing first to the east wall, then to the table and finally up toward the outer cellar door. "But for now, let's take a look topside," he spoke, as if on a submarine.

Pennypinch and Ima quickly climbed the steps to the alley but stopped when their eyes came *flush* to the dumpster. They saw Cash's crew surrounding him.

"Oh no, Cash got shot!" Ima frantically climbed the remaining way out the cellar.

"Don't worry, Ima. I'll live, but I couldn't save Lionel or Wes. I'm so sorry. Those thugs sped off in a terrible hurry," said Cash, obviously in pain.

Dollar continued with breathy details, "They were all bound and gagged and blindfolded, stumbling out in front of the gunman. Cash leapt at him with a crowbar, but that weapon could not match a firearm."

"Someone, call an ambulance," ordered Ima. "Dollar, tell me about the getaway car."

"It all happened so fast. I didn't get the license, but I can tell you the culprits' car is a Black Caddy with a broken windshield," he said, proudly waving his crowbar.

• • •

Ima dashed to the head of the alley and jumped into a taxi. Dollar ran behind her and then followed on foot alongside her cab until the corner. When the light changed, Dollar ran on across the street. However, looking back, he saw that Ima's cab never made it across because congested traffic made the intersection totally *impassable* from all directions. He realized the dilemma but did not want to lose sight of the culprits' caddy nor of Ima's cab back in the previous block.

Therefore, he jumped on top of a mailbox to gain extra height. From that *vantage point*, he could now keep up with both. Finally, he eyed the caddy up ahead, now boxed in and unable to change lanes. Dollar began to wave his hands wildly back toward Ima's taxi and pointed until she waved back from the car window.

"Driver, follow the signals from that man waving atop the mailbox," directed Ima.

Although a typical cabby might have argued, this one picked up on the urgency and *adroitly* eased up to the traffic light at the end of his block, hoping to make it across in this cycle. Just as the light turned yellow, he took a chance to complete a crossing and managed to get to the other side safely. Unfortunately, the tail of his cab hung out in the intersection. That rather unpopular *maneuver* set dozens of horns to honking.

To correct the problem, the cabby began creeping toward the car in front of him. In so doing, he slightly knocked the next bumper. The driver of that car whirled out and ran back to Ima's cab, cursing *a blue streak*, shaking his fist at the driver, and claiming a personal injury.

"Hey, what's the big idea? You wrecked my bumper and my neck hurts. Someone's gotta pay for the damage."

"Aw, your mudder wears flannel pajamas!" said Ima's driver.

"Well, your mudder's bald and wears a wig!" said the bumper's driver.

Ima mused, watching another unforgettable New York moment. The drivers exchanged insults until the traffic cleared from the left lane. *Without further ado*, the Bumper King ran back to his car.

Ima's cabby quickly moved into a better position and announced he could now see the culprits' car. Ima hung out the window and waved a grateful goodbye to Dollar. "Go on back to the Friars Club alley to check on the other fellas!"

Debts and Deals

Ima's cabby had a new task now: keep the Black Caddy in sight until its destination. He followed it through a couple of illegal turns, one west on 57th and another heading south on Broadway. The big car stopped at West 46th Street, which ran only one-way. Ima's cabby followed a short distance behind.

Ima saw the two Pollibos get out of the Caddy. The hostages followed, both gagged, blindfolded, and with hands tied. Ima strained to identify the fifth man emerging. *Dismayed* and in disbelief, she saw Shelton Grape crawling out! She wondered, had the Pollibos also taken him hostage?

Had she gotten this whole thing wrong? However, seeing Shelton had free hands, she returned to her original supposition that he was in *collusion* with the Pollibos. Projecting how the whole scheme might unravel at the theatre, Ima asked the cabby to let her out a half-block away. Like a real detective, she would *pursue* her prey from a safe distance, keeping both gangsters and victims unaware of her presence until the right time

With the evening performance of *1776* already in progress, Ima noticed a security guard at the front doors of the 46th Street Theatre. She respectfully approached and described the men who had just gone past toward the stage door. She gave a quick rundown of the urgent situation and asked the guard to call Officer Allrest at the local precinct, feeling sure the police would respond quickly.

Then *stealthily*, Ima headed toward the alley and arrived just in time to watch the Pollibo group slip in the side door. Keeping her distance, she mused as Sal Pollibo entered the backstage door first, as if he owned the place. She suspected that Lionel and Wes, now with blindfolds off, realized that actually two Pollibos existed and two had caused today's drama. The victims followed dutifully behind Sal Pollibo; and Val Pollibo followed them *unabashedly* letting his revolver show. She figured...that he figured...a gun provided him the most persuasive way to *keep under wraps* the prisoners.

Once the group disappeared inside, Ima made her move to enter as well. Hanging far enough back in the shadows to be unnoticed but staying close enough to observe the action, she saw Val nervously *bristling* as a theatre employee approached. The man held up his hand to block the trespassers.

"You can't come back here during a performance."

"Oh yeah, who says?" asked Val, bullishly.

"I'm the stage manager, and I say so."

"Well, this says we can do whatever we want." Val held his gun to the man's nose.

"So there. Now call Primo and tell him Sal Pollibo is here to collect," demanded Sal.

Soon thereafter, Primo, a *stocky* fellow with horn-rimmed glasses and a cigar gripped in his teeth, walked up and shushed the Pollibo *entourage*. "Follow me."

Primo led the two hostages and the two gangsters downstairs and into his private office. Whether ignored, unseen, or uninvited, Shelton Grape lagged behind outside Primo's door. He looked as bewildered and exhausted as the two hostages. He too had been awake for almost three days.

Even though Ima stayed on the top landing, she still kept her *teacher eyes* on Shelton. As soon as the security officer came to confirm he had actually contacted the authorities, she went on downstairs to the office level. Outside the production manager's door, Shelton Grape paced a few steps to and fro.

Shelton glanced at Ima with *contempt*. Then, quite unexpectedly, his look of *disdain* melted into desperation and then a weak quest for sympathy. She wanted no conversation but only stared blankly at him, trying to interpret his changing countenance. She had not decided yet if he was a true *turncoat* to Wes, a recent rival for Lionel or a forever two-faced friend to the Pollibos, ready to turn into a *snitch* against his childhood buddies or anyone else who tried to *implicate* him in this nasty business. Then suddenly Shelton looked *dazed* and seemed to *hallucinate*:

•   •   •

He raised his hand as if volunteering in class. The play's producer pointed to him and announced that Shelton Grape was the only one who could rescue the play. Shelton bowed and saw a headline run across his mind. "Grape replaces Longwind in *1776* Cast." Somehow Lionel's downfall had answered all Shelton's dreams and had *catapulted* him onto the Broadway stage! The surroundings all re-enforced his delusion. The tops of scenery bowed down to him and then leaned against the stage walls. Wardrobe people with tape measures scurried down the hall to make costumes to fit him perfectly. He imagined that he stood outside his own dressing room, waiting for the stage manager to put a star on the door. He looked around and saw the director arrive to ask him to take over all the roles and to make this musical into a one-man show. Shelton bowed again and again until he grew dizzy and almost fainted.

•   •   •

Closing the office door and standing with his back to it, Primo looked at the two hoodlums and then at Lionel and Wes. "Lionel, what's this all about? Is this supposed to explain why you missed rehearsal today?"

Unable to talk with his mouth gagged, Lionel nodded and pled with his eyes. Primo wagged his finger at Sal. "A terrible thing you have done to our major *understudy*. He's our backup plan to get out of trouble, not to be the cause of it."

"Then I hope you consider him valuable enough to *redeem from the pawnshop*. As I said earlier on the phone, I require your answer to my proposal by the end of the play tonight," Sal *reiterated*.

"Well then, I've got a whole act yet. That says to me, I can do whatever I want until then," quipped Primo, unwilling to let anyone bully him.

"Don't mess with Sal or me. We have ways of getting precisely what we want," said Val waving his gun.

"And I have ways of thwarting what you want. The theatre has its customs and traditions. No one bullies his way into show business. So, I suggest we discuss your proposal like civilized men."

"Oh, shall we drink tea and eat lemon cookies?" Sal asked sarcastically.

Primo ignored Sal's attempt at humor and seized the floor, "First off, I insist you remove the gags from these men."

Val looked at his brother. "He insists? That's funny."

Sal held out his hand to take Val's gun and then nodded for him to remove the hostages' *encumbrances*. Lionel and Wes sputtered a little and rubbed their faces. Sal returned Val's gun.

"Okay, let's *talk turkey*," said Sal with *cunning*. "The two men before you have run up a heavy debt which I expect someone to pay. You're as good as anyone since you have a contract with them. I believe we discussed a figure of $30,000."

"You delude yourselves! The *1776* producers have no intention of paying blackmail. As a policy, we never involve ourselves in employees' private matters. We especially don't stoop to rescuing actors from gambling debts." Primo declared. "So I consider your demands *moot*."

"What? They're not mute. I took off their gags," said Val, obviously not knowing what the word "moot" meant.

"Val, let me handle this. Now Mr. Primo, surely you don't want Lionel to lose his life over our inability to come to satisfactory terms," said Sal. "I am a businessman above all and quite willing to *negotiate*."

"Negotiate? I see no written agreement on the table!" said Primo.

Val *bristled* and pointed his gun directly at the production manager. "You better listen. Sal starts with the best deal and moves down to the worst."

"Put your gun away Val. We will handle this like gentlemen, right...gentlemen?" Sal said dispassionately. "I think my little arrangement should *entice* you? What if I extend the due date on my debt, and you send Lionel's weekly paychecks directly to me."

"How did my paychecks get into this?" Lionel said to Sal.

"Do you expect me to forego my commission on his checks?" asked Wes.

"I see no other way," Sal said with a fake sigh.

"Wait a minute," exclaimed Lionel. "You asked my new employer to pay a ransom without telling me how much I owed or giving me a chance to get the money." He paused and laughed. "You are so foolish to make me a bargaining chip."

"I'd say he's made a foolish, fatal mistake," added Primo.

Sal bristled at Primo, "You dare call me a fool?"

"Primo is right. You gambled that your plan would *jeopardize* the play. But you misjudge the value of my reputation. I'm not the only actor in town who can do this," admitted Lionel.

"What a trouper! At least one clear thinker stands in our midst," said Primo, swatting Lionel on the back.

"Look Primo, I know the show's position. It's in business to make money, not to save some actor's neck from gangsters," admitted Lionel.

"Lionel, you know we love your work! But honestly, you've put yourself in a tough spot. Missing today's rehearsal is enough for you to *get canned*. Frankly, we'd rather release you from your contract and reopen auditions to replace you."

"Good plan. I've got a few actors to send over," Wes chimed in, grabbing the floor away from the Pollibos.

"I'm always interested in new faces," said Primo, his own face showing that he liked playing this *game of keep-away*.

"Besides, a new play is in the works," said Wes, keeping the ball in the air.

"A new play?" inquired Lionel, catching on to the strategy and *volleying* the ball back.

"I hadn't mentioned it because you had this job," Wes responded quickly.

"Great. Who's the *playwright*? Do I know him?" Lionel asked.

"A new one!" said Wes.

"What's the title?" asked Primo, seeing the Pollibos' loss of command.

"It's in early stages, but it's called *Out of This World*," replied Wes, not giving a second chance for either Pollibo to speak.

"Good title. What's it about?" asked Lionel.

"Astronauts going to the moon!" replied Wes.

"Sounds like it has good plot potential to me," said Lionel.

"Right, so I want you to start researching the role tomorrow when NASA puts a man on the moon," Wes suggested.

Wes, Primo, and Lionel delighted in seeing the Pollibos' heads swivel back and forth as if watching a hockey match. The showbiz veterans showed no sign of weakness and had no plans to yield back control to these goons.

"Sounds perfect for Lionel," chuckled Primo, slowing the conversation and directing it so the two goons would realize the *extortion* plot had failed.

"I can see you in the role of a distinguished navy test-pilot," said Wes, completing the exchange of power from the Pollibos to Primo.

"So can I. Our producers might back that play. When can I see a script?" Primo asked.

"I'll keep you posted. I might even put in a little of my own money too."

Wes wanted to tantalize Val and Sal with the thought that the Westerly Agency might still have money behind it, which they would never touch. That *ploy* brought expected glee to the enemy's eyes, *deflecting* their focus off Lionel. Wes had succeeded in protecting his client in an unusual manner. "Hey, Primo, let's do lunch next week to discuss this."

"Good idea. Well, everything has turned out fine for us all." said Primo, pacing back and forth in front of the office door. Having *defused* the Pollibos, Primo needed a way to end this meeting without any violence.

"You know if Lionel gets the astronaut part, which no doubt he will, we here at *1776* would look more *magnanimous* if we released him for that reason instead of his missing a rehearsal. So, do we have a deal, Wes?"

"Good publicity all around. And no penalty for canceling contracts!" added Wes.

"Agree!" declared Primo.

"Sounds good to me," said Lionel, looking at the Pollibos who shook their heads, totally baffled how this talking game had left them out in the cold.

Primo heard a scuffling which momentarily stopped him. Nonchalantly, he pressed his rump against the door and heard a low whisper from outside.

"It's the police. Give us a signal when you're ready," said Officer Onfoot.

Primo hit his heel against the door but began talking again, "So, there we have it, gentlemen. I can't say it any better than Mr. Shakespeare '*All's well that ends well*'!"

"Looky here, you're jumping ahead. You're not consulting me. You can't negotiate among yourselves and exclude me!" said Sal, *discombobulated* by these showbiz men who had cut him out completely.

"But we just did!" said Wes, smiling.

"You mean you don't want Lionel back?" asked Sal.

"Nope. He's gonna do a new play," replied Primo.

"So, that opens up his job, right?" inquired Sal attempting to recover from Primo's *power play.*

"Open— as if never filled!" Primo declared.

"Well, let me think," Sal said, a bit confused by the introduction of the other play idea. "Look, I'd be willing to let Lionel's wages from this new play repay me if you promised to hire my client."

"How does that deal secure the money you just tried to *extort* from me?" asked Primo.

"I think my client would be willing to pay me a large commission to be in your cast," Sal intoned.

"Funny, I've never heard of the Pollibo Talent Agency. Yet, you have a client? Hmmm. Are you licensed?" asked Wes.

"We can't deal with anyone except licensed agents." Primo began to string the Pollibos along again. "And by client, I assume you mean that pitiful character creeping outside this door?"

"My client Shelton Grape is a solid professional, as good as Lionel Longwind any day of the week," declared Sal.

"Sir, you are not only foolish but confused," remarked Wes. "Shelton Grape is my client! I'd be happy to let you pay me to release him from his contract."

"He's under contract to you?" asked Sal. "Well, still I bet my lawyer can break—"

"A contract as solid as the Rock of Gibralter," replied Wes. "But for a fee, we might *negotiate* a deal. Besides, in polite circles, Shelton is what we call a *has-been*: dead wood, not good for building, just burning."

Primo turned to Val, then Sal, and last to Wes. "No matter who represents him, he—"

"Don't fret, Primo. If you accept Sal's deal, I will *relinquish* all claims to Shelton," said Wes.

Sal Pollibo knew how to make very fast changes in card games, but this showbiz talk seemed jet-propelled. He didn't know which end was up or which side to claim as his. Sal turned to Primo. "Well, so tell me what you will offer for Shelton?"

"Offer? No-no-no! That's not how showbiz works, Mr. Pollibo. While I grant you Shelton is a charming fellow, he knows the usual ropes," said Primo.

"Though your so-called client counted on your naiveté to threaten *1776*, he misled you to think a little threat or back-stabbing would get him a job and you some money. But in showbiz, there are no such short cuts, no side doors, and no quick offers," said Wes.

"Wes is right. Besides, I have no authority to cast Shelton in a play. He must *pass muster* before the whole production staff. He must compete for the spot and audition on equal terms. All the *hoofers hit the boards* and do their little soft-shoe routine. Then we decide whether or not to make an offer," iterated Primo.

"But that hardly seems fair since I'm letting you *off the hook* with Longwind and providing you an equal replacement!" Sal added.

"Equal? With combat boots on, I could still out-hoof Shelton Grape," said Lionel confidently.

"Fair? The dictionary would not define as fair how you two pretended to be one person to scam us at poker! I knew something smelled fishy when you kept needing to go to the restroom," Wes said, trying to put it together. "I bet you met each other outside, shared information, and exchanged places at the table, unbeknownst to us."

"Those bets you would have won instead you still owe us lots of money," said Sal, regaining a little strength. "Only Lionel is off the hook."

"Well, all may be fair in love and war, but not in cards," Wes declared.

"Don't get smart. Our deal with Primo does not let you off," Val reminded.

"What deal?" asked Primo, kicking the door twice.

Instantly, the police unit broke in and grabbed the two gangsters while Officer Onfoot recited their Miranda Rights.

"Sal and Val Pollibo, you're under arrest for running a gambling operation in a private club, *abducting* these two men and holding them against their will, attempting to *extort*, and causing bodily harm to Cash Underground. Anything you say may be held against you in a court of law."

"Cash? Who's that? I don't know anyone by that name. How can I be arrested for hurting someone I've never even heard of?" said Sal.

"That's how the law works!" replied Onfoot. "Okay men, handcuffed the two louses and get them to the precinct. That ought to wake up Officer Allrest from his evening nap."

While the police wrestled to cuff the two lugs, Shelton poked his nose into the *fray*, saw things going *awry*, and quickly slinked away unnoticed. But Ima remained watching from the doorway pleased to see Onfoot taking charge. Once the police had the culprits ready to tow, she rushed in, much to Lionel's surprise.

"Eema, what are you doing here?" asked Lionel.

"Don't be mad PapaLi," she begged as she hugged him and then Wes. "Riina and a whole group of us have been trying to find you two all day. And Uncle Wes, I just heard your analysis of what happened. It matches what I discovered in my investigation. And thanks for the clues you gave on those phone calls."

"I'm glad you understood them, especially on how deep we really were," said Wes.

"It took some figuring, but it finally dawned on me," she said.

"Investigation? Clues?" inquired Lionel shaking his head. "I don't understand anything you're saying or how you found us."

"I'll tell you the whole story later. Just know that after Wes called from that echo chamber, we've been on your trail," replied Ima.

"Oh, Ima, ever since you arrived in Manhattan, we have not been very *hospitable*. We've offered nothing but *mayhem*," remarked Wes.

"At least the mayhem did not result in *melee* or *malaise* which might have landed many folks in the hospital," she grinned and winked at her father.

"Right, Eemagene, no hand-to-hand battle or *dazed* illness here," said Lionel proudly.

"I can't believe you're like both your mother and father about exact words," said Wes.

"Our family never met a word it didn't like...to use," added Lionel.

"Well, all I want to say is please forgive Manhattan for its very unwelcoming welcome party. I promise you more fun from now on," said Wes.

"Actually, in a way it has been fun. I'd forgotten how exciting New York can be. This has been my most dramatic case so far," Ima remarked.

"Case? What do you mean?" Lionel asked, looking more bewildered than ever.

"It's a long story; but *suffice it to say*, I plan to be a full-fledged sleuth one day," Ima announced as if she had a large audience.

"And I'm here to attest to her skill," declared Officer Onfoot cracking a slight grin in her direction.

As the police squad escorted the Pollibos off, Officer Onfoot turned to the freed hostages, "Now, gentlemen, I know you've been through a lot; but we still need your statements down at the station."

"Well then, sweetheart, I'll see you at home," Lionel said to Ima.

"Probably not until quite late! I have to go back to the Friars to verify some details on the case and to make sure an ambulance came for Cash. Did you know one of those Pollibos shot my friend from the Park?"

"Oh, I'm sorry. I heard a shot but didn't know what happened," said Wes.

"Cash is that guy at church, right? Well, looks like trying to be good didn't exactly pay off for him," said Lionel.

"PapaLi!" said Ima, shocked.

"I'm kidding, just trying to lighten the mood. We all need a good laugh."

"It's not at all funny that he took a bullet for you," declared Ima.

"You're right. I meant no harm. I'm sorry, Eema. The man probably saved my life."

Cash and Carry

Concurrent to Ima and Sam going to check out the wine cellar and the *ensuing* alley scene behind the Friars Club, Riina sat at the front desk feeling antsy and a bit left out of the action. Wondering what to do to help, she decided to look for a policeman, perhaps even find Officer Onfoot on his regular beat nearby. It would be easier to explain this suspicious ordeal to a familiar, if not friendly face!

Around the corner from the Friars, Riina *serendipitously* saw Onfoot standing by the manhole in which she and Ima had previously hid. She began to flirt shamelessly, focusing her acting talent and persuasive powers to convince him to radio his precinct.

"Officer Onfoot, I'm so happy to find you on duty. Would you please follow me to the wine cellar of the Friars?" she pleaded in earnest.

"Why?" he asked, cocking his head and staring at Riina in her *stereotypical* reporter's garb. "I take orders from the precinct, not newspapermen."

"But I'm a newspaperwoman and sort of a *damsel in distress* who wants you to prevent a possibly dreadful development down there." She moved closer and patted his chest with her hand.

"Hey, lady, we classify touching an officer as *assault*." He pushed her away and straightened his uniform shirt to regain his dignity. "Back off, or I'll drag you to the precinct."

"Like you did a few days ago?" Riina reminded him.

"What?" he said *querulously.*

"Don't you remember me and my friend crawling out of this same manhole a few days ago?" she said, pointing to the lid by the curb.

"Yes, I remember; but no, I still won't follow you into the Friars' wine cellar. Why do you have such a fascination for deep places?" asked the officer.

"Because they hold danger and dark secrets," said Riina.

"I've had my *quota* of danger for the day."

"Oh, please, Officer Onfoot, I promise if you follow me, it may make you a hero."

Reluctantly, Onfoot *acquiesced,* "This better not be a wild goose chase!"

Riina and Onfoot walked in the Friars' front door and almost collided with Sam who was yelling, "Someone's been shot. Get the police. Get the police."

"I am the police, sir," said Onfoot.

"Someone has been shot out in the back alley. Go through the kitchen and down to the wine cellar," he said pointing franticly to the elevator. "I've got to call for an ambulance."

When Officer Onfoot and Riina descended into the Friars wine cellar, they did not find Ima. But after ascending the backstairs to the alley, they did see Cash bleeding *profusely,* almost unconscious.

"Don't fret, Cash. An ambulance will be here pronto. Just rest," Riina said.

"Ima's cab caught up with those creeps who shot Cash," reported Dollar, just running up. "I don't know where they're headed in their Black Caddy, but I could see her cabby driving like a Manhattan maniac to keep up with it."

"Okay guys," said Riina. "Here's what we're gonna do before anything else. Since Ima's not here, I can tell you she's gone really big on this praying jazz. So guys, bow your heads and let's give it our best shot and ask God that she doesn't get herself shot and that Cash, who actually was shot, will recover without having to get too many shots at the hospital where they give lots of shots. So, amen." Riina prayed with her eyes open, used her regular, feisty *palaver*, and waved her hands to make each point. "Oh, by the way, even though I'm Jewish, Ima always ends her prayer in Jesus' name. So, this time, so do I. Amen"

Within five minutes, a squad of policeman had arrived; and an ambulance waited at the head of the alley. The EMT team rushed to the dumpster scene on foot. The medics eased Cash onto a stretcher, carried him to the street, and loaded him onto the vehicle. Riina and Dollar insisted on going along. The rest of the crew waved them off.

• • •

"Where are you taking him?" Riina asked.

"From the look of his clothes, I'd say he's *destitute*. We'll take him to the emergency room at Bellevue. Let them sort it out," said the EMT in charge.

"But sir, if you take him to a charity hospital, you'd be making a big mistake," said Dollar, the new-man-in-charge. "Old Cash Underground did not get his name from his parents but from his reputation. He and his father owned the contracting firm that built most of the sewers of New York. The man's *rolling in dough like Rockefeller!*"

"What? You've got to be kidding," remarked Riina. "Why does he hang around all of you-you-you...men of leisure?"

Dollar laughed heartily. "You mean us bums? It's plain and simple! He lives in a luxury condominium across from the park but just enjoys our company."

"Well then driver, take this man to the Waldorf-Astoria and have the doctor make a house call over there!" quipped Riina.

"No miss, we must follow regular procedures until we can check his insurance coverage," said the EMT.

· · ·

Ima said goodbye to PapaLi and Uncle Wes and caught a cab back to the Friars Club. Just as she arrived, the clock struck eleven. As Sam punched out his timecard, he pointed her to Nelson, the night man now punching in.

"Were you the one on duty early this morning?" inquired Ima.

"Yes, who wants to know?" Nelson said *testily*.

"My name is Ímagine Purple, and I'm collecting witnesses in a case involving my father Lionel Longwind. Can you tell me what happened to him in the marathon poker game? Did you see or overhear anything unusual in the card room? Did anyone knock him about?"

"Look, young lady. The Club tells employees to keep their eyes and ears on service. We don't gossip about members' business," remarked Nelson.

"Just like the *three little monkeys* who hear and see and speak no evil?" she said.

"That's how we do it," said Nelson.

" Well, that may sound like the loyal thing to do under normal conditions," Ima said pointedly, "But—"

"Look young lady, important people played here last night. Stakes ran high and so did feelings. Truthfully, only one thing mattered to me about the poker marathon. The winners promised to donate a large percent of the proceeds to the actors' pension fund. I don't care who won last night because everyone here will benefit somehow, members and employees. Don't you see?" Nelson iterated.

"Did the Pollibo twins tell you to say that neat little speech? Did they buy you off so you wouldn't give evidence against them?" Ima boldly inquired.

"I don't know any members named Pollibo," he said *callously*.

"You mean to tell me that your job kept you so busy you never saw two men switching places during the night? You never thought to call the police on them?" Ima *goaded* the night man to make him confess.

Beleaguered and off guard, Nelson asked, "What exactly do you want, Miss? I'd like to help, but—"

"But what...someone *strong-armed* you or offered you a nice cash incentive?"

"Are you saying I took a bribe?" asked Nelson.

"I'm saying you've *clammed up*."

"Well, you can't just come in here and start accusing loyal employees. You have no right," Nelson said *officiously*.

"When someone kidnaps my father from this Club, you can bet I've got a right to find out what happened. And so far, I'd say the employees around here either neglected their duties or got bought off," declared Ima. "Now are you going to be *forthcoming* or not?"

"Miss, you're asking me to risk my job and my neck," Nelson said sheepishly.

"Look, did you or did you not tell Sam you'd speak to me but only in person. Well, here I am...in the flesh with notebook in hand, all set for any details that could *nail the coffin shut* on those goons."

"Okay. I can tell you that those are normally pretty good guys, a little rough around the edges. But they're *natty* dressers. You gotta give 'em that," Nelson declared.

"Actually, I don't 'gotta give 'em' anything. Right now they're down at the precinct getting themselves fingerprinted and sized for striped uniforms. I hope that fashion stays in their wardrobe forever," Ima said rather sharply. She had let herself get too tired.

That usually caused her to get *exasperated* or make mistakes. She needed to hush before *going overboard* and regretting her words.

Still standing close by, Sam signaled Ima to come over. "You're barking up a dead tree. Nelson has *clammed up* because he is also in deep to the Pollibos, same as half the staff here. Right now, I think it's more critical that you go to the hospital to check on that man who got shot."

"Oh, of course, I almost forgot about Cash. How is he? Which hospital?" asked Ima.

"From the looks of him and his friends, I'd say Bellevue for charity cases," Sam said, sadden by how events had turned.

"Of course, you're right, thanks," she said and ran to hail a cab.

• • •

Within ten minutes, Ima stood at the Bellevue admissions desk. The clerk sent her to the ICU where she learned that Cash had gone into surgery. She went to the visitor's area to wait for more information. When she saw Dollar and Riina already there, she felt relieved. At least Cash had had familiar faces with him during this horrible ordeal.

While waiting, the friends watched television to see if the midnight news might mention the capture of the Pollibos or the shooting of Cash. They heard nothing. All the networks rallied around one headline: Tomorrow's Moon Walk.

Reports of the spaceship reaching its destination jammed the airwaves. The crew now encircled the moon and the walk remained on schedule. National excitement had reached a fever pitch.

• • •

Without explanation, Ima left the ICU in haste. Ima caught a taxi home, walked in, and unplugged the portable television set. Lionel lay dozing on the couch and suddenly woke with a start.

"Hey, where are you going with my TV?" he asked.

"To the hospital so Cash can watch the Moon Walk tomorrow."

"Well, how about me? If I'm going to play an astronaut, don't I need to watch all this backup material before the walk?" inquired Lionel

"Maybe you can catch it at Teresa's apartment," Ima suggested.

"I had hoped after my ordeal, she would come here. Must you take the TV right now?"

"Yes, because I want Cash to have it when he wakes up from surgery," retorted Ima.

"But what about my character background study tonight?" asked Lionel.

"PapaLi, don't you think it will do your own character a world of good to remember that Old Cash just took a bullet trying to save you? We owe him. It's our time to do something nice for him?"

"You're right. After being tied up all night, I'm not thinking very straight. So, do you think Cash will pull through all right?" said Lionel, now looking a bit embarrassed.

"I'll leave the *prognosis* to the doctors. All I want is...when Cash comes out of recovery and gets taken to a ward, well... well...you know...charity wards aren't like private rooms," said Ima emotionally.

"Can't say that I do know," said Lionel.

"PapaLi, charity wards don't have the luxury of a TV," she said angrily. "There's one in the lobby, but it'll be days before Cash will feel like going there. So, I don't want him to miss one moment of this historical event! Understand? He needs something good to happen in his life after giving so much for our sakes!"

"Boy, are you mad!" said Lionel.

"Yes, you can bet I am! No, I take that back," she corrected herself. "Please don't bet on it or anything else ever. Betting caused this whole problem in the first place. Look, you'd be mad at me if this were reversed. What if I had let my finances *flounder* and lost money I couldn't afford to lose?"

"You'd never do that. You're as *frugal* as your mother," he said.

Ima choked back some tears. "Look PapaLi, I'm overjoyed that you and Wes weren't hurt more than you were. But as for the rest of your shenanigans, I'm shocked at you. You may be my famous father; but frankly, I expect better things from you!" She broke down uncontrollably.

Lionel stood up and put his arms around her. "Eema, please forgive me. I feel awful about what I've done. I've disappointed you more than I ever thought possible. I'm going to change, starting here and now."

"Well, you better. I'm your family, and I have to love you. But Teresa may come to her senses and change her mind," Ima surprised herself by speaking so forcefully to her father. "And now," her words sounded like dialogue from a play, "please, excuse me! I have a taxi waiting." Grabbing the portable TV, Ima headed down the elevator.

• • •

Riina and Dollar were still *keeping vigil* for Cash when Ima returned. They repeated what the doctor had told them. It seemed that Cash had no complications after his surgery but still required monitoring for a few days.

"So, what's the TV for?" asked Riina.

"For tomorrow's Moon Walk. I didn't want Cash to miss a moment of the big day."

Riina looked at Dollar and started laughing hysterically. "You brought a TV from home when one sits right in front of our noses?"

"Why is that so funny? He might not feel well enough to come out here, but he certainly deserves to see history in the making" explained Ima.

"Well, that's very sweet and considerate of you. I know it will touch Cash deeply," said Dollar winking at Riina.

Ima did not understand why each looked like the *cat who ate the canary*.

• • •

About 8 o'clock the next morning, orderlies rolled Cash from the recovery room to a ward. They told his friends he could receive visitors after his bath. So while waiting, Ima called Marsha at AAH and asked her to monitor the calls at the office.

"Wes is probably exhausted after his ordeal. I'll be in the office shortly. But for now, I'm at the hospital."

"Good, you finally found which hospital admitted Lionel," said Marsha.

"No, PapaLi is fine. I'm here for a friend who tried to protect Lionel and Wes but instead got shot himself behind the Friars Club last night."

"Protecting Lionel and Wes? Got shot behind Friars? What a story! That's more excitement than that place has had in years," said Marsha.

"It's a long tale. Tonight's paper will probably have all the details. Thankfully, everyone is fine, much to your help," remarked Ima. "I'll call you when I'm back at the office. Bye."

• • •

After the nurses bathed Cash and put him in a fresh hospital gown, they said he could receive visitors. He looked quite surprised and delighted when three tired faces poked their noses in to say "Hi."

"What's all this, a welcoming party or buzzards hoping for a corpse?" he said weakly but with a smile.

"Cash, you're such a crazy old man," said Dollar.

They all laughed. Riina hugged Cash. Dollar shook his hand, and Ima set the TV up on his portable table at the foot of his bed.

"So, how do you feel?" Ima inquired as she then gave a hug too.

Cash looked at the TV curiously and then at Dollar who shrugged his shoulders, "Like I said, I'll live. I'm just mad those gangsters got away."

"You can believe me they got stopped in royal style. Thanks to Dollar smashing their Cadillac's windshield and tracking the car in traffic, I could follow them to the 46th Theatre where they eventually got arrested."

"So, they're going off for a long time?" Cash asked.

"They will if justice is served and I have anything to say about it," said Ima.

Riina chimed in, "Here's hoping the judge *sets bail* so high that those hoods must do chin-ups to earn every dollar."

"No. Higher than that! As high as the moon so no one has enough money to get them out before the trial," said Ima.

"Glad to hear it. And now tell me the story behind this television set?" Cash asked, amazingly *coherent* after his bad experience.

Ima beamed as she spoke, "Well, there's one good thing about your not having to sleep in the Park tonight. Since you're in the hospital and the wards don't usually provide individual TV sets, I wanted you to be able to see the historical Moon Walk this evening."

Old Cash just sat there overwhelmed, cocking his head curiously. "Why, Missy, that's a mighty nice gesture you've made, but—"

"Well, just enjoy it! And now, I must go to work."

"Disguised like Lois Lane?" asked Riina.

"I guess so," Ima hugged the old man again. "Now mind the nurses. I'll check on you later," she said before dashing away.

"But I won't be here," he called out to her, but the door had already shut.

Goons Around Town and Men on the Moon

Maria Mobley sent her lawyer to represent the Pollibo twins. Val and Sal Pollibo both pleaded "not guilty" at the 10 o'clock *arraignment*. Since they had serious multiple charges against them, the judge set bail at $50,000 each. Maria had a beauty appointment and arrived a little late to the courthouse. She paid the required ten percent of bail and promised to keep an eye on her brothers until their trial.

On the way home, she fussed at them. "Boys, does this have anything to do with that project down in my cellar?"

"Don't get your hair all frizzy," said Val.

"That's the least of my worries. Do you want New York society to *blackball* me? I may never get my picture in the paper again." lamented Maria.

"Ah, cool your toes, Maria," said Val. "This bum rap will never stick, and the police know it."

"You got that right," said Sal. "What they really want to do is charge us with *bookmaking*. But that'll never stick either. The police are so stupid to keep sending undercover men to *entrap* us at P.J.'s. Those guys *stick out like sore thumbs* and might as well have 'fake' written on their foreheads."

"Well, I'm warning you two. Stop all your shenanigans for at least a while. Remember when you *sully* your reputations, you tarnish mine as well. Some day one of your regulars will get fed up and turn you in," Maria predicted.

"Not a chance," said Val. "The guys doing business with us won't squeal because they have their own reputations to worry about. Besides, most of them are in deep...really deep. We've got a *failsafe system*. The police can't keep us locked up, and our regulars stay too hooked or scared to squeal."

"And anyone who does, well, let's just say, I wouldn't want to be in his bed that night!" Sal warned, without emotion.

When the car pulled in front of the Mobley Mansion, Val nudged his sister out and said, "Give me your gun. They confiscated ours as evidence."

Maria *complied*, pulling from her handbag a jeweled pistol. "Handle this with care. It's the last treasured gift Papa gave me."

"See you later, Sis. We've got business to tend to," Sal said in a flat tone.

• • •

Obviously having just awaken, Wes met Ima at the door when she arrived for work. He stood there in his bathrobe, holding a coffee cup in his hand and looking like *death warmed over*.

"Oh, Uncle Wes. I'm glad the nightmare is over for you and PapaLi."

"Me too, sweetheart. After all that has happened, I'm surprised you even came in today," he said.

"I wouldn't have, but I got so little work done yesterday. Besides, since all bets and debts are off with the Pollibos, I wanted to mail those client checks," she surmised.

"By the way, if Shelton calls, tell him to come in to discuss his future. No excuses accepted. It's a *command performance*," Wes said.

Ima called Marsha at the answering service to say she'd take over the calls now. Then, as soon as Wes went to his room to take a shower, she heard loud banging on the inner hall door and came from behind her desk to answer the door.

The Pollibos simply brushed past her and headed to the back bedroom but returned quickly.

"Where's Mr. Westerly?" Val asked gruffly.

"He's unavailable at the moment. And how did you get in our front door?" she said, trying to disguise that she shook like a leaf.

"I find ringing doorbells wastes my time. I can open any door with my nifty key tool," said Val holding up his key kit.

"I think it would be best to call later and set an appointment," she spoke words which sounded unconvincing, even to her.

No thanks. We'll wait right here. And tell your boss that we're here to collect the dough he owes," said Sal.

"Well, then may I get you some coffee or tea?" she said but thought...or *arsenic?*

Both men mumbled "coffee," so she went downstairs to fix a pot. While it perked, she picked up Line #1 and dialed Line #2. It started ringing. She figured the Pollibos would not suspect anything unusual in that. After all, this was an office; and offices normally received many calls during a workday.

Usually when super busy, Wes and Ima let Marsha field calls. She hoped that Marsha would leave it alone and that Wes would realize that this time no one intended to catch the phone. Surely the *incessant* ringing would make him react. She had gotten his clues and now hoped he would get hers, yet without making the Pollibos suspicious.

She put both lines on hold so that they kept blinking. Whichever light went to steady first, she would quickly press the other button. Closing her eyes, she asked quietly for peace to do the right thing. Then, one blinking light went to solid. She pressed the other. Wes answered. "Westerly Agency."

"Wes, it's Ima," she whispered. "The Pollibos are sitting up in the office. I wanted you prepared for whatever."

"Okay. Keep them occupied. I'll finish dressing and come in shortly," he said.

To look normal, Ima put her line on hold to indicate an on-going call that needed her attention. With that *tactic* in place, Ima carried a tray up to the office, poured cups of hot coffee for the two thugs, and resisted the temptation to dump it in their laps rather than serve it. Instead, after *cordially* offering them sugar and cream, she returned to her desk and pretended to call the answering service on the other line.

"Hi, Marsha, did y'all catch that call? I had busy hands, and I think Wes may have taken his phone off the hook while he showered. You know how he hates us to miss any calls." Ima *feigned* listening and wrote down a phony message. "Thanks, bye." She looked up and saw the two men thumbing through issues of *Variety Magazine*. Her little *feint* had worked.

Ostensibly looking for business, she called Tinker & Partners, mostly because she loved to hear the operator say that company's name. It always made her smile. She asked for an account rep and acted normal about everything. When Wes walked in, she felt relief.

"Good morning gentlemen. I'm surprised to see you out and about so early this fine morning," he said in an upbeat tone, pulling on his years of acting.

"We came for our money," said Val, flashing Maria's small pistol.

"What for...to pay your bail?" Wes replied with a bit of sarcasm.

"That's done; so don't talk smart. Just give us our money, or we'll tie you up again." Sal retorted equally *sardonically*.

"This time we'll put you where no one can guess," Val remarked.

"Look guys, after three days out of the office, I have more pressing matters than gambling debts," intoned Wes.

"Well, nothing's more pressing to us than our money," Sal said.

"Yeah, and no one *stiffs* the Pollibos and lives to talk about it," said Val.

"So, *fork over the dough*; or your assistant will take a ride farther than her father did," Sal warned.

"Hmmm, I wonder how much he'd pay to get her back?" Val asked.

"Or to prevent seeing her carrot-haired head on a *charger* like John the Baptist in *Salome*," declared Sal, obviously proud that he had *upped the ante* of threats.

"Yeah, like that opera Maria took us to as kids!" said Val, looking proud that he could remember that long ago.

Sal's threat had gotten the proper effect. Both Wes and Ima stood there, horrified by the *prospect* Sal had just suggested. Ima wondered how these hoodlums could possibly think about opera at a time like this or even knew about it.

"Uncle Wes, I have $8,000 in traveler's checks in my purse," Ima offered.

"No, Ima, that's your trip money. You need it," Wes advised.

"I can cancel my trip," Ima said to Wes and then turned to the Pollibos. "Would you take that as a down payment, and I'll get the rest somehow?"

"I'll take it, but we will all go to Wes's bank for the remainder," said Sal.

"No. She stays here! Only I'll go with you," Wes said firmly and then turned to Ima. "Ima, write me out a $3,000 check on the business account and hold back some client checks. I think my banker knows me well enough to make a loan on the rest."

"Oh, please, Uncle Wes, don't borrow anymore money," Ima implored. "Use my travel checks now. We can figure this out later."

Then with checks in hand, the Pollibos followed Wes out the door. That provided Ima with a short *reprieve*. Intuitively she knew that after the Pollibos got the money from Wes, they'd head for the Amherst, muscle past Arnie and go straight up to the Lionel's apartment. Taking no chances of that, she dialed home. Lionel answered.

"PapaLi, just listen. The Pollibos got out on bail and have taken Wes to his bank to get cash. I know they'll come for you next. You must leave and hide somewhere safe. You need money to get out of town or to pay them...whichever works. I don't know how much you lost recently in the *stock* market, but call Teresa and ask her to sell some securities right now. All of them if you have to! You must be ready to leave New York if necessary. I'm going back to the hospital to check on Cash, and then we can make more plans. Call me at Bellevue if you need to and please be careful. Forgive me for fussing so at you last night. This whole thing is totally out of control."

· · ·

Teresa felt shock at Lionel's summary of his encounter with the Pollibos. She regretted that *1776* had released him from his contract but simply got angry at his request for her to sell $20,000 of his investments.

"You mean you lost that much in a friendly poker game? What kind of friends let you bet so recklessly?" exclaimed Teresa.

"One like Shelton Grape?" replied Lionel.

"What nerve lies behind his false face! He even called me yesterday to say that you were *indisposed* and asked if I planned to stay engaged to you."

"And-and-and, do you?" asked Lionel, afraid to hear the answer.

"I'm mad at you, Lionel, not out of love with you. Why didn't you call to say you were in deep with those guys? I could have helped avoid this crisis."

"No one needed to know. I expected to win back the money. As it turned out, Shelton's word indisposed, served as a *euphemism* for my being bound, gagged and blindfolded with a gun to my head. I don't deserve sympathy. I just wanted to explain it to you," said Lionel reiterating his points.

"At least your sweet Ima called me yesterday to say she planned to help your budget by making more home-cooked meals. She even invited me to dinner but never called me back to say when. It's funny she never mentioned a word about all this."

"She probably didn't know anything yet," he surmised

"It baffles me that anyone would strip his savings over a few nights of cards," Teresa declared in exasperation.

"Eema is as furious with me as you. You both have every right to ask a million questions. I've made a mess of things with my regular bills but never dreamed I'd end up *beholden* to gangsters."

"You're right. You were only dreaming...and not thinking, at all!" she said in tears, venting at the man she had agreed to marry. "What about our future?"

"Oh Teresa, please forgive me. I'll make amends somehow. But for now, will you just do as I asked and leave your anger until later? Ima just called to say the goons have taken Wes to his bank. Most likely their next stop is here. They aim to collect their debt from me one way or another. So, please, I must pay up or flee."

"Okay. Go to my apartment. I'll call the doorman to let you in. I'll meet you there at around 2:00 o'clock. If you change your plans, leave a message with him and at my office so I can find you."

"Does that give you enough time to get some *stocks* sold?" Lionel inquired.

"Yes, even if I have to hold onto them myself. Look, I have to hang up and get busy." She hesitated, "I do love you, Lionel; but Ima was right. You haven't a clue about money."

Teresa hung up and sat for a moment, gripped with anger and heartbreak. When her anger subsided, a quiet wisdom calmed her and gave her a new insight. Maybe Lionel had to learn this lesson in front of everyone he loved. She had worked with all types of investors. She knew how *seductive* quick money sounded and how *vulnerable* people fell for that lie. Her secretary interrupted her thoughts, saying a rather insistent man was on the phone.

"Take a message. I just had a huge project plopped on my desk."

"But it's Shelton Grape, you know, the 'Crossword Puzzle' announcer," she said, obviously impressed with that tag. "He seems very anxious to talk to you."

"Well, I'm not anxious to talk to him. Just say I can't be disturbed."

· · ·

Lionel packed a few clothes and buzzed Arnie to arrange a taxi pick-up down in the garage. Once in the cab, Lionel felt tempted to tell the driver to head for an airport...to Newark, Kennedy, LaGuardia...any airport to catch any plane to go anywhere. It didn't matter. He simply needed to escape the scene! Yet he quickly confessed to himself that such an irresponsible thought would only *compound* his recent reckless behavior. How could he so easily consider throwing away everything he once held dear: his sanity, sanctity, and stability? He knew why...because he had been just like those people Teresa had described...those who *got suckered-in* by the fast money lie. His naiveté had gotten him in deep with people who held no regard for decency.

"Where to, mister? The meter's running." the cabby said abruptly.

Lionel came to his senses and told the driver Teresa's address. In no time he felt safely *secreted* inside her apartment. After a quick shower and shave, he flopped on the sofa to watch TV. Fortunately, tonight's moon walk topped every network's coverage. Lionel simply decided to watch current history unfold and stay calm until Teresa arrived.

· · ·

Ima grabbed her valise and tried to hail a taxi outside Wes's office. Finally, she walked quickly to Second Avenue to catch a downtown bus to Bellevue. Arriving, she returned to the ward where Cash had been that morning but soon learned of his transfer to Sloan Kettering Hospital. Good grief, she thought, they sent him to the monkey place?

She hopped an uptown bus on First Avenue to East 66th Street and then walked over to York Avenue. Upon entering the attractive lobby of this big research hospital, she puzzled over how the *impoverished* Cash could end up here. Maybe something had gone wrong this morning? Had they found something serious that required a consultant?

The receptionist gave her Cash's room number. Tiptoeing in, Ima could not believe her eyes. Cash lay resting quietly in a private room that had a big TV hanging on the wall. Hers sat on a chair. What was going on?

Cash stirred and opened his eyes. "Well, there she is, Miss Lending Library or should I say Miss TV-On-Loan," he said, with his eyes twinkling.

"Are you okay? I mean why did they move you here? Do you have to see some high-powered specialist for a gunshot wound?" asked Ima.

"No, I'm fine. It's just closer to the park so my friends can visit me."

"And here, you get a big room with a big TV? I can't believe it." Ima said, feeling a bit foolish.

"No Missy, what you did, showed me who you really are. You did one of the most caring things ever done for me. I'll love you forever for it. I ought to put you in my will." Cash laughed, reaching to pat her shoulder.

"Like PapaLi's will?" Ima said, tittering. "I told him not to lose my whole inheritance in a card game, but it looks like he did." Still not understanding, she remained a bit embarrassed. "I expect him to join your crew at the Park any day now."

"Ima, your dad's been through a lot lately. He needs your love and forgiveness," Cash said with wise tenderness. "By the way, without your own TV, have you heard any of the build-up for the Moon Walk tonight?"

"No, you might say I've been otherwise engaged," she said, kidding him.

"Do you want to stay here and watch it with me?" asked Cash.

"Thanks. I'd love to, but I only came by to say hello," she said.

"Just think, by tomorrow, every school kid on the globe will have two new heroes. I mean, absolutely everyone will know the names of Neil Armstrong and Buzz Aldrin, our super spacemen," said Cash, seeming quite animated.

"I'll have to catch up on it later. Right now, I've got my hands full," said Ima, scrunching her face. Her teasing manner had turned into bewilderment.

"Tell Old Cash about it. What's got you so worried now?"

"I only told you half the story about what happened after you were shot, but some other things you still don't know. I followed the culprits to the theatre where Lionel rehearses."

"I remember, you said Dollar saved the day. He's a good man," said Cash.

"But there's more. See, the Pollibos intended not only to hold Lionel hostage for money that he lost in the poker game, but also to get a ransom paid by the producers of the play Lionel's in. However, the production manager *foiled* their plan by releasing Lionel from his contract. That shocked the Pollibos...no, that humiliated them so much they didn't even resist when the police came and took them away."

"So, there. The bad guys are in jail. It's all over," declared Cash.

"Not quite. They're free again!" she revealed.

"How's that possible?" asked Cash.

"The Pollibos made bail and came to Wes' office this morning."

Cash shook his head. "Determined to get their money, aren't they?"

"Yes, they even said they'd cut off my head like John the Baptist if Wes and PapaLi don't pay what they owe," Ima whispered, laying her head on the bedside and weeping.

"What a *despicable* thing to say to a pretty face like yours. Believe me, they only said it to terrorize you...to make you give them what they want," Cash iterated.

"You're right. I gave them $8,000...in travelers checks."

"Of your own money?" Cash inquired.

Ima nodded. "I thought it would satisfy them until payments from our clients' jobs came in. They took it but forced Wes to go to his bank...for still more. Now, I'm almost sure they're headed to Lionel's apartment by now."

"How much does he owe?" asked Cash.

"I never knew. No one said. I think about $18,000. Some friendly card game, huh! Who needs friends like that!" Ima lamented.

"Like you said yesterday, your big star father was their *cash cow*."

The old man got very quiet, but then his face *flushed*. "Well, there are some things you don't know as well. Do you recall how speechless I was over the TV you brought last night?"

"I was happy to do that. I figured you needed it."

"Yes I did, but not in the way you think. You see, Missy, my name's Old Cash for a definite reason. I'm sort of a *cash cow* myself. I have plenty of it. I've saved almost every dime I have ever made. I am what you call *well-heeled* and can afford any hospital in town. When the EMTs took me to Bellevue I hated to sound uppity and demanding. Anyway, I have another ailment; so, Bellevue contacted my regular doctor who wanted me moved to Kettering. So here I am."

"Then I don't understand why you pretend to be poor," said Ima puzzled.

He could see his news had scared her. "I just wanted people to get to know me, not my money. Look, Dollar told Riina last night, but they kept it secret from you because they thought this should come from me."

"Cash, I'm so glad you're not poor like I thought. It makes me happy that you can have whatever you need or want," remarked Ima.

"Well, there is something I want," Cash said, slowly and deliberately.

"Just name it. I'll try to get it for you," declared Ima.

"Not for me, for you! I want you and Lionel to *get out of Dodge* immediately," Cash *sagaciously* advised.

"I know what you say is wise, but if I think I can strike a deal with—"

"Strike a deal...with *card sharks* and kidnappers? Do you want to believe if you find the money and pay them off, all this will blow away?" asked Cash.

"But their family knows about opera, so they're not totally uncivilized or unreasonable."

"Oh, Ima, being reasonable is not how these hoodlums work. They come from a mean family and do mean things whenever they want."

"Well, if they hurt people, how to they get away scot-free?" asked Ima.

"Because, when Pollibos get convicted for a crime, they don't stay in prison long."

"How's that possible?" asked Ima naïvely.

"They have a few city *officials in their pockets.* And to make it worse, some official will simply tell some clerk to *expunge* all the crimes from those goons' file.

"Oh Cash, no. If supposedly good guys...are on the bad guys' side, that means the whole city may have grown corrupt," surmised Ima.

"Exactly. That's why I want you to leave town now. Don't stop to look over your shoulder. Just go," Cash said, as if giving orders to Dollar and the crew.

"It's a nice idea to think about leaving; but if Lionel and I pooled all our nickels right now, we couldn't afford a subway ride to Grand Central Station," she admitted.

"What I mean is I'll give you the money to leave town if you'll go now, today, tonight, tomorrow at the latest. I'm not asking you. I'm almost demanding it," he said.

"We can't let you do that, Cash. You need your money for your old age."

"It's my pleasure. You've brought life and love back to this old soul. I don't have to wait to die for my money to do some good for folks."

"But where would we go?" asked Ima.

"Get on the first plane leaving and go as far as it takes you," Cash advised.

"Strange. I started my adventures with that philosophy!"

"Well, good! Let my gift carry you from this adventure to a better one."

"Thanks Cash. You've become like another godfather to me," she said.

"Now, listen to me carefully. Don't go home for clothes or anything. Go directly to Riina. I'm sure her family won't mind. Give me her number. I'll ask my financial advisor to make things ready ASAP."

Get Out of Dodge

Cash picked up the phone and dialed his financial advisor, "Teresa, this is Cash Underground, I mean Caleb Underwood. Do you think you can sell some *stock* for me and have the money ready by four o'clock?"

"I can't believe you're asking that. I'm doing the same thing right now for someone else. Has America undergone an attack, and no one told me?"

"No, I need $30,000 in cash for two friends in desperate *straits*."

"Okay, let me think. I'll put in a *sell-order* now and bring papers by as soon as possible. I have an outside appointment at two, but I'll do my best to meet your schedule," she said, shaking her head at the work ahead. Teresa did not act or feel at all *serene* this afternoon. Two difficult requests had interrupted her normal composure.

"Oh, by the way, I'm not at home. Just call me at Sloan-Kettering Hospital."

"At Kettering? Are you okay?" asked Teresa with concern in her voice.

"I'm fine, and I'll be even better if you can do this for me, pronto." After he gave her his room number and Riina's phone number, they said good-bye.

The Pollibos dropped Wes back at his office and headed up First Avenue to the Amherst. Left temporarily *off the hook*, Wes called to warn Lionel but got no answer. He hoped Ima had called her father to inform him of this new development. Searching Ima's desk for a note to that effect but finding none, he grew worried and began to grab at straws. He called Riina, hoping that maybe Ima had checked in with her.

"Hi Wes, what's up? Is my public *clamoring* to see more of me?" said Riina trying to act flippant.

"Not yet! I just called to see if you knew where Lionel or Ima might be?" asked Wes.

Actually, Ima stood right in front of Riina's nose. Realizing Wes was on the line, she quickly held her finger over her lips which meant *mum's the word*.

Since Riina now knew half the plan and was helping Ima pack clothes, they had made already a *pact* with Cash to wait to hear from him for the next step.

"Nope, can't say that I do," Riina replied in her usual manner but *divulged* no details.

"Well then, you need to know that the Pollibos made bail and are looking for her and Lionel." Wes sounded sad.

"I can't believe a judge let those crooks out of jail," she *feigned* complaint. "It sounds like they know more important people than their silly sister does!"

"Maybe so! Anyway, do you have any idea where Ima or Lionel might go?"

Riina feared to say very much in case the Pollibos were again feeding him the questions to *extract* information, as done once before. She *begged off*. "No, but I sure will let you know if I learn anything."

"Oh, by the way, Riina, I saw the Smooth-On contract. It looks like a fair deal. I see no reason to bargain. Okay, talk to you later," said Wes.

"Thanks for keeping me a secret," said Ima.

"Absolutely, the Pollibos seem *ubiquitous*. There's no telling where they'll pop up again. I won't feel relief until you're on the road," said Riina.

"Can you believe Cash wants to give us money and send us out of town?"

"Dollar told me about Old Cash's stash. How I'd love to go also," said Riina, doing her *Garbo pose*, now a *stock* gesture. "But alas, I must stay here. Such is the life of the new spokeswoman for Smooth-On Soaps," Riina bragged.

Ima yelped. "Wes approved the contract?"

Rinna nodded. "Yes, just now on the phone! At last I'm a well-paid, employed actress."

"Wouldn't our old drama coach drop his jaw if he knew?"

"He'd probably pass out," Riina began to *preen* and strut about the room.

"I say *gloat* all you like. I'm *pleased as Punch* for you," declared Ima.

"You won't believe the script of the first spot. There will be suds all over a sliding board. I'm wearing white duck pants with dirt on my bottom. The camera pans in on the stains as I climb up the ladder. Then I slide down, bound off, look directly into the camera and say, 'And you thought washboards went out of style with log cabins. I 'm here to tell you that Smooth-On Soap will scrub out any grime your kids can get on their clothes," iterated Riina as she performed the commercial for Ima.

"Sounds great!" Ima said but then stopped abruptly. "Oops, I forgot to call Teresa to cancel any sell-order of PapaLi's *stock*." Ima quickly called E.F. Hutton and asked for Teresa.

"She's busy. May I take a message," said Teresa's very protective secretary.

"No, it's vital I speak directly to her. Tell her it's her fiancé's daughter." Ima thought the title sounded *pretentious*, but the *ploy* worked. The secretary put her through.

"What's the crisis now? I'm up to my chin in crocodiles. Can this wait?" asked Teresa.

"No. Did Lionel ask you to sell stock for him today?"

"Yes, why?" asked Teresa, sounding puzzled.

"Well, don't. We're going to be okay. A friend wants to give me enough money to pay off the Pollibos and get out of town. So, there's no need for you to continue."

"I usually can catch anything thrown, but a rare coincidence has my head spinning today. By any chance is your friend's name Caleb Underwood...I mean Cash Underground?"

Ima dropped to the floor and then *retrieved* the receiver, stammering, "Yes-Yes-Yes. How did you know?"

"He's also my client," Teresa said. "No one's supposed to know he's wealthy. This is all too crazy to explain right now. Where are you?"

"At Riina's near 65th and Madison. Can you bring Lionel and the money over here as soon as possible?" asked Ima.

Riina jumped up and down and whispered. "Don't give out my address. The Pollibos may *get wind of it*. Give her somewhere more general."

"Like what: General Delivery 'The Sidewalks of New York' somewhere off Madison Avenue " Ima asked *facetiously* but then stopped suddenly with a good idea. "How about the sewers of New York?"

"Great. We've been in them so much lately we ought to join the union," joked Riina.

"Okay, but where in the sewers?" asked Ima.

"Make it where we began the tour; but this time, I'm taking a crowbar to pry the lid," added Riina. "An on-camera spokeswoman needs to have perfect fingernails."

Ima turned back to the phone. "Teresa, we can't chance another phone call. Can you bring Lionel and the money to the south end of the Park across from the Plaza, at four?"

"You mean in the wide-open," said Teresa, *incredulously*.

"Not exactly, but it is safer with lots of people around. I'll be by a manhole," she replied freely, figuring the Pollibos could not tap Teresa's work phone.

· · ·

Meanwhile the Pollibos were *strong-arming* Arnie at the Amherst. Sal poked Maria's small, jeweled pistol into the doorman's ribs. "You don't want to be a hero! Just take us to where Lionel Longwind and his daughter live."

Without a struggle, Arnie *complied*. He took them up in the elevator and without their noticing, he locked the automatic doors open. Then he used his master key to open the Longwind apartment. As soon as the Pollibos entered, Arnie quickly pulled the door closed and locked the deadbolt with his key. That *maneuver* gave him a slight lead even though he could hear someone fumbling with the lock.

As Arnie ran back to the elevator, Sal stepped from the apartment in time to fire a shot at this interfering doorman. Then Val scooted down the hall in time to stick in his arm to prevent the elevator doors from closing completely. Brawny himself, Arnie twisted Val's arm into an awkward position until the gangster *cried uncle* and withdrew his arm.

With the doors shut and the elevator moving steadily to the lobby, Arnie checked a wound on the side of his neck and found it only *superficial*.

· · ·

"Forget him for now," Sal yelled from the apartment door. "Come back in here and help me search for a stash of cash or bonds or jewelry. Surely a famous star like Lionel has some valuables."

Stumbling around, Val happened on some investment papers and saw nice big numbers. "Look what I found."

Sal grabbed them and saw certain figures circled. Then he noticed in the corner of a statement page, the name and phone of Teresa Latimer, financial advisor for E.F. Hutton. He called the number and asked for Lady Latimer. After being told she had *sequestered* herself for an afternoon of work, he called information to get her home number but found it unlisted.

Sal paced the floor. Just then, Boofy strolled from the kitchen hoping someone would feed her. She brushed up against Sal's leg, but he kicked her away which made the cat very mad. She tackled his pants leg with her teeth and claws and tore off a flap of fabric.

Trying to shake Boofy loose, he said "Val, shoot the blasted thing."

Val grabbed at the kitty, trying to coax it to release Sal's leg, "Sal, I might hit your leg. Besides, I can't shoot a poor dumb animal!" Val picked the creature up, petted it, and looked for its food in the refrigerator.

Sal looked through Lionel's personal directory but did not find what he wanted. Then he spoke aloud, "Teresa Latimer. That name Latimer sounds very familiar. Where have I heard it before?"

Val came back in the room, set down a saucer of milk for Boofy, and began to drink from the carton himself. "Aw, I know who that is. It's Shelton Grape's girlfriend."

Sal quickly dialed. When Shelton answered, there was a loud crash as if a lamp had fallen down.

"Shelton Grape here!"

"It's Sal."

"Oh, I was hoping for an audition call about *1776*. Besides, I thought you got arrested and sent to jail?"

"Believe me, if that were true, my first phone would be to my lawyer, not to you."

"So, why did you call me now?" asked Shelton.

"I need Teresa Latimer's home phone," said Sal.

"Why must you involve her in this mishmash?" asked Shelton.

"Don't ask so many questions."

"Look, I'm getting tired of all your intrigues and *strong-arming* and bullying. None of it has helped my career *one iota*."

"Shut up Shel, and just give me her number. You don't need to know everything."

. . .

Lionel heard the phone jingling and figured it was Teresa with more instruction. So he picked it up quickly, "Teresa?"

"No, it's Sal! And I'd recognize your British accent anywhere. So you're hiding out in Teresa's apartment. I've got an operator friend who can cross-referenced any phone or address in town. See ya soon," said Sal, slamming down the receiver.

Lionel sat there in shock, *miffed* at himself for picking up the phone. How did those goons know where he was? His *safe haven* had proved as unsafe as had his own home. Immediately, he ordered another cab to pick him up, this time in Teresa's apartment garage. With that done, he quickly called her office, hoping she had not yet left for their two o'clock appointment.

Unfortunately she had. He could think of no other way to relay the change in plans except to leave a message in case Teresa checked back with her secretary, "Tell her, the Pollibos traced me to her apartment which forces me to go elsewhere. I'll call again when I find a *place to light*."

"Mr. Longwind, I think Mrs. Latimer may have switched your appointment at two with her four o'clock. She mentioned going by Sloan-Kettering Hospital to get a signature from Caleb Underwood who needed paperwork," the secretary related. "If so, she'll be late to meet with you. I'm sorry, but she insisted on risking to do it this way."

"Would you call over there and give this same message to that Mr. Underwood. I absolutely must connect with Teresa. Thanks for whatever you can do," Lionel said, his anxiety now mounting.

He started writing the same message to leave here but had second thoughts. If those goons did come to her apartment, he'd be giving away the plan. That could only endanger other people. No. He would have to trust that Teresa kept in touch with her office.

Having covered all bases, Lionel grabbed his suitcase and dashed downstairs to the basement as fast as he could move. His legs still had some numbness from being tied to a chair the day before. When the cab arrived, Lionel got in and told the driver to circle the block until he decided where to go.

Jan Hus Church advertised itself as an *asylum* for those needing protection, which accurately described his situation. He knew the soup kitchen ended at two, but the building might still be open. After thinking more about it, Lionel changed his mind. The church stood only half a block from the Amherst. So, maybe he should go by Sloan Kettering and try to meet up with Teresa. That might truly confuse the Pollibos if they tried to follow him, yet Lionel hated to risk possible violence around sick people.

Then he thought about Ima's best friend Riina who lived only a few blocks from Teresa. He needed time to think so he told the cabby to continue driving around until he decided on the best place to go. Finally he said, "Go to Madison at 65th Street but watch for anyone following us."

As more and more cars *encased* the cab, Lionel envisioned how traffic could help or hinder Teresa en route. Reaching his destination, he paid the fare but requested the cabby to wait. Lionel looked around *stealthily* before entering the building. The doorman rang the Feingold apartment, announced the guest, and sent Lionel hightailing upstairs.

"Lionel, how did you know to come here?" said Riina, opening the door.

"A long shot is often a good guess! Listen, the Pollibos seem to know my every move. Even though I don't think they've figured out this place yet, I can't stay. I've got a cab waiting. But first I must try one last time to find Teresa and to tell her the plan has changed a second time."

"But PapaLi, it's all set. We've already arranged with Teresa to bring you and the money to the foot of the Park. So, you're just ahead of the plan."

"I hope there's enough money," he said with a worried look.

"Didn't she tell you? My friend Cash Underground is giving us enough to take care of your debts and to leave town for a while."

"Cash Underground?" Lionel repeated excitedly. "Her secretary said Teresa might be going by the hospital to get the signature of a Mr. Underwood. I didn't understand what she meant."

"That's Cash's real name. Let's call him right now."

• • •

Ima rang the hospital and within seconds, her friend picked up.

"Cash Underground here!"

"This is Ima. By any chance has Teresa Latimer been in to see you?"

"Teresa's right here. She just mentioned about needing to confirm with you. I'll put her on," said Cash, feeling sprite from all this activity around him.

"Everything is set here. How about at your end?" asked Teresa.

"Teresa, so glad to hear your reassuring voice. I'm happy to report that we three scattered sheep have assembled; but I won't say where. The Pollibos seem to know Lionel's steps no matter where he goes. So, let's just say the plan at the watering hole is still on. Watch for our heads popping up about 4 o'clock," said Ima, confidently *encoding* the meeting place.

"See you there. Till then, stay safe," said Teresa with a long sigh before hanging up.

Lionel waved, indicating his desire to talk to Teresa; but Ima felt relief that the phone had already gone dead. One more conversation might make Teresa very uneasy or delay the prearranged rendezvous.

"What incredible coincidences...Cash...Teresa...the money... this whole thing," said Lionel in total disbelief.

"Believe me, Mr. Longwind, it's more than coincidences. You see, Ima is on a big prayer jag. So, stop dragging your feet, get on the bandwagon, and expect miracles," declared Riina, opening a few random closets. "And speaking of miracles, I'm going to need one to find LeoPop's crowbar."

With everything set, Lionel grabbed Ima's valise full of Riina's *hand-me-downs*. They all headed to the lobby and then outside to the faithful taxi still waiting.

"Where to now, Mister?" the cabby asked.

Riina answered instead. "To the bottom of the Park and hurry."

The second leg of the trip proved little more than around the corner. Even so, with the long wait and heavy traffic preventing much progress, the total fare with tip ran $20, quite a lot for having gone less than a mile.

The cabby handed Lionel a card and tapped his hat. "Anytime you need special treatment, just call that number,"

When let out across from the Plaza, the group now felt relief. Lionel admitted he would rather take these two young ladies across to the Plaza Hotel than hide in a manhole, but that was not an option. With all their lives currently in jeopardy, he remembered his promise to be more prudent from now on.

Lionel set about prying open the manhole cover with the crowbar. While he sweated, Ima and Riina put the suitcases on the sidewalk and distracted pedestrians by dancing an Estonian polka. A few people asked if they were advertising a folk festival in the Park. The two friends smiled and pointed to the trees, pretending not to understand English.

Soon Ima and Lionel awkwardly descended the manhole. They remained just below the surface, at the top of the ladder. Riina left the cover off and stood just off the curb, beside the hole. She intended to make sure no one accidentally stumbled into it and no car stopped or parked over it. That would block her friends from exiting on time.

Riina glanced at the nearby suitcases and then the street jammed with cabs. Any minute, she expected to see Teresa arriving in one of them. Lionel had described her as the most gorgeous middle-aged lady in Manhattan. Riina figured a dame like that would be easy to spot.

With brains exhausted from scheming and rushing around all day, Lionel and Ima remained down the manhole, silent so as not to draw attention to their strange location. Very soon, they heard brakes, a running motor, and the click of high heels that approached and then stopped.

"Are you Teresa?" asked Riina.

"Yes." Teresa replied. "Are they here?"

Up popped Ima's head like a jack-in-the-box. The two manhole monitors helped her out first.

Lionel quickly climbed out behind. "Well now I have three lovely ladies to take across the street for a cocktail."

"Oh, no, you don't." said Teresa, hugging him and looking up into his eyes. "I've not risked-life-and-limb to move-heaven-and-earth so we could have a party at the Plaza."

"Just kidding! I'm gonna stick to my promise...not my problems. Thank you for everything, darling. I'll call you when we get to...wherever we're going," Lionel said, hugging Teresa.

"Don't thank me. Thank your *benefactor*, Mr. Cash Underground. I've held onto over half of this money in case the Pollibos try to *put the screws* to me. I'll see that your debts get cancelled and your bills get paid. For these services, I expect a country wedding and a honeymoon in England!" Teresa said with no apologies for the tears beginning to fall.

"Good idea. I'd like to go home for a while anyway," he said.

"Perfect, PapaLi. I just read in *Variety* that a revival of *Anything Goes* opens in London this fall. Maybe Wes can arrange an audition for you," said Ima.

"How about you arrange getting your father out of here, right now," said Teresa.

"I am surrounded by incredibly intelligent business women, who still all love me on a summer's afternoon, in spite of what I've put them through."

"Yes! Lionel Longwind remains a charming matinee idol," declared Riina.

"Hey, bud, are you going or staying," called out the cabby that had brought Teresa to the Park. "Someone's got to pay for this meter running."

"Those two are going, and we two are staying," said Teresa.

While everyone hugged everyone else, the driver grabbed the baggage. Then Lionel and Ima crawled in and waved to their friends as the cab pulled away.

Ima saw Teresa and Riina jaywalking across to the Plaza and said, "I'd say that today they both added a new job line to their resumes."

"What, Rescuers of Dumb Animals?" asked Lionel, still acting embarrassed by his behavior that had gotten everyone in this mess in the first place.

"Well, that's one title but more so, they're Real Friends in Time of Need," said Ima.

"Okay Mister, I'm at a light. Which way?" asked the cabby.

"To LaGuardia Airport!" Lionel and Ima said together.

"Which airline?" asked the driver.

"Delta! I want to go to Atlanta," declared Ima. "I have a friend there, and she's in a time of need too."

"We can go to the moon as far as I care," said Lionel. "But, no, I'd settle for anywhere with a big TV screen so I can see every single moment of tonight's Moon Walk! Are you as excited as I am, Eema?"

"I guess so," Ima said, looking at her very complex, uneven, yet delightful father. She had to admit again having never known anyone else with such eternal *exuberance* for life. "It seems that everything must happen in this July of 1969: from the Last Passenger Train Across Newfoundland to the Scary Ferry across Cabot Strait; from the marijuana ring in Maine to a poker game in Manhattan; from a walk on the moon to my next adventure. So far, it's already been quite a month for me," Ima remarked, her voice fading.

"And it's not over yet," added Lionel.

Ima suddenly sat up straight, yelping, "Talk about dumb animals, we forgot Boofy."

"Sorry, darling Eema. We dare not risk returning to the apartment!"

Epilogue: Holding Down the Fort

While the cabdriver fought traffic to the airport, Ima and Lionel sat in the backseat and began to relax from the tension of the last few hours. Upon arriving, they got on the stand-by list for Atlanta and headed for the proper gate area.

Most passengers clustered at one end, watching a television that hung from the ceiling just like at the hospital. After about an hour or so, Lionel left Ima with the TV watchers and stepped to a pay phone to call Teresa.

"Thank you, darling, for remaining true during all my stupid decisions that caused so much difficulty," said Lionel.

"Then you made it safely to the airport? No *clandestine* goons on your trail or no men jumping from luggage conveyors to shoot at you?" Teresa asked, anticipating the worse.

"I'm happy to report we had no followers, goon or otherwise," Lionel added.

"What a relief! Now I have a tale to tell. I just got back home from going to your apartment to pick up bills."

"Oh good. That's one reason I called...if you'd look after—"

"The mess?" Teresa interrupted.

"Well, I did leave in hurry."

"No. Someone made this mess on purpose...had scattered papers everywhere!"

"Why would anyone want to look through my bills?"

"For some reason, those horrid Pollibos forced Arnie to open your door and then shot at him."

"Oh, no, they shot Arnie too. Why?" Lionel despaired at how wide the repercussions had spread from his mistakes. "Please tell me he's okay."

"The bullet only *grazed* his neck. Anyway, he called the police. They staked out the apartment house and captured the Pollibos the minute they came swaggering out the front door."

"Two arrests in two days! I hope this one sticks. But with such guys, there never seems to be enough evidence to convict them," surmised Lionel.

"I'm not so sure this time, Lionel. Your doorman has sharp eyes and identified them right there and then. Even better, he saw the man use a jeweled pistol. How many of those exist?" explained Teresa.

"Right," said Lionel laughing. "Or maybe we should ask how many men have jeweled pistols?"

"The best part is Arnie *serendipitously* saw a similar jewel on the lobby floor...a good clue to trace directly to the Pollibos," said Teresa. "But, you'll be so proud of me. I discovered the best piece of evidence of all. Even the police missed it completely."

"What? A handkerchief with a P for Pollibo monogrammed on it?" asked Lionel.

"No, darling. When I went to your apartment, I found what looked like a piece of trouser fabric. Guess who was sitting on it, purring like a motor?"

"Boofy?' asked Lionel.

"Absolutely!" Teresa replied.

"Boofy is one reason I called," Lionel admitted. "On the way to the airport, we remembered...we'd forgotten the cat but figured we didn't dare return to get her."

"You figured right. Tell Ima I'll hold down the fort and keep her kitty until you return. Besides, Boofy may have to go on the witness stand. Just imagine the headlines."

Lionel laughed and teased, "It could read, 'Kitty Cat Testifies Against Cellar Rats!'"

"I think my clue will seal the fate of those goons," Teresa declared.

"You and Ima should team up as sleuths!" Lionel remarked.

"Sleuths? A stockbroker and a schoolteacher?"

"Ima has already solved a few mysteries on her trip. She said this case was her best one yet. But that's another whole story. I better get back to her. I'll call you when I can."

Lionel returned to the waiting area and related to Ima what Teresa had said.

Ima jumped up. "But PapaLi, if we're going to Atlanta, I need to take Boofy back to her rightful owner. Call Teresa again and ask her to bring the kitty here!"

"Absolutely not, Ima. It's too risky! The Pollibos will most likely *make bail* again and then they'll try to find us or hurt her if the evidence gets reported in the news."

"Of course, you're right, PapaLi." admitted Ima. "I don't think clearly when I'm tired. We'll figure it out later. Let's go watch men walk on the moon."

More to come in

IMASODE V

Anti-Belle of Antebellum Atlanta

APPENDICES

Biographies

The Feingold Family

Leo and Marianna

Kuld Finantsid (who changed his name to Leo Feingold) and Marianna Rannet married just as World War II spread through Europe. To escape Hitler's inevitable capture of their homeland in Estonia, Leo and Mariana risked all to take a boat across to North America. Through many hardships, they crossed the Atlantic and eventually settled in New York City where they started a new life. Soon after, Riina came along. (You can read their full biographies in Imasode-VII, *Escapades in Estonia*.)

Riina

By the time Riina grew old enough to go to nursery school, her family had moved up east of Central Park on 65th Street and Madison. On her first day of school, she met Ímagine Purple. They soon became constant playmates and forever friends.

In school, they gave each other silly names. Riina called Ima Longwind, Ima Longnose. Ima accepted that *moniker* as long as Riina didn't call her Ima Pickanose or Ima Picklenose. If Riina did that, then

Ima got to call her friend, Reena Finklegel because she ate a lot of jello or Ringa Fingergold because her daddy made gold rings.

Riina took tap and ballet and became the star of the school's talent shows. Her wiry hair formed a curly cloud encircling her head like a swarm of bees. Whereas Riina was more the performer, her pal Ímagine Purple took a quieter role. Learning to play piano, Ima liked to accompany while Riina sang and acted out Hit Parade songs. Their favorites were "Mares eat oats and does eat oats, but little lambs eat ivy" or "A you're adorable, B you're so beautiful, C you're a cutie full of charm." The constant repetition of their repertoire almost drove their parents insane or as the girls called it, going *Bonkers in Yonkers.*

Both only children, Riina and Ima pricked their fingers with a pin to make themselves blood sisters. They wore each other's clothes *much to the chagrin* of their mothers and practically moved into each other's apartments on weekends. It broke Riina's heart when Ima moved away to Michigan. Burying herself in her studies, she decided to become the next Greta Garbo. Sarah Bernhardt, or Fanny Bryce, depending how her face looked when matured.

The Longwind Family

Ímagine or Ima

As the main character, she belongs to her own family, the Longwinds and to her in-laws, the Purples. During Imasodes I and II, you had available her complete biography alphabetized under her first name Ímagine Purple.

Lionel

Born in London and orphaned by the age of ten, Lionel went to live with his Aunt Lottie, a young, vivacious lady who had loved him from birth and took him in gladly. A handsome boy with an incredible singing voice, Lionel had "star" written all over him. Lottie hoped to *nurture* that hope by insisting Lionel take voice lessons once his adolescent voice deepened.

Lionel's aunt had an enormous influence in his life. Since she was an *inveterate* hostess and now had built-in entertainment, the talented nephew soon found an adoring *entourage* among her guests. To keep the boy balanced, she showed him off to a wide circle of friends from both ends of London's *social spectrum*. Some came from the House of Lords; others, from a local *public house* (a pub).

With Lottie's connections, Lionel got into the best schools and finally into Eton College. There he rubbed elbows with the old and new rich of England. Wherever he went, Lionel joined the boys choir. He developed an interest for all kinds of music but especially loved operettas by Sigmund Romberg and Rudolf Frimml. He knew all the words to every song of these composers.

Lottie designed elaborate theme parties based on whatever songs her nephew could sing. When he starred in a school production of the *Student Prince*, she brought the whole cast to her home for a private audience to hear her young songbird. Lionel enthralled her guests with his brilliant *renditions*. Lottie always joked that he had to *sing for his supper* to pay for his keep, a phrase which Lionel wondered might be true.

In reality, his Aunt Lottie wanted to groom Lionel for a concert career. However, his teachers recognized his baritone voice would better suit musical revues than opera. Once, when he performed at Covent Gardens, a visiting American director hired him on the spot for a new show presently in rehearsal in New York. With the promise of stardom on the *Great White Way*, Lionel took a ship to America to seek his fortune.

Although very scared and lonely upon arrival, he was soon the Toast of the Town. Rich women and Broadway producers flung party invitations, marriage proposals, and singing contracts at the handsome young Englishman. Lionel soon found his *renown* brought a life far too busy for casual chitchat or a showbiz social life.

He had several women friends but had no serious intentions of looking for a mate. That option remained in his distant future. He first wanted to enjoy success in his chosen career. Besides, the demands of the theatre taxed him far more than outsiders realized. If he overtired himself, his voice faded. So, he protected the tool of his trade, a tool which had brought him great fame since his late teens.

Lionel easily adapted his style to the American musical theatre. He went from operettas to Ziegfeld type revues to stories like *Roberta* with musical scores. Although he landed a few singing roles in Busby Berkeley type movie musicals and had to move to Hollywood, his first love remained the live stage. Finally in the late 1930s, in order to get back to Broadway, he tried out for an experimental mystery musical. The show had many troubles. The script stunk, the cast kept changing, and the scenery wobbled. Not wanting a flop, the producer dared not open the show in New Haven, much less New York.

Instead, the producer shipped the entire production as far north as he could imagine, all the way to Newfoundland. The theatre company ventured to the Rock to practice far away from the critics' ears. There the play went through heavy-duty rewrites and rehearsals. The night of dress rehearsal, Madge, a schoolteacher on vacation, just happened to attend the performance. She fell head over heels for Lionel. It proved love at first sight for him as well. By the end of the play, he summoned her on stage and proposed. Very romantic, indeed!

Lottie

Lionel's Aunt Lottie loved raising him. The story of her fascinating life will appear in her complete biography available in Imasode VIII, *Aunt Lottie's London.*

Madge

In the summer of 1937, an English teacher named Imágine (Madge) Lovelace vacationed to Newfoundland. It just so happened she stayed at a hotel where rehearsals for a new play were being held in the ballroom. She met Lionel Longwind and fell in love at first glance. Lionel had the male lead in the play and saw Madge in the audience. At the final curtain, he brought her up on stage and proposed. Given such an unforgettable gesture, she could not resist accepting!

Madge had Ímagine (Ima) on the last day of 1939 but still managed to keep up with Lionel who had to continue on a tour. Finally, they settled into an apartment in Manhattan. The whole family loved living in New York. Ima went to a girls' school. Madge taught at a boys' school, and Lionel continued acting in Broadway plays.

A woman with great wisdom and humor, Madge took in stride the life of being married to an actor. She gracefully juggled the two worlds: the practical and the theatrical. She managed Lionel's finances because *money burned a hole in his pocket.* Although dying in her 40s, she left an indelible mark on her husband's heart and her daughter's personality.

The Pollibo Family

Benito married Veronica in Italy and immigrated to the U.S.

Maria, eldest child born in Italy, married David Mobley in NY

Valentino, one of twins born in NY

Salvatore, one of twins born in NY

Dominic, Benito's brother moved to Detroit and married Gloria Rossellini

Calverti, an only child

Delgado, the only grandchild

Benito

In the Roaring Twenties, Benito Pollibo, a prosperous shopkeeper in Genoa, Italy, decided to immigrate to America for a new start. He, his wife Veronica, his baby girl Maria, and his younger brother Dominic all prepared for this big adventure. Everyone had high hopes. The Pollibos brought with them many fine antiques and settled in a rare, free standing home of Little Italy in Lower Manhattan. Even so, they struggled with the language and made many sacrifices. Before he got his import business established, Benito still had to feed his family. Sadly, he sold off the furniture, piece by piece. Though he kept a roof over his wife and children, they ended up sleeping and eating on the floor.

Still, never giving up hope that America would answer his dreams, Benito kept plugging. He worked as a *stevedore* down at the docks and learned what happened when an improperly packed box traveled across the ocean. Things fell out or got destroyed. What remained *salvageable* but unclaimed, Benito simply took home. When he saved enough money to buy a warehouse close to the docks, he stored these goods. He also began making regular trips back to Europe to buy antiques for his intended business.

Maria

Maria liked living in New York. English came easily to her. It made her angry when her parents only talked Italian with their neighbors. Drawingg pictures of houses and buildings became her favorite pastime. She thought of herself as a budding Leonardo da Vinci. However, when Veronica died giving birth to twin boys, young Maria had to give up her dreams and become an instant junior mom.

While Papa stayed at work for long hours, Maria did her best to keep house, cook meals, do laundry, and tend to the twins. By the time she was fifteen, Benito's business flourished. Once her father could afford a nanny, Maria went off to *finishing school*. He hoped that advantage would help her rise to a higher social class than first generation immigrants usually held.

Maria met and married a rich playboy named David Mobley. Benito did not bless the marriage and almost disowned her for mixing with non-Italians. Gradually David settled down, became a *stockbroker*, and made his own fortune. Maria admitted to herself that her husband's money meant nothing to her. But the Mobley family name brought her the prestige and social status she craved.

Valentino and Salvatore

As the twins got old enough to go on the subway alone, they would visit their sister in her big fine home on East 55th Street. Always delighted to see them, Maria took them to the theatre for a bit of culture and refinement. Afterwards, she always let them have an Italian ice. They loved the treat but only *feigned* interest in the plays. Strangely though, they did enjoy going to operas, especially those sung in Italian.

Such familiar sounds reminded them of when the whole family still lived together.

Back in the neighborhood, the Pollibo twins turned into rascals and bullies. They broke into candy stores, beat up non-Italian kids, and hogged the ball when playing street ball. At fifteen, they dropped out of school and lied about their ages to join the army. They tried their shenanigans in the military. Whereas at first, they only did pranks like *short sheeting* their buddies' cots, later on they began to pocket ammunition when they went for target practice at the rifle range. When their sergeant discovered the theft, both Pollibos received dishonorable discharges.

Upon returning to Little Italy, they fell in with a local gang of hoodlums. Sal started *selling protection* to small businesses. If any shop *refused* to pay, he would break their display window into a hundred *shards*. While Sal ripped off small businessmen, Val worked the *numbers racket* with the tenants in the neighborhood.

Knowing every poor man dreamed that one day his number would come up or he'd win the Irish Sweepstakes, Val *pandered* to that dream. Occasionally, a neighbor would announce winning twenty or thirty bucks. Such small wins would excite everyone. For a few days afterwards, Val's business boomed. People would buy more numbers, hoping their *ship would come in* also.

As children, Sal and Val could not stand the idea of anyone who was not Italian. As they approached their thirties, they began to have irrational hatred for all non-Italians, especially if someone in the neighborhood married outside the ethnic group. Just as Papa Benito had expressed sadness and anger because Maria married someone from midtown, other families felt the same way. Having trained as a *sniper* in the military, Sal hired himself out to get rid of non-Italian family members.

He even decided on a very daring deed: to *knock off* his own brother-in-law, David Mobley right in the middle of Grand Central Station with crowds of people walking around. Using a silencer on his gun, Sal shot David with *impunity*. No one noticed anything until the body dropped to the floor. While everyone fussed over the dying man, Sal dashed away, scot-free. That success moved Sal up to *the big time* as a hired killer.

With her husband gone, Maria felt *bereft* and needed company. She invited her twin brothers to come live with her in her huge mansion. Now living in a swanky area, Val distinguished himself by progressing from selling chances at the numbers to *upscale bookmaking*. He made bets on anything: baseball, football, horses, and even the space race success.

When people *welched* on bets, he used his brawny body to convince them not to risk that again. If so, he'd threaten to *sic* his brother Sal on them. For a while, both Pollibo brothers made money by breaking the law.

Dominic, Caliverti, and Delgado

The Detroit branch of the Pollibo Family will have their full biographies given in Imasode VI – *Danger Starts in Detroit*. So look for Ima to have more trouble ahead.

Shelton (Vino) Grape

Born with the last name of Vino, Shelton never fit in with the other kids on his block of Little Italy. A rather bookish boy, he was tall, skinny, and almost frail-looking. The tough Pollibo twins teased him unmercifully, and even beat him up to get his *allegiance*. Although *dominated* by these bullies, he rarely went along with their pranks.

As Shelton matured, his face filled out and his voice deepened. The drama teacher cast him in the senior play which made him more popular at school. From then on, the draw of the stage hooked Shelton.

He took acting lessons and soon got bit parts in *off Broadway* plays. Although handsome enough, he lacked the *edginess* that great actors like Orson Wells or John Barrymore had. His voice seemed too big for the stage and too loud for films but better suited for radio. Therefore, Shelton attended disk jockey school and found his professional *niche* as a broadcast announcer. Even so, that did not satisfy his ego to perform in front of a live audience. To keep his theatre dream alive, he took lessons with a vocal coach. After toning down his booming voice, he won a few minor roles on Broadway.

During a tour of one play, he met and married Dee Ann Jones of Tulsa, Oklahoma. It upset her family that she had married an Italian, so he changed his name from Vino to Grape, figuring at least his name still meant fruit of the vine. One evening the bad-news Pollibo twins from the old neighborhood attended a performance in which Shelton had a part. They recognized him but not the name listed on the program. When they came backstage to congratulate him, Sal asked, "What's with the name Grape? Are you ashamed of being Italian?

"Of course not. It's a stage name," Shelton said, lying about the true reason. "I'll tell you about it sometime."

Shelton had mixed feelings about reconnecting with the old gang. He enjoyed the *camaraderie* but not the memory of their cruel teasing. One afternoon, he visited the old neighborhood and learned that the Pollibo twins had moved to a *posh* midtown brownstone. Old friends told how their sister Maria needed their comfort since someone had murdered her husband.

On another occasion, Shelton bumped into the Pollibos having drinks at P.J. Clarke's. Watching Val exchange money with several *patrons*, he surmised that this hangout served as a place to collect and pay off bets. After a couple of drinks, all their tongues loosened. By evening's end, they had exhausted the subject of old times and had drunk themselves into a *stupor*. Shelton learned about Val's becoming the local bookie and about Sal's running a "missing persons" business.

"Isn't it hard to find missing people," Shelton said naively.

"Precisely, and I make sure they stay missing," Sal explained.

"Oh," Shelton said, not understanding at first. "Do you work for the Police or the FBI?"

"No, I work solo," said Sal.

Finally feeling comfortable enough to share his own history, Shelton admitted having to change his name to pacify his in-laws. "They objected to Vino sounding too Italian."

Val jumped up and flexed his muscles. "Well, how about Pollibo? I object to anyone objecting to names that sound too Italian."

"Yeah, that someone may find his name missing from the phone directory," said Sal.

Suddenly Shelton realized what Sal meant about "missing persons" and "working alone." When he got home that night, he told his wife about his old bullying neighbors now had illegal jobs as a bookie and a hitman.

"Do you think my folks might end up on a *hit list*," she asked anxiously.

Shelton shook his head, deciding not to worry about Sal's idle threat but to keep Pollibos' chosen careers tucked away for future use. Maybe, after all these years, he'd find a way to bully the bullies. Better yet, maybe he'd hold this secret over their heads to get their help to advance his own career.

Although achieving modest success in New York, Shelton grew bitter about Dee Ann wanting to climb the social ladder. She insisted they rent an expensive loft in the Village. He reminded her that after paying the rent each month, they had little left for entertainment, much less for a bigger apartment. She grew very dissatisfied. Hoping to keep her happy and to boost his income, he began to bet on the horses and arrange card games with high stakes. Once he lost too much money, Shelton lost his wife as well.

Dee Ann disappeared without a trace, leaving him lonely and heartbroken. He suspected her parents had influenced her to divorce him, anything to *extricate* her from this marriage, even going against his church rules.

Teresa Latimer

Teresa Gutierrez came from a family of five and grew up in Harlem's Puerto Rican neighborhood of New York City. Her Latin eyes, blue-black hair, and shy nature made her an adored child at home and at school. Her folks recognized her intelligence, wanted the best for her, but had no idea how to steer her into her *destiny*.

Teachers praised her bright mind and directed her toward a serious academic career. Teresa adapted well to individual attention and strove to please everyone around her, as well as herself. She won the school's spelling bee in the sixth grade and became the champion of all Manhattan.

While attending high school, she had a major setback. Her father became seriously ill. Her mother took a job in the garment district to support their family. At first, Teresa and her two brothers alternated staying home to take care of the father. Finally, it fell to her to drop out of school entirely. But inside, she *refused* to give up her dream to know more about life. Once a week, she ran to the library to check out new books.

When Mr. Gutierrez grew strong enough to be left at home alone, Teresa went back to school. Having missed more than two years, she found that most of her classmates had graduated. Others had quit to join the army at the tail end of WWII. Very motivated, Teresa studied hard, went to summer school, and finished within a year.

More than anything else in life, Teresa wanted to go to college. Her folks had no money for such a venture. They told her that people had to accept whatever lot life offered. Teresa refused that idea. Discouraging words did not *squelch* her desire to know more. So, in the mornings, she helped her mom sew uniforms for soldiers. In the evenings, she took a few business courses at City College.

In the newspaper, she read that Columbia University gave scholarships to a few deserving students every year. Her application *essay* showed the school that her early sacrifices had matured her into a truly remarkable girl. The entrance exam proved quite difficult, but she passed. Soon Teresa entered the famous school and carried no other thought with her than to study hard to pass every course in her degree plan. She graduated with honors and soon got a job at Chase Manhattan Bank.

Then, for the first time in her life, Teresa relaxed and thought about dating. At work, she met Terence Latimer, a young man *destined* to be a vice president before he reached thirty. Of course, with identical nicknames, their *colleagues* teased them about being Terry2 and figured they were also destined for each other. They fell in love and married the summer of 1948.

Because Terence just missed the World War II *draft*, he felt pressed to serve his country when the Korean Conflict started. He went to OCS to become an army lieutenant and planned for Teresa join him if he got stationed in the States. But once he completed the training, his whole outfit *deployed* to the Korean front.

In the dead of winter, Terence and his men got cut off from the rest of the company. His radioman worked furiously to get through to HQ. *Munitions* ran low. Food grew scarce. He and many other soldiers developed frozen feet. When rescuers finally arrived, they whisked Terry's unit off to a hospital in Tokyo. Because of delayed treatment, an infection set in his legs and spread throughout his body. He died before coming home.

Devastated, Teresa took a leave of absence from her job and moved back with her family for a few months. She needed time to recover such a loss so early in her marriage. Upon returning to her job, she made work her chief desire and outlet. In the *ensuing* years, she distinguished herself in the banking world by writing articles about how customers could save for retirement.

For her achievements, she received the top employee award many years in a row and advanced to higher positions than usually offered to women. However, no one could deny her abilities. Building upon her success, Teresa left banking and went to work on Wall Street to sell *stocks*. She continued to develop her idea for how regular folk could retire with more savings.

Although a beautiful young widow who often attracted men's eyes, Teresa stayed single. However, when she met Lionel Longwind, a light turned on in a room that had been dark for almost twenty years. At first glance, she could not resist the matinee idol.

The Underwood Family

Among New York City's earliest civil engineers, the Underwoods started the Underground Construction Company at the turn of the twentieth century. The city streets already bulged with people, horse carriages, and garbage. The fallout of such *profuse refuse* became enormous. Whoever solved the city's huge dilemmas would need to work quickly and economically. The Underwood brothers saw the issues of transportation and sanitation as similar challenges and opportunities. They hoped to improve city services, to create employment for many, and to prosper their own business.

Since many companies *vied* to build the city's subway train system, the Underwood family sought the less glamorous underground project: the sewers. Heavy rains caused floods in the city. Muddy streets made it not only impossible for trolleys and horse carriages to move about but also difficult for common folk to walk to work.

Although for decades the city's underground *infrastructure* had existed in some areas, it was composed of inferior concrete. Much of it had begun to crumble into disrepair. Also the sewer system needed expansion to reach to each end of the island and then onto the other *boroughs*.

With a high *work ethic* and willingness to get their hands dirty, the Underwoods unknowingly made the lowest bids to rebuild the city sewers and won the project. Year in and year out, New York City awarded them more and more sewer contracts. Before long the sewers gained the name of the Underwood Undergrounds.

Caleb Underwood aka Cash Underground

Into this very successful family, Caleb was born. As a boy, he grew up down in the *dank* sewer passages. He considered them his own special kingdom. After a big rain, he'd bring down his fishing pole and hope for a fish to swim by. He ran between parts of the underground job and saw how hard the men had to work and how risky the projects were.

One time, when a tunnel caved in, a man died. Caleb's father never recovered emotionally from that loss. From then on Mr. Underwood did everything in his power to make it safe for his workers. He knew that without them, he could neither build nor maintain the *catacombs* of tunneling beneath Manhattan.

As Caleb's body grew stronger, he worked for his father in the summers and enjoyed going down below to cool off. Now older, he began to appreciate his father's engineering knowledge. However, that side of the business did not fascinate him because his talents lay elsewhere.

Caleb went off to university to study economics and accounting, instead of engineering. He thought it more important to determine why his family made money *hand over fist* because so far, no one seemed clear on which projects proved the most *lucrative*. While at school, Caleb invested his allowance in *stocks* and picked up the nickname of Cash. Thrifty to a fault, he rarely spent a dime. His friends spread a rumor that he buried the Underwood money underground. Hence his *moniker* grew into Cash Underground.

By the time he graduated, he had saved a lot of money. Some advised him to start a new business, but Cash did not have the *entrepreneur* spirit. He preferred to manage the finances of the Underwoods' business interests. That way he could conserve the fortune his father and uncle had struggled to create. He began tracking each expense made on every tunnel constructed by his family's company.

Cash brought to his father's attention the duplicated or wasteful *expenditures* on certain projects. His insights helped save on production costs. That, in turn, increased their profits. With revenues up, they could afford to continue making low bids and often hit right close to a city's project budget. That accuracy in turn brought them more projects, and more projects made the company more money with which to hire more workers. He kept that cycle going for many decades, and the company grew even more prosperous.

Although Cash never married nor had a family, he bought a huge condominium apartment on Central Park East for a place to entertain customers. Upon retiring, he knew he did not need so much space but liked that address for a different reason. Every day he toured the Park and handed out money to the vagrants.

When he realized many of them bought liquor instead of food with his handouts, he asked a nearby delicatessen to deliver *hero sandwiches* at noon. Soon, a booming picnic went on daily. Believing his appearance in expensive suits had looked *off-putting* to his new buddies, Cash began to buy his clothes at thrift stores. He never looked down on anyone who was *down on their luck*. He simply became one of the fellows.

Wes Westerly

Burt Westerly was born to be an entertainer. His parents owned one of New York's first moving pictures theatres in the East Village, so he grew up watching the silent movies and then the talkies. With no need to buy a ticket, he would see them over and over until he could dance every step, sing every song, and tell every joke. Burt planned to make movies or be in them when he grew up.

Just as he prepared to go university, the Great Depression hit. Although many families pulled their children out of college to save money for more important things like food and shelter, his folks insisted Burt go on with his education. They had observed a strange fact: people, poor or not, kept going to see movies. In the face of lost jobs and lost homes, movies served as an escape from their misery. So, the Westerly Picture Show not only stayed open but prospered.

By the time Burt finished his degree, the movie production business had mostly moved to Hollywood. With no interest in going west and knowing only big names could find enough work in movies to stay in New York, he decided to make his fame and fortune in broadcasting. The *Big Apple* still reigned as king of radio, and most American families at least owned one of those. Radio tagged Burt as Wes Westerly, the *novelty* actor. He excelled in doing character voices and *dialects* and even did cartoon characters for Saturday morning kid shows. Although not a household face or name like a movie star, he became one of radio's most famous and familiar voices.

Preferring to work every day, he played many different roles, ages, and nationalities from afternoon soap opera villains to evening detectives. Soon he became the highest paid and most sought after radio actor in America. Since radio shows were live broadcasts, Wes would finish one program at CBS studios, go down the elevator to a waiting taxi, and be zoomed over to the NBC network housed in Rockefeller Center.

Most radio actors could stand in front of a microphone and sight-read a script with no mistakes. Producers often handed them local commercials to read at the first, middle, and last of a show. This saved the station money for not having to hire a separate spot announcer. In the early 1950s, television became the chief form of home entertainment. Things began to change rapidly.

This new medium proved expensive to produce. TV shows had only 22 minutes to tell a story that sponsors would buy and audiences would watch. Producers hired Wes to help design commercials. He also taught writers how to time their story scripts to fit the exact slot allowed for commercials. Although his radio experience made his advice invaluable to this growing industry, Wes craved a more active role.

Big companies like Ivory Soap, Kellogg Cereals, Texaco Gas, and Lucky Strike Cigarettes *clamored* to sponsor TV shows. But having their names splashed over the new small screen meant going through advertising agencies. Television spots required more sophisticated ad specialists. Wes sensed TV ads needed better actors and announcers to bring them alive. Agencies knew how to write and produce radio and print ads. But they had not polished their skills at making TV commercials. These short ads required hiring both visual and vocal talents. Seeing a unique opportunity, Wes called together all his old radio *cronies*.

At their first gathering, they *reminisced* about the radio *heyday*. No one disagreed that their faces did not looked young or handsome enough for the new visual medium of television. So, the next step proved easy. Wes proposed a new concept by which he would represent his radio buddies as their agent and explained how it would work. TV needed these accomplished voice-over announcers to talk behind the new commercials. He convinced them that they would make more money behind the scenes than they ever had in front of a microphone. Even if individual commercials did not pay very much, he foresaw they would have steady voice-over work.

Wes left the advertising business and set up the Westerly Talent Agency. He helped to expand AFTRA to protect television as well as radio performers from *unscrupulous* producers. From his new *vantage point*, he provided a great service to professional actors and ad agency casting departments alike. He had a master's touch for matching the perfect voice to a particular commercial. His taste, reputation, and integrity attracted the best ad agencies for contracts and the best actors for clients.

One of his prize clients was Lionel Longwind, the longtime Broadway singing star transplanted from England. Wes also represented well-known local announcers like Shelton Grape, several jingle-writing musicians, a couple of documentary producers, as well as a few budding actresses and fashion models. Amateurs beat down his door to get on his list, but he kept his *stable of clients* to a size he could handle with care and represent properly.

Cliché, Idioms, & Phrases

About face: pivoting feet to turn 180° the opposite way
Above board: legitimate/legal
Actor's aside: words meant for audience's ears only
Add fuel to the fire: make inflamed situations grow hotter
A-line: Jackie Kennedy type dress forming A shoulder to knee
All growed up: (Slang) for "grown"
All's well...ends well: things begin badly yet work out
Arm-twisting: ploy to persuade; shy of strong-arming
At odds with: out of harmony; in conflict
Attempted assault: start of a malicious attack

Backhanded compliment: disguised ridicule to mislead
Baked Alaska: ice cream encased in hot meringue
Bawdy dive: bar/hangout for drunks/lowlifes
Begged off: politely declined; asked to be released
Big Apple: a nickname for New York City
Bill of fare: items on a menu
Blue streak: non-stop; rapidly
Body metaphors: references alluding to body parts
Bonkers in Yonkers: going crazy north of the Bronx
Bookie style: betting code of .25=$25; .50=$50; one=$100

Bowler hats: derby; small brim/rounded crown hat
Bread and butter: main source of income/livelihood
Break a leg: good luck phrase to give actors a boost
Break character: actor drops illusion; changes face/voice

Can-can: chorus line dance done by Follies Bergere
Can't make a silk purse... sow's ear: frills don't erase nature
Carbon copy: marks duplicated on paper by ink sheets
Card shark: player who cheats or plays tricks in a game
Cash cow: product to bring fast/easy profit
Casting couch: directors offer a role in exchange for sex
Cat who ate the canary: one who looks guilty
Cater the wake: provide food before a funeral
Chief cook and bottle-washer: one who does everything
Chomping at the bit: eager for an event to start
Clammed up: said nothing; stopped talking
Classic crime formula: weapon/opportunity/motive
Close shave: almost caught; a near accident/death/injury
Coast was clear: nothing dangerous seen either direction
Comp Your Dinner: offer meals with no charge
Con artist: one who tricks people out of their money
Cooler heads... prevail: less emotional folk give calmer ideas
Command performance: required attendance
Counter-flow: opposite direction from everyone else
Coward die...: reliving old failures; fearing future ones
Cried uncle: code words for surrender or giving up
Cross to bear: Roman criminal carried his own cross
Cupboard was bare: no food on hand; empty larder
Cutthroat poker: turning game so certain ones win
Cutting up the rug: old phrase for dancing

Damsel in distress: desperate lady needing a rescue
Dangle a carrot: tempt someone with a reward
Daylight basement: lower level under front entrance steps

Dead giveaway: a clue no one should miss
Death warmed over: looking gravely ill/at point of dying
Delicate ego: one easily shaken/offended; unconfident
Den of iniquity: hidden place where instincts yield to evil
Dime a dozen: item gets cheap if supply outstrips demand
Dog-eat-Dog: succeeding at all cost even if it hurts others
Don't borrow trouble: don't invite/take on others' problems
Double standard: rules applied unevenly to people
Down on their luck: covered in misfortune/poverty
Drill sergeant: one training soldiers to perform their duties
Drop of a hat: for slightest reason; done without delay
Dropping all pretense: stopping a ruse/feint used to mislead
Drown his sorrows: getting drunk until one forgets sadness
Drum up: direct more interest in a cause
Dying on stage: actor keeps forgetting lines and gets booed

Easy girl: one who gives in to men's desires
Egging on: urging/daring someone to continue
Empire waist: high place below bust line on bodice
Empty larder: no stock or staples in the pantry
Even keel: emotionally stable/balanced; boat keel upright

Façade of propriety: false image of being good/above board
Face the music: admitting guilt; accepting results
Failsafe system: if one thing breaks, a backup exists
Falling out: disagreement that breaks up a friendship
Far cry: conditions way different from the expected
Femme fatale: one using her beauty to lure men to danger
Fight for the King: imaginary book about Loyalists
Finishing school: place where girls prepare to join society
First rodeo: where a greenhorn learns needed skills
First watch: nautical term for first day shift
Five boroughs: Manhattan/Bronx/Brooklyn/Queens/Staten Isle
Flash in the pan: no lasting fame; one-hit wonder

Fork over the dough: pay money; forced to give
Friars Club roasts: banquets to satirize guests of honor
From the frying pan...fire: from bad things to worse ones
Frugal to a fault: saving to a point of almost penny pinching
Full count: two strikes and three balls on a baseball player
Full house: Two+three cards of a kind (See Poker Terms)
Full-run contract: offer to stay with a show till it closes

Game of keep-away: tossing ball only among certain ones
Garbo pose: Greta laid a hand across her chest in Camile.
Gaping holes: obvious gaps; logic erros seen/unseen
Get a quick fix: needing a hit of narcotics
Get canned: to fire a person
Get out of Dodge: leave town
Get the picture: grasp what's going on in a situation
Get the scoop: be first to report a news story or latest facts
Get wind of it: hear a rumor; learn of an event
Go to such lengths: work hard to accomplish a task
Going overboard: doing more than is needed/expected
Golden calf: Moses' brother Aaron helped make this idol
Got suckered in: drawn into an unwise/illegal arrangement
Gourmet goulash: superb Hungarian stew of veal/veggies
Grease your palm: buy someone off with a bribe or favor
Great White Way: showbiz name for Broadway
Green with envy: jealous of another's good fortune

Hand-me-downs: clothes worn by siblings before you
Hand over fist: money/product coming in quickly
Has-been: a hack using old routines, whose career is over
Hero sandwiches: submarine or poor boy sandwich
Hide nor hair: missing; no sign/evidence can be found.
High stakes: lots of $$ risked on a bet
Hit list: targets to be murdered
Hobnob with the hoity-toity: hang out with pompous folk

Hoi polloi: the common folk
Hoodlum attire: stereotyped mob dress; dark suit/shirt/tie
Hoofers hit the boards: old soft-shoe dancers on a stage
Horning in: going where you're not invited; nosiness

In tune: play along; have a good grasp of things
Incessant comparisons: constant description of differences
Inject some levity: put a joke into the conversation
Innocence stolen: loss of simpler/purer thoughts
Intensive Care Unit: place for emergency/surgery patients
It-girl: old phrase for hottest new female star
It was...best...worst of times: Tale of Two Cities' first line

Johnny-on-the-spot: one always ready and on time
Jump and jive: jazz version of Lindy/Swing/Jitterbug
Jump to conclusions: decide without all the facts
Just the facts, ma'am: line Joe Friday oft said on Dragnet

Keeping vigil: watching/waiting if someone's sick/dying
Kept bad company: associated with the wrong crowd
Kill two birds...: solve two problems with one action
Knock off: (Mafia) to kill someone
Known by company...: choice of friends sets my reputation

Last bats: team starting in field, gets last inning at home
Last straw: unable to handle any more problems
Let the chips fall...: do what's needed, results will follow
Limbo contest: dance when folks go under a low pole
Lily-livered: not brave; weak willed
Lose Your Shirt: gambling/bad investing took last dollar
Low class outfits: clothes of prostitutes or cheap/easy girls

Maître d: headwaiter/steward at restaurant or hotel
Making a mountain...: treating small matters like big deals
Man-killer: lady with a kiss of death or looks that slay men
Man of the Year: annual award for most outstanding man
Marijuana grow-op: farm raising illegal cannabis
Matinee idol: male stars over whom women swooned
Mob bosses: heads of various Mafia families
Moosey women: aggressive *proselytizers* of lesbianism
Money burned a hole in his pocket: never saved a dime
Much to the chagrin: causing dismay/disappointment
Mum's the word: keep it a secret; don't reveal anything
Musical revivals: redoing plays with prior long runs

Nail the coffin shut: ironclad facts proving a case
Nest egg: money saved for future wants or hard times
Nighty-night: (Slang) good night; sweet dreams
Nip in the bud: stop something before it starts to grow
No biggie: easily done; not a bother
Non sequitur: not following or fitted to what's been said
Numbers racket: chances sold only to local area suckers

Off Broadway: theatres in Village or lower/upper Eastside
Off the hook: relieved of duty/suspicion/responsibility
Off-limits: not allowed
Officials in their pocket: city leaders on the take giving favors
Off-putting: offensive/repellent/repugnant
On a roll: a series of events going your way
On a tight leash: short rope; no length to get into trouble
On her high horse: uppity; in a haughty mood/manner
On the fly: done while something else is occurring
On the horizon: happening very soon
On the sly: secretly/deceptively; out of view
On the spur: spontaneous; without a plan/appointment
On the take: accepting bribes to overlook illegal acts

One iota: not even a little bit
One's own worst enemy: harming self more than others can
One-way glass: mirror prevents the observed to see observers
Oom-pa-pa: polka music described in onomatopoeia
Open sesame: phrase Ali Baba used to open magical cave
Orchestra section: seats after orchestra pit and below balcony
Out damn spot: Lady MacBeth had guilt of unseen blood
Out of commission: something's wrong/broken
Out of kilter: not in balance; uneven; out of whack
Out of sync: uncoordinated; not in same rhythm/harmony
Out of whack: not working properly

Panders to human frailities: encourages others in their vices
Pass muster: satisfy all rules/requirements by examination
Peace pact: treaty/truce whereby two parties agree
Penny ante poker: fun poker with low stakes/penny bets
Penny pinching: frugal to the point of being cheap/stingy
Perennial favorite: best liked each year
Photo composites: multiple poses of a model or actor
Picture paints a 1,000 words: a visual image saves time/talk
Pie-in-the-sky: unreal expectations of future; rainbow's end
Pillar to post: moving between a series of places
Pilot of a new TV show: idea tested before being produced
Pins in a voodoo doll: occult punishment of person's image
Place to light: somewhere to land on and stay
Pleased as Punch: in Punch & Judy, he delights in hitting folk
Plunging V-neckline: stylish bodice in the 1950s and 1960s
Poker terms: flush; straight; two of a kind (See Lookups)
Police action: UN's term for undeclared war
Police precinct: law enforcement stations spread over a city
Ponder and pray: Ima weighs clues to not jump to conclusions
Pound of flesh: get revenge/extract payment for an act done
Power play: maneuver to undercut/usurp whoever rules
Profuse refuse: lots of garbage/rubbish/trash/debris

Prosecuting crime: collecting facts to convict a criminal
Public House: pub; drinking establishment
Pull is better than push: get noticed by those with influence
Pulled the wool...eyes: fooled/deceived/misled by someone
Purse strings: means control of how money gets spent
Put the screws to: blame another/force him to do your will
Putty in my hands: one so malleable to do another's will

Quid pro quo: (Legal/Latin) do one thing to get another

Rain check: postpone invitation to another day
Reconnoiter the rear: survey/observe/inspect events out back
Redeem from the pawnshop: buy back an item earlier sold
Residual paychecks: income from reruns of a show/ad
Rich uncle dies: unearned money drops from sky; ship comes in
Ride the rails: hopping on a freight train for a free ride
Ringside table: tables surrounding a stage or dance floor
Right off the bat: immediately, at first
Robbing the cradle: dating/marrying someone a lot younger
Rock of Gibraltar: Africa/Spain landmark; term for immoveable
Rolling in dough like Rockefeller: rich man covered in money
Run amuck: goes along smoothly but ends out of control/in a frenzy
Run-of-the-Mill: average, without flare
Russian roulette: risky spin of gun chamber *stocked* with only one bullet

Safe haven: a place to light; remote hideout/asylum
Sandwich man: one wearing a bi-fold placard advertisement
Saxon blockheadedness: ancient German seemed thickheaded
Score movies: write music to run under film dialogue
Scores to settle: revenge; get even; clear up an issue
Sea legs: walk upright on a boat, given wave action
Seething hostilities: anger underneath/unknown/unseen
Sell-order: client's demand that his broker sell some stock
Selling protection: mafia insurance sold to shops to avoid fire

Sergeant of arms: club rep who keeps order/security
Serve that girl a syrup sandwich: Louisiana sports cheer
Set the stakes of the game: limit bets; assign amounts to chips
Sets bail: amount one arrested pays to avoid jail till trial
Sexton of a cathedral: maintainer of church's buildings
Shrink's couch: sofa where psychiatrist's patients lie/talk
Ship Comes In: unearned windfall if rich uncle dies
Shoo-in: no contest; no one else has a chance to win
Short sheeting: top sheet becomes bottom by special folding
Sides split: laughing so hard it hurts
Since Hector was a pup: it's been going on for a long time
Sing for his supper: perform to get fed; quid pro quo
Social spectrum: arranging folks by low/middle/upper class
Some kind of pull: influence that can get you out of trouble
Spit and polish: orderliness; restoring an original situation
Split the scene: leave quickly to prevent being caught
Square one: back at the beginning; starting over
Stable of clients: an agent's group of actors/performers
Stacked deck: method dealer uses so only he wins
Stance of dominance: bullying/lording over one who seems weak
Stand-in: placeholder on a movie set until star is required
Stars in her eyes: enthralled by famous folks or personal fame
Stars before her eyes: knocked unconscious and seeing stars
Stashed away: hidden/stored away for future use
Sterling characters: people thought to have no flaws
Stew in her own juices: leave someone to suffer alone
Stick out like sore thumbs: easily seen; very obvious
Stood on deck: next batter waits in sideline box
Stood her in good stead: was useful/gave a good reputation
Stop the presses: if news breaks, editor calls printing to a halt
Street-level buildings: entrance is even with sidewalk
Strong-arming: forcing someone to act against his own will
Suffice it to say: enough said; no more words needed
Tagged his shoulder: cutting in to dance with someone's partner

Take his marbles and go home: one not getting his way, leaves
Taken its toll: a cost beyond money, wearing you down
Talk turkey: get down to business; discuss without frills
Teacher eyes: with eyes in back of their heads, they see all
Ten percent commission: fee for getting clients new jobs
Tenements tomorrow: some apartments *deteriorate* into slums
Tenor of the conversation: implied tone/mood of talk
The big time: rising to the top of one's career
The ropes: learning/knowing what to do in a certain situation
Theatre District: W. 44th to 47th considered on-Broadway
Three little monkeys: Japanese statues advise best behavior
Top billing: headliner; first name on marquee or in lights
Topsy-turvy: turned upside down
Train of thought: sequence/order of ideas following each other
Trench coat: heavy canvas overcoat with many pockets

Under scrutiny: closely watched/observed/examined
Union book: outline of worker rules and pay rates
Union scale: amount paid performers, prescribed by unions
Up and comers: those neither at the bottom nor top of careers
Up the ante: add money in start-up pot; fuel to the fire
Up the stakes: raising bets higher
Up to my gills: so full, it won't hold more or I can't breathe
Upscale bookie: one taking bets from well-heeled clients
Upscale bookmaking: art of feeding on rich gamblers' vice
Utopian pipedream: vain, fantastic nowhere; pie-in-the-sky

Vantage point: view from an opportune angle/position
Variety Magazine: weekly trade magazine for show business
Vice-versa: other way around

Waiting for his lawyer: a crook is quiet till an attorney comes
Well-heeled: wealthy; describes one with lots of money
Wild abandon: in a reckless manner; beyond carefree

Wilted endive salad: pouring bacon drippings on greens
Wiggle out: (aka Wriggle out) get out of a tight spot
Windmill delivery: pitcher circles arm before releasing ball
Winning pot: all money out on a table in a card game
Without further ado: No more delay or fanfare needed
Work ethic: skill/desire to finish task completely/expediently
World is your oyster: free to do whatever; life with a pearl inside
Wreaked havoc: caused chaos/confusion all around
Wrecking ball: equipment to demolish buildings
Write jingles: compose musical ditties to advertise products.

Lookup Suggestions

Abbreviations

AAH	Actors At Home, fictional answering svc.
AFTRA	American Fed. of TV and Radio Actors
aka	Also known as (alias)
Amend.	Amendment (e.g. Constitution)
&	Ampersand means "and"
Apt.	Apartment
Arch.	Architecture
ASAP	As soon as possible
Assoc.	Association
Bldg.	Building
BOI	Born on the Island, *exclusive* designation
CBS	Columbia Broadcasting System
°	Degree (angle or temperature)
Dept.	Department
eg.	(Latin) for example
Fed.	Federation (or Federal)
Govt.	Government
Eng.	English
EMT	Emergency medical technician

ICU	Intensive Care Unit
i.e.	(Latin) that is
LA	Los Angeles
LP	Long Playing Album
Mkt.	Market
Mtnc.	Maintenance
NBC	National Broadcasting Company
NYC	New York City
#	Number (or pounds in weight)
OCS	Officer Candidate School
PJs	pajamas
P.J.'s	Short for P.J. Clarke's
Presby.	Presbyterian
RCA	Radio Corporation of America
SAG	Screen Actors Guild union
Sq.	Square
Svc.	Service
TN	Tennessee
UN	United Nations
w/	with
w/o	without
Y	Nickname for YWCA & YMCA
YWCA	Young Women's Christian Assoc.

Dances

Fox Trot	1, 2 & 3 (step, step, quick-quick)
Jerk	abrupt torso motion with neck whips
Jitterbug	oy lifts/spins girl like a yo-yo
Jump & Jive	rough jitterbug or solo in zoot suit
Limbo	dance whereby person goes under a pole
Lindy Hop	softer/sophisticated version of jitterbug
Morris	ancient dance to tune like "Greensleeves"
Polka	fast, alternating side steps in 2-beats
Soft-shoe	vaudeville shuffling without taps on shoes
Swim dance	with swim like arms movements

Food Establishments (1960s)

Choc Full 'o Nuts	franchise coffee shops
Horn & Hordart	automats around Manhattan
La Toque Blanche	French Restaurant on E. 50th
Nedicks	chain of hotdog stands
P.J. Clarke's	bar and casual diner
Sardi's	theatrical & advertising hangout
Sloppy Louie's	famous fried-fish cafe near wharves

History

Eng. Renaissance	revival of art & architecture, 1400-1600
Great Depression	financial crash brought crisis, 1929+
Historical Society	group preserving landmarks, 1968
NYC Blackout	big loss of electricity, 1966
Korean War	UN police action, 1950-53
Roaring 20s	frivolous living era till 1929 crash
Valley Forge	Washington's troops wintered,1777-78
World War II	Hitler's quest to subdue Europe,1938+

Hospitals

Bellevue	charity and psychiatric hospital
Columbia Presby.	heart hospital
Mount Sinai	multi-specialty hospital
Sloan-Kettering	large research cancer hospital

Housing Types

Apartment House	building with individual units to rent
Brownstones	3-4 story homes with daylight basements
Condominiums	apts. to buy but had mtnc. fee
Cooperatives	residents buy *stock* in owning the bldg.
Flats	term for apts. on one level
Free standing	a few private homes remain in NYC

High Rise	tall towers with multiple apartments
Lofts	apartments built inside a warehouse
Public Housing	govt. built apts. with reduced rent rates
Rent Control	old bldgs. with multifamily units
Resident Hotels	room sharing bath; no kitchens
Slums	units neglected due to high taxes/greed
Storefront unit	flat over business, oft-owner occupied
Sublease/sublet	one already leased by another renter
Tenements	dwellings with low upkeep standards

Laws

Blue Law	laws keeping stores closed on Sundays
Sanitation Codes	regulations of a city health dept.
Miranda Act	statement of an arrested person's rights
Prohibition	18th Amend., forbade alcohol brew/sell
Rent Control	Freeze on landlord's ability to raise rates

Locations in New York City:

Bowery	once Manhattan's worst *vagrant* area
Brooklyn Yard	spot for ships to dry-dock for repairs
East Diamonds	cluster of Central Park softball diamonds
Ellis Island	past NY's immigrants processing point
Erdmann House	built 1929 on E. 55th in NY arch. *heyday*
Fifth Avenue	home of Berdorf's/Lord&Taylor/Saks
Friars Club	showbiz hangout; hosts Celebrity Roasts
Fulton Fish Mkt	big fish exchange in Manhattan
Grand Central	NY Central Railroad terminal
Great White Way	another name for Broadway
Jan Hus Church	Presby. Church with Moravian roots
Little Italy	Italian immigrant settlement
Penn Station	Pennsylvania Railroad terminal
Port Authority	NY bus terminal
Rockefeller Center	business/broadcast area built in 1930s
Sing Sing	major penitentiary in NY
Studio 54	famous nightclub in its prime

| Times Square | Junction where Broadway cuts at 47th |
| Waldorf-Astoria | elegant high-rise hotel on Park & 50th |

Maps to research

| New England | check distance from Maine to NYC |
| New York City | check all 5 *demarcated* boroughs |

Miscellaneous

Camel Cigarette	huge sign puffed smoke in Times Sq.
Chicken Licken	aka Henny Penny in nursery rhymes
Eton College:	English *exclusive* boys school
Grosse Point, MI	wealthy area east of Detroit
Irish Sweepstakes	lottery set up in 1930 to help hospitals
Jenny Lind	bed with spooled legs & headboards
Joy Perfume	top product of Jean Patou from 1930s
New Haven	where shows open first to correct trouble
NY Times	America's most prominent newspaper
Poker Terms	see below–winning hands broken out
Rock of Gibraltar	famous landmark of Spain off Africa
Sidewalks of NY	famous song by Lawlor/Blake, 1894
Stratford, Ontario	Canadian Shakespeare Festival home
Tony Awards	top honors given in theatre
Variety Magazine	weekly magazine for show business

People-Actors

Betty Hutton	trapeze artist-*Greatest Show on Earth*
Fanny Bryce	Ziegfeld Follies & radio comedienne
Greta Garbo	Swedish actress, major role in *Camille*
Gene	Autryradio/film cowboy bought LA Dodgers
Howard di Silva	actor, played Benjamin Franklin in *1776*
J. Carrol Naish	radio actor played *Luigi* & did accents.
John Barrymore	major film actor for 2 decades
Maurice Chevalier	French star known for role in *Gigi*

Orson Wells	actor, *Citizen Kane* & *War of the Worlds*
Ron Holgateactor	won Tony, Richard H. Lee, role
Sarah Bernhardt	French stage/film actress

People-Musical Producers

Florenz Ziegfeld	NY *impresario* of revues, 1900s
Gilbert & Sullivan	collaborated on 14 operettas, 1890s
Rudolf Frimml	wrote operettas into mid 20th century
Sigmund Romberg	wrote operettas to mid 20th century

People-Real or Fictional

Ali Baba	main character of book *The 40 Thieves*
Cisco Kid	radio/TV character w/sidekick Pancho
Clarence Darrow	defense attorney, Scopes monkey trial
Juan Merishal	great windup pitcher for the Giants
John the Baptist	last prophet of Israel, beheaded by Herod
Lady Astor	first woman in Great Britain's parliament
Karl Marx	author of *Communist Manifesto*, 1848
Lady Macbeth	character who said "out damn spot"
Mad King Ludwig	young Bavarian built a fairytale castle
Marilyn Monroe	skirt blew up in *Seven Year Itch*, 1955
Martin Erdmann	built grand home in Renaissance style
Mata Hari	spy in WWI for Germans, Dutch woman,
Mickey Mantle	star fielder/hitter for NY Yankees
Moliere	French farce playwright, 1622-1673
Moravians	oft-persecuted Christian group, 1500s
Nathan Detroit	gangster character in *Guys and Dolls*
Pablo Picasso	famous Spanish artist 1881-1973
Richard Henry Lee	first to urge the colonies to revolt
Rockefeller	American family, oilmen/philanthropists
Rothschild	German-Jewish family, European bankers
Shakespeare	English playwright, 1564-1616

Poker Terms

Flush	5 cards/same suit in sequence, high card wins
Full House	2 of a kind & 3 of a kind
Royal *flush*	5 cards, same suit, ace ends sequence
Straight	5 cards in mixed suits
Three of a kind	3 cards with same number or face
Two pairs	two sets, w/same number or face.

Songs

"A you're adorable, B you're so beautiful, C you're a cutie"
> (Music by Sid Lippman, Lyrics by Buddy Kaye, sung by Perry Como & the Fontaine Sisters on RCA, 1949.)

"Daring young man on the flying trapeze."
> (Music by Gaston Lyle, lyrics by George Leybourne, 1867)

"Everybody get together, try and love one another right now,"
> (A theme for the 1960s, composed by Chet Powers)

"Greensleeves"
> (Traditional folk tune, now mostly known as "What Child is This?")

"Mares eat Oats, and does eat oats, and little lambs eat ivy"
> (Words & Music by Milton Drake, Al Hoffman, Jerry Livingston)

"Thank Heaven for Little Girls"
> from *Gigi* (Music and Words by Frederick Lowe & Alan Jay Lerner, 1955)

"They're gonna put me in the movies."
> (Written by John Lennon for Ringo Starr, topped charts in 1968)

You ought to be in pictures"
> (Guy Lombardo & his Royal Canadians, Brunswick,1934.)

Theatre Productions: Musicals/Operas/Plays/Movies

Anything Goes	Cole Porter, play on a cruise ship, 1934
Busby Berkley	Director, giant film musical, 1930s
Camelot	Lerner & Lowe, King Arthur tale, 1960
Camille	Greta Garbo, Oscar-nominated role,1936
Citzen Kane	Orson Wells, film of Hearst empire
Damn Yankees	Allen & Ross, baseball stage play, 1955
Dragnet	Popular radio/TV cop show, 1950s-60s
Front Page	Ben Hecht, play of newspapers, 1928
Gigi	Lerner & Lowe, play 1948; film, 1958
Guys and Dolls	F. Loesser, 1950 play about gangsters
La Bohème	G. Puccini, opera about bohemians, 1896
Oklahoma	Rogers & Hammerstein, 1st musical, 1943
Oliver	L. Bart, musical of Dickens' tale, 1960
Punch & Judy	Show with puppet hitting each other
Roberta	J. Kern, musical on fashion world, 1933
Rockettes Show	Radio City Music Hall chorus line on stage.
1776	Sherman Edwards, 1969 musical of Independence War
Salome	Richard Strauss, 1905 opera of Biblical story
Student Prince	Sigmund Romberg, 1924 operetta
War of Worlds	Aldous Huxley, end-of-world portrayed on radio
Ziegfeld Follies	burlesque revues & vaudeville acts 1910-20s

Theatrical Companies & Musical Venues

Carnegie Hall	concert & recital center
Covent Gardens	London *venue* for various style concerts
46th St. Theatre	Broadway Theatre District off Times Sq.
Metropolitan	America's most *renown* opera company
Phoenix Repertory	theatre to showcase actors
Radio City	movie theatre inside Rockefeller Center
Savoyards	Gilbert & Sullivan operetta company

Punctuation Review

1. Of course, the following are the easy ones you already know: a period (.) ends a normal sentence; a comma (,) separates single items in a list or clarifies phrases.

2. A question mark (?) indicates a type of sentence called an interrogative. To remember that word, think about how a policeman might interrogate a suspect. An interrogative does not declare information but asks for it. In addition to a question mark following a speaker asking something, a writer of fiction often uses it to signal doubt in an event; the main character faces many options; or the reader needs to dig deeper on a certain issue.

3. Semi-colons (;) separate long phrases in a list. A semi-colon mostly accompanies a conjunction to join two independent clauses when one clause already has a comma. In this book the semi-colon often separates two independent clauses even when no conjunction appears. That signals for readers to read two separate ideas, as if simultaneously, instead of linearly! A semi-colon can separate two short independent clauses when one has only an understood verb: (e.g. One said yes; the other, no.)

4. A colon (:) means the next word, phrase, or clause clarifies or equals the previous one. It can *precede* a whole section or often gives signals with phrases: "the following" and "as follows."

5. Ellipsis dots (...) mean the writer purposely left something out, the speaker has paused to think, or the speaker is stammering to express his idea.

6. An Em dash (–) means the speaker got interrupted. An en dash (-) is stronger than a colon and also means the next word, phrase, or clause clarifies the previous ones. Single dashes (—) can also indicate stuttering, stammering, or sputtering.

7. An exclamation point (!) can be used for emphasis as in an interjection that adds ungrammatical information to a text to help understanding: (Well then! Heavens to Betsy!) It can also signal an expletive (Wow! Drat!). The most important use in this work is to signal the reader that the writer has intentionally written an incomplete sentence called a fragment. Although Ima, as an English teacher, allows her students to write fragments in stories and dialogue, she advises that you be very careful to use them ever so sparsely in your own class *essays*!

8. Normally an asterisk (*) is used to denote that an explanation will follow at the bottom of a page. At the bottom of the List of Characters, you will see just such a notation.

Vocabulary

abduct (ed, ing): kidnap/carry off by force; away from midline
acclaimed: applauded/saluted/highly approved
accost (ing): approach aggressively; start talking first
acrimony: bitterness/*animosity*
acquiesced: agreed to give in; *complied* w/o protest
adept: exhibit great skill & coordination
adhere (s, d): stick to like glue; closely follow rules
adroit (ly): clever/skillful/*agile* movement of body
aesthetic: quality of looking artistic/pleasing/balanced
agenda: list of issues to discuss at a meeting
agile: (adj): nimble/being *adept*
agility: (n) ability to move quickly/easily
alleged: asserted/declared as true; unproved/thought guilty
allegiance: loyalty/obligations to a cause or ruler
alluding: indirectly referring to folks/events/books
altercation: noisy/unfortunate disagreement or fast change
Amazons: mythical female warriors in man-less society
ambiguous: unclear/indefinite; may *imply* two meanings
ambivalent: unsure/conflicting feelings toward something
amenity (ies): niceties that add pleasure/comfort
amplified: extended/increased/made more powerful
animosity: open hatred/hostility
antebellum: before the Civil War

antics: mischief/shenanigans/pranks; odd gestures
apparition: sudden appearance like a vision; ghostly image
apprehend (ed): capture; take into custody; grasp meanings
arcane: understood by those with special knowledge
ardent: passionate/*fervent*/very enthusiastic
arraignment: time to hear pleas/set charges for a crime
arsenic: a dangerous poison
ascertain: discover/analyze/figure out what's definite
askance: a side glance; look of surprise
assailant: violent attacker; one who assaults
assault (ed, ing): (v) to attack or assail someone
assault: (n) violent attack physical/verbal
asylum: place offering protection
attesting: to affirm/assure/validate as true
audacious: bold/outlandish/daring; lacking restraint
audible: capable of being heard
august: majestic, awesome
austere: bare, without frills; strict/stern/severe
avenge: seek revenge/payback; *exact* vengeance
awry: turned/twisted/gone amiss

badmouthing: criticizing/talking ill of someone
bag (ged, ging): catch/kill an animal by hunting for it
bail: amount accused person pays to remain free until trial
bailiwick: area of expertise/interest/authority
balustrades: row of poles with railing along stairs
banshees: Irish mythic spirits screaming to announce death
barrage: artillery for protection; *onslaught* of words/bullets
begot: have *sired*/ cause a child to be born
beguile: delude/deceive
beholden: indebted to someone; owing something
beleaguered: surrounded/*harassed* by
belie (s): misinform/tell lies/speak falsely
belligerent: easily shows aggressiveness or picks a fight

benefactor: one who gives financial aid

bequeath: pass on property/money to heirs as per a will

bereft: grieved beyond hope; *inconsolable*

besmirch (ed): *taint*/tarnish/ruin someone's reputation

blatant: obviously offensive/unpleasant/too loud

blackball: negative vote; blocked membership to a club

blurb: short comment to summarize a story/information

bodice: top section or blouse part of a dress

bookmaking: taking/recording bets in a payoff book

boon: pleasant outcome; a benefit/blessing

bootlegger: unlicensed person who makes liquor *on the sly*

borough: a large district of a city

bourgeoisie: name Karl Marx gave capitalist/tradesmen

bristle (d, ling): react stiffly/angrily as if brushed roughly

brusque (ly): coarse/blunt in word & deed, w/o apology

buffaloed: easily *intimidated*/fooled/confounded

bushwhacked: pushed through thick woods; ambushed

cacophony: noisy/*discordant*/unharmonious sounds

cajole: to coax someone by using humor

calisthenics: organized exercises

calloused: (v) to let oneself harden and grow tough

callous (ly): unfeeling, hard, tough like a *callus*

callus: (n) hard rough patch on skin

camaraderie: friendship/fellowship/oneness within a group

cantankerous: very *ornery* and unwilling to cooperate

capish:(Italian Slang "kapish") Or you die, understand?

captor: one who takes another captive

catalyst: last item added and that changes mixture radically

catapulted: hurled to the front; launched/exploded abruptly

cater: to provide anything wished for, like food/amusement)

catacombs: burial caverns/tunnels with tomblike *niches*

cavalier: (adj) acting haughty/arrogant/casual about matters

chaos: complete turmoil/confusion; no order
chagrin: (n) displeasure/embarrassment/humiliation
charger: a platter or plate
chic (ly): stylish; fashionable without flashiness
civility (ties): polite, daily courtesy we extend to each other
clamor (ed, ing): (v) gather/demand in disorderly manner
clandestine: hidden, secretive
coddling: treating one too carefully like slow-cooked egg
coherent: intelligible/sensible/logical; hangs together
cohort (s): co-worker; associates
colleague (s): fellow members in activity or on job; *cohorts*
collusion: in cahoots; join secretly for a deceitful purpose
comply (lied): agreed to request/followed instructions
compound: to combine/add to/make more complex
comprise (d): consists/composed of; contained within
compromise (d): (v) sacrifice principles/settle differences
compromise: (n) disagreement resolved
conceded: gave in; admitted another's argument won
conscription: forced enrollment in a nation's military
concurrent: simultaneous; occurring at same time/place
condescendingly: acting as if coming down to a lower level
conduits: pipes/channels in which fluids/electricity travel
consummate: completely fulfilled; *proficient*
contemplate (s, ed, ing): ponder/meditate/think long on
contempt: bitter/vile disrespect for someone/something
contemptuous: scornful; acting with *disdain*
contentious: argumentative; *quarrelsome*
cordial (ly): kind/friendly/sincere
cordialities: warm expressions/courtesies used in society
corollary: result/follow up *inference* with little proof
covet (ed): to desire what another owns
cranium: skull/head/enclosure of brain
cravenly: miserably fearful; cowardly
crony (ies): close friend/buddy/pal to hang out with

cunning: *shrewd*; crafty; artful; wily
curlicue: fanciful jots on alphabet letters or architecture
curtly: done in a rude manner; cutting short; sharp-tongued
cynical: mocking/not trusting the motives of others

dank: wet/damp/cold
dastardly: cowardly; often misused to mean cruel
dawdling: wasting time
dazed: bewildered; stunned as in shock from a heavy blow
debacle: sudden ruin or collapse
debutante: girl formally introduced in high society
decipher: decode/analyze/figure out
defiled: violated another's purity; *sullied*/tarnished
deflecting: swerving/turning aside from hitting a surface
defused: diluted an argument; removed a comment's power
degenerate (s): immoral or antisocial person/deviant
demarcated: set limit/line between people/lands
demure: shy/reserved; may *feign* timidity
denomination: an item's classified values (dollar, quarter)
depicted: described/represented in words or pictures
depleted: exhausted/used until nothing remained
deployed: spread/sent out
derelict: a vagrant/outcast of society
dereliction: neglect on purpose
deride: scoff at; treat with mirth *tainted* with *contempt*
derisively: in a mocking/scoffing manner
despicable: mean/vile/hateful
destined: headed for a predetermined success/result
destiny: fate/place that holds necessary events/success
destitute: desperately poor; lacking all ways and means
deteriorate: to fall into disrepair/lose its value
dialects: speech variances–southern drawl, Texas twang
digress: to leave/stray from the subject at hand
din: loud, sustained noise/*cacophony* of sound

discombobulated: thrown off balance; confused/*disconcerted*
disconcert (ed, ing): upset; feel deeply disturbed/*perturbed*
discordant: disagreeable/not in accord.
disdain: reject with *scorn*; show *contempt*
dismay (ed): (v) to be filled with anxiety/dread
dismay: (n) sudden dread/fear/alarm
disoriented: lost one's sense of direction; felt imbalanced
dispose: to get rid of
dissent: disagreement/disapproval/difference of opinion
distraught: very upset/anxious/almost *inconsolable*
divulge (d): give out information
domicile: one's home; where one lives/resides regularly
dominated: proved more powerful; bullied/ruled over
dolt: dullard/stupid person
dote (d, ting): show great affection/attention yet not *fawning*
dowdy: poor style, dullish without flare
draft: requirement to join the army; *conscription*
dredging: digging up unhappy thoughts; deepening a canal
drift: general meaning; gist/trend/direction
ducts: pipes that carry water, air conditioning; *conduits*
duvet: comforter/coverlet w/o sides, which lies atop covers

edginess: uneasiness, anxiousness, sharpness
effusive (ly): abundantly emotional/gushy over a matter
emulate: imitate/excel in a flattering way
encase (d, sing): to enclose/box in
encoding: sending message in secret signals
encumbrances: items/duties that prevent free movement
ensuing: following immediately
entice (d): attract by promising a reward; *dangle a carrot*
entourage: group accompanying an important person
entrap (ped): set decoy to disguise danger and to trap *prey*
entreated: beg/plead/*implore*
entrepreneur: one risking money to start a business

essay (ed, ing): (v) to try out or make an attempt
essay: (v) trial/testing; literary paper analyzing a theme/topic
euphemism: pleasant word for a offensive term
exact: force/demand a payment from another; *extract*
exasperated: provoked/irritated/irked
exclusive: separated out; allowing entry for only a few
exempt: excused/freed from duty
expedient (ly): suitable/fitting/appropriate for task at hand
expenditure: amount spent; expense; cost
expound: explain with great detail
expunge: erase from a file; remove completely
extort (ed): to blackmail/solicit a ransom/*exact* money
extortion: use of power to obtain money
extract: pull out; take away forcibly; withdraw from
extricate: cause a release from difficulty; be disentangled
extrapolate: extend from a known fact to an extreme end
exuberance: unrestrained, *effusive* joy pouring out
exude (d): to ooze/leak out of an opening as sap from a tree

façade (s): front of building; fake appearance of something
facetious (ly): unserious/playful/flippant
failsafe: backup idea/device so things work no matter what
fascia: flat wood in door frames/between moldings
fawning: making over a person, but wanting favor in return
fedora: pinched crown hat with medium brim worn up/down
feign (ed, ing): pretend; act in a fake manner
feint: pretended air/*ploy* to mislead from intended goal
fervent: passionate/warm/strongly felt; *ardent*
fink: betrayer/double-crosser; one seeking his own good
flatfoot: (Slang) old name for a policeman on the beat
flophouse: cheap, fleabag hotel
flounder: move clumsily
flush: (adj) two even surfaces/items or on same *plane*
flush: (n) a sequence of five cards in same suit

flushed: (v) face grew red

foiled: spoiled; prevented plan from working

forte: area in which one excels/has expertise; *bailiwick*

forthcoming: about to appear; available soon

fray: (n) argument/battle

frayed: (v) unraveled edges; worn out threads of material

frugal: very thrifty; never reckless with money

furrowing: making wrinkles in one's brow

futile: useless/vain

genial: pleasant/*cordial* manner

gibberish: nonsense language

gigs: scheduled performances for bands/singers/actors

glowered: glared at

goad (ed): shove, gently force

goon: thug/hoodlum used to *intimidate* others

gossamer: very sheer/thin fabric; airy as a spider web

gratuitous: unearned/freely given; at no cost

grazed: barely struck/brushed/skimmed as a stone on water

greenhorn: one with no experience learns to do a task

grip: small suitcase; valise

grouse: complain/murmur

guffaw: huge outburst of uncontrollable laughter

hack: *has-been*; hackneyed performer who does same *shtick*

hallucinate: to be deluded; to see/perceive things not there

harass (ed, ing): disturb/irritate *persistently*

harbor: hold/keep/nourish/shelter

heed: pay attention; follow/do as required

heinous: incredibly wicked

heyday: top time of a fad/success/career

highbrow: one with superior learning/culture

hodgepodge: mixture of unlike items; disorder

hoodlum: mobster/*goon*/gangster

hoodwinked: fooled; *pulled the wool over someone's eyes*
hubbub: uproar/lots of noise/babbling voices
hybrid: two dissimilar items combined to form new product

ilk: same type/kind
imbroglio: very complicated situation
immutable: not subject to change
impassable: impossible to cross or go forward
impasse: dilemma; no exit from or continuation
impeccable: spotless; flawless; without blame
impecunious: without money; penniless
imperious: overbearing; once meant regal/imperial
impervious: unable to be penetrated; unaffected by danger
implicate: *imply*/involve/*incriminate*; point to possible guilt
implored: begged/*entreated*/asked for reason or mercy
imply (ied, ying): suggest/hint/express indirectly
impound (ed, ing): seize/take into legal custody
impoverish (ed): reduced to poverty till even *impecunious*
impresario: producer of huge entertainments
impromptu: performed without rehearsal; done *on the spur*
improvise (d): act without a script like ad-libbing dialogue
improvisation: an *improvised* act/skit/dialogue
impunity: without punishment; *exempt* from consequence
inadvertently: not intended or on purpose; accidental
inauthentic: not genuine or trustworthy
incentive: reason/spur to act; promise of a reward
incessant: contining/unceasing; with no relief in sight
incognito: avoiding recognition; travel under new name
inconsolable: unable to be comforted
incorrigible: not trainable or correctable
incredulous (ly): disbelieving
incriminate: suggest guilt/involve others in crime
indisposed: unavailable or slightly ill
indubitably: too obvious to be doubted/questioned

infer (red): conclude/ determine from evidence
inference: conclusion from events/facts observed
infernal: abominable; hellish
infractions: violation of rules
infrastructure: bridges/roads/utilities form basics of city life
insinuate: worm a way in; *imply*/slant facts a certain way
insipid: dull/uninteresting; lacking flavor
instigate (s, d): stir up trouble; to *goad*/urge
insufferable: not to be tolerated/endured
intercom: speaking/listening device between rooms
interjected: interrupt flow to insert/add information
intimidate (d, ting): make timid; frighten/inhibit/threaten
intimidation: act of curbing someone's word/action/safety
intruder: one who imposes or enters uninvited/unwanted
inveterate: long standing, like a deeply held belief
irascible: easily angered
irate: outraged; angry
irk (s, ed): to irritate/annoy someone
ironclad: rigid; definite proof; no loopholes
irrelevant: does not fit; not *pertinent* right now
italicized: words printed in italics

jeopardize: injure/endanger/cause loss of valued item

kibitz: to watch/comment on an activity
kinescope: film of live broadcast or from videotape
kiosks: small sales booths
kosher: food prepared according to Jewish law

lavish: luxuriant/abundant/plentiful
levity: light-hearted speech/frivolity/humor
lingo: specialized language/jargon within a group
lodged: to be stuck/embedded
loiter (s, ed): linger/stand idly about w/o permission

longevity: length of life; long duration
lowlifes: folk with questionable morals
lucrative: able to produce wealth/profit
lure: (v) entice/attract/tempt as with a fishing *lure*
lure (n) irresistible attractor; a decoy

magnanimous: noble/generous/forgiving/gracious
maître d: head waiter/steward at restaurant
malaise: feeling of being ill/depressed/even *dazed*
malleable: easy to persuade or to mold like clay
maneuver: a skillful change; *adroit* movement
marathon: event/race/contest of great endurance
marker: promise to pay; debt owed by a gambler
marquee: signboard on front of a theatre/bus/train
mayhem: violent disorder/confusion/havoc
meander: wander about with no definite destination
melee: confused hand to hand combat; violent free for all
mellifluous: mellow/flowing quality of a man's voice
metaphor: item is its own description: He's (like) a dog
miffed: to become peeved/annoyed
milk: drain the last drop from a situation
mockup: model of something; look-alike
moderate: make reasonable within limits; not extreme
modify: change form to less severe; *mollify*
mollify: make gentler/softer
moniker: nickname/label given one by close pals
moot: left unresolved; with no need to decide
mortified: caused shame/humiliation; wounded pride
moxie: energy/pep/courage/knowhow
munitions: war weapons; group of guns/bullets
muster (ed): gather/assemble together

naïveté: lack of worldly guile; simple/unsophisticated
narthex: foyer/front lobby of a church
natty: suave/dapper/neat; describes a good dresser
negotiate (d): make terms of a deal; get around a tight spot
niche: small shelf in a wall; place fitting one's talent
nix (ed): (Slang) to say "no"
novelty: unusual stage act/talent
novice: beginner at an activity; similar to *greenhorn*
nurture: nourish; encourage/direct someone in right way

oaf: obnoxious/clumsy/mulish man
oblivious: unaware/forgetful
obsequious: too flattering/complimentary; *fawning* over
obstinate: sticking stubbornly to one's path/opinion
obvious (ly): unavoidably clear; leaving no doubt
officious (ly): excessively forward in giving advice; bossy
offing: in the near future
omnipresent: always/forever nearby; around everywhere
onomatopoeia: word sounds like its meaning (gong/buzz)
onslaught: violent attack; unstoppable outpouring
opportune: more fitting/suitable/*expedient* for an occasion.
opulence: extremely elegant/lavish/abundant
ornery: stubborn; difficult to deal with
ostensibly: seems one way but is another; outer *belies* inner

pact: formal bargain/agreement
palaver: idle chatter
pander (ed): promote evil *vices*; agree for favors in return
passé: out of date; not in fashion
pate: top of the head
patron: customer; champion of others, supporter of the arts
patronage: continued support/encouragement of an activity
patronize (zing): act in a demeaning way; often shop same store
pedant (ic): one influenced more by books than experience

pejorative: downgrading a thing to make it sound worse

pensive (ly): in deep thought

perceptible: ability to be taken in by the mind or senses

perception: impression/viewpoint/insight of something

perennial: happens yearly; lasts indefinitely

persevere (s, d): keep at something even in hardships

persistent (ly): won't let go/give up; almost *obstinate*

persona: real/false image one projects, hoping others believe

pertinent: currently important/relevant/fitting to a situation

perturbed: greatly upset/disturbed/made uneasy

peruse (s, d, sing): examine/review a matter carefully

petulant (ly): very irritated/ill-*tempered*; in a childish way

phenomenon: *perceptible* fact/event; oft-used for rare event

philanthropists: donors to charity improve society/the arts

pine (s, d, ning): to feel great longing/yearning for something

pinwale: corduroy fabric with narrow rows of nap

pirouetted: (v) body turning totally about on toes as in ballet

pitch (ed): present/try to sell an idea to another

plane: two surfaces on same/even level

playwright: one who crafts/writes a play

ploy: approach to gain a certain result/advantage

plum: the top choice; best of anything

pommeled: pummeled; struck/hit repeatedly

posh: fashionable/*exclusive*/expensive

poulder: built-up land reclaimed from the sea as in Holland

precarious: dangerously unstable/unsafe; lacking security

precede (ding): go before in time/rank; preface/introduce

preclude: prevent need of any further action

predator: an animal seeking to *prey* on weaker ones

preen: take pride in oneself; primp

prestige: status/success/fame achieved by *prominent* people

presume (d): to take for granted; assume without evidence

pretentious: outwardly showy; putting on air of importance

prey: (n) animal stalked by hunter

prey: (v) stalk/make a victim
prig: know-it-all; *pedant* who is overly precise
prior: before present time; previous/*preceding*
proficient: excellently/skillfully performing a task
profuse (ly): plentiful/overflowing/abundant
prognosis: probable course of disease; prediction of outcome
prominent: widely known/noticeable/sticking out; *renown*
proselytize: convert; influence another to adopt your beliefs
prospect: future possibility; expected event *on the horizon*
protestations: strong expression of *dissent*
prudent: wise; using common sense
prurience: extreme interest in improper topics (i.e. sex)
publicity: information to gain favor/attention for something
pugnacious: *quarrelsome*/eager to fight (pug-nosed boxer)
pursue: chase/go after; follow intending to overtake

quarrelsome: tending to argue/be *belligerent*
querulous (ly): peevish; always complaining
quizzical (ly): puzzled; with a teasing/questioning look
quota: amount allowed/assigned to others

ramshackle: falling apart; rickety
random: haphazard; with no pattern
raucous: rough/harsh sounding; describes loud laughter
recessed: indented; placed in a secluded alcove
recommend (ed): give approval/counsel on a worthy choice
reconnoiter (ed): survey/observe/inspect a situation
recoup (ed, ing): recover a loss; regain a favored position
recourse: turning to another for aid/security/second chance
recumbent: lying relaxed/stretch out
redeem (ed, ing): exchange; set free/recover ownership
refuge: shelter/safe place
refuse: (n) useless discards; worthless rubbish
refuse: (v) reject; deny access/entry; say "no"

regale: entertain/delight; decorate with medals

reiterated: said over again; repeated a list

relinquish (ed): yield/surrender/give up power

reminisced: recalled old times/sentimental memories

render (ing): offer/deliver; give what's due

rendition: version/interpretation/*rendering* of another's work

reneges: fails to keep a commitment; breaks promises

renovations: restorations/repairs to recapture original idea

renown: (adj) being widely acclaimed; well known

renown: (n) celebrity; fame

repast: food/meal/nourishment

repellent: offensive/mildly *repulsive*

repent (ing): change behavior 180° to go in opposite direction

reprieve: period of relief; postponing a punishment

reprimand: severe order to correct behavior

repugnant: being very offensive/distasteful/*repulsive*

repulsive: degusting/obnoxious/*repugnant*; worth rejecting

resilient: able to recover quickly; with great endurance

retrieve (d): regain; fetch something cast off

revival: new production of an old play

ridicule: *deride*/mock/make fun of

rigged: fixed a game; manipulated/cheated by plan

risqué: suggestive of a scandalous/sensuous idea

ruefully: causing great regret/sorrow

ruckus: loud noise/commotion

rummaging: searching thoroughly; disarranging

ruse: trick/charade/diversion to fool/mislead others

sacrosanct: when a topic is so sacred, it is rarely mentioned

sagaciously: wise/shrewd; judging with keen *perception*

salvaged: saved; *recouped* leftovers from disaster

salvageable: worthy of saving/reusing/*recouping*

sardonically: cynically/mocking; with poisonous *scorn*

savvy: (Slang) comprehending; with common/street sense

scenario: outline of how a plot may unfold

schmoozing: (Yiddish/Slang) chatting idly or to gain favor

shtick: (Yiddish) trait/characteristic; oft means old joke/act

score: write music for a film/ad/show/background

scorn (ing): (v) mock; treat as unworthy

scorn: (n) *contempt*; strong show of disrespect/*disdain*

scruples: moral objections to evil; principles to live by

scuttlebutt: gossip/rumors; talk around ship's water fountain

seasoned: experienced with what to expect

secreted: hidden away/set out of view

seductive: tempting/*enticing*/using the *lure* of sex

segued: moved/ transitioned from one topic to another

senile: mental abilities diminishing in old age

serene: calm/composed; unruffled

sequestered: separated from/set apart for a reason

serendipitously: when unplanned things converge/combine

serendipity: pleasant discoveries with a happy result

shards: broken pieces of glass/pottery/metal slag

shrewd: tricky/sharp/astute/discerning

sic: to urge a dog to bite/fight; leave error in as it is

sinister: suggesting a wicked/evil intent

sired: fathered; *begot* a child

skulking: lurking/hanging about idly; moving *stealthily*

snidely: acting with a malicious/sarcastic/superior attitude

sniper: one who fires on a target from a concealed spot

snitch: (n) a tattletale; petty thief

solicitous: concerned/thoughtful; often over eager/anxious

spanned: spread over a given space

Spartan: very stark/disciplined; *austere*

squelch: to crush/squash/quash/silence/snuff out

stabilize: make stable/balanced/unmovable

stealthily: with secret/unnoticed/hidden movements

steeled: strengthened; made hard/strong against conditions

stereotype (d): fixed model of an idea oft-copied by others

stevedore: one unloading cargo at a dock; longshoremen
stiff (s): ignore a debt; purposely not paying money owed
stilted (ly): overly dignified/formal; stiff/unnatural
stock: (adj) typical/usual; stereotyped
stock: (n) shares owned in a company; warehouse inventory
stockbroker: one who buys/sells *stock* of many companies
stocked: (v) filled with supplies
stocky: sturdy/thickset; often barrel-chested
straddle: sprawl/spread legs apart on either side
strait (s): narrow/difficult place to pass through
strategize: put together a plan; coordinate actions
strategy: plan/group of actions to accomplish a goal
stupor: unresponsiveness; state of *dazed* unawareness
sublease (s, d): renting one's apartment to another
subtle: vague/slight/often devious differences in two ideas
sully (ied): *taint*/spoil/defile
superficial: trivial; near surface; no depth
suppositions: unproved statement; assumption
surpassed: excelled beyond; exceeded expectation/limits
svelt: stylishly slender/slim
swindled: cheated; obtained money by fraud

tactic: special attack on a problem to meet a goal; *ploy*
taint (ed): stain/infect (e.g. *render* evidence impure/useless)
temper (ed): (v) *modify*; smooth out unevenness; *moderate*
temper: (n) composure; often means a huge show of anger
temperament: one's usual behavior/manner/attitude
tenement: residence for poorer tenants but not quite a slum
tentatively: with uncertainty; holding back
timbre: distinct quality one sound makes over other sounds
tome: one book in a work of many volumes
traipsed: intruded by walking idly through an area
traverse: travel across; to cross back and forth
trooper: one member of a military/police team

trouper: one actor in theatrical group
tufted: dents made by sewing buttons in a cushion/pillow
turncoat: traitor; one who switches *allegiance* to enemy
turnstile: gate that slows folks passing to various areas
truce: treaty; settlement of differences

ubiquitous: seeming to show up everywhere; *omnipresent*
unabashedly: without embarrassment
undercurrents: contrary forces beneath *superficial* fact/view
understudy: one learning a role of an actor who may fall ill
unison: singing together on the same note without harmony
unorthodox: not according to tradition or regular ritual
unscrupulous: no honor/principles; *contemptuous* of all good
usurp: take power without rightful authority

valiant: brave; acting with courage
venue (s): special place where a performance/trial occurs
verge: (n) extreme edge/brink/point where action occurs
verge: (v) approach/come near
viable: capable of developing; can stay alive
vices: worst habits; immoral practices
vie: to compete for attention/favor to win a victory/prize
virile: very alive; masculine/courageous/strong
Voilà: (French) There it is! There you are!
volley (ed, ling): move balls/words/ideas back and forth
vulnerable: having a weak side that someone can invade
vying: (to *vie*) contending/striving for prize at contest's end

waned: declined/decreased/dwindled gradually
warrant: deserve/justify/be worthy of such notice
welch (ed): (also welsh) to *stiff* debtor; not pay off on a bet
welcher: (also welsher) one who *stiffs* debtor/won't pay bets
whiplash: neck injury from a fast back/forth neck motion

Yiddish: (Jewish) blended dialect of German/Slavic/Hebrew